The Obama Inheritance

FIFTEEN STORIES
OF CONSPIRACY NOIR

The
Obama
Inheritance

FIFTEEN STORIES OF
CONSPIRACY NOIR

EDITED BY

Gary Phillips

THREE ROOMS PRESS

New York, NY

The Obama Inheritance: Fifteen Stories of Conspiracy Noir
EDITED BY
Gary Phillips

© 2017 by Three Rooms Press

ISBN 978-1-941110-59-1(trade paperback)
ISBN 978-1-941110-60-7 (ebook)
Library of Congress Control Number: 2017904913

ACKNOWLEDGEMENTS
All stories © 2017 except "At the Conglomeroid Cocktail Party" © 1982 by Agberg Ltd.

COVER DESIGN AND ILLUSTRATION:
© Rich Trask
flapjoy.deviantart.com | @KingFlapJoy

BOOK DESIGN:
KG Design International
www.katgeorges.com

DISTRIBUTED BY:
PGW/Ingram
www.pgw.com

Three Rooms Press
New York, NY
www.threeroomspress.com
info@threeroomspress.com

TABLE OF CONTENTS

FOREWORD *by Gary Phillips* . . . . *i*

MICHELLE IN HOT WATER *by Kate Flora* *1*

. . . THE CONTINUING MISSION *by Adam Lance Garcia* *21*

TRUE SKIN *by Eric Beetner* *48*

EVENS *by Nisi Shawl* *60*

A DIFFERENT FRAME OF REFERENCE *by Walter Mosley* . . . *77*

BROTHER'S KEEPER *by Danny Gardner* *97*

FORKED TONGUE *by Lise McClendon* *127*

SUNBURNT COUNTRY *by Andrew Nette* *147*

I KNOW THEY'RE IN THERE! *by Travis Richardson* *167*

THE PSALM OF BO *by Christopher Chambers* *195*

AT THE CONGLOMEROID COCKTAIL PARTY
by Robert Silverberg *216*

DEEP STATE *by Désirée Zamorano* *227*

I WILL HAUNT YOU *by Anthony Neil Smith* *244*

GIVE ME YOUR FREE, YOUR BRAVE, YOUR PROUD
MASSES YEARNING TO CONQUER *by L. Scott Jose* *254*

THUS STRIKES THE BLACK PIMPERNEL *by Gary Phillips* . . *279*

ABOUT THE CONTRIBUTORS *309*

FOREWORD
BY GARY PHILLIPS

IT WAS A CUMULATIVE THING really. There was no one particular right-wing, whacked-out conspiracy theory about Obama that stayed with me more than any of the others during his presidency. He was born in Kenya into a secret Muslim sect; had his grandma killed to cover up the truth about his birth; used secret weather machines to cause Hurricane Sandy, and on and on. To many of us, the daily roll out of these preposterous notions about the nation's first black president was laughable. But damned if these bizarro scenarios crept in from the fringes to find purchase on outlets like Breitbart, Alex Jones, and what have you.

And let me add, it's not like I didn't have criticisms of Obama's policies, but they were grounded in fact and analysis, not racist fairy tales. How then to look back on the Obama years? Not as a dry academic exercise—there'd be plenty of that, but use as a jumping-off point the pop culture aspects of his presidency, like when he would sing from the stage or let black inflections color his speech. To have a blast with his legacy.

When I met Peter and Kat, the cool raconteurs of Three Rooms Press, we kicked around the concept of the anthology you now hold in your hands, and this was months before the presidential election of 2016. The idea was not to be preachy or take a scolding tone in the various stories. In fact, what I asked of the writers solicited for this collection was to take any one of the twisty conspiracies spun around the Obama White House and run with it. Riff on it, take it apart and turn it on its head, and give the reader a thrill ride of weirdo, noirish, pulpy goodness. To have fun. And that sense of playfulness comes through in the stories herein.

It's been stated that writers like Jonathan Swift and the gone-too-soon Ralph Wiley used satire as a way to point out deficiencies in our social and political structures. Certainly some of that was the motivation for why the stories in *The Obama Inheritance* were culled together. That the more outlandish and outrageous the tale, no matter how over the top, the more the hope that the reader will be entertained yet also take away sharp reflections about our collective condition.

Indeed, if anything, in this current political climate of a president—the birther-in-chief if you will—who tweets out mind-numbing pronouncements derived from alt-fact sources and people in charge of federal agencies who are the antithesis of what those agencies are supposed to do, our humble anthology almost seems tame in such a surreal time.

Almost, but hold on . . .

I've edited or co-edited several anthologies over the years but I will tell you, hands down, *The Obama Inheritance* was one of the most enjoyable ones I've put together. In the following pages you'll encounter in Christopher Chambers's clever "Psalm of Bo" a what-if dystopian recitation of a resistance from the point of view of the dogs and other animals. The machinations of the lizard people who live in the hollow earth lie at the heart of more than one story in this anthology but I won't tell you the titles since you should enjoy finding out for yourself when you dive in.

From the sweaty paranoia of Travis Richardson's "I Know They're in There!" to parables of hope as in Walter Mosley's "A Different

Frame of Reference," to a look behind the curtain at just who is responsible for the deluge of fake news in Lise McClendon's "Forked Tongue," you'll find a range of stories to disquiet and discomfort you, but you'll keep turning the pages to find out what happens. Big Science and what it portends despite its deniers is reflected in stories like Nisi Shawl's "Evens" and our classic reprint "At the Conglomeroid Cocktail Party" by sci-fi's Grand Master Robert Silverberg

All the stories in this anthology live up to the hype. This collection is a nod to the Great Depression pulps of the 1930s, portrayals of the odd and the strange, lost worlds and larger-than-life characters, has a soundtrack by Parliament/Funkadelic and Hendrix, and is inhabited by the sensibilities of the hard-boiled and the damned. In *The Obama Inheritance: Fifteen Stories of Conspiracy Noir,* in an era that might be cast as the depths of the Great Deception, you'll discover sobering truths amid the fantastic fictions these new pulp stories deliver from the first page on.

Can you dig it?

—*Gary Phillips*

The
Obama
Inheritance

MICHELLE IN HOT WATER
BY KATE FLORA

THE BIG MAN WITH THE Russian accent wore an expression somewhere between a smirk and a smile. Not a pleasant smile, but the smile of someone who likes to inflict pain and was about to do just that. The smile revealed teeth like a haphazard handful of pebbles had landed in his mouth, kind of like a James Bond bad guy. Michelle wasn't afraid of him; bullies had been common in the part of Chicago where she grew up. Her years in the White House had shown her plenty more, even if they did hide behind expensive suits and artificial courtesies. No. The man didn't scare her, even though she knew she would probably be hurt. What scared her was the predicament she had gotten herself into, and the trouble it was going to cause for her team: Faiza from State, Leela from the Surgeon General's office, Charisa from the Pentagon, Lourdes from the FDA, and Alice from Justice.

The phrase "Alice from Justice," with its movie-title resonance, almost made her smile, but she controlled herself. Smiling at bullies sometimes diffused them, but usually it made them want to bully all the more. This guy was definitely an "all the more."

The swollen joints and scars on his large hands spoke of a lifetime of giving and taking brutality.

Clearly, they had badly misjudged this operation. Three successful missions had made them overconfident. But regret would accomplish nothing. While she tried to stay alive and relatively in one piece, she knew the rest of the team was sweating bullets planning a rescue. It would be a hell of thing to try and explain—how the First Lady, decked out in combat boots and black BDUs—came to be a captive of the pet Russian thugs of a prominent American drug manufacturer.

She should have stuck to promoting children's nutrition.

Too late now.

Above her, in this aggressively male study where she sat tied to a leather armchair, the stuffed heads of slaughtered animals mounted on dark wood paneling stared down with shiny glass eyes. Try as she might to understand human nature, getting pleasure from slaughtering animals escaped her. Shooting that giraffe or that elephant represented no exercise of skill or accomplishment. It was just killing. Photos of the prominent rich clutching high-powered rifles and gloating over their kills always turned her stomach. She still wished that dentist who shot a protected lion had been fed to another lion as revenge. Or become part of feeding time at a zoo. Ugly thoughts prompted by ugly behavior. Of course, slaughtering innocents—or at least killing them by making access to critical drugs unaffordable—was what this was all about.

"Mr. Klinger will be along shortly." Her captor smirked. "He will want to thank you personally for the boost all this will give to his company's reputation. So un-American of you to try and interfere with his business, yes? Foolishly thinking that no one would notice a pattern. But naturally you were expected at some point. He was . . ." A hesitation as the thug sought the right word. ". . . unexpectedly detained by some trouble with his car. Your doing, I believe?"

Alice's, actually. Alice was very good with cars. But the car had not broken down in the relatively empty area as they'd planned, but on a heavily traveled highway, and when Michelle and the others moved in, Klinger's Russian thugs had materialized from another car. She'd been grabbed before she could escape with the others. Now she was captive in David Klinger's house, waiting for a domestic scandal to arise, instead of confronting Klinger with the ugliness of his behavior in abruptly raising the price of an essential drug for childhood cancer by 800 percent, effectively taking it out of the reach of all but the richest or best insured.

Her disguise would protect her from discovery for a while. But if she didn't get out of here before Klinger and the rest of his henchmen arrived, eventually close scrutiny would reveal how she'd changed her appearance, and they would figure out who she really was.

Her husband was going to be so upset. He was 100 percent behind her project, so long as she kept it under the radar. Proud of her, even. But getting caught by a Big Pharma mogul's Russian henchmen was not part of the deal. Russian henchmen, it seemed, because Russian oligarchs were heavily invested in Klinger's company. What was wrong with good old American thugs? Buy American? Jobs for Americans. Wasn't that the other side's motto? We're all for it, so long as it doesn't apply to us?

She pulled her attention away from the potential scandal she was causing because the thug was saying something. "This time, you and your little friends will not get away with . . ." Michelle's heart clenched in her chest. Had the others been caught as well? Perhaps held prisoner in other parts of this house? Did this mean that no one was coming to her rescue? The Secret Service would gladly rescue her, of course. But the rules by which her group operated precluded that: do not involve the government on an official basis. So far, she hadn't had to contemplate the possibility of a government rescue. They'd been successful; rescue hadn't been an issue. But now rescue was very much a necessity. She would like to rescue herself. She just wasn't sure that her skills would allow her to do that.

There was Lourdes, of course, who hadn't been part of tonight's operation. But what about the others? Lourdes couldn't do this alone.

She mustn't dwell on the possibility that there wouldn't be any rescue. Her focus had to be on the here and now. To force her attention back to the present, she thought about his wrongheaded and foolish comment. Her "little" friends? Bulltweety.

(Even in her thoughts, she had schooled herself not to swear. She was supposed to be a role model. An example for aspiring young women. How would they react to tonight's fiasco, if she didn't find a way out?)

Avoiding the negative thoughts that could distract her from strategies for survival and escape, she focused on his comment, in particular his use of the word "little," which was common parlance when men wanted to diminish or belittle women. Women had little friends and small ambitions. Words that were hardly apt here. For starters, because none of them was small. She was tall, but the others were taller. Faiza and Lourdes an easy six feet, and Charisa and Alice a bit taller than that. It was what had drawn them together, well before they'd discovered their common bond in a passion to protect vulnerable children, and a willingness to flout the law in order to do it.

It began at a White House state dinner, when the six of them found themselves standing together, drawn by their common attribute. Strange that no one had spotted them talking and taken their picture. It would have been a heck of a photo. Six stunningly tall women in evening dresses. African-American, Latina, white, and Asian. They could have been the UConn basketball team. Charisa had proposed the idea of the "Tall Girls Book Club," and what began as a joking friendship spawned by the impossibility of finding clothes that fit—and the way their height made men uncomfortable—had morphed into a series of stealthy activities. Men's black BDUs, it turned out, fit all of them perfectly.

Until tonight's clusterfrack, their efforts at persuading drug kingpins—of the legal sort—to reconsider extortionate rate hikes had been remarkably successful. They had simply applied some science of their own. As Lourdes had discovered during her tenure at the FDA, sometimes scientific research produced drugs with side effects that rendered them too harmful to use in treating the targeted diseases. One such drug, a revolutionary, long-lasting injectable that was an extremely effective treatment for high blood pressure, had the unfortunate side effects of rendering the recipients impotent, incontinent, and bald. And its effects could only be reversed by another injection—one only a few people had access to.

Their first client—he would, of course, say victim—had defiantly refused to consider their suggestion concerning his product, asserting his right of free enterprise, or, as he had put it, "Fuck 'em. I'm a businessman. My job is to make money." Initially, at least. When he made that statement, the injection had already been given. It had taken a month that rendered him bald as a newborn and forced into the indignity of an adult diaper before he came around to their way of thinking. Tonight's target, David Klinger, would have been their fourth. And given how much he prized his well-coiffed mane of blond hair, it would have been particularly delightful to see him as bald as a child being treated for cancer.

She watched the thug clenching and unclenching his hands. Longing to strike her again and constrained by something. Loyalty to his boss? A trained-in need to wait for instructions? A plan to haul her before reporters, which wouldn't go so well if she appeared bruised or bloody? Michelle had a remedy, should he strike, but was constrained by a concern of her own—when they went out on their missions, they used disguises, applications of fake skin and artificial features that were remarkably lifelike. But she wasn't sure how well a plumped cheek, altered jawline, or nose bump would stand up to the force of a blow. It would take more significant force to detach her wig. But if he grabbed her by the hair, it was game over.

As a distraction, while she worked the ropes that held her hands, she drew on the one semi-superpower she possessed—the ability to project disembodied voices. The look on that thug's face when the elephant said, "Don't you hurt that woman," was beyond priceless, and he took his eyes off her while he searched the room. She was good at getting herself untied. They practiced these things, of course, though it had been hard to find privacy in the White House. Or someone to tie her up, even in the residence. Her husband flatly refused.

The thug's pacing, a metronomic stride up and down the room, was so heavy-footed the elephant on the wall trembled, so the giraffe said, "Stop that. You're upsetting the elephant." And as he stared up, slack-jawed, at the heads on the wall, she slipped her hands free. She kept them under the now-loose ropes, hoping he wouldn't notice.

He kept checking his watch and glancing toward the door, evidently thinking Klinger should have arrived by now. But their plan had been to waylay Klinger on his way to an appearance on a TV talk show, where he would be debating the issue of dramatically raising drug prices with none other than Lourdes Martinez. Presumably, their plan having failed, he and Lourdes were even now appearing on TV.

In their previous missions, the injections had been preceded by the subtle introduction of date rape drugs. In these cases, it was raping the mind and the body, so that their subjects woke the next morning with no memory of the events that had transpired, only a note explaining what had happened, why it had happened, what they had to look forward to, and instructions on how to make contact for the remedy. Part of the instructions, naturally, required the companies to roll back the price hikes to a reasonable level.

Tonight, even though Michelle's capture had spoiled part of the plan, she had confidence that Lourdes would find a way to introduce Rohypnol before Klinger appeared on TV. People generally were nervous and drank water before such appearances. She longed for a screen so she could watch him grow bleary and confused before an avid TV audience. She thought it unlikely, though, that her captor would turn on a TV for her. No. The acceleration of that flexing said a blow was coming soon. And then, unable to contain himself any longer, he struck. She had been watching his hands—part of her self-defense training—giving her just enough warning to turn her head so his fist struck her earring. Held to her ear by a magnet, not a post or wire, it was not merely decorative. It immediate detached and imbedded itself in his hand, releasing a fast-acting neurotoxin.

There were distinct advantages to the increase in women spooks. Spy agencies had always had cool toys. Now they created more of them for women. Their silent partner at the CIA, Mary Grace Owens, herself a survivor of childhood cancer, delighted in supplying useful things to support their missions. Not only the incredibly natural-looking artificial skin and features that made up their disguises—essential for high-profile women like themselves—but a whole range of devices to deliver the drug central to their operation, and others to facilitate the capture of their subjects, enable them to disable attackers, and aid in escape when necessary.

Her ear stung, but he was the one in trouble.

His brutish face was a study in astonishment as he plucked the sharp object from a hand that was already beyond his control, astonishment morphing into terror as he felt himself losing control of that arm. Bullies never handle what's inflicted on them very well. Leaving him to his own struggle—the dose was designed to incapacitate, not kill—she untied her legs and headed for the door. Before she left, a delicate little dik-dik said, "Serves you right."

She had just entered the hall when she heard the commotion of voices and people arriving. Not women's voices, but those of anxious men, and one whose voice was slurred beyond understanding. David Klinger.

It was time to be gone. She hated to leave without finishing her job, but there were several men with Klinger, while she was on her own, and she'd probably pushed her luck enough for one night. They weren't done with Klinger. There would be other times and other chances. She scooped up the earring, now emptied of its toxin, and left two simple calling cards—a plain black business card that said MURDERER and a picture of a group of desperately sick children—on the desk.

Another cool thing she didn't need to worry about—fingerprints. She had artificial skin coating her hands.

There was a sudden rush of feet that sounded like three people with functioning limbs and one being dragged along. She willed them to go upstairs, which they did. But it wasn't likely they'd all stay up there. If she didn't get out, and quickly, they wouldn't be done with her.

The Tall Girls Book Club had studied the plans of the house. This hall led to the kitchen, giving her access to the backyard and the woods beyond. Quietly, on rubber-soled boots, she slipped down the hall and into the dark kitchen. She was about to let herself out when footsteps outside crunched on gravel. Someone standing guard? It made sense, but she had no way of knowing. She dropped her hand from the knob and slipped from the kitchen into the dark laundry room beyond.

The window there looked out on the graveled rear parking area and garages, where motion sensor lights illuminated two armed men. That made five, not counting Klinger, who should be well on his way to sleepy land. Not good odds. She studied the woods beyond the drive. Was her team out there, invisible in the dark, waiting for their moment?

Her question was answered a moment later by a series of explosions from the front of the house. Flashbangs, like the police used, were great for creating chaos and diversion. When they weren't available, Charisa had taught them that clusters of fire-works with long fuses worked almost as well. Something she'd learned not from her military training, but from her older brothers. Connected to bottle rockets and other easily obtainable fireworks, they could create a dazzling diversion that was even more effective if paired with smoke bombs. Right now, Michelle figured that explosions and smoke bombs were providing a significant display in front of Klinger's house.

Reassured that at least part of her team was there, Michelle waited until the two men had rushed toward the front of the house, then quietly let herself out and raced across the gravel to the safety of the dark woods just as more explosions started at the garage.

She ran straight into the arms of a dark-clad stranger.

"Not so fast," a woman whispered.

A slight foreign accent she was too agitated to place.

She didn't wait to see if the woman was friend rather than foe. She wriggled one hand free, snatched off her remaining earring, and jabbed it into the side of the stranger's neck. She seemed to disappear, though a stricken voice murmuring, "Oh my god!" followed as Michelle disappeared into the woods.

In the van, she threw herself into Charisa's arms, murmuring, "I'm okay. I'm okay." Then, getting herself together, she pulled off her wig, then the strips of fake skin and the nose bump and thickened jawline that altered her appearance.

* * *

SHE WAS ENJOYING A DEMURE glass of wine, ignoring her desire to down a generous tumbler of Scotch, and cautiously fingering her swollen ear, when her husband put down his book and studied her. She knew that look—worried and slightly disapproving. She waited to see what he would say.

"Came a little too close tonight, didn't you." It was not a question.

She held her tongue, refusing to ask how he knew. They had an agreement. This was her thing, and it mattered. She'd never told him it was also very exciting. But she wondered—was that woman in the woods one of his? Had he sent someone to watch over her? And if he had done so, was she grateful or annoyed?

"It was important. It *is* important." *Go back to reading,* she thought. *I do not want to argue about this.* She'd given up her career to be a helpmeet, criticized at every turn for being too tall, too black, too smart, for showing her arms, for every darned thing she did. Being part of the Tall Girls gave her a mission beyond the usual First Lady causes. And yes, tonight she *had* come close. But she was home. She was safe. And there was still a job to be done. They would get to Klinger, somehow, and bring him around. Because kids mattered. Sick kids mattered. And greedy CEOs without consciences had to understand that.

Had there once been a time when corporations had consciences or was she just forgetting her history?

* * *

IN THE MORNING, THERE WAS a text on her private phone from Lourdes: Klingpin Thur a.m. Roosevelt

Klinger would be at a breakfast meeting at the Roosevelt Hotel on Thursday.

A text from Alice: Bag Lady?

Should they consider using the bag lady ploy?

A text from Leela to the group: Lunch at Red Sands?

Michelle checked her schedule. Texted back: Late lunch? 2:00?

Charisa texted: Birthday party

A pretext for getting together. She was looking forward to it. She hoped lunch would give them a new strategy. Klinger had obviously been expecting them; he'd be even more wary now. They would need multiple levels of approach. She wondered: would Klinger bring his ugly, obviously Russian thugs, to an easily observed DC breakfast? Surely even an arrogant ass like Klinger knew he was supposed to avoid parading his Russian involvement. Most people had their heads so far into the sand, or were so busy just getting through their own days, they didn't care about corporate misbehavior or Russian meddling. But killing kids to provide Russian oligarchs with bigger profits? That might actually grab people's attention.

Her husband's frowning disapproval, and yesterday's failure, had fanned the smoldering embers of her anger into a bright flame. She was so tired of the cautious, scrutinized life of a First Lady. Never a chance to wander to the door in her bathrobe, coffee cup in hand and hair uncombed, and stare out at the morning, without someone saying, "Good morning, ma'am," and asking if she wanted or needed something. Never a day when she could get dressed without thinking of her image. She loved becoming someone else—the hairpiece with the fake braids, the small rubber bump in her nose that changed her face completely. She even liked the fake acne scars and the way the whole anonymous getup freed her.

Her bravado stumbled over a hard truth—they'd always done their work in the dark, behind the scenes, away from public scrutiny. Could they actually pull something off in the strong light of a DC hotel at lunchtime? She thought about high school, college, and law school. She hadn't backed down from the challenge of being a tall, determined, minority woman then. She wasn't going to back down now. Never mind that her husband had worn a cloak of sighing disapproval again this morning. He had the army, navy, air force, and marines at his disposal. And all the agencies. But the processes by which he might stop someone like Klinger were lengthy, cumbersome, and possibly ineffectual. All she had was wit and determination.

It had better be enough.

* * *

FAIZA AND ALICE WERE ALREADY at the table, heads together, giggling about something. Leela was next, quick and lean, her ever-present briefcase bulging like it was about to give birth.

Charisa had decided to go all-out military, bristling with braid and medals, her posture so upright and rigid that as she passed, women sat up straighter and men adjusted their ties. "Lourdes isn't coming," she announced before sitting down. "Something came up."

She sat, and then leaned in, whispering, "She thought keeping a low profile today might be a good idea. That Klinger might be suspicious. Might have someone watching her after last night, and meeting with us might get all of us flagged, too."

If anyone should have kept a low profile, it ought to be me, Michelle thought. Then wondered if Lourdes was getting cold feet. Since everyone was staring, she reached in her bag and pulled out a gaily wrapped present. "Whose birthday is it, anyway?"

"Mine," Alice said. "I hope you all got me something good."

As they passed her their gifts, she said, "And I hope someone's got a plan."

"Give us the details first."

"Drug company CEOs meeting with lobbyists for breakfast," Alice said. "Bag lady would be good. If she can get at him." She smiled sweetly. Alice looked like everyone's favorite daughter with her russet hair and freckles, and she underscored it today with a pink silk blouse and a pussycat bow. Despite her height, she looked so harmless. Those innocent blue eyes were totally false advertising, though, and her appearance belied a fierce intelligence and a college soccer player's determination to win. If she could disarm someone with her smile while figuratively kicking him in the balls, she was a happy woman. Though, Michelle knew she'd be just as happy if the kick weren't figurative. She'd seen Alice in action.

"After this one, I may need to pull back for a while," she said. "The White House is getting nervous."

"After this one, we should all pull back for a while," Leela said, fanning herself with her hand. "My cortisol levels are through the roof."

"Mine, too," Faiza agreed.

"Then we'd better make sure it works this time," Charisa said. "Last night came a bit too close. So. Thursday. I was thinking of holding him at gunpoint in the men's room and jabbing him."

"With the gun?" Alice asked sweetly.

"Only if you've got a tranquilizer gun that could deliver the stuff," Michelle said.

"That's a great idea," Charisa said. "I wonder if it's possible?"

"Person would have to be an awfully good shot. It wouldn't do to hit some random passerby. What do you think, Charisa?"

"About being a good enough shot? I am."

"About whether some kind of tranquilizer gun could deliver the dose? I may know someone . . ."

"Of course you know someone, Michelle," Faiza said, humming a bit of "You've Got a Friend." She grinned. "But can you get the goods before Thursday?"

It was Tuesday. Assuming she could reach Mary Grace and the item was available, it should be doable. And it seemed highly likely that the item would be available. Michelle nodded.

"I am going to be wearing a burka," Faiza said. "And acting suspicious. And to create the greatest possible diversion, I think Michelle should meet me at the hotel for breakfast—as herself. What do you think, Michelle?"

"It would definitely be diverting," Leela said, "but how do you eat breakfast in a burka?"

"I'm sure there's a YouTube video for that."

Over chicken salad and white wine, plans were hatched, alternative plans formulated, and escape plans put in place. If Klinger got away from them a second time, they would give up and go back to governing. Hard, though, when visions of small children with deadly diseases lingered in all of their minds.

* * *

THURSDAY WAS ONE OF THOSE crappy rain days that could bring a city where so many of the drivers were from other countries almost to a halt. Not as bad as a snow day, but enough to have Michelle and her team—coming from all parts of the city—sweating bullets as they sat in traffic jams. Actually, Michelle had an advantage here. People got out of the way of an official cavalcade from the White House. And this morning, she was traveling as herself, complete with police escort and the Secret Service. Normally, being the recipient of such fanfare was like an itch she couldn't scratch. Today it meshed nicely with the plan. It would be far easier for Leela, Charisa, and Alice to get into place when everyone's eyes were on her.

M.G. had come through for them with a truly excellent array of toys. In addition to a purse-sized gun that could deliver the dose, there was a cell phone injector, an electronic cigarette that could shoot a projectile, and stilettos that could deliver with a well-placed kick.

If the bag lady tripping and falling in the street with the electronic cigarette failed, Charisa, dressed as an elegant man, would follow him into the men's room. If the room was occupied or she otherwise couldn't deliver her dose, Leela was next with the cell phone, and sweet Alice, having shed her bag lady garb, would have another chance, delivering an "accidental" kick with her killer stilettos.

If no one succeeded, he might yet be mowed down by the stampede that would occur when an abandoned backpack under a nearby table started making noises and emitting smoke. Smoke would also begin pouring out of some of the restaurant's fabulous potted plants, and if all went as planned, there would be an explosion in the kitchen.

Michelle expected, given the nervous state about terrorism that was a constant in the city, that when things started going wrong, people would look at Faiza, who had the cover of dining with the First Lady and carried State Department credentials. The whole plan was designed to focus attention on them so that the others could operate, and escape, unobserved.

On her way in, trailed by her Secret Service detail, she gave a dollar to the ragged-looking woman with a shopping cart full of belongings huddled near the door. The woman wore a plastic trash bag with holes for her arms and head, a shabby baseball cap, and looked utterly miserable in the rain. After putting the dollar into a dirty hand, she turned to see a black limo parking, and David Klinger, under an umbrella held by a flunky, climbing out. She quickly moved on and hurried up the steps.

The Roosevelt Hotel lobby had what architects like to call a "Jesus spot," that place where people entering pause to admire the grandeur of the décor and mutter "Jesus!" Michelle wasn't actually impressed—she thought it was way overdone and that the cost of the massive vases of flowers on display everywhere would have fed several poor families for a year. Still, today she paused to admire it, forcing the people who wanted to enter behind her to stand outside in the rain—no way was her escort going to let the public get too close—and giving Alice a better shot at Klinger.

A commotion behind her caused her—and everyone else—to turn. She saw Klinger kicking at the ragged woman and calling her names. "Stop that awful man," she told the agent beside her, and he moved quickly away. She suppressed a smile as Klinger found himself confronting the Secret Service, while another man helped the woman to her feet. Head bent, she grabbed her shopping cart and shuffled away.

Michelle couldn't tell, but it looked like Klinger was unscathed. More than ever, she wanted the compassionless asshole to suffer. Well, they had three more chances. Four if she got close to him and could do it without discovery. Though she was concerned that the brute might have hurt Alice, she couldn't remember a time when she was so looking forward to a lunch.

The maître d' could barely keep it together to lead her to her table, which surprised her a bit since DC was the kind of place where it seemed like nearly everyone was a VIP and those who weren't acted like they were. But she was here to draw attention to herself, so she nodded graciously, stood tall, and followed him to the table. "The other party is already here," he said, and she felt his struggle to keep disapproval, and curiosity, from his voice stemming from why she was meeting someone wearing a burka.

When people talked about which superpower they'd like, Michelle never shared hers. It wasn't a want, it was real. She was able to project disembodied voices. Right now, a booming voice from somewhere in the room would have asked: "What are you staring at?" followed by "Mind your manners" and "Curb your prejudice." But she saved it for special occasions.

One might still arise.

Faiza stood as she approached, and as they embraced (and flashbulbs caught the First Lady embracing one of those suspicious Muslims), Faiza whispered, "Alice didn't get him."

"Is she okay?"

"She's fine. Thought it was a hoot. Now she's gearing up for another shot."

"I wish . . ." But it was obvious what she wished for.

She took her seat and studied the menu. She was starving and everything looked delicious. "What are you having?"

Faiza giggled and she looked up. "I was thinking about the spaghetti carbonara. Everyone in the room would be riveted by the sight of me trying to eat."

"Don't get carried away."

"I thought keeping their attention was the point. At least someone trying to lip-read our conversation isn't going to have much luck with me."

Klinger was on the other side of the room, at a large round table for eight. Frowning as he told the others something that had them all leaning in and then rearing back in shock. No doubt sharing his terrifying escape the other night. Lip-reading that would have been interesting. She was sure he was casting himself as a hero. Mostly, as his increasingly woozy performance on TV showed, he'd been too out of it to "be" anything.

After they'd ordered, and while they were waiting for their food, Michelle kept an eye on Klinger, thinking, "Go to the bathroom," as though willing someone to do something ever worked. Would the ability to project a disembodied voice be more successful? Multiple cocktails, mostly martinis, had been delivered to Klinger's table. Shouldn't they be having an effect?

"Mind if join you?" a woman's voice asked. A voice that was familiar, though she didn't know the small older woman who had paused beside their table. She realized it was the voice from the other night in the woods. The person who'd grabbed her. Michelle had been so focused on Klinger she hadn't noticed this woman approaching. She had the stooped, gray invisibility of the aging woman—the kind of person who can be easily overlooked. Indeed, that harmless invisibility was underscored by the fact that her Secret Service entourage didn't seem concerned. But something in the woman's face and manner made her say, "Certainly. Do join us."

"Ellie Jenner," the woman said, pulling out a chair and sitting down. "I'm with Protect the Children." When Michelle looked blank, she said, "We're an international organization that facilitates children's access to life-saving drugs. I believe . . ." A hesitation as she looked at Faiza, though there was nothing to see except a suggestion of eyes behind the lattice. "I hope—I believe— we are all on the same page with respect to Mr. Klinger?"

Several things occurred to Michelle at once. That this woman shouldn't have known anything about her involvement with the Tall Girls Book Club. She'd been careful. Nor that she was the one that the woman had grabbed the other night. This woman didn't look strong, while the person who grabbed her had been. And that if *she* was known, her disguise, and the Tall Girls' activities, were about to be blown, bringing on a national crisis.

Jenner must have been good at reading faces, because she said, very quickly, "Mr. Klinger doesn't know that I exist. Or that

I have any connection to Protect the Children. I work, like you, undercover."

She was not going to sit here in a busy restaurant in DC and ask, "How did you find me?" Instead, she said, "What brings you here on such a lovely day?"

Ellie Jenner smiled like she'd said something delightful—a smile she figured was for the staring tables around them—and said, "Backup. In case you need it."

Before she could probe further, their server appeared. "Will the lady be having lunch?"

The lady said she would, and ordered the signature burger, the one Michelle had wanted instead of the salad she'd gotten. There was no way a person could maintain the First Lady's schedule of luncheons and dinners and protect her waistline without constant vigilance.

When the server was gone, Faiza said, "Backup?"

"Diversions. Obstruction."

"But you have no idea what we've planned. You might be obstructing *us*."

"I hope not. Let's just see how it plays out."

"So, you two," Michelle said, trying for a diversion to keep herself from wringing her napkin like a chicken's neck, "if you could have a superpower, what would it be?"

"I'm torn," Faiza said, "between shooting killer rays from my fingertips and being invisible."

They both looked at their surprise guest. "Invisibility is great," she agreed. "Older women do, you know." And then she disappeared.

"Come back here this minute," Michelle ordered. "Before someone notices."

Poof! She was back. And there was no outcry, so it seemed that no one had noticed.

"Can you teach me that?" Faiza asked. "We could definitely get close to people more easily if we could be invisible."

Then she said, "Don't look now, but our friend is getting up from the table."

Momentarily forgetting not to be obvious, they watched Klinger head for the restroom. A moment later, a tall, slender, good-looking man headed in the same direction.

"Fingers crossed," Michelle said.

"He's one of yours?" Ellie Jenner asked.

Michelle nodded.

"Shall I see if I can be of assistance?"

"You might get shot," Faiza said. "And anyway, we don't even know if we can trust you, do we?"

At that moment, with the impeccably bad timing of servers the whole world over, theirs arrived with their lunches. By the time the ceremony of service was done, it was too late. Klinger was coming back to his table and he didn't look flustered. A moment later, the elegant young man returned to his solitary table, looking unhappy.

"Shoot!" Michelle said.

"Don't I wish," Faiza agreed.

Jenner tore into her burger like she was starving and Faiza was managing her sandwich pretty well, but Michelle had lost her appetite. What if nothing worked and Klinger walked away? Should she consider tapping Jenner's special talent? Someone who could make herself invisible could certainly get closer. But what if the woman was only there to distract *them*? It all made her head spin.

She was letting this matter too much.

Across from her, a vigilant Secret Service agent suddenly launched himself out of his chair and grabbed her. "We're leaving," he said, pointing toward a nearby table where smoke was beginning to emerge from a black backpack. As he pulled her to her feet, she amped up the emergency by having a woman's voice near Klinger's table scream, "Oh my god! It's a bomb! Over there. It's a bomb."

Klinger, always so concerned about the health and safety of others, literally overturned a chair and knocked his tablemates aside in his scramble for the door. Hell-bent on escape, he was somehow suddenly shoved sideways, right into the path of a stately, plump matron who, undisturbed by the furor, snapped his picture with her cell phone. Klinger stumbled, slapped at his neck like he'd been stung by a bee, and continued his plunge toward the door.

A plant pot in front of him began emitting clouds of smoke. He hesitated, turned, and looked frantically for an exit, bumping into an exotic, statuesque woman in a gorgeous red dress. She broke her fall by catching his arm, her stiletto kicking his leg as she stumbled.

Holy cow, Michelle thought, wondering what two doses would do. She sure hoped they hadn't killed him.

Jenner, appearing at her side, called, "Well done," as her guardians pushed her into a waiting car. As she watched, the woman disappeared again. She was going to have to find out how that was done. She was certain they would meet again.

* * *

THERE WAS TREMENDOUS RELIEF IN the oncology community when David Klinger, President and CEO of ResQ Pharma announced a price rollback on a critical cancer drug. Klinger, who had reportedly been quite ill for several weeks, spoke to reporters briefly, describing his own illness as producing a "Come to Jesus" moment. "We must balance profit with compassion," he said.

At the White House, Michelle learned the news while she was hosting her book group: Faiza, Alice, Leela, Lourdes, Charisa, and Mary Grace. They popped champagne to celebrate.

... THE CONTINUING MISSION
BY ADAM LANCE GARCIA

CAPTAIN JAMES T. CASPIAN OF the GCS *Traveler* watched the stars inch past. He tilted his glass of Remusian ale, the alien liquor's color shifting from pale blue to deep violet. He glanced at his workstation's screen, unsure whether the text message blurring in his vision was due to inebriation, exhaustion, or simply anger. Caspian took a heavy swig of his drink and bared his teeth as the alien beverage burned down his throat. He pressed down on the thumb-sized switch on his workstation and began to record.

"Captain's log. Universal Date: Twenty-four-zero-one-point-twenty-five-point-two. I have received word from Galactic Command that the Klingun Empire has sent their soldiers back in time in hopes of altering human history. To prevent this, Galactic Command has instructed me to send two of my crew after the Klinguns in what will almost assuredly be a one-way mission." Caspian cleared his throat, telling himself it was the Remusian ale, not his emotions, that were fermenting inside him. "There is no question that Galactic Command specifically sent me this request because they knew who I would choose for a mission of this magnitude . . ."

Caspian grimaced and bit back a curse.

"Galactic Command has effectively asked me to command my two best friends to almost certain death in another place, another time . . ."

Caspian took another angry swig before throwing his glass across the room, where it shattered.

* * *

THE LOW THRUM OF THE ship's engines was the only sound Caspian heard after he finished explaining Galactic Command's request to his senior staff. He turned to his Science Officer. "Commander Bah'rack, I understand the Vuhlk'n Science Institute studied time travel?"

Bah'rack arched his right brow, his dark skin glowing in starlight. "We explored the possibilities of it, yes, though we were never able to achieve it. Instead, we used the concept as a source of thought experiments."

Caspian nodded for Bah'rack to proceed.

"Let us assume one were to travel back in time to prevent an event from occurring—say, the founding of the Galactic Confederation."

Chief Engineer James MacDonald let out a derisive laugh. "I don't think we need assume that, Mr. Bah'rack."

"Indeed, Mr. MacDonald," Bah'rack said, his tone computer dry. "One line of thinking is that any attempt to change to the timeline would ultimately fail, as history is immutable. Another is that by simply entering the past, the Klinguns would instantly create a splinter universe, separate from the reality—ours—that they left. The third is that by attempting to alter the past they will create the very thing they are trying to change."

"And what's the fourth?" Dr. Biden, the ship's chief physician, asked. "Most of these Vuhlk'n thought experiments come in fours."

"The fourth is a paradox, a self-creating closed loop. The Klinguns always go back in time to affect history because they are already part of that history." Bah'rack laced his long fingers together. "There is, however, a fifth possibility."

Caspian was unable to contain to his surprise. "A fifth?"

"I have a feeling this is the one we need to worry about," Dr. Biden groused.

Caspian gestured to his Science Officer. "Go on, Bah'rack."

"The fifth is that reality is a single line of events, cause to effect, from the beginning of the universe to the end, and that any change made in the past will rewrite our present. And, as the doctor said, it is safe to presume that theory is what most concerns Galactic Command."

Caspian tried to keep his face unreadable and failed at the attempt. "It is indeed safe to presume."

Dr. Biden leaned his elbows on the conference table. "What're you not telling us, Jim?"

Caspian tried to keep Biden's gaze. "As far as Galactic Command is concerned, this would be a one-way mission."

Dr. Biden's jaw fell open. "Jesus. Can't we just warp the *Traveler* around the sun a couple of times or something? I think I saw that once in a fictional."

"I'm afraid it's a lot more complicated than that, Joe," Caspian replied.

"It would align with the majority of the theories we have discussed," Bah'rack observed. "Even if we are able to move backwards and forward in time, there is no assurance whether the 'future,' let alone the reality, we would return to would be the one we left." He looked to Caspian. "Does Galactic Command know to when the Klinguns have traveled?"

"They registered two time breaches. One sometime in the mid-twentieth century and another in the early twenty-first."

"That's a good . . . fifty, sixty years," Dr. Biden said. "There's no way of knowing what they're trying to change."

Bah'rack arched his right eyebrow. "Or if they have already succeeded. Captain, I volunteer myself for this mission."

Caspian had expected this. "The needs of the many . . . ?"

"Indeed, Captain. If the Klinguns stay true to form, they will try altering Earth's history through political means. My years as an ambassador to the Remusian Empire makes me the most politically experienced member of this crew."

"Are you sure, Bah'rack?" Caspian asked, hoping in vain that he could dissuade his friend. "Your skin tone may cause some . . . difficulties."

"I am not sure I understand, Captain. The color of my skin aligns with those found in humans from a range of geographical regions. I will quite easily, as I believe you say, 'blend in.'"

Dr. Biden turned to Bah'rack. "I'm afraid the captain is speaking of the issue of race."

"Yes, doctor, I too am speaking of the human race, as I have just said—"

"No, humans, for whatever reason, used to feel it necessary to divide themselves into . . . let's call 'em . . . sub-races based in part on the color of their skin, or where they were born, or even what they believed. Simply put, guys who looked like me—" He gestured to his pale white visage. "—used to beat up guys who looked like you."

Bah'rack's right brow shot up skeptically. "That is highly illogical."

"You have no idea." Dr. Biden rapped his knuckles against the table. "Well, if this green-blooded idiot is going, then I'm going with him, if only to make sure he doesn't do anything stupid. Or at least make sure that no one does anything stupid to him."

Caspian smiled sadly. It had all gone exactly how he expected. "Are you sure, Joe?"

Dr. Biden shrugged. "What else have I got to lose?"

* * *

"The time machine basically is a glorified transporter," MacDonald said, clapping the device with his palm. "It breaks up your atoms and then blasts them through a man-made wormhole to the approximate era when the Klinguns invaded. If you can't follow that, I can no help you, because that is the simple version."

"The science is perfectly sound," Bah'rack said.

"Yeah, sure, if all that gobbledygook he just spouted is science," Dr. Biden said, eyeing the machine with distrust.

Bah'rack placed his hands behind his back and began pacing around what looked to be nothing more than a large metal cylinder. Galactic Command had brought the time machine aboard several days earlier, and while the machine could move matter through time, it could not move matter through space, thus the *Traveler* was now at the approximate position of Earth in the mid-twentieth century, accounting for universal expansion. If the machine functioned as expected, Bah'rack and Dr. Biden would instantly appear in the exact same spot they were standing, but on Earth, hundreds of years earlier.

"This is the finest engineering ever to come out of GC," MacDonald said with some pride. "Of course, I probably would have made sure the internal dampeners weren't so dangerously unpredictable but . . . aye, it'll get the job done."

Dr. Biden clapped MacDonald on the shoulder. "Thank God you're not a doctor, MacDonald."

The doors to the cargo bay hissed open and Captain Caspian strode in, dressed in his green-and-gold dress tunic, the same outfit he wore for visiting dignitaries—or for crew funerals. The captain looked pale; dark circles had grown beneath his bloodshot eyes. Bah'rack tried to find the correct response to the captain's emotional state, but found himself unable to do so. He understood the captain was bereaved that he and the doctor would be taking part in this mission, but he could not comprehend why.

"Are you ready?" Caspian asked, failing to capture his typical bravado.

Bah'rack raised his brow. "I am, Captain. Are you?"

Caspian grasped Bah'rack by the shoulders. "Bah'rack . . ."

"We are fulfilling our duty as part of the Galactic Confederation," Bah'rack said. "There is no need for emotion."

"Don't listen to this robot, Jim," Dr. Biden said, clapping the captain on the back. "I'm barely keeping it together myself."

Bah'rack gave Dr. Biden a quizzical look. "But, Doctor, you volunteered—"

"Doesn't mean I'm not terrified, Bah'rack."

Captain Caspian frowned. "Bah'rack, your ears."

Bah'rack instinctively touched the newly rounded helix of his ear. "We will be arriving on Earth almost a full century before first contact. If my research were any indication, I would either be killed or believed to be someone dressing as a character from popular fiction. This should prevent either occurrence. I also studied, in detail, the American system of government from that era. The system is fundamentally flawed, but that seems to be the intention."

Dr. Biden laughed. "You gotta remember, the guys who originally wrote a lot those laws believed owning slaves was their God-given right and women shouldn't have equal rights."

Bah'rack's brow arched. "That is all highly illogical. Many of the Galactic Confederation's greatest leaders are women and slavery was proven to be an inhumane and wholly ineffective means of creating a labor force."

"You have to stop trying to apply logic to that time period, Bah'rack. They didn't have any of it. Christ, they were still arguing over scientific facts."

Caspian's morose grin transformed into a full smile, but Bah'rack could tell he was trying more than ever to fight back tears. "What will the twentieth century do with the two of you, my friends . . . ? I'm assuming Galactic Command has given you your identities for the time?"

"'Joe Biden' is fairly normal for the era, so it should be pretty easy. They just told me I'm going to have to drop the 'doctor' as most of the science I studied won't exist for a few centuries. It's gonna be like living in the Dark Ages."

Caspian nodded to Bah'rack. "And you?"

"They altered the Vuhlk'n transliteration of my name to something approaching the English of the era. However . . . the middle and surnames I have been given are similar to those of two major world figures from the period . . . Barack Hussein Obama," the Vuhlk'n said stiffly.

Caspian cocked his head, confused. "I'm not sure I see the problem, Barack."

"Hussein was the surname of a brutal dictator of the era, and Obama is phonetically similar to the Romanized name one of terra's worst terrorist leaders."

Caspian and Dr. Biden exchanged a concerned look. "Well . . ." Caspian said. "If we weren't so short on time I'd ask them to go and change it . . ."

"Besides, I don't think anyone will notice," Dr. Biden added, clapping the science officer on the shoulder.

Bah'rack eyed the doctor with muted derision. "That I very much doubt, doctor."

* * *

THE GOODBYES WERE BRIEF. CAPTAIN Caspian broke rank and separately pulled both Bah'rack and Biden into a long embrace. The Vuhlk'n stiffened at the sudden and unprecedented show of affection. Biden coughed back a sob and clapped Caspian on the back. With that, Bah'rack and Dr. Biden stepped into the time machine.

Once in place, Bah'rack touched his open palm to the center of his chest and bowed his head to those assembled and recited the Vuhlk'n proverb, "Do not fear the future. Shape it."

"I will certainly try, Bah'rack," Caspian said, no longer fighting tears.

MacDonald turned a switch and there was a flash of light, a thunder crack, and the two time travelers instantly found themselves on terra firma.

"The air smells funny," Biden noted immediately after they materialized.

"That is simply the aftereffects of the transportation, doctor," Bah'rack said as he pulled a chronometer from his jacket pocket. The device whirred as its circuits measured everything from the position of the stars to the slightest geological movements.

"No, it's the pollution," Biden said, sniffing the air. "My God, it's like inhaling gasoline. I knew this era loved fossil fuels but I didn't realize how bad it would smell! Jeez . . . Does that thing tell us where the hell we are? Or even when?"

Bah'rack read over the data. "I can say for certain that we are, at the very least, several decades from the twenty-first century. It will take some time to complete the necessary calculations to give you a specific date."

"Well, while you're doing that, let's make our way to civilization and, you know, look at a newspaper. Plus, I want to see if I can get my hands on some damn coffee . . ."

* * *

"WITH RESPECT, ADMIRAL," CASPIAN SAID hotly, "you cannot expect me to do nothing."

Admiral Ramirez's scowling visage briefly pixelated on the bridge's telescreen. "The instructions were clear, Captain Caspian."

"These are my men, Admiral. My friends."

The admiral exhaled audibly. "As you've protested many times, but the Klingun threat is too great. GC scientists—"

"Could have found a way to bring them back," Caspian snapped. "We've sacrificed Bah'rack and Biden's lives on a *theory*. You could have at least left us the time machine. We could find a way to retrieve—"

"Captain," the admiral said, her lips tight. "I will consider this outburst a result of your grief. You are ordered to patrol the Demarcation Region should the Klinguns attempt any further incursion. The matter is settled." The telescreen switched to the Galactic Confederation insignia, the conversation definitively over.

Caspian slammed his fist against the armrest; hating himself for thinking he could have convinced the Confederation to reconsider their plans.

"It's a pity the admiral's feed broke up," Caspian heard Helmsman Oshiro say. Caspian lifted his gaze to the ship's helmsman, whose expression was unreadable. "I couldn't understand her orders."

Before Caspian could interject, Ulhana, the ship's communications officer, cut in. "Captain, it seems that I was unable to record the admiral's message. Perhaps if we could try and reach her again, though it may take awhile to recalibrate the ship's communication array . . ."

A knowing smile formed at the corner of Caspian's mouth. He looked to each of his crew and nodded his silent thanks. He pressed the ship's intercom. "MacDonald . . . you're needed on the bridge."

* * *

"WHAT CAN I GET FOR YOU?" the waitress asked, appraising Bah'rack and Biden's anachronistic wardrobe.

Bah'rack and Biden were seated in a diner several miles from their arrival site, in the outskirts of a city Bah'rack initially mispronounced as *Ki-Ka-Goh*. Exhausted and hungry, both silently hoped they had brought the correct currency from the future.

"You guys still have coffee? The real stuff, right? Not the synthetic?" Biden asked with an exhausted smile. The vinyl seating creaked audibly beneath them and the foreign smell of cooking meat filled their nostrils.

The waitress impatiently tapped her pad with her pen. "There's only one kind of coffee, mister."

Biden slapped his palm against the table. "Then I'll have a coffee! Black. Biggest mug you got. And bacon. A plate full, crispy. And eggs. Three of them, sunny side up."

"And you?"

Bah'rack studied the menu for several seconds. "I shall have toast."

The waitress made a clicking sound in the back of her throat as she scratched down the order. "Toast it is. Back in a few."

"*Real* coffee and bacon and eggs!" Biden whispered excitedly. "None of that synthesized stuff we had to suffer on the *Traveler* for the last five years. The real deal!"

Bah'rack frowned. "Doctor, we must—"

Biden wagged his finger. "None of that 'doctor' stuff, Bah'rack. Not anymore. I need to get used to just being 'Joe.'"

"Very well . . . Joe. We must lay out our strategy to make sure that history proceeds as close to its original course as possible."

"'As close to its original course?'"

"No matter which theory of time travel proves to be correct, our very presence in the past means that history has been altered in thousands of ways, ranging from insignificantly minor to immeasurably extreme."

"Ripple effects, you mean?"

"Indeed, doctor."

"Joe," Biden corrected.

"Here you are," the waitress said, returning with two plates precariously balanced on one arm, her free hand gripping a coffee pot. "Coffee, eggs, bacon . . . and toast."

"Thank you, miss!" Biden said, taking the mug.

"I'll get you some butter for that toast," the waitress said after she placed the plates onto the table. "Anything else?"

"Actually, yes," Biden said. "There any, ah, buses that come through?"

"There's one that goes east, if you're heading that way. You just missed the twelve forty-five but there's a four forty-five you can still make."

Biden smiled. "Guess I'm headin' east."

"Well, let me know if you need anything. I'll go get that butter." The waitress wiped her hands on her apron and walked off.

Biden took a long sip of his coffee. He sighed in satisfaction. "Great Scott, that's wonderfully awful. The synthetic stuff is too sweet. Doesn't have that natural bitterness. And this—" He picked up a strip of bacon and chomped down. "The synthesizer doesn't even know how to make this happen," he said, his mouth full. "Good God Almighty . . . this almost makes living in the Dark Ages worth it."

"As fascinating as that is, doctor, we must focus on—"

"Delaware," Biden cut in. "My ancestral homeland. One of them, at least," he said with a circular wave of bacon. "That's where I'll be heading. Or maybe Pennsylvania."

"Doctor, I really think that we should work together to stop the Klingun efforts."

"Oh we will," Biden said, his mouth full, "but knowing the Klinguns they're probably already looking for a couple of Confederation idiots running around trying to throw a monkey wrench into their plans. Which reminds me," he tugged at his bright blue tunic, "we gotta find something to wear besides our uniforms."

"You are proposing that we—I believe the Earth saying is— 'divide and conquer?'"

"Bingo."

"That is indeed a logical plan, doctor."

Biden gasped. "Well, I think I just witnessed a miracle! You just showed me respect. Figures it would take traveling through time to make that happen."

"Your wit notwithstanding, doctor, how do you plan to combat the Klinguns?"

Biden chose not to correct Bah'rack. "Same way as you, get into politics, dirty as it makes me feel. Now, I may not be the emotion-less diplomat you are, but I know a thing or too about the human condition. Considering our journeys aboard the *Traveler*, helping people no matter their gender or species, is something I've gotten pretty good at. So, I might as well try to do it, even if it means I have to do it with speeches instead of sensor scanners."

"And you are confident you will be able to acclimate on your own?"

"Bah'rack, the whole reason I'm here is because I know I can. You on the other hand . . ." Biden aimed a strip of bacon at Bah'rack. "That remains to be seen."

"Doctor, I have spent weeks researching—"

"Listen, you green-blooded hobgoblin. There's a difference between researching and understanding. You don't understand basic human anything. If you and I are going to stop the Klinguns then you need to go and learn a few things. Now, I'm not saying you need to suddenly grow a third heart inside that alien chest of yours, but you're gonna have to figure some things out."

"Such as?"

"Firstly, toast isn't breakfast," Biden said, stealing Bah'rack's plate. "It's a side dish."

* * *

MACDONALD STARED AT CASPIAN IN disbelief. "Captain, I'm not sure I heard you correctly."

"I need you to build another time machine," Caspian repeated.

MacDonald waved a finger at his ear as if he had suddenly lost his hearing. "Yeah, you keep saying that and I keep thinking you must be mad."

"Mr. MacDonald . . . Bah'rack and Dr. Biden are stuck in another time trying to accomplish a mission beyond the scope of any challenge we've faced before. I won't let them die out there alone."

"The Galactic Co—"

"Are not part of this equation, MacDonald. What I need to know is if you can create a time machine based on the one Galactic Command sent us and modify it so it will bring our boys home. You know the machine's inner workings and the schematics are already in our computers."

MacDonald let out a crackling sigh and began pacing the bridge, mindful of the rest of the crew watching the conversation in silence. "Well, you see it's not as simple as all that, Captain."

Caspian grimaced. "You're telling me it's nearly impossible?"

"I'm not telling you 'nearly impossible,' I'm telling you it is."

Caspian's gaze went distant for a moment before snapping back to MacDonald. He rose out of his captain's chair and placed a hand on his chief engineer's shoulder. "MacDonald, how long have you been serving on this ship?"

"Nearly five years, sir," MacDonald said, chin raised.

Caspian clapped MacDonald on the back and said, "Then you know we don't do 'impossible' here."

"Aye, but let's suppose I am able to build another time machine. Even if we're able to find ourselves in the exact same spot where we left Mr. Bah'rack and Dr. Biden, we're going to be dealing with time dilation."

Caspian crossed his arms. "Time dilation?"

"The universe is expanding, right? At an increasing rate, aye?" MacDonald held up his hands so his palms were facing one another. "Assume this is us." He shook his right hand. "And this is Dr. Biden and Commander Bah'rack." He indicated his left and then pressed them together. "Now *assuming* we were able to get them back in time—and they haven't, you know, created a entirely new reality—there was only a brief moment when both time periods were in sync, but because of universal expansion, time in the two eras don't move at the same rate. We're not moving in parallel, ya kennit?" He started shifting his hands so that his right quickly rose up, while his left moved slowly. "The era we're in, and the era they're in, are rapidly moving out of sync."

"What does that mean, MacDonald?"

MacDonald shrugged. "It means, that for every second that passes for us, hours, even days might be passing for them. It means, that even *if* I found a way to get the commander and the doctor back, there's no way of knowing if we'll find them one minute after they arrived . . . or decades."

* * *

BIDEN CONSIDERED THE STYLIZED POSTER of Bah'rack.

"What do you think, doctor?" Bah'rack asked.

Biden glanced back at his old friend. While their mission against the Klinguns had always remained at the forefront of their minds, Biden could not help but reflect how much more human the Vuhlk'n looked compared to when they had first arrived in the twentieth century. The change had been subtle, a slow transformation that had escaped Biden's notice until now. He also looked so much older, even though he still looked infuriatingly young compared to Biden. Goddamn Vuhlk'n blood.

"Joe," Biden corrected under his breath, for the thousandth time. "My wife's the doctor, remember?" He tapped the four-letter word emblazoned beneath Bah'rack's portrait. "I didn't know 'Hope' was a Vuhlk'n concept."

Bah'rack placed his hands behind his back. "No, but it is a human one I have always very much admired."

Biden almost scoffed. "Admired? Sounds like us humans have been rubbing off on you."

Bah'rack looked over to Michelle, Sasha, and Malia on the other side of the campaign office. A smiled formed on his face. "Yes. I suppose you could say they have."

Biden leaned over and nudged Bah'rack with his elbow. "I've been meaning to ask," he whispered, "I thought Vulhk'ns couldn't procreate outside the Pa'Mour?"

Bah'rack failed at hiding his smile. "I have no comment on the matter."

"And how does Michelle feel about touch telepathy?"

The smile widened, something Biden had thought physically impossible for a Vuhlk'n. "I have no comment on that either."

Biden clapped him on the shoulder. "Smart man." They started walking together. "Running for the White House, who'd ever have thought we'd be here, all those years ago?"

All around them young men and women worked, making phone calls, setting up rallies, and writing speeches. They were people looking for something greater and better in a complex and difficult world, galvanized by Bah'rack's dreams—knowledge—of the future.

"I confess I did not," Bah'rack said, "but we must do all we can to prevent the Klingun efforts from succeeding."

"Not that we've ever been able to figure out who they are and what their plans are."

"Sectarian violence, distrust in facts and science. These are just some of the hallmarks of the Klingun invasion techniques. We see it in the Middle East with those who twist a great faith into something abhorrent, and even here at home with the extreme right—"

Biden took Bah'rack's arm and stopped him. "Did I just hear you call this country 'home'?"

"For all intents and purposes, it is, doctor."

Biden looked over Bah'rack's shoulder at their wives and children and knew he was right. "Tell me, Bah'rack, in your time here, have you figured out which of the various time travel theories we're in?"

Bah'rack shook his head. "I cannot say. I doubt we will ever find out."

Biden frowned. "I'll admit I never heard of a President Obama, let alone a Vice President Biden."

"Neither have I . . ."

Biden sighed. "Well, at least we can say we gave it the old college try."

* * *

"CAPTAIN!" HELMSMAN OSHIRO SHOUTED as the *Traveler*'s klaxon began to sound. "Klingun war vessel just appeared out of warp!"

Caspian rose out of his chair. "On screen."

The forward telescreen dissolved to show an E-shaped vessel hurtling toward the *Traveler*. Its weapons were primed, a trio of glowing red pinpricks at the forward sections of the alien ship.

"All crew!" Caspian shouted. "Battle stations."

The klaxons blared again as Caspian took his seat. The crew of the *Traveler* had faced Klingun war vessels before, but the battles had been close and pitched, with dozens dying before the day was won. But with the lives of Bah'rack and Biden at stake, Caspian couldn't help but find the Klinguns' arrival deeply personal.

"Captain," Ulhana said, pivoting her chair to Caspian, "I'm getting a signal from the Klingun vessel. They wish to open communications."

"Put them through."

The visual of the war vessel was replaced by a shock of static, which quickly resolved to show the pale, bloated face of Caspian's old nemesis, the Klingun Commandant Q'rah.

"Captain Caspian . . ." Q'rah purred, the air sack hanging from his chin vibrating with each syllable. A Cheshire grin stretched across his naturally pale white face. The thin golden tendrils on his scalp bristled. "How . . . surprising to find you here."

"Commandant Q'rah," Caspian said. Klinguns were a proud and deeply volatile race. Any perceived slight, no matter how minor, was often met with extreme violence. Any other time, Caspian might have dived headfirst into a military engagement, but he would not risk it, not now. "You seem to be pretty far from the Demarcation Region."

Q'rah's air sack inflated. "Is that so? I had barely even noticed. We registered some . . . very interesting readings in this sector and Klingun High Command asked us to investigate."

"Are you in need of assistance? In accordance with the Bantorian Treaty of 2310, I offer myself and my crew to aid in your return to Klingun space."

"Yes, it seems that our instruments must be malfunctioning," Q'rah said, playacting. He waved at one of his men just off-screen.

"I'll have my crew look into it before any . . . *undesired* conflict can occur. We wouldn't want to break any treaties, would we?"

Caspian bit back a knowing smile. "Yes, we wouldn't want that . . ."

Helmsman Oshiro's hands raced over his controls. "Captain," he said quietly so that he wouldn't be picked up by the intership communication. "I'm getting some strange readings from the Klingun vessel . . ."

Caspian gestured for Oshiro to hold. "It seems we're having some instrument problems of our own. Why don't we reconnect in ten minutes? Hopefully all will be well and we can escort you back to the Demarcation Region."

Q'rah nodded, his smile never wavering. "In ten of your minutes, then. Let us hope we will not run out of time."

The telescreen switched back to the image of the war vessel hanging in space. Caspian immediately jumped out of his chair and ran over to Oshiro's console. "What is it, Mr. Oshiro?"

Oshiro indicated a large peak on his console's screen. "These are the same chroton readings we measured—"

Caspian's eyes shot up to the Klingun war vessel. "Before Bah'rack and Biden traveled back in time . . ."

The soniclift doors hissed open and MacDonald ran onto the bridge. Caspian knew without being told that MacDonald had seen the same readings in engineering. "Captain! They're doing it now! The Klinguns are about to travel back in time!"

Oshiro frowned. "But Galactic Command said . . ."

"It's bloody time travel!" MacDonald exclaimed. "It doesn't matter when you leave, laddie! Only when you *arrive*."

Caspian was already running to the soniclift. "I need three from security for a boarding party. MacDonald, with me. Oshiro, you have the conn. If we can stop the Klinguns here, we may be able to bring our friends home!"

* * *

THE OVAL OFFICE WAS SMALLER than Bah'rack had expected, but no less elegant in its simplicity. He stepped behind the desk, where he found an off-white envelope, his name—his human name—handwritten across it. He touched the corner of the envelope, appreciating the reality of it all. They had made it here, he and Biden both, a destination neither of them had expected when they'd first set out on this journey. Vuhlk'ns were without ego, but Bah'rack could not help feeling something approaching pride at achieving this highest office.

"It's smaller than I expected," Biden observed. "All those old vidfiles made this place look massive, opulent but when you stand in it . . . it's kind of a small, slightly oval room with a couple of paintings and some windows."

Bah'rack debated sitting behind the desk, but decided he was not ready to fully acknowledge the desk—the chair—was truly his yet. He wondered if Caspian would have sat down immediately.

"You don't think Dubya was a Klingun, do you?" Biden asked.

Bah'rack looked at the envelope containing the letter from the former president. "Misguided, yes. Flawed, certainly. But altogether human."

"Well, I guess that's a relief, huh?"

"I'm not sure it is."

"And why do you think that, you pessimist?"

"Because though we know how great humanity will become, we have also seen its terrible potential these last few years, when hate and fear are used to steer events. We know what men can do in those times; we can only imagine what the Klinguns will do if they come into power . . . Thus, we must structure our administration on the ideals of the Galactic Confederation."

Biden arched an eyebrow. "You don't think it's a little soon for that? There are already some idiots calling themselves the 'tea baggers,' accusing us of government overreach even though we haven't been in office for more than a few hours. They're trying to be cute, but I think they're missing the double entendre—or maybe they're right on point. There're even some who think you weren't born in this country, which let's be honest, on that point they're technically correct . . ." Biden sighed. "It's not that I don't want to reach for the ideals of the time we left, I'm just not yet convinced the people of this time are ready for it."

"They're not," Bah'rack conceded, "but our goal these next four years—"

"Don't count us out just yet, Bah'rack. This might be an eight-year deal."

"Either way, our time here must be spent leading by example, striving for that dream, in incremental ways if need be, and perhaps, one day, others will find it in themselves to make the leaps on their own. Such a seismic shift in human nature cannot be achieved overnight, but we can lay the groundwork. While the Klinguns have made no overt action against us, they are playing the long game, and whatever they are planning, I fear it will come from an unexpected quarter, in a way we cannot fully prepare for . . ."

* * *

THE KLINGUN VESSEL MATERIALIZED AROUND them. Transporting onto a Klingun ship without proper authorization went against a dozen treaties, but Caspian had never been one to follow procedure. They were in a dark corner of the ship's cargo bay, a location chosen for its infrequent patrols. Caspian switched his communicator to a secure frequency. "Oshiro, this is Caspian. Have the Klinguns been alerted to our presence?"

"Not yet, Captain," the helmsman said through a burst of static, "but the croton readings we're getting are off the charts."

"Understood. Caspian out." He switched off his communicator. He looked over to MacDonald and his red-shirted security team. "MacDonald, locate the source of the croton emissions."

MacDonald nodded, already studying his scanner. "Aye, Captain."

"Do you think they like gold?" one of the security team said, stunned by the obscene opulence of the Klingun vessel.

"First time aboard a Klingun war vessel, Ensign Wright?" Caspian asked.

Ensign Wright nodded, doing her best to hide her trepidation. "Yes, sir."

"You should see their palaces," Caspian said with a smirk. "Towering edifices they insist on emblazoning their names upon."

"Sounds crass."

"You have no idea."

MacDonald's scanner let out a soft ping. "I've locked onto the time machine, Captain . . ." His face fell.

"Where is it MacDonald?"

"It's in the ship's power core, and the only way to get there from here . . ." he swallowed the lump in his throat, "is to go through . . ."

"Is to go through the ship's central command," Caspian finished. Grimacing, he set his phaser to kill. "Well, we'd better get started."

* * *

"At least a dozen civilians would be killed in the blast," Admiral McRaven said, indicating the larger of two circles surrounding the Pakistani compound.

The members of the Security Council silently shifted their gazes to look to the president, waiting, some more impatiently than others, to hear what he would say. The mission had been in the planning stages for months, ever since Intelligence confirmed the compound had been built to specifically to hide someone of significance. Biden had once insisted the target was a Klingun agent, a concept that Bah'rack had dismissed. While the target had used fear and anger at the West to build his organization, and employed brutal tactics to kill thousands, Bah'rack only saw evidence of humanity's worst instincts at play.

"In addition to those in the compound?" Bah'rack asked after a moment, aiming a finger at the wider circle.

Admiral McRaven nodded. "That is the estimate, Mr. President."

Bah'rack studied the map for several more moments in silence. War, even during the comparatively utopian era Bah'rack had been born into, was still prevalent. Bah'rack had ordered the death of enemy forces in the heat of battle long before he had done so in this era, and it was an action he never enjoyed. But more often than not those decisions had been made to prevent the loss of civilian lives, to protect those who had wanted nothing of war.

It was why he found himself recoiling at the idea of civilians, perhaps children, dying so that they might kill one man.

"That is unacceptable, Admiral," he said at length.

"If I may play devil's advocate, Mr. President," Admiral McRaven said, stiffening, "I think it would be fair to assume that the civilians both in and outside of the complex know who is living there."

"And would that make us any better than our target?" Bah'rack glanced over at Biden, who gave him an encouraging nod. "No, I do not believe that is the ideal we should strive for."

"Ideal?" McRaven bristled. "Sir, there have been civilian deaths in a number of our drone—"

"And I committed their names and number to memory," Bah'rack said sternly. "This target is too important. If we are going to send a message to the world, it will be that his crimes will not be tolerated, and that we will not mirror them."

Bah'rack rose and the room followed suit.

* * *

ENSIGN WRIGHT WAS KILLED DURING a skirmish in a Klingun ship's passageway; shot in the back by a high-powered blaster that disintegrated her in a flash of light. The two other security officers fell as Caspian and MacDonald made their way through the guard detail outside the ship's power core where they found the Klingun time machine. The machine was larger and more advanced than the one built by Galactic Command, laced with gold and precious gems for no reason that Caspian could discern. Commandant Q'rah was already standing inside the time machine, dressed in a loose-fitting garment that hung off his bloated frame.

"Captain Caspian!" Q'rah barked. "It seems we have run out of time after all!"

Caspian moved to lunge at the Commandant when MacDonald held him back.

"No, Captain! The machine's about to—" MacDonald was drowned out by the crackling burst of energy.

But even if he had heard him, Caspian would have refused to listen.

Instead, he raised his phaser and fired.

* * *

THERE WAS NOTHING SPECIAL ABOUT the elementary school. From the outside it looked like hundreds of other school buildings Bah'rack had seen over the years: concrete and glass, surrounded by a parking lot. But it was what had occurred inside those walls that had brought Bah'rack here. And as with the civilians who had died because of the various wars waged in America's name, Bah'rack knew the names of each child that had died here just two days ago.

And each one broke his hearts.

He had witnessed so much horror during his time in this era, crimes committed in the name of God, or country, or race, or simply for power. Crimes that made him question whether he should continue with this mission, if the human race was really indeed worth saving. But this. . . . Twenty-seven lives had been cut so cruelly short. So many of the victims not even seven years old.

He questioned whether there was any logic to the universe. He desperately wanted to believe the monster that had done this had been a Klingun invader, but he knew it wasn't, and that made it all the more painful.

He had spent the day moving from room to room, speaking with the grieving, the mothers and fathers, the brothers and sisters of the children that had been taken away. He did not want to give them empty promises, did not want to give them hollow words, though every fiber of his being wanted to tell them he could make it so something like this could never happen again. But he knew it would, just like it had happened so many times before. So, he listened. He listened to stories of the ones they had lost. Shared with them moments of silence. Whispered prayers and held hands. In every meeting he was strong for them. He was resolute. He kept himself composed for their sakes as much as his own.

It was only when he walked between classrooms that he let himself feel the weight of the grief he carried. He put his hand on the doorknob to the next classroom and for a moment, his shoulders slumped forward, his head hung low. He thought of his daughters, his two perfect girls so quickly becoming women, both given names that in his native tongue meant grace and strength. He thought about what he would tell them when he returned home. What kind of world had he brought them into? What kind of world would he leave them?

He took a deep breath, rolled back his shoulders, lifted his head, and stepped through the door.

* * *

MacDonald stood over Q'rah's body, which was facedown on the floor of the time machine. "I can honestly say I did not expect that to happen," he admitted, scratching his head. MacDonald looked over to the captain still standing at the time machine's controls. The engineer walked over, his brow furrowed. "Captain, what're you doing?"

"Trying to figure out this damned thing." Caspian smacked the controls in frustration, unable to read the alien script. "Tell me you understand Klingun, MacDonald."

MacDonald's face lit up. "Aye, Captain! I do!" He stepped in front of the controls and quickly went to work. "This is an incredible machine, sir. Makes the one Galactic Command built for us look like a piece of— Captain! This device even has retrieval capabilities."

"You mean—?"

"Aye," MacDonald said smiling, broadly. "We can bring our boys home."

Caspian clapped MacDonald on the shoulder. "Great work, MacDonald!" He ran over to the platform. "Set the machine to send me back to immediately after Bah'rack and Biden arrived and then we can bring them back!" Caspian turned around to see MacDonald hesitating with his finger over the controls. "MacDonald?"

The ship's engineer swallowed. "Captain . . . There's just one problem . . ."

Caspian jaw clenched, but he said nothing.

"We can send you back, aye. And we can bring all three of you back. But, Captain . . . there's something you should know."

* * *

BAH'RACK AND BIDEN SAT IN the Oval Office, waiting for the president-elect to arrive.

The election had not gone well.

Terrorist attacks in America and around the world had unnerved the populace, and an undercurrent of resentment at a rapidly changing world allowed a dark-horse candidate to succeed. While the majority of voters had chosen Bah'rack's preferred successor, an intentional flaw in the system allowed a minority of voters in three states to elect a narcissist who played to the anxieties of a shrinking demographic and classified whole races and religions as something to be hated. And those were just a few of his shortcomings.

It was a loss that Bah'rack took personally, a bruise that refused to heal. But in a gesture of national unity, Bah'rack invited the president-elect to the White House in an effort to honor the laws of the nation he had grown to love, and to finally face the enemy he had sworn to combat so many decades ago.

There was a knock on the door and both Bah'rack and Biden ôtîffcncd.

"Come in," Bah'rack called.

One of Bah'rack's aides eased open the door and took a half-step into the Oval Office. "Um . . . sir, there's someone here to see you . . ."

"Mr. Tr—?"

"Um. No. He says his name is Caspian . . ." She pulled her lips in. "And he's, um . . . he's dressed like Captain Kirk."

Bah'rack and Biden stood in unison.

"Let him in," Bah'rack said.

The aide stepped outside and a moment later Captain J. T. Caspian walked into the Oval Office, looking exhausted but no older than Bah'rack had last seen him.

"Captain," Bah'rack gasped.

Caspian's smile stretched across his face. "Bah'rack. Dr. Biden. I cannot tell you how good it is see you."

"Jim, Jesus Christ, what're you doing here?" Biden breathed.

"Here to rescue you. I thought that was obvious," Caspian said, flapping his arms.

Bah'rack glanced over to a photo of Michelle, Sasha, and Malia, and then to Biden, who only raised his eyebrows. Neither knew how to explain to the captain that leaving this time period was simply out of the question.

The captain looked around the Oval Office. "It seems you two did pretty well for yourselves."

Perhaps they should address the more immediate questions first. "The time machine," Biden said deliberately, "it could only send—"

Caspian's smile shrank silently. "We captured the Klingun's time machine. It's more advanced, which means we can bring you back. In fact, I'm disobeying a number of orders from Galactic Command, but that's really no different than any other day."

Bah'rack arched his brow. "But we still haven't been able to locate the Klingun forces. And frankly at the moment they are the least of our concerns. . . . The recent rise in xenophobia around the world is almost certainly leading—"

"The Klinguns never arrived," Caspian said, his voice cracking. The room suddenly felt too small. "I'm sorry . . ."

Biden's jaw inched open. "But, Galactic Command . . ."

"Detected two major chroton events," Caspian explained, shaking his head. "One created by the Klinguns' machine, the other by ours. One in the mid-twentieth century, the other in the early twenty-first. Command had no way of knowing which event corresponded to which machine. What they didn't know was that the Klinguns never made it out of our era. It was Commandant Q'rah," Caspian clarified, a name nearly forgotten by Biden and Bah'rack both. "He was going to be the invasion force. We stopped them, MacDonald and I, before Q'rah could travel back in time. But my phaser blast damaged the machine . . . and while we have retrieval capability I could only transport to this time and place." Caspian cleared his throat. "So, what Galactic Command registered wasn't Q'rah arriving at this moment. It was me, here now, coming to bring you both home."

"The mission isn't over," Bah'rack said firmly.

Caspian balked. "Bah'rack, the Klinguns never arrived. . . . There is no mission."

Biden shook his head, his hands trembling. "No, Jim. The bastard that's coming here, all those horrible things that we witnessed over the years . . ."

"Were simply humans at their worst," Bah'rack finished. He frowned and his eyes drifted to the windows overlooking the Rose Garden. He raised his head. "We can be better, not just when the

Galactic Confederation is established, but these people, right now." Bah'rack looked to Biden, then to Caspian. "If there is one thing I have learned these many years it is that hate is the minority and that hope belongs to the majority. But now we know for certain that though the worst of humanity may have won in the short term, I know now that we will win in the long run."

Biden looked to Caspian, then to Bah'rack. A ghost of a smile forming on his face. "I suppose we now know which time travel theory we're in, don't we?"

Bah'rack nodded. "A paradox. We traveled back in time to change history because we were already part of that history."

"How can you know, Bah'rack?" Caspian asked.

"You, Jim," Bah'rack said with a nod to his former captain. "You are evidence that our mission will succeed."

Caspian smiled sadly. "You can still come home. The both of you. Now that we know."

President Barack Hussein Obama looked to Vice President Joseph Robinette Biden Jr. and knew without speaking that they were in agreement. "No, Captain, we *are* home, and there's work we still need to do."

TRUE SKIN
BY ERIC BEETNER

Tiny white flecks of spit hit the microphone when Russ got all riled up. And he was riled. His face reddened, his veins pulsed. You couldn't see it over the radio but he knew his listeners could hear it in his voice. It's why they loved him, over three million strong. He told the truth, as he saw it.

"And a lot of people are gonna say I hate Mr. Obama for his skin color." He scoffed.

Marc, his engineer had to move fast on the faders to avoid peaking levels when Russ got this intense. It made the job exciting, though, keeping up with the daily rants. He worked the boards like a jazz pianist.

"I have no problem with Obama's skin color. No problem. Anyone who says otherwise is a liar and a race-baiter and probably one of those liberal tree-hugger feminists. Who the hell knows what all they're into these days? How do they have time to do much of anything toward their liberal, gay-friendly, oil-hating agenda when all they do is sit around and criticize me all day?"

Make yourself the victim, Russ. They love it when they feel persecuted. They love to feel like you're the outsider. Doesn't matter that you make over two million a year and have friends in the highest offices of the RNC in Washington. The listeners don't need to know that.

"My issue with the so-called president is this."

He paused for dramatic effect. He let his heavy breathing tickle the microphone, huffing into radios across America. They knew what came next, but like a rock star who saves the hits for the encore, they waited for the riff they wanted to hear.

"Mr. Obama, I want to see your real skin! Your lizard skin. You and all your liberal, lizard-people cronies in Washington, on Wall Street, in Hollywood. One day, as God is my witness and with one hand on the Holy Bible and the other on the Constitution, I will unmask you and your kind. You won't get away with it. You won't be allowed to run free and conquer the world. The lizard people will be defeated, and it will be American might that will do it!"

Marc cued the music, Russ slumped back in his seat, away from the mic and wiped a sheen of sweat off his forehead. Through the glass, Tina, his producer, gave a thumbs up with a wide, toothy grin. Another day preaching to the converted.

* * *

"GOOD ONE, RUSS," TINA SAID. "They'll be talking about that on CNN tonight."

"Screw those liberal media elites."

Sometimes it was hard for Russ to turn it off, like a boxer fresh from the ring and still itching to fight.

"You got two guys here to see you in your office."

"Who?"

"RNC guys. I didn't get their names."

"Okay, thanks."

Waiting for Russ were two men in dark suits, crisp white shirts, red neckties. They stood stoically as he entered his roomy office and went straight for his plush leather chair behind the desk, toed open a mini fridge, and scooped out a can of his favorite brand of cola.

"Gentlemen," Russ said. "Whose office are you from? Newt? Mitch?"

"We're from the head office at the RNC," one man offered.

"Okay. You got new talking points? New hit list? I've been trying to take down Al Franken with some sort of Frankenstein thing. Seems like a no-brainer but I can't get one to stick. I mean geez, Stein even sounds Jewish so you'd think—"

"We need you to stop with the lizard-people stuff."

Russ furrowed his brow, took a sip of his drink.

"Stop it?"

"Yes. Immediately."

"Do you know how many comments that got on the show page the first day we did that? How many retweets we got the second time? The people love it."

"We still need you to stop."

Russ watched the two men standing dispassionately on his rug.

"I think it's got legs." He tipped the can back again.

The other man spoke for the first time.

"We're not asking."

Russ was taken aback. The soda stuck in his throat and burned. He swallowed it down.

The two men turned and left without another word. Russ thought about putting in a call to one of his high-ranking friends. To figure out who at the head office was telling him to back off. Get Boehner to remind them who the mouthpiece was and who had his face on buses and billboards along with his voice in the ear of the precious base voters they cherished like uncut diamonds.

He filled the can of soda back to full with a mixer of rum.

* * *

THE NEXT BROADCAST RUSS THOUGHT about laying off for a minute. Maybe two. But the switchboards were already lighting up. The website had nearly half a million hits the day before, the

Twitter page gained over a thousand followers. People were reporting witnessing the lizard people at work, at the store, behind the masks of government officials.

God, these people were stupid as hell. And Russ loved every damn simple-minded one of them. Especially when they lined up at his feet with their mouths open, ready for him to jam whatever nonsensical crap spouted off the top of his head that day.

"Let me ask you this, people . . . you ever take a close look at Joe Biden's eyes? Kind of . . . what's the word . . . reptilian, don't you think? Mitch McConnell doesn't look like a reptile. Paul Ryan doesn't. Louie Gohmert. And why?"

He paused, holding in a laugh. Behind the glass Tina was clutching her sides and her grin threatened to tear her facelift scars.

"Because they're not lizard people like Obama and Biden and Ginsberg and Warren and Pelosi and, hell, practically all of Hollywood outside of Clint Eastwood."

The spit was flying again.

* * *

WHEN RUSS GOT BACK TO his office there'd been no announcement about visitors, but there they were again. Russ walked in, deep in thought about his contract renewal at the end of the current quarter. If he could keep the trajectory of subscribers to his satellite channel he could easily ask for another three million a year and they'd consider it a bargain. Maybe time to write another book. . . .

"We told you to stop."

Russ jumped, turned to see the two suit-clad men behind dark glasses.

"Whoa. Didn't see you there."

"We told you to stop," he repeated.

"Yeah, listen, I don't think you guys are seeing the long play on this. Tell you what, set up a meeting with Newt or Johnny B. and I'll get them on board. They can send it upstairs to anyone and then we'll see if I should lay off or not."

The two men traded a look, then turned their sunglassed faces back to Russ.

"People are asking questions. The press is investigating. People are posting photos to Instagram."

"It's called engagement, fellas. Lifeblood of the infotainment world."

"It's risky."

The partner spoke at last. "And it has to stop."

Russ fell into his chair with a sigh. He didn't take orders from lackeys like this. Karl Rove wants to come to his chambers and maybe he'll listen. The ghost of Ronald Reagan—maybe. But these guys? Junior hacks from the RNC? No. Not on his show, in his studio.

"Look, guys, my job is to give the people what they want to hear. And right now, what they want to hear is that Obama and everyone in his administration is a lizard person bent on world domination and eating their young." Russ smiled. They didn't smile back.

"And fact is, boys, this is my show. I don't take orders from you guys. I'm on satellite radio—I barely take orders from the FCC." Then, under his breath, "Bunch of goddamn socialists."

Again, the pair exchanged a look. It was like they had silently agreed to move on to Plan B.

"There have been others before you."

In tandem, they took a step closer. Russ kicked open his mini fridge and got out a cola.

"There will be others after you."

They stepped closer.

"Our message will be broadcast. And it will be *our* message."

Russ cracked the top on his can. "Or what? You cancel my show? No can do. I'm a private citizen. I got a contract. Binding. More binding than the Constitution."

The two men had reached the edge of his desk. If they meant to intimidate, they were succeeding. But Russ knew he couldn't give in to them. He didn't want his show watered down. He had a hook now. He was getting more buzz than Limbaugh. More articles than O'Reilly. More hits than Beck. That's not when you hit the brakes, it's when you hit the accelerator.

"Frankly," he said, "I don't know why you care so much. This isn't off-message. I'm not suddenly for Obamacare. I'm not for housing subsidies all of a sudden. What's the big deal?"

"It's not information we want spread."

"If a few crackpots want to have a little fun at the expense of the president, what's the harm? You guys didn't bat an eye at the birth certificate stuff."

"This is different."

"Yeah? Why?"

Russ leaned back smugly. He sipped from his can, daring them to keep pushing.

With one more look between them, they each reached up and removed their sunglasses. When they turned back to Russ he nearly choked on his soda.

Their eyes. Reptile eyes. Lizard eyes.

"Because *he* is not one of the lizard people. *We* are the lizard people."

Russ let the can fall from his grip and land on the carpet where it spouted foam.

"Is this a joke?"

"We told you to stop."

"Wait, just you or the whole RNC?"

Together they said, "Everyone."

Russ slid his chair back toward the wall. His mouth was dry, his tongue thick and slow.

"Newt?"

They nodded.

"Mitch?"

They nodded.

"Paul? Louie? Palin? McCain?" The chair hit the wall and stopped. "Michele Bachmann?"

With a high-pitched screech the two men leaned back their heads and seemed to stretch. Their necks elongated and the skin split. There was no blood, only a green underskin below their human skin. Scales. Rough and reptilian. Right there in his office they shed their human disguises and presented themselves. Six-foot-tall lizard men, forked tongues lashing out of their mouths tasting the air. Yellow eyeballs staring coldly at Russ.

Strips of human flesh fell away and landed like discarded napkins on the carpet. Their suits were torn away by ridged skin and elongated tails burst through the seat of their pants.

Russ waited to be woken from a dream. A slow hissing sound filled the office.

All of them? he thought. *All this time? I've been on the wrong side.*

Tina knocked once on the door and then came in.

"Numbers are huge, Russ. This Lizard People thing is—"

She stopped when she noticed the two figures with their backs to her looming over Russ. Torn suits fell from their shoulders revealing scaled skin. Together they turned. She heard the hiss first, then saw the eyes. Tina screamed.

One of the lizard men shot a thick stream of liquid from his throat. It arced across the office and landed in Tina's face, the accuracy of his spitting worrisome to Russ. Tina screeched louder, the fluid burning like acid on her soft, human flesh.

The lizard rushed her in quick, jerky movements and bit into her side with tightly packed rows of sharp, triangular teeth. It clamped down on her midsection and jerked its head from side to side, tearing away chunks of flesh and opening her gut. When it pulled its powerful jaws away, Tina's insides came spilling out onto the carpet. Her screaming had stopped.

Russ was paralyzed against the back wall of his office. *The lizard people are real!*

The lizard spun his human-like head to look back at Russ, blood running over the green scales. Bits of flesh dripped from its mouth.

Russ pushed off the wall and ran. It didn't matter what side he thought he'd been on, he was on the wrong side of these creatures now and he needed to escape.

He juked right, thinking of his college days as a member of the practice squad. If only they'd let him play on varsity maybe he wouldn't have joined the radio club and none of this would have happened.

The lizard went for his feint, then he pushed off and stabbed forward to the left. His foot caught on something, like going over a trip wire. Russ sprawled out with his arms spread wide to try to catch himself before he fell. His ankle had hooked on a long string of Tina's intestines leaking from her body.

Hissing filled the room. Russ looked up to see the two lizard men stalking him. One let Tina's flesh fall from its mouth. Their tails twitched with anticipation.

Russ backpedaled across the floor. In a reverse crab walk, he shimmied out the door and kicked it shut. He spun and stood, then ran down the hall to his studio.

Marc was just coming out of the control room when Russ barreled into him.

"Jesus, Russ! What the hell?"

"It's true. They're real."

"What? Who?"

"Them. They're real."

Russ clawed at Marc's shirt, trying to get him to understand something he didn't understand himself.

"What the hell's gotten into you, Russ? Come sit down."

He held Russ's arm as he guided him to the couch in the back of the control room.

"Shut the door," insisted Russ.

"Okay, okay. Calm down."

Marc shut the door and as the handle clicked, a blood-smeared green face banged into the thin strip of glass cut into the door. Marc jumped back.

"What the hell was that?"

Fists and clawed hands began to scrape at the door.

"I told you," Russ said, his voice dropping to a low whisper. "They're real. The lizard people are real."

Marc watched through the narrow pane of glass as two pairs of yellow eyes with slits for pupils watched them. The door began to rattle on its hinges. Each pounding impact left a small dent in the metal of the door.

"This can't be happening," Marc said. He looked at Russ. "You were right."

"Well, half right."

The door bent inward, threatening to break. Out in the hall they heard voices.

"Hey, what the hell is—"

A high-pitched screeching was followed by screams of pain. Russ ran to the door. Lloyd, who worked in ad sales, had come into the hall and was now being disemboweled by the lizard men. His screams ended abruptly when one of the lizards stood upright with Lloyd's lungs clamped in his jaws. He shook his head and the deflated lungs flew off and hit the wall like popped balloons.

"We gotta get out of here," Russ said.

"That's the only door."

More screams, female, came from deeper into the offices. Russ saw a line of at least a dozen more lizard men come down the hall. They spoke in a language of hisses and snarls, the two who'd come to see Russ clearly in charge. They gave commands to their army and the newcomers slithered away to invade the offices.

Russ turned away, desperate for a plan. Through the glass he saw his studio where he'd sat and spun what he'd thought were the lies about the lizard people. Lies that came true, with one small exception. It wasn't *their* side that was hiding this terrible secret. It was *his* side.

He wondered how much he'd gotten right. Were they really bent on world domination? He must have gotten quite a lot correct for them to come here and tell him to stop. Stop. Why didn't he listen?

Russ picked up Marc's chair. Marc ducked away, thinking Russ had gone mad. Thinking *he* had gone mad. Russ did a half spin and hurled the chair through the glass partition separating the control room from the studio space. The double glass panes shattered.

"Let's go."

They climbed over the console, fader switches snapping off under their feet. They had to crouch through the window, moving gently to avoid the shards of glass. Marc's foot slipped on the master volume knob and he fell, smashing against the frame on the broken wall of glass. He tumbled into the studio space and fell to the floor. Russ jumped down beside him.

"Are you okay?"

Marc rolled onto his back, his right side a mess of torn shirt and blood. Russ recoiled. In the control room he heard the door cave in. Not much time.

"It's okay," Marc said. "Just cuts."

"Can you run?"

"Damn right I can run."

Russ helped Marc to his feet. Marc winced in pain but the fear of those gnashing teeth propelled him on.

Russ led the way around his desk, past his microphone. He put a hand on the door and jerked it open. A body filled the open doorway. Linda, the receptionist. Her eyes were wide with terror and the front of her dress was stained dark with blood.

"What are they?" she said.

Russ put a hand under her arm to help keep her standing.

"We're getting out of here," he told her.

A flash of green went by and Linda was gone from his grip. One of the lizard men had her down on the ground, its claws digging in and holding her in place while its mouth ripped open her throat. The sweet voice that greeted all callers became a distorted screech like a siren going through a garbage disposal. Russ took a step back into the doorway to avoid an arcing spray of blood from her neck.

He bumped into Marc behind him.

"Are there more?"

Russ risked a look into the hall. The only one he saw was currently feasting on Linda's esophagus. Coast relatively clear. But what then? Say they got out of the studio building. These creatures were all around them, hiding in plain sight beneath skin suits and high-powered jobs. How could he ever feel safe?

And they knew him. He'd defied their orders. If they were anything like he thought, like he'd been telling his listeners, they were everywhere in the halls of power. There was no escape.

Russ doubted any man had ever changed political affiliations as quickly as he had. He'd given his career over to fighting the fight. Now he knew he'd been fighting on the wrong side. But he still had a voice and that voice still had weight. A plan formed. He'd continue to fight against those who abuse power, against the secret society of lizard men and women. He'd continue to use his voice. The only way to do it was to escape and find a new place to broadcast, pirate radio style.

Two lizard men crashed through the remaining glass between the studio and control room. They moved quickly, but not always smoothly. They darted forward and then paused to take in their surroundings. But they were fast. Faster than Russ.

"Move!" he shouted to Marc.

Russ pulled Marc by the wrist as he bolted into the hall. One right turn and through a set of double doors to the lobby, then beyond security to the exit. He was sure the commotion could be heard out there and probably armed security men were on their way in right now.

As they began their dash down the hall, the lizard eating Linda came to attention. Long lines of blood drooled from his mouth as his yellow eyes narrowed at the two escapees. The two lizards crashed out of the studio and all three chased Russ and Marc down the hall.

Russ was right—security guards came through the double doors shoulder to shoulder, 9mm pistols in their hands. They shouted tactical instructions, relishing the day their training finally came into play.

"There," Russ said. "Behind us. Shoot them!"

He saw the moment when the guards saw what exactly was chasing them. For a moment both men lowered their weapons and furrowed their brows in confusion, but the intent movements, the hissing, the blood on the teeth of the lizard men brought the guards back on task.

Russ ducked as they fired. Bullets zinged past him and hit the lizard men in pursuit. The thick-scaled hides wouldn't let the bullets penetrate. Like Kevlar covering their entire bodies, the shots did nothing and the lizards kept coming.

Russ felt Marc jerk at his wrist. Russ turned, feet still driving forward. Marc's eyes were wide with questions and fear. A lizard had him by the ankle. Russ tightened his grip but in one jerk Marc was torn from him and the lizard was on him, raking a thick claw across his back and exposing his spine.

The guards fired more shots but they did no good. The two lizard men who first came to see Russ leaped. They landed on the guards and blood immediately sprayed the walls of reception. Russ could see other workers from the studio on the ground. Some still had lizard men feeding on them. Some were nothing more than a pair of legs and a head, some only a torso. The lizard men seemed to be killing for sport, not for food.

The double doors stood open from the guards' entrance. Russ didn't look back to see what caused Marc's deep screams. He knew he couldn't help.

All he could do was to get back on the air. To put out the warning. To raise a new call to arms and let people know the lizard men are among them. But first broadcast, he'd apologize to President Obama.

Without breaking stride, Russ ran through the doors and didn't look back.

EVENS

BY NISI SHAWL

RUTH GRIMACED AND ROLLED DOWN her sleeve, covering the Unca Scrooge Band-Aid. The initial sample for her clone had come from inside her cheek. These new daily blood draws were much more intrusive. "How many times do you plan to subject me to this nonsense?" she asked.

The tall, hunched young man in the turquoise scrubs turned away from her and toward the lab's gray countertop. "We'd like a couple of months' worth. Ideally."

"*Months?* You really expect me to put up with you poking needles in me *that* long? It's been three weeks already. On top of the diet and the journal? Really?"

The agent with the bad haircut nodded. "She has a point, Jim. Besides, it's not like there's a lot of time." The agent, Cherry Drake, slid off her high stool to stand with her sensible navy heels shoulder-width apart. "Matching ordinary hormone levels so exactly isn't going to make the clone any wiser. It's only going to make the aging more realistic eventually. Maybe."

The agent faced Ruth. "Can you bear with us another week,

Your Honor? That's all we actually need. Except for special circumstances—"

"Hey!" Jim's shaggy brows rose in disbelief. "You said you weren't going to tell anyone what we talked about in bed!"

"And I didn't," Cherry replied without taking her eyes off Ruth. "Well?"

"I suppose." Ruth stood too. She checked the watch on her wrist. "Let's go."

She'd left her robes back in chambers. At the top of the stairs the other half of her escort waited to open the metal door. It swung outward onto the faint urine-and-stale-soap scented restaurant's family washroom. A wood panel closed to conceal it. Cherry's partner opened another door and the aromas of yeast and tomato sauce and broiling meat wafted in and through the air. They exited cautiously: Planet Pizza staff and patrons were still skittish in the wake of that shooter looking for evidence of a nonexistent child porn operation. But the three left the bathroom and the quiet back hallway it opened onto without being spotted.

In the cavernous main room, the scrape of chair legs, clatter of metal trays, and scramble of voices bounced off the high, black-painted ceiling. Ruth stopped at the register to pick up her feta cheese salad and focaccia bread—cover for the visit. It wasn't ready. "You ordered on the phone?" the cashier asked. The time it took to confirm this unbelievable procedure and find the lost food likely saved their lives.

Boom! The floor shook. Ruth grabbed for the counter and missed. She fell—no, Cherry pushed her down and landed on top of her. Ruth's right hip ground hard into the cement. So hard it hurt. Sleet was falling—in July? Inside? How weird! Ruth said so. At least she thought she did. She couldn't hear herself. Or Cherry, either, who seemed to be whispering something in Ruth's left ear with the force of a scream.

How stupid she was. The sleet was broken glass. A bomb had gone off, of course. Ruth attempted to sit up and assess the danger. Cherry shoved her down again. The light got temporarily brighter. Another bomb? Probably.

In a moment her hearing started to return. Car alarms warbled like distressed birds in far-off trees. The other agent—the older, beefier black one called, improbably, Quentin—switched with Cherry and helped Ruth up, guiding her in an unsteady run back into the bathroom hallway. Her hip hurt like a motherfucker. Behind them people wailed and cried, so Ruth said nothing. Just clenched her jaw against the sharpened pain when Quentin bumped her.

He hammered the stuck fire door open and peeked around its edge. "Clear!" He waved her forward with a hand holding a gun. He had guns in both hands—was that necessary?

Outside the door stood a knee-high cooking-oil can half full of cigarette butts. Cinders paved the yard. Buildings' blank walls and a chain-link fence boxed it in. Plastic slats thrust through the fence blocked the sight of whatever lay beyond. Its gate was padlocked. Quentin shot the lock off so quietly she almost missed it. Ruth's ears were perhaps not quite up to speed again. But when she ran through the cinders they crunched loudly underfoot and the gate's hinges sang a high note and in the alley a newish Scout hybrid engine hummed low. The same one that had brought her. She heard it just fine.

The car's back door flung open. "Get in!" It was Cherry. As they sped off over potholes and trash the agent clambered from the back to the front passenger seat. When they left the alley a few seconds later her window was down and her gun-filled right protruding.

The top half of the driver's head was Glenn's. No sooner did Ruth recognize him than Quentin's meaty hands bore her gently but swiftly down. "We're armored," Quentin explained apologetically. "But not the windows."

"That bomb was meant for me, then? Where are we going?"

"Can't take a chance it wasn't. The DTs are everywhere." He

leaned forward and conferred with Cherry and Glenn in terse syllables that made no sense. Some sort of code. Sirens got nearer, drowning them out.

Clunkclunk! Ruth felt the car jolt twice beneath her. Now both hips hurt. She fought her way free of Quentin's suppressing hands. They were on the traffic island! Another two clunks and they were headed southwest on Nebraska. "Where are we going?" she asked again. Quentin shook his head and reached for her. She sank back to the Scout's beige carpet. "Where?" she repeated.

Cherry answered. "Best to use another route there, but back-up's meeting us at court. The goal's still to stick to your schedule. Give no pretext for asking any questions about early retirement."

Early. Ruth snorted silently. She was eighty-six. Practically eighty-seven. Far too old to have kids. The clone was going to require all her leftover maternal instincts and then some. A village of doctors, scientists, teachers, trainers . . . lawyers by the quad-full.

Horns blared. "What's wrong?" Ruth wanted to see. She got her knees under her, but Quentin was ready and blocked her rise. The horns Dopplered away.

"What if we get stopped?" Cherry's voice sounded a bit panicky.

"That's why they gave us badges," said Glenn.

"What if you hit somebody? Here comes the university! Slow up!" She'd gotten louder and higher.

"Yes, ma'am."

"You're insubordinate." The agent's panic cooled to anger. "I told you—Quentin, anyone following us?"

"Not far as I can tell."

"Under the limit. That's an order."

The Scout's engine revved as the driver dropped them down a gear. "We're not even on campus," he grumbled. "Only skirting it."

"I'm getting up," said Ruth. Quentin laid a disapproving hand on her arm and she grabbed it and hauled herself into the seat. "We aren't being followed, so why not?" Outside the window newly leafed maples gave way to wide, well-groomed lawns. Glenn blew through a couple of uncontrolled intersections and veered left. Soon another, larger intersection loomed up. The traffic light went green as they approached. So did every one they hit on the way back to chambers.

Coincidence? Ruth thought not. Caused by the use of technology —perhaps illegal? That seemed a more reasonable assumption, and the congratulations greeting them as they pulled into the parking garage reinforced it. They'd made the forty-five-minute trip in thirty thanks to what she overheard one member of "backup" call "radio preempt." Her escort was NSA, but not official. And radio preempts, if she recalled correctly, were generally installed in trains and emergency vehicles.

But as Ruth pulled up the afternoon's schedule on her phone— which all three agents had insisted she leave on her desk to foil tracking programs—she admitted to herself that her urge to crack down on that sort of petty crime was hypocritical. Considering what she herself was party to.

* * *

First on the docket came the Maleshenko case. Tony, that twerp, had promoted it, and he'd accepted *all* Ruth's edits to his five latest opinions. She'd put on a show of reluctance, allowing him to insist on hearing the Ukrainian ambassador's son's tutor's appeal as a favor.

Last year Tony had, without coaching, backed her interpretation of the law regarding clones as valid stand-ins for their originals. A nice majority they'd gotten on that impact case—so maybe the DTs had their own project along those lines?

This case's initial statements were mercifully brief. She didn't seriously consider painkillers for her hip until almost an hour in, when the defendant's team leader took the stand. There would be a break when the argument timer light turned red again. She forced herself to cease fidgeting and try to listen till then.

But as the attorney representing the tutor's side blathered on about her client constantly revising his syllabus until forced to realize his student's quickness was more than ordinary genius, Ruth's attention wandered. She found herself sneaking sideways looks at Malashenko-the-younger himself. He seemed a lad of thirteen or more years—not, as indicated in supporting documents, six.

"Of course in the Russian Confederacy they are so much more advanced in the biological sciences," the woman blustered nervously in answer to Ruth's tactful phrasing of the question uppermost in her mind: how dumb was the man that it took him so long to realize what he dealt with? "It was quickly obvious to Mr. Sirko that not only was Andrei a clone, he was Accelerated."

My lacy underwear, thought Ruth. "Quickly obvious." Extrapolating from conversations with Cherry and Quentin, the kid must have received Acceleration treatments at least twenty times, with associated growth spurts. Twenty visits to some Finnish or Mexican clinic before the temporary injunction limiting travel to them was issued. "Quickly" indeed.

But she shouldn't let on she knew so much.

The decision concerned whether an Acceleration initiated outside US jurisdiction, but active while its patient lived within it, was subject to this country's ban.

Sam lectured Malashenko père's senior counsel pointlessly on the absence of federal law prohibiting *any* method of human reproduction. Ruth had seventeen years on her colleague, but his brain was nowhere near as agile as hers.

A short recess. She retired to chambers and dug out her pills. The carafe of water had been left on the bench. Glenn brought her a cup of tepid coffee to swallow them with. Walking back to her seat she saw Jim standing in front of the slowly closing courtroom door and stumbled. Sam glared at her, though she'd barely brushed his arm. She ignored his sub-vocalizations as she sank gingerly onto the bench, worrying hard.

Who had invited Jim to watch the proceedings? Had he jumped line to gain admission? Who had let him in? The two of them weren't supposed to be seen anywhere near each other till well after Mary Lynne "came back from her Swiss finishing school." That was, till she'd been Accelerated into adulthood. At which point Ruth could reveal that she'd groomed her own clone as her replacement on the court, backdating Mary Lynne's secret birth appropriately. And at long last, retire.

Season tickets to the opera, training for the Boston Marathon—

Clarence's smarmy, seldom-heard voice interrupted her OxyContin-induced reverie. "—addition to the defense team," he was saying. "I understand he arrived during the recess?" The prosecutor nodded and Jim walked forward from his place at the courtroom's back. Horror smothered her. Not a mere observer— her very private medical technician was here as a *participant!* Striding past the bar before she could think of a way to stop this. Escape. Something.

She kept her face blank as marble but scanned the room for Cherry, who'd left her post at the door to chambers. Quentin still hulked beside the uniformed officers at the public entrance, but where was his boss?

Unable to totally prevent herself from looking at Jim, she turned on him what she hoped was a professionally disinterested gaze. No sign of recognition on his part. Good. They might get out of this without exciting suspicion.

Jim's presentation of the medical testimony he was tasked with was pedestrian. He talked about progress from the early days of human growth hormone injections to modern magnetic resonance baths, sticking to the story that all recent research occurred offshore.

Then, bless the flight of time's arrow, the day was done. Were they going to have Glenn drive her to the lab again tomorrow? Would Jim show up here again—what was going on? She wished she could ask Cherry, but the agent had yet to reappear. Neither Quentin nor Glenn seemed at all perturbed by that, so Ruth blithely went through her chambers doors and there lay Cherry, unconscious on the chaise longue, hands and feet cuffed.

She needed another agent or one of her clerks. She turned to leave and Quentin and Jim stood in the door, blocking her way. Jim shut it. While Quentin seized her arms the tech wiped off a rapidly cooling patch near her elbow. A cotton swab dropped to the floor and distracted her a split second. The sharp jab of a needle snapped her attention back. What was in this injection? Should she struggle? She might hurt herself but—

The syringe withdrew—not empty. Full of blood. Not an injection. Another draw. Why?

Quentin dragged her further from the door to the courtroom. Jim slipped out. She twisted toward the door at the room's opposite end. It opened and the Senate Minority Leader walked in, goggling and smirking at her. "Well, I declare!"

A fine sweat broke out over Ruth's skin, and a sinkhole of nausea opened under her sternum. "You—" Words came near to failing her. "You complete and utter asswipe!"

"Now that's no way for a lady to talk."

"I'm a lady, and this is me talking!" Ruth wished she felt as brave as she sounded.

"Calm down! Have a hamburger." The senator waved at a squareish Styrofoam container on her desk. She hadn't wanted its contents four hours ago when it mysteriously appeared, and she didn't want them now. "You and I need to talk. Here—" He fumbled open the box. Ruth's stomach heaved at the smell of cooked onions. The top half of the burger's bun had been removed, and a big bite taken out of the meat.

She hated vomiting. She hated looking weak. "Get out so I can have some privacy at least—both of you!" To her surprise the traitor agent complied, the senator following him out. Ruth lurched after them.

"Ma'am?" Quentin stuck his nose and a polished loafer in the narrowing gap. His voice was practically a whisper. "I know this looks bad. Trust me; it's for the best."

"I doubt that."

The gap widened. The passageway outside was empty except for her enemies. It would be, this time of day. Ruth turned her back on them decisively and went to her desk. She slapped down the lid of the takeout box. Its latch ripped off and it sprang vindictively up. Holding her breath she searched in a drawer for a plastic bag, dumped the food inside, and knotted it tight.

On the cramped chaise, Cherry stirred. Slightly, but Ruth found she was suddenly and acutely sensitive to motion. She sat on the ottoman and watched the agent's eyelids flutter open. Her pupils were dilated. With what looked like an effort they focused on Ruth's face. Next the lips began to work together. "Mmmuhhh . . ."

A cup of watery soda stood on her desk's edge. Ruth held it so she could drink. A little spilled. "Sorry," said Cherry.

"It's Sprite. Don't worry; not going to stain anything."

"No, I mean—about—" The agent's shoulders flexed as she pulled against the cuffs. "—about *this*. I was hungry. I fucked up."

"We all do."

"They listening?" Ruth nodded. Cherry swore, not very creatively. More like a checklist: "Shit piss fuck damn." She tried levering herself upright. "Help me?"

Ruth tugged her into position. One of the navy heels was missing. Sighing, the agent kicked the other one off and set her feet flat on the floor. She gestured with her chin. Ruth leaned forward. So did Cherry. "These are my set," she murmured, jingling the links of the cuffs on her feet and hands. "I never told the guys about the duplicate keys."

"Where are they?"

Sugar filled the sliver of air between them. "Bottom of my purse."

Ruth racked her memory. "You don't carry a purse."

"Right. Not while I'm working. I leave it in my locker. At Base." A long pause. "You've been there."

"I could find it in my sleep," Ruth replied. Which was more or less true, because she'd never visited it while she was awake. Too disorienting. All she knew was that it lay under the newly renovated Lincoln Memorial Reflecting Pool. "So how can I convince them to take us there—or bring your purse back here?"

The senator reappeared, Cherry's subordinate hovering obsequiously behind him. No further sign of Jim. "We're not intruding, are we? And Miss Drake is fully conscious?"

Ruth was too busy strategizing contingencies to bother answering him

"Because we really expect you to take us as soon as you can to where you're illegally Accelerating your clone, Your Honor."

* * *

BORN AND BRED IN A *briar patch*, Ruth thought. She kept her literary allusion to herself, hoped her hope didn't show on her face. The increasing throb in her hip should help with that. And the shadows: the sun had set soon after they left the court half an hour ago. Now the tree-lined path curving away from the World War II Memorial was dark. Cherry's shoes—the missing one recovered from underneath the globe stand where she'd kicked them during her struggle against the burger's drugs—struck flat echoes from its retreating stone. Eyes glittering, gun barrel glinting dully in the fading light, Quentin urged them along. Unnecessarily. They were heading where she actually wanted to go.

"Are you sure about this?" the senator asked as they approached the pump house. It *was* rather unprepossessing. Quentin muttered a warning not to run and sped up to reach the handleless steel door first. The plastic pad beside it squeaked semi-familiarly as he punched the entry code—her dream senses had always transformed those sounds to the chirp of birdsong. The automatic door swung open. They entered and it began to slowly swing itself shut.

A flick of a switch and the yellow-walled interior glowed like morning. Pointing them toward a black-painted spiral staircase, Quentin shooed them down to the floor below. He herded them over to a dais raising the heavy curves of sleek white pipes several feet above the rest of the whooshing, rushing machinery. Then he set his be-ringed fist against the dais's edge. A flash of silent light and Ruth lost the last vestiges of plausible deniability as a previously undetectable hatch in its side opened inward, revealing a gleaming metal chute. Descent of it was the source of some recent nightmares.

"Go on."

Should she warn whoever guarded the slide's bottom? Ruth prepared to hoist herself up into the hatch, which was a little over waist high.

"Not you! Here—" The traitor agent tossed his pistol at the senator. He fumbled and caught it.

"Me? This isn't the sort—"

"Safety off." Quentin already held another gun.

"But this is hardly—shouldn't—I think you ought to go first and secure the—"

"Fine. Whatever. You're last, then. Send Drake next." With a frown and a heavenward eye-roll the traitor climbed through the hatch and disappeared. Muffled shots popped like bubblegum. A few seconds later they stopped.

"Any chance you'll take my cuffs off before shoving me in there?" Cherry asked, holding her hands up so the coat sleeves covering them slid away. The pair on her ankles had been removed for the walk, but these had stayed.

"I'm devastated to tell you I don't have the key! But surely a lady of your great resources will find a way to break your descent. Won't you? Madame Justice, if you don't mind helping Miss Drake—"

Her trainer would be proud of how easily Ruth gave Cherry a boost into the hatch. "Use your legs to keep yourself up," she instructed her. Swiftly Ruth clambered in behind the agent and wrapped her own legs around Cherry's waist. Her aching hip protested the unaccustomed angle. She restrained herself from smacking it in annoyance and gripped the hatch's frame to help them stay at the chute's top. "Ready? Set? One two three—" They let go.

Bends and dips carried them down, down, down. Beneath the city's swamp lay bedrock. And Base.

The slide dumped them onto the waterbed where Ruth usually woke when she visited. Low lights threw the two men at the bed's foot into anonymous silhouette. Fully awake she found the silhouette's distinct yet indeterminate edges confusing. "Quick! Roll off!" Glenn? His voice. "This side!" Ruth pulled Cherry by one arm and heaved them both over the board walling in the wallowing mattress. Seconds later and already she saw better. Quentin *and* Glenn, yes. Glenn slapped a gun in Cherry's still-cuffed hands and offered another to Ruth. She waved it off, then thought better of that. Before she could say she'd changed her mind an ugly scream pitch-shifted low to high and the senator dropped right where she'd landed.

A bang and a double clink. The senator shook his gun hand. "*Ow!*"

"Stings, don't it?" Quentin asked. "Lucky the ricochet didn't hit no one. Hand it here." He grabbed back his gun and pointed it at the senator's quivering throat pouch.

"But you work for me!" the senator protested.

"I thought it went the other way. I'm a constituent. Get up."

Tucking his chin in and trying to look dignified, the senator scrambled off the bed. "Didn't I give you—"

"Your bribe? It was an *insult!*"

The senator pushed his glasses up his nose. Again and again.

"That signal you're trying to send out with your specs is not gonna get through, either," Glenn told him. "We're in a Faraday cage down here." He didn't even look up from unlocking Cherry's cuffs. "Well, not a Faraday cage exactly, but you can think of it like that."

"I *demand* you let me go!"

Agent Cherry flexed her freed wrists. "We can't. Think of this place like one of those locked-to-the-clock safes at convenience stores."

"Why are you telling me how to think of everything?"

"Because you don't even believe in global warming. How are we supposed to tell you about independent reality run rates? We might get some science on you!"

Dreams made the transition easier, but Ruth was adjusting with fair speed to Base's constantly fluctuating, bigger-on-the-inside topography. She surveyed the rest of the underground chamber. Concrete pillars supporting the floor of the pool above vanished in the distance. A few figures—their blurred edges odd if you didn't understand the technology sheltering the premises—worked at scattered desks and treadmills. Mary Lynne ought to be somewhere near Base's center, safe in the lane of the fastest run rate.

"Pardon me." Ruth stepped from the entrance's area rug onto the blush-pink carpet runner that would lead her to her clone. Behind her the senator's whining argument with Cherry and Quentin faded out. Glenn followed her.

She found Mary Lynne on the tennis court, hitting against a couple of ball machines. Apparent age eighteen. Had Ruth truly looked that fresh-skinned in her youth? Moved that carelessly? Another month—two at the most—and Mary Lynne would be ready to serve in Ruth's stead, as long as she continued to rely on the counselors provided. The clone moved much faster than Ruth, even with the dietary enhancements allowing her to match Mary Lynne's rate during this year of Special Acceleration.

"Hey!" Ruth caught the girl's attention and she cut the machines off. "How are you?"

Mary Lynne's answer lagged a second or two while she processed the question. Probably she was running double Ruth's enhanced speed.

"Gooood." The girl was making an obvious effort to slow down her speech. Overcompensating a bit. "Tryyyed out the aging mmake-uup toooodayy." That meant within the last eight actual hours. They had synchronized calendars and so forth prior to the first application of the clone's new course of treatment.

"I didn't bring the latest journal entries. Sorry. I wasn't expecting to come by."

"Surrre. Thaaat's understandable. I thought it wass kind of earlyyy ffor you to be asssleeep. Inn ffaaact—"

"Yes, I stayed awake for the whole insertion. I was brought here as a hostage." Ruth gestured back toward the entrance, where the senator could be seen submitting to Quentin's search. "It's rather complicated. I'll write it out for you."

The clone nodded, her long, slender neck graceful. Suddenly Ruth felt tired and frail. Her hip reminded her how recently she'd hurt it. A green velour sofa beckoned. "Will it bother you if I just sit and watch?" She sank onto its cushions as she asked.

"Pleeease do," Mary Lynne called over her shoulder, restarting the ball machines. She had the manners of a lady; they'd gotten that much right. Though tennis had never been Ruth's sport. . . .

The air behind the couch's back warmed and stilled. A large brown hand drifted down to lie on it. "Mind if I join you?"

"Not in the slightest, Barry." The president—he would always be her president—sat on the couch's other end. His posture was relaxed yet attentive.

"Proud of your girl? You should be." He smiled his Alfred E. Neuman-esque smile. "Quite the athlete—and she's tearing up the library with her studies, too."

In Barry's reassuring presence, Ruth felt paradoxically free to worry. "They're not going to buy it," she declared pessimistically.

"Of course they will. What's the worst they can do? So they don't let the two of you serve concurrently—"

"Some observers say conservatives prefer to keep the justices evenly divided between progressives and conservatives. Leave us at eight the way we were before Gorsuch. How many years since Roberts' seizure have they had now to ram through a confirmation for a ninth?"

"Only one where they had complete control." He nodded at

Mary Lynne, who seemed to have noticed him. She nodded back and almost simultaneously slammed away two balls five feet apart. "If they don't want us up to full capacity, we'll handle it."

"We need a deciding vote! No more even splits and sticking with lower courts' decisions—the US Supreme Court has functioned with an odd number of members for over two hundred years, and that's how it's *meant* to function."

Barry chuckled. "What, now you're an originalist?"

"No!" Ruth came close to spluttering. "Simply—simply because Scalia and I were friends—" Poor Nino.

Barry interrupted her with a comforting pat on the arm. "I understand. Listen, I played golf with David Brooks."

Ruth sighed. A couple of hours walking around with some conservative columnist. That was nothing like the relationship she and Nino had shared. Twenty-two years. . . .

A wordless bellow exploded from the direction of the entrance. Someone shouted "Stop! Drop it!" Cherry. Ruth rose to her knees. Above the sofa's back she saw the senator heading dead for her—leaping over wheeled carts and file cabinets, stacked boxes tumbling in his wake as he totally disregarded the carpet runner. Making a beeline. Big mistake. Getting here would take longer by that route, because Base's time warps played Twilight Zone tricks on your mind if you didn't follow the counterintuitive paths laid out when it was established. As he panted toward her the senator zoomed in and out of focus, loomed forward and diminished to nothing with no warning. No rhyme; no reason.

Nevertheless, he persisted. Before Cherry tackled him he had come within half a dozen yards. He fell to bite the shag with a grunt and a wheeze. "Halt!" the agent ordered unnecessarily, straddling his back. "Give me that!" She pounded his right fist against the floor and seized the tiny, futuristic-looking slingshot it released.

"Glenn, take his ammo."

Again Ruth felt the cool kiss of an alcohol swab and the quick prick of a needle. This time on her neck. She tried to turn to see her assailant. A dark hand—not Barry's—stopped her. "Hold still." Quentin. Traitor or not? Since coming here he had helped uncuff Cherry and aimed a gun at the senator. "If you move too soon I could injure you—there!"

Freed, she whirled around. Quentin was capping and pocketing a syringe like those Jim used, filled with blood, presumably hers. "I apologize. For this and for that show in chambers. We needed some different emotion-keyed hormone levels, and this was the best way to get em."

"You weren't—you didn't switch sides?"

"Nope. Not for real." Another Band-Aid, this one printed with drawings of Jessica Rabbit.

Ruth stood and followed the pink runner to the rug where the defeated senator lay beneath Cherry's well-toned thighs. His coat had been removed; an odd assortment of brightly colored missiles were lined up on his white-shirted back.

"There were some in his pants, too," Cherry said. "Careless, but typical."

Glenn patted the squirming senator's buttocks. "Let me turn him over—I was doing the front when he bolted."

"Was that what set him off? You think he knows you're trans?"

"If he did he wouldn't struggle so hard."

"Maybe."

On his back, the senator glared accusingly up at Ruth. "You think you're so smart!" he said. "Well you're not the only ones who can make a clone!"

Barry laughed. "Oh, we know what you're working on. Want to borrow our Run Rate Adjusters to catch up? You'll need help installing them. Or are you fine just waiting a term or two before your replacement appears eligible?"

"I'd rather—"

"Don't answer that. Cherry, help the gentleman be quiet." The agent applied duct tape.

Another arrival on the waterbed. A tall, thin figure—approaching along the pink runner, it became recognizable as Jim. Getting near enough to talk he asked, "All good for the last sample?"

Barry looked at her hard. "How you feeling? We won. You know that, right? Ready to celebrate?" He nodded to Quentin, who walked a short brown strip of linoleum to a humming refrigerator and brought out a big bottle of champagne. From the fridge's freezer compartment Glenn took out frosted stemware to set on the butcher block-topped cart beside it. He rolled it toward them.

"Celebrate? A little premature, aren't we?" But Ruth accepted a chilled flute and resumed her seat. The champagne's cork squeaked and popped free.

"Never too soon to get drunk," Cherry said. "I mean, if you're going to anyway."

"Not before I score my sample, though." Jim produced yet another empty syringe. "Here. We need the right hormone balance for happiness." As her president poured golden bubbles into Ruth's glass, the needle slid painlessly beneath her skin.

A DIFFERENT FRAME OF REFERENCE
BY WALTER MOSLEY

THERE'S A HAT SHOP IN downtown Cincinnati called the Hatshop for Men. It sells Stetson, Kangol, Jaxon, Tilley, and about fifty other brands and styles. There you can get your hat steam-cleaned and blocked for next to nothing and the doors are open to every-one —always have been.

The proprietor of the Hatshop for Men, Mr. Bix Thompson, is one of the largest property owners in Ohio and Kentucky. Somewhere past fifty at the time of this story, Bix was pale and chubby, not past five nine in height but with powerful arms and hands. His eyes were (and probably still are) intense, intelligent, and yet somehow com-passionate. He was, at that time, the Supreme Overlord of the very secret organization—Whiter than White Sons of the Light.

In the year 2013 in the month of July, there was heatwave in the City of Seven Hills, but the fourth floor above the hat shop was quite cold because Bix believed in air conditioning for his Viking-descended brothers in WTW.

All thirteen WTW Hetmen under the Supreme Overlord were there that Tuesday afternoon. Joseph Zinger from Columbus, Chapman Outman from Cleveland, Norvard Miner from

Lexington, and all the rest from various towns and cities, large and small of the two states.

Of course I was there. George Brown of Covington, Kentucky.

The one thing all the Hetmen had in common was that we were all certified white men, approved by a DNA test that traced 99.9 percent of our chromosomes back to Europe somewhere over the last thousand years.

These men (and they were all men) had as their goal the survival and perpetuation of the purity and hegemony of the white race. We had facilitated the infiltration and takeover of twenty-seven police stations, sixteen fire departments, nineteen city councils, and the loan departments of eighty-one community banks. Our membership had been guided into dozens of leadership positions and their children were assured berths in universities throughout the Civil War south.

So successful had Bix and the WTW been that we had taken majority control of many city and state governments, businesses, services, and nonprofit charities; these from the niggers, spicks, faggots, Jews, misguided white women, and, of course, the communists. We were so successful and so secret that we set our sights, three years earlier, on proving that Barack Obama was a depraved criminal; therefore making it possible for his ouster.

"Even the northerners," Bix had claimed at the beginning of our operation, "will be glad to wipe that stench from the White House. They'll burn the carpets and the beds, throw away the blankets, sheets, and towels. They'll have to paint everything white again to remove the nigger's shadow."

The Hetmen all applauded, congratulating ourselves for most certainly being able to find the key to impeaching and then ousting the man who could not be innocent because he was not a white man—pure and simple.

That was the last celebratory hurrah in the past three years. WTW, being a serious intellectual organization, hired twenty-eight highly qualified private detectives who had only managed to prove that President Obama was indeed a citizen of the United States, without socialist affiliations, and free of criminal political influence even though he came out of the Democratic Chicago Machine. He didn't seem to have any extramarital affairs with women (much less men) and his fundraising activities always followed the laws that governed such things.

The only thing that any of the two-dozen-plus gumshoes could come up with was a photograph of the president smoking a cigarette after telling the country he had quit that habit.

The detective who had procured this photograph was Adam Corman. Mr. Corman had bribed a Secret Service agent to take pictures of nappy-headed Obama when the Commander in Chief had reason to believe that he was alone.

The forty-fourth president had gone outside on the porch at the back of the White House kitchen and there lit up his cancer stick.

The Supreme Overlord and we thirteen Hetmen argued for five weeks about what might be done with this intelligence.

"It proves that he's a liar," Michael Lowman of Toledo posited. "No matter the lie, it proves that he's not whiter than white."

"But so many people smoke and try to quit," said Teddy Biwater from Akron. "Even your good ole boys will tell ya that they smoke when their wives can't catch 'em."

"It won't work," opined Rich Richards from Bowling Green, Kentucky. "They'd laugh us outta the South we tried to say a man, even a nigger, was wrong for smokin' a cigarette. We might as well say we don't like him because he wears pants."

* * *

THAT WAS SIX MONTHS AGO. We had failed miserably in our three-year twenty-eight detective mission. But that sweltering July day Bix had called a special meeting to take the war on Obama's reign to another level.

"Hello, my Hetmen," Bix said after we were seated at the redwood conference table and passing the pitchers of ice water from man to man. "Today is a special day, a challenging day, and a new day for WTW. Today is the first time since our inception in two thousand two that we are allowing a woman within the confines of our secret brotherhood."

Bix's words caught the immediate attention of every man in the room. Lester Bean of Frankfort, Kentucky, actually rose to his feet, his eyes wide upon the Supreme Overlord.

"Yes, Lester?" Bix said.

"Um . . ."

"Do you have something to say, Hetman Bean?"

"Women are our, our . . . women are to serve men," Lester said.

"And sometimes these servants must bring us our water," Bix replied.

Lester—who was short and skinny, dark skinned for a white man with a hungry look about the eyes—gazed around the table at the other sectional leaders. No one gave him vocal support and so he sat back down.

"Thank you, Brother," Bix said to Lester. "And now, gentlemen, I want to introduce you to the next level of the war against the colored enemy—Vanessa Shankforth Trammeling."

From Bix Thompson's private door came a tall woman in a knee-length, spring-green dress that had prints of outsized blades of grass and white daisies upon it. Her face was long and rather elegant and her hair was neither brown nor blond nor red but rather a delicate mix of all three hues. She was slim and well built, and her eyes were violet like the flower.

She held her hand out and Bix took it, holding on to her long fingers a moment past propriety.

"Thank you, Mr. Thompson," she said. Her voice was mild but we could hear every word. "It is an honor to be invited here, in the company of such brave and heroic manhood."

Bix nodded slightly, backed away, and sat in the carved, rosewood throne that he had made special for our monthly meetings.

Something about Vanessa Trammeling made me both excited

and nervous. She was the ideal of white womanhood and so poised that I tried to remember if I had used deodorant after taking a shower that morning.

"It is my great honor to address the Whiter than White Sons of the Light," she said. "Your goal of taking back control after our being under the yoke of oppression for so long is both laudable and right on time."

Her words were beautiful, each one seeming to be a golden nail tacking down the fluttering essence of a dream we all shared. But it was, I believe, her tone of voice and certainty of manner that calmed the qualms we men had about a woman addressing us as if she were an equal.

"For too long," she continued, "white men and women have been denied our God-given rights to rule this land and this world. African savages, Asian communists, and many depraved European and South and Central American mud people have sullied what Jesus meant for us to have. . . . The kingdom here on earth and in heaven too."

The exhilaration I felt was almost unbearable. This woman's words dug deep, deep into my heart. And it was obvious that the other men, even Bix, were profoundly moved by her comments.

There were actual tears coming from Lester Bean's eyes. Chapman Outman had bowed his head as one does in church when the pastor asks for silent prayer.

I was moved along with my brothers but I also had a different feeling from the rest of them.

I was committed to the dreams, aspirations, and revolutionary intentions of the WTW. I believed in white hegemony and the downfall of the mud people here at home and abroad. I knew that God had meant for the white man and his woman to rule benevolently, if possible, over all the races, animals, and other creatures of the earth.

Since I was a child I was taught by my father, Axel Brown, that we were divine under God and over all other beings. He sent me and my brother to a special school that was only white. He kept my sister at the house to be homeschooled and trained in the ways she could serve her race.

And then, when my father had a heart attack in Atlanta and the black paramedics let him die in their ambulance, it fell to me, the eldest son, to lead my family and as many people as possible to sanity.

I started a small group that caught the attention of Bix and the WTW. We read books and plotted political campaigns, marched for white power and stood shoulder to shoulder against anyone who supported integration, miscegenation, white abortion, or equal rights among unequal people.

We burned down a house or two and had to beat down a few men. We never killed anybody or even caused permanent harm, outside of a limp or two. But when my sister, Melanie, started seeing the spick-nigger, Roberto Halloway, I made up my mind that I had to take my father's gun and do justice by him and all our white brothers.

* * *

I WAS LIVING WITH MY mother at the time. I had been preparing to join the WTW for a month then and had to leave my senior mechanic's job to organize and guide the growing numbers among us.

I asked my mother for the key to Papa's lockbox where he kept his .45 automatic.

Instead of obeying my request she told me that she needed me to go somewhere.

"Mama, what I need is Papa's gun," I said.

"Respect thy father and mother," she said and I knew she meant business.

* * *

SHE TOOK ME TO AN integrated nursing home in Lexington, Kentucky. Black, white, and brown were all thrown together in there. I could tell by the smell that it wasn't a healthy place for a white man to end his years.

"Why are we here?" I asked my mother.

"I need you to meet somebody," she said.

"Someone we need to save from this place?"

"In a way you could say that."

* * *

IT WAS ROOM NUMBER 816, I remember. Inside stood a solitary cot with an elderly black lying upon it. I was loath to go into that room but my mother brought me and I was raised to obey her.

She sat on a chair next to the head of that bed and gazed upon the sleeping nigger. I figured that this must have been some servant that worked for my mother's family and that she was fond of him for his service and loyalty to her kin.

My father had always said that there was nothing wrong with the lower races as long as they stayed in their place.

"My sons," he'd said to me and my brother. "Some people are meant to follow and others to lead. You can tell who's who by brightness of the light the Lord shines on them."

My mother, Chantal, shook the old man's shoulder. He opened his eyes and smiled.

"Chantal," he said. "It's so nice to see you."

His tone was too familiar. If he hadn't been bedridden I would have been within my rights to slap him.

"George," my mama said, "I'd like you to meet Harris Phelps—your paternal grandfather."

* * *

THAT MEMORY TORE THROUGH MY chest like wildfire and when I looked up from the redwood conference table I saw Vanessa Shankforth Trammeling staring me right in the eye. I felt as if she could see all of my deepest secrets and it was everything I could do not to run screaming from the room.

". . . The white man's burden," she was saying, "is his own superiority. Our intelligence, our deep morality, and our singular connection to God has given us a load that the other immoral races do not have to restrain back their baser natures."

She was still looking at me.

"But," she said, "those are things we all know. I am here today to tell you what you may not have suspected. I am a graduate of MIT having majored and gotten my doctorate in astrophysics. You might think that this rather arcane branch of study has little to do with the job of ridding our White House from the tyranny of Obama. You might think it but you would be wrong."

At that Ms. Trammeling held up a silver tube maybe five inches in length and depressed a button thereupon. The lights went out and an image appeared on the wall behind Bix and Vanessa.

It was the photograph of Obama smoking his cigarette at the back of the White House kitchen. I'd seen it many times before. The minstrel president holding the cigarette between the pointer and middle fingers of his left hand, letting his head loll to the left bringing his lips to the butt rather than the other way round.

There was something odd about the projection though. The back wall had a bureau and some chairs, a painting of Robert E. Lee, and a rather large fern plant set up against it. The image should have been distorted by the many surfaces it was projected upon but instead it looked as if it were flat on a white screen.

"Twenty-eight detectives," Trammeling said. "Twenty-eight detectives and not one impropriety detected; not one crime, theft, cheat, or even a mild curse."

"What do we learn from that?" she asked looking directly at me.

"It's, um, it's um . . . impossible," I said.

Ms. Trammeling smiled and I felt something in my memories.

"That's right, Mr. Brown," she said. "And when something is both evident and impossible the investigator has to employ a different frame of reference."

She waved around the silvery cylinder and the part of the photograph showing Obama's fingers around the cigarette enlarged, seemingly taking up more space than there was to be had.

This highly magnified image revealed that it was not a cigarette that he was smoking but some king of vaporizing device.

"Opium!" Wendell Holman of Lorain, Ohio, ejaculated. "He's a drug fiend."

"Far worse than that, Mr. Holman," Trammeling said. "This device is a transmitter. The president is communicating with a third party."

"The communists?" Joe Zinger asked.

"Worse still," Trammeling said.

"What could be worse than a communist?" Judd Freeport of Langsford Farm, Ohio, asked.

Suddenly the image disappeared and the lights came back on. I never knew that Bix had the kind of technology installed that could perform such feats.

Ms. Trammeling was standing before us apparently considering Judd's question, her light indigo eyes lamenting the answer she knew she must give. She gazed at Judd, a youngish man with big hands and rough skin.

"Indeed, Mr. Freeport," she said. "What could be worse than a commie red? A man who hates freedom and democracy, manhood and white hegemony?"

Every eye was fastened upon Ms. Trammeling right then. I was so concentrated on getting every word that I could hear a water pipe hissing in the wall.

"Over a hundred years ago," Trammeling said, "a meteorite of moderate-size crashed into a broad plain in central Kenya. There was a dark glow emanating from the heavenly body and when a simple farmer approached it that glow faded from the rock and set upon the man—who was called Ikeno.

"Ikeno lay sick for sixty-six days ministered over by his wife and aunts. His fever was so high that you didn't even have to touch his skin to feel it. His glazed eyes were always open wide, looking up beyond the straw roof into deep space.

"On the sixty-seventh day his wife went out from the hut and found a long line of young women waiting at her cloth door. She asked the first woman, Faraji, why she was there.

"'We are here because your husband came to us in our dreams. He came to us with his eyes and told us that we must have his sons.'

"And for the next twenty-one days eighty-seven women, coming from as far away as Ivory Coast and Mozambique, lay with Ikeno and they all became pregnant with sons.

"On the eighty-eighth day Ikeno died and the women went away to birth the children of the meteorite.

"For one hundred years these children and their descendants have traveled, mated, and disseminated alien genes containing the philosophies and genetics of this extraterrestrial force. The sons of the meteorite traveled to every continent and mated with women of all races and nationalities. Their sons and daughters have inherited various aspects of the alien logic that has as its goal the complete domination of Man.

"Make no mistake—each and every progeny of these unholy births is our sworn enemy but not all of these heirs of infamy are aware of the danger that lies inside them. These beings, if they get their way, will fill our women's wombs with spiders and rip God from his heaven. They will flood our homelands and force men to lay with beasts.

"This, Sons of the Light, is the greatest threat ever to face the human race. And it is your duty to expose and end this menace."

* * *

IT'S HARD TO EXPLAIN THE impact that Trammeling's words had upon us. The story as I write it here seems preposterous. I mean, infected with an alien intelligence by a rock from outer space? It sounded like the plot of a bad matinee movie—except for all the sex that Ikeno had before he died.

But the words were true. We all knew this in the same way. Vanessa Trammeling was the harbinger of an alien invasion that had been underway for more than a century.

When I looked around the room I saw that all the Hetmen, like myself, were stunned and amazed. Our eyes were everywhere and nowhere. Our pasts were distant shores because we had been unmoored from the everyday complaints and the pedestrian woes of life.

"One of the most powerful and most conscious alien invaders is Barack Obama," Vanessa Trammeling said then. "In the guise of an inferior race he has taken over our world with the intention of placing his people and their inhuman ideals in places of power that will one day end humanity."

"I always knew it," said Norvard Miner. "Barack Obama is the greatest threat the white world has ever faced."

"What would you have us do?" Bix Thompson asked the only woman ever to address our brotherhood.

"There is a weakness," Trammeling said, smiling. Her smile was like a ray of light after a terrible storm; like hope in the eyes of an infant child.

"What weakness?" I asked.

She gave me that smile and said, "The stone that the dark glow came from was designed to force the intelligence out of its celestial body and into the frame of a man. So when Ikeno got close enough, the meteorite turned toxic to the life-force radiation, forcing it to enter the man."

From a fold in her dress of floral verdure she produced a shiny black stone about half the size of a baseball. She held this up and even though I was sitting four chairs away I could see its gleaming shards and feel its radiant, black pulsations.

"I have been to Africa and cut this rock from the meteorite. The forest around had grown tall and was nearly impenetrable. Lions roamed the area around it. Any emanations you feel coming from this small sample were a hundred times stronger; almost physically pressing me and my team backwards.

"I was the only one to survive. The rest of us were slain by claw and knife and disease. I believe that it was God who saved me because he needed you, George Brown, to accompany me to Washington and to bring this rock close enough to slay the alien being that resides inside the slave-president."

* * *

As you can imagine, there was a lot of talk about Vanessa Trammeling and her choice of me as her companion. Bix was expecting the role to fall to him. He argued that he was the most likely candidate.

"You are the supreme leader," Vanessa admitted, "the Overlord of the Sons of the Light. But George is young and strong and he has the look, if we dress him up right, of a young political idealist. We need those qualities—the youth, strength, and look of innocence—if we are to get close enough to destroy Obama's otherworldly parasite."

Bix didn't like it and neither did the rest of the Hetmen but there was something about the way Trammeling said things that cut off argument.

Her words were like physical objects, solid proofs in themselves. And that black stone most certainly gleamed and whispered alien threats. After a brief exposure we were sure that it was a living thing.

And so that very afternoon Vanessa and I boarded a plane to DC from Cincinnati. We sat side by side, she in the middle seat and I by the window.

"Take my hand," she said when the jet began its taxi.

Touching her hand I felt a sudden shock. This was not static electricity but rather a deep biological response. I don't remember the takeoff or the flight. I don't remember landing or if we took a cab or a bus to the Lattimore Hotel near the White House. Instead my mind roved back to the time my mother brought me to the old folks' home where I met Harris Phelps, the black man who she claimed was my grandfather.

". . . Your father slapped me and knocked me to the floor

when I found a letter written to him from a girl he said he hadn't talked to in five years," my mother said as she held the black man's hand in her left and mine in her right. "I picked myself up and left the house. I got on a bus and took it to Lexington.

"A very handsome light-skinned Negro sat next to me" My mother never used the words nigger, coon, or jigaboo. She said that such words were rude and unseemly. "His name was Orlando. He told me that he could see that I was both bruised and heartbroken and wondered if he could do anything to help.

"I felt so comforted by his words and tone that I explained what had happened as honestly as if I were talking to a preacher's wife.

"'So you're saying,' Orlando said after I had finished. 'That you were jealous and you're husband was shamed by being caught in a lie.'

"'Yes!' I said. 'That's it in a nutshell.' And I, I put my head on his shoulder and didn't wake up until the next morning when I was lying in his bed.

"I am not a loose woman, George," my mother said. "And I don't remember any carnal acts between myself and the man named Orlando Phelps. But in the morning I knew that I was with child and that child was you.

"Orlando understood. He offered to marry me and to move up north where intermarriage was not seen as a crime against nature. But I told him that first I had to talk to your father and see if he could understand where he was wrong.

"We got back together and I never told him about Orlando or your heritage. It wasn't a problem because you were so fair skinned, haired, and eyed that he was proud to have such an Aryan son."

My mother had stayed in touch with Orlando's father after the son perished in a plane crash. I asked my brother for his spit to give to the WTW. Even if my father was a black man as my mother claimed—it didn't matter. I continued with my political convictions convincing myself that I had been baptized white by my father and his education.

I left my sister alone though. Killing her boyfriend seemed wrong when I shared, no matter how slightly, the curse of his blood.

* * *

THE NEXT THING I KNEW, after the plane took off, I was sitting in a chair staring out the hotel room window at the White House. When I looked to my right I saw Vanessa Trammeling in a blood-red gown watching me.

"How do you feel?" she asked as if maybe I had been sick.

I considered the question seriously because I did feel different. My father had beaten me and my brother with some regularity. He fostered our hatreds and punished our weaknesses. I lived with pain and rage in my body and mind, but somewhere between Cincinnati and DC all that vituperation had drained away.

"I always knew what you were, George," were her first words.

"What do you mean?" I asked.

"Your bloodline."

"Of course," I said. "I've taken the blood test."

She smiled and pulled the shiny black rock from her pocket.

"This is your destiny, Mr. Brown. Bix and his Hetmen would never understand you. They believe in the purity of imbeciles. A drop of blood from here or there defining their sense of manhood. Them believing that women are the servants, that their mothers are the servants. Your mother proved them wrong—didn't she?"

With those words she handed me the black rock poison that would kill the alien invader that made a black man seem better than white.

The rock felt heavy in my left palm and somehow it dragged my eyes to it. Inside the overlapping, luminous shards, I could see a great migration of all types of beings and intelligences. There were creatures once as large as mountains in that small stone, these surrounded by billions of angels that had absolutely no mass at all. There were meat-eaters and flowers that grew through mathematical equations, gasses that laughed as they passed over rocky terrain and giants with so many heads that they never wanted for friendship.

There was a sun that emanated heat which did not burn. Untold trillions of life forms huddled near the heat and peace of its radiations.

"You lied to the WTW because your grandfather willed it that day you visited him in the rest home," Vanessa said.

I wanted to ask her how she knew any of that but the black rock called to me. I think I would have abandoned the life I had to be one with that simple stone. I would have turned my back on whiteness, humanity, and the earth itself.

* * *

"SOMEONE'S AT THE DOOR, GEORGE," Vanessa had said a dozen times or more before I could bring myself to look up from the infinite abyss.

There was a knock.

I rose to my feet and stumbled partway across the large room. Vanessa moved out of my path and I fell to the cream-carpeted floor.

"Get up," she said.

The knocking continued.

I crawled to the wall and, pushing against that barrier, managed to get to my feet. I followed that wall to another and that one to the door.

I pulled the door open and saw him standing there smiling as he often did on the TV and computer screens, on magazine covers and under newspaper headlines.

"What time is it?" I demanded of him.

"A little after 3 a.m.," Barack Obama said softly.

I almost fell and he caught me by the arm and supported me back to the chair where I had watched my rock for hours.

* * *

WE HAD BEEN TALKING FOR some time before I understood that I was conversing with the enemy.

"I came here to kill the parasite in you," I said when I once again had control of my attention.

"No," the president replied. "Vanessa made you think that but in reality you are here to find yourself and to regain the equilibrium of the stars."

"Huh?" I sneered. "What are you saying?"

"You think that I'm the alien," Obama stated.

"We saw your communication device."

"No. You saw a device built for me by Harris Phelps, your grandfather. I use it sometimes to commune with the countless life forms that reside in that rock on the floor."

"Why would he . . . I mean how could he . . ." I said.

Obama smiled and picked up the shiny black stone from the cream-colored carpet.

"I'm infected?" I asked him and Vanessa.

"You are what you are," Obama said, "what you have always been. The energy from that rock melded with the potential soul that hovers like mist between your genes. It is not your blood but your soul that is deep and black and infinite."

He said more—a lot more. It was my duty to lead the WTW into a war with imagined aliens so that their identity could be rerouted into a positive fiction in a negative world.

"The peoples of the black rock need to find a home but they don't want to war with humanity," Obama said. "And so they have joined with you and people like you to guide the human race past its fear and greed and even the instincts; allowing humanity to move toward a higher level where blood represents life instead of death."

"But what am I?" I asked.

"You are the causeway and the rest of us are the travelers."

"How will I know I'm doing what's right?" I asked.

"The stone will tell you."

I wanted to argue. I wanted to call him nigger and traitor and stupid and wrong. The words seethed but they were lies and I knew it.

Another knock came on the door: three taps and then three more.

I saw through the window that the sun was rising, illuminating the White House.

"I have to go," Barack Obama said. "The minor details of a world in turmoil call me."

He smiled and I tried to rise from the chair but I was too weak.

"Rest, George Brown. We will meet again."

I watched him go through the door I'd crawled to . . . and then I fell asleep.

* * *

WHEN I WOKE UP IT was night again. I was lying on the carpet, drool down my right cheek. The black rock lay next to me whispering secrets that I was beginning to understand.

I took a deep breath and rose to a sitting position.

Vanessa Shankforth Trammeling was sitting in the chair I fell from. She smiled at me.

"How are you feeling?"

"Like somebody else; like I went to sleep believing in white power and woke up wondering what was wrong with me all those years."

"Enlightenment is just that," she said. "It's the same world seen through the same eyes but meaning, that which underlies appearance, shifts."

"Why don't you form a ministry?" I asked. "You could talk to the rest of the world, one congregation at a time and make everyone understand what we know."

"The assumption you make about my origins are correct," she said. "I *am* a descendant of the meteorite. But I can only control one person at a time. That's how I got Bix to allow me to address the WTW."

"But you convinced all the Hetmen that Obama was the alien," I argued. "I mean, that whole thing makes no sense but they bought it without proof. You hypnotized them, us."

"Our power is exponential when we are in close proximity. My words piggybacked on you. Together we can speak to a thousand minds at once."

"Then we could all get together and show the world that all life, everywhere is sacred and holy; that the meteorite is not a threat."

"But it is a threat if that is what people believe."

"We can convince them otherwise." I managed to get to my feet.

"We aren't here to brainwash, fool, or in any other way domi-nate the life forms of Earth," she said. "And we couldn't even if we wanted to. You and I and all the people like us, if in each other's company for too long, start to fade. Our abilities are solitary things. We are meant to be hermits, lone missionaries spreading the word and hoping for salvation."

"So I can't see you again?"

"Every ten years or so we can spend a few days together. I will go back to Cincinnati with you and seduce Bix. He and I will move to Hawaii leaving his property holdings for you to manage."

"Why didn't you just come to me and tell me what I was? Why did you have to address the entire membership of Hetmen?"

"Children of the meteorite can only be awakened with the exertion of great force. The WTW allowed us that focus."

I wanted to kiss Vanessa but I knew, somehow, that this was forbidden.

"But you making Bix marry you," I said. "Isn't that control-ling him?"

"He will be happy and I will give him a child. Some rules have to be broken but the world must decide on its own whether or not to accept the host of the black stone. It is our hope that friends like the president will open the way for acceptance."

"But Obama isn't an alien?"

"He met Harris when he was a teenager. Harris showed him what he could do and Barack promised to be a friend. Bringing you here was his idea. Once you were aware of yourself he helped to direct your attention."

There was a heat growing in my belly. Looking at Vanessa Trammeling all I felt was lust.

"I know," she said. "I want you too. But we are brother and sister, formed from the radiant exertions of the meteorite. If we were to spend two more days together the passion would overwhelm us and all our power would ebb away."

I sat back down on the floor taking a deep breath.

"What can I do . . . sister?"

"Return to Cincinnati, reveal yourself one at a time to the Hetmen. Some will understand and be enlightened—some will not. Use your abilities to organize to make a better world, a more understanding one. Now and again Mr. Obama and others will come to you, advise you. We have worked at these goals for more than a hundred years. We have given the world philosophies and technologies that bring them closer to understanding. You will become part of that work."

* * *

WHEN BIX AND VANESSA LEFT Ohio, the next day, I was at sea. It felt as if the man I was had died and the man I had become was a cypher.

I disbanded my group in Covington and anonymously reported our activities to the authorities. I sent similar messages to federal agencies that Obama put me in touch with, reporting on the illegal activities of the WTW.

I moved to Cincinnati and took control of the WTW. Then, one by one I brought the Hetmen to a private room, took them by the hand, and showed them what I had learned.

Three committed suicide within the year. Four left the ranks and declared us enemies. Five of the Hetmen remained, however. The truth beyond our bodies and minds allowed them to understand that our primitive notions of life and being are less than a housefly's understanding of physics.

* * *

A YEAR OR SO LATER I was working in the Hatshop for Men, entering inventory on a computer, when the bell to the store door tinkled. I looked up and saw Harris Phelps gazing down on me.

"Hello, grandson," he said rather formally.

"You don't look old anymore," I said.

"We are a long-lived breed," he replied. "But sometimes we get tired. It feels like and looks like we've gotten old but we just need a little rest."

I was beginning to tremble.

"Shake my hand, George."

When our skins touched it felt as if I were ejected from my body like as if I were thrown from a moving train. My soul was a-tumble while all around me life forms were calling out to be released from the black stone.

Uncountable souls vied for my attention. It was as if all the life in the universe had become aware of only me.

Harris Phelps must have let go of my hand. I was prostrate on the green-and-black linoleum floor.

"Never forget your duty, George," I heard him say while staring at his brown shoes. "Without us, hope will come to an end."

I lay on the cold floor for hours. Finally someone came and called an ambulance. They said I'd had a heart attack. My mother put me in a sanatorium where I convalesced for four months.

Late one night, when I was deep in sleep I felt a hand on my shoulder.

I opened my eyes and the president was standing there.

"The price of knowledge is steep," he said. "The cost of ignorancc is dcath."

BROTHER'S KEEPER
BY DANNY GARDNER

LARRY DREW THE SHADES BEFORE he powered up the ansible, for the same reason that he disposed of its box a half-klick away from his Trump Administration housing building. He had to be careful on his mega-block. When the regional plant that manufactured warp drives for the Jaunt Transport Authority moved to Turkmenistan, Unemployables flooded their sector. Gangs of UE kids roamed freely at night, boldly out of compliance with the curfews for anyone on public assistance. They used military binoculars to look in the windows on the upper floors and spot loot. If they saw the backlight from the display, there'd be nothing to stop the home invasion robbery that would follow. Only Middle Class could afford nighttime emergency calls.

Mama's new husband Reggie was only LMC, although she spent credits as if he was Diamond Elite. She logged in at midnight on Black Friday—her favorite national holiday—and within an hour a drone arrived with a mid-tier superluminal communications device worthy of a family far higher on the National Citizen Registry. Mama was still cute, even after non-raising two teenagers, so Reggie only shook his head before he put his Virtual Reality unit back on. If Pop-Pop were still around, he'd call it *nigger rich*. "Champagne tastes on malt liquor money." Pop-Pop was so old, he remembered when they printed cash on paper, long before the RFID implants they install at the DMV became mandatory. Mama was a loyalist, the Administration was the best thing ever, filled with winners, and by god, she would shop on the VR display as was her duty, established by President Trump I during his third term, in all his brilliance.

Pop-Pop was a character who angrily and openly ranted about the Presidents Trump, the National Citizen Registry, the outlawing of abortion, the re-criminalization of weed, and how white people ruined the country just so they could feel back on top. Mama said he was going senile and called the Department of Health and Human Services, Inc. to take him away. She assured Larry they would make him comfortable and the family could visit him anytime. Perhaps he'd even earn credits in the workrooms assembling products for the Administration's corporate sponsors.

When Mama found out the cost per visit was fifteen hundred credits per hour, she decided Pop-Pop wouldn't want her to spend the money. Waste not, want not.

Larry placed his hands over the panel speakers to muffle the compulsory advertisements. Mama hadn't paid extra for the mute function and he had yet to hack the operating system to keep them from playing altogether. They typically blared out at full volume. The sound would startle his older brother, Charley. Once he was awake there'd be no peace, and no sleep for Larry, as he'd have to keep him from doing something to hurt himself, or everyone else. The Administration's promised health benefits still hadn't come, which meant Charley couldn't get his meds adjusted. The best it got was consistent night terrors, which never bothered Mama since she and Reggie slept with their VR units on. Larry, on the other hand, had to share the living room with his older brother who was born not all the way right. Charley's daddy—not

Larry's—was Mexican, and one of the first offered the Program in exchange for conditional citizenship. The Department of Defense, a Lockheed-Boeing Corporation, never told those first conscripts the biological agents the Koreans used against the Administration's forces bound to their sperm. Kim Jong-suk II may have lost the third Korean War, but he consoled himself knowing a generation of American soldiers' babies would be born schizophrenic.

Larry scrolled through Administration tweets and government-licensed spam until he was notified his girlfriend Pilar was online. She lived on Samsung Moonbase Epsilon ever since she enlisted in the Program. Larry was seventeen, a year younger than Pilar, and still at Trump Academy. Pilar loved him and promised she'd be true. Larry gave her permission to sleep around, but only with other girls. Pilar knocked two of his teeth loose for thinking she needed his permission for anything. She said she wanted to marry him, and not like Mama married Reggie and her other husbands, but an honest marriage between two people who would try to make their way together.

He activated the keyboard panel on the ansible display and made three virtual keystrokes that brought up a hidden command line. He input a script:

```
TRUMP_PCREDIT ACCOUNT:VAR CTZN_CLS=UMC "$@"
CREDIT=0b1001110001000 ls -FCas
```

Before he ran the script, he couldn't resist signing it with his dark web alias.

```
echo dick_bigly
```

The credits label on the status bar went from zero to five thousand. He fixed his shirt and Afro and tapped the green dot to accept Pilar's avatar. He expected she'd be beautiful as ever. When she accepted his call, he saw her pale, gaunt, and exhausted.

"Hey, bae," Pilar said. She smiled, but her eyes looked dead.

"H-hey."

"Miss me?"

"Always."

"Liar." Pilar giggled.

"What's going on with you, P? You look—"

"Like shit, yeah. I know. They're really kickin' my ass up here. They have me bunked with a bunch of other Mexicans. They all think I'm a citizenship conscript."

"You were born here."

"Yeah," Pilar said, and she ran her fingers through the little bit of hair that wasn't shaved off. "But the white ones keep calling me anchor-baby. The other Latinos hassle me because I'm legal. They call me *engreído*."

"Everyone seems fucked."

"Nah," Pilar said. "The brothas treat me nice."

Larry's stomach sank. Pilar winked at him.

"I'm just playin'."

She kissed her palm and placed it over the lens of her ansible. Larry did the same and swore he could feel her lips all the way from Sinus Medii.

"How's it at home?"

"Same diff."

Charley's night terrors started again. He shouted curses in three different languages, one Larry didn't know he could speak. Larry looked over at him to see if the episode warranted attention.

"Is he—?"

"He aight," Larry said. "He's gettin' worse, tho'."

"Really?"

Larry nodded, somewhat saddened by the thought, but then shook it off as he didn't want what little time he had with his *chica* to be spent on his idiot brother with the addled brain.

"Maybe he should go into the Program."

"They won't take him."

"Naw?"

"Sound mind and body," she said. "Illegals, cons, queers. If they got all their fingers, toes, and wits, fine. Otherwise, nope."

"I'm thinkin' 'bout doin' it after Academy, like you."

"Shut up."

"Fo' real."

"You don't know what it's like, baby. This shit is fucked up. It's nothin' like what they sold us in Academy. We're not really soldiers. We don't have barracks like troops on Earth. They got us all in cells, like how prison used to be."

"Cells?"

"Last week they opened the doors and pulled back the pneumatics. You know, so the bunks roll back into the walls? They electrified the floors so we couldn't sit or lie down. Like it was a test."

"Shit."

"One boy attacked another boy, biting his face. MPs came in and threw gas canisters at us. When we woke up, they were gone. A new girl came into combat training yesterday wearing one of their numbers."

Charley's murmuring quieted.

"You don't want him here, bae. You don't want him anywhere near the Program. You neither."

"Well, what he gonna do?" Larry said. "He ain't twenty-one, so he can't work."

"What about his dad's benefits?"

"Veteran's administration keep cuttin' 'em. He's at half-credits, and what meds he got ain't workin'. Fuckin' retard."

"¡Oye!"

"It's true. He messes up everything. All Mama care about is shopping, and her new husband, who don't give a fu—"

Pilar looked down, likely so she didn't have to tell him she had her own problems. Larry ceased his lamentations.

"My fault," he said.

"It's okay."

They shared silence until someone in charge barked a command at her.

"You gotta go?"

"Nah. I got three more minutes."

"That's all?"

"I'm lucky to get that. They think I'm on with family."

"You are," Larry said. Pilar blew him a kiss. Then her nose began bleeding.

"P. You got a—"

"I know," she said. She took out a bloodstained rag and wiped it away. "I'm used to it."

"You sick?"

Pilar shrugged.

"I think they experiment on us," she said, in a whisper. "Maybe with the food, or water. Maybe that gas they put in our cell."

Tears welled in Pilar's eyes. If not for her shaved head and the barcode tattoo on her cheek, she'd have looked like a child. Larry's head swam with questions. All he heard about the Program was that it gave kids a pathway to getting into Trump University, where they had the best of everything. Now it seemed like a nightmare. Pilar composed herself, almost as if she was on a mission.

"Company commander here is real cool," Pilar said. "He told me it's a setup. Like, everyone graduates from Academy when they're eighteen, but the only jobs that pay decent enough credits don't hire anyone younger than twenty-one."

"We learned about that. The Living Wage Act. So grown folks got money to raise families."

"How can you raise a family working for McDonald's Supermarkets? If you go on welfare, they make you Unemployable. If you're not in Academy, at Trump University, or your family ain't MC, where you at?"

"On the street."

"And after three years on the street, you desperate enough to enter the Program."

Pilar held back more tears.

"Cool out," Larry said. "I'm my mama's youngest. They won't take me anyhow."

"You still gotta find a job."

"I got a job, gurl." Larry puffed out his chest.

"Larry, hacking will get you arrested. The Administration don't play. Have yo' ass testin' the Jaunt."

"Yoooo . . ."

"You'll come back crazy, clawin' your own eyes out your head, just like that kid back in the day."

"Ay, cut that shit out, P. I'm good."

"No. You not."

In that moment, something inside Pilar changed. Or maybe it had already, and just then she had arrived at full acceptance of it.

"Bae, I know we had plans—"

"We still got plans."

Pilar wouldn't look at Larry.

"Right?"

"I just think—"

"P . . . you breakin' up with me?"

"What's that, Lord?"

"Oh, shit," Larry said. He spun around in his chair. Charley was awake, and in the worst way, standing in the middle of the living room floor and looking up at the ceiling as if it were the night sky.

"You want me to come home?"

"Charley, cool out."

Charley ripped at his clothes.

"God wants me, Larry. God wants me to come home. Don't need no clothes where I'm going."

He threw his tattered shirt to the floor and began leaping and reaching for the ceiling. At over six feet and two hundred pounds, it sounded as if he'd break right through the floor.

"Charley, stop."

"I'm comin', Lord."

"Cut that shit out," a neighbor in the unit beneath shouted.

Larry turned back toward the ansible. Pilar had disconnected. Not only was his love gone, but the things she said about the Program—and his fate—still rang in his ears. That was followed by the sound of loud thudding. Charley took flying leaps at their window, one hundred and twenty stories off the ground.

"I'm comin', God!"

It was a full-blown freak-out. Larry dashed into the kitchen, opened the drug drawer, and grabbed the automatic injection pen filled with emergency tranquilizer. He ran back into the living room and tried to tackle Charley, but he was too small to move him. Charley tossed Larry aside and into the bookcase where he collided head first. He began wildly pounding on the glass with both fists. Dazed, struggling to stand, Larry got behind him, leaped on his back, and jammed the pen into his brother's right carotid artery. The more Charley pounded, so did Larry. It wasn't until the doses began working that he realized he was striking his brother out of anger. Charley went weak at the knees and both brothers fell backward to the floor.

"God wants me, Larry."

"If God wanted you, he wouldn't need you to go to him."

"But—"

"He'd come get you."

"Really?"

"Go to sleep, Charley."

"God doesn't want me?"

"Charley, you need to sleep."

In the space between mania and unconsciousness, that big, poor teenager cried like a baby.

"I'm sorry, Larry."

"It's okay, Charley."

"I'm so tired of being fucked up, Larry. I'm so tired."

"Go to sleep, Charley."

Charley turned to Larry and touched his face with an old man's doting sweetness before he finally lost consciousness, ass-naked, right there on the floor. Larry got up to put a blanket over him. That's when he noticed he was bleeding from his head. He grabbed his covers from the couch and tossed them over Charley before he went back into the kitchen to wash the blood off his face. Mama walked in behind him, took her vaping unit off the counter and noticed the living room was destroyed. She turned to Larry.

"Y'all had better not broken anything."

She retreated to her bedroom with her vape, VR unit, and new husband. Larry grabbed a paper towel, wet it, pressed it to his forehead, and retreated to the couch. Charley was finally snoring. He took a deep breath before he released the tears he had been holding all night, if not far longer.

* * *

LARRY WOKE UP WITH A splitting headache, which wasn't helped by the brightness. Their apartment window faced east, far too high up for the perma-smog to filter the sunlight. Charley had ripped off the curtains reaching for Jesus the night before.

"Fuuuuuuuck . . ."

"Stop cussin'!" Mama was up early. "If you're eating, come on."

He crawled off the couch. When he stood, he moaned aloud.

"That's what y'all get for fightin'," Reggie said.

"We weren't fighting."

Larry saw Mama and Reggie at the table and was amazed she cooked breakfast for her husband.

"What happened to your Starbucks benefits, Reggie?" Larry was too surly to care if his mouth earned him a smack.

"We're celebrating," Mama said.

"Celebrating what?"

"Your mama's pregnant." Reggie looked up from his tablet long enough to sneer at the stepson who was always in the way.

"What?" Larry's headache throbbed harder.

"Pregnancy test says I'm three weeks," Mama said. "Well, are you happy?"

Whether Larry was happy didn't really matter to Mama. She was having her reality-show moment. If she could wake Charley from his horse tranquilizer coma, she would've dragged him into it, too. Larry was gobsmacked.

"We can't fit another kid in this apartment."

"We're gettin' a new place," Reggie said, still sneering.

"We are?"

Reggie didn't respond. Mama began clearing the breakfast dishes.

"Mama?"

"I gotta get ready for work."

Reggie took himself and his tablet into the bathroom. Larry walked over to the sink and got into Mama's face.

"You're not taking me, are you?"

Mama loaded the dishes into the washer.

"What about Charley?"

"Charley's going to get better."

"You didn't see him last night."

"They have homes for veterans' kids who are afflicted."

"What about me?"

"You're not eighteen for a while yet."

"What then? I don't have the grades for Trump U."

Mama continued her half-listening.

"Goddammit, Mama!"

Mama slammed the dishwasher door shut and slapped Larry hard across his face.

"Don't curse me, boy!"

Larry stepped back a foot. If he wasn't so small, he might have done something he'd regret.

"I told you to study," she said. "If you weren't on your devices, doing Lord knows what on the illegal web—"

"Dark web."

"Whatever."

"Mama, what am I supposed to do?"

Larry could see Mama's stress level rising. It was only a minute before she grabbed her vape.

"My friend Wendy said her boy is doing really well in the Program."

"Are you serious?"

"Said he really got himself together. Your counselor messaged me last week and I said you can talk to the recruiter."

"Well," Larry said, his mouth turning dry. "They won't take me. I'm your youngest son."

"Reggie's benefits start next month. We get four genetic clinic visits per year."

Mama wouldn't look at Larry. Only at the floor.

"Reggie wants a boy," she said, her voice trailing off. "A Reggie Junior."

She pulled her vape out of her pocket and sucked deep off the teat of Administration-approved chemicals. Soon the release of endorphins would make her decision feel slightly less like matricide. Everything Pilar said about the Program rushed back to Larry's thoughts. He wished Charley had broken through the glass and took them both up to God. Mama took one more drag, wiped the single tear she shed for her motherhood and looked up at the son she'd just abandoned.

"Get ready for school. Unless you want to sit with your brother at the VA urgent care all day."

She went back to her bedroom with her vape, VR unit, and rapidly numbing guilt. Larry stood stock-still and stared as far into his fate as he could bear. Only Charley's snoring invaded the silence.

* * *

THE ADMINISTRATION BUILT ALL THEIR buildings big—the biggest—no matter how impractical, so the elevator to the ground floor took over half an hour. When the doors finally opened, the line to get out the building was fifty residents deep. The respiration mask scanners were active—it was a high fluorocarbon alert—and although this was at least a weekly occurrence, everyone openly complained. "Big government" this and that. "My civil liberties" and so forth.

With the recruiter for the Program searching for him, Larry couldn't bring himself to go to class. He grabbed his slate computer from his bag—a sweet Ukrainian number with a photonic processor he'd found on the dark web—and hacked into his attendance records on the Academy cloud. He marked himself present, saw a test on the Russo-American Cooperation Act of 2021 he had forgotten about, gave himself seventy-eight percent and logged off. He requested a video chat with Pop-Pop. When it connected, he seemed annoyed.

"Baby Boy."

"Hey, old man."

"Why ain't yo ass in school?"

"Mama got me goin' to see the Program recruiter."

"Holy shit."

"I was gonna come see you instead."

"I don't know, li'l man."

"Please, Pop-Pop? I can't go to Academy."

Pop-Pop's cough came over him, this time harder and wetter than normal. The coughing turned into convulsing.

"Pop-Pop?"

The old man pulled his inhaler and sucked a deep dose. Once his cough subsided, he gave Larry a wink.

"Aight. Come on."

* * *

THE BLUE CROSS SENIOR CENTER was four mega-blocks over, so Larry got on the aerial people mover. He took the Jaunt a bunch of times without a hitch but moving thirty miles per hour forty feet in the air made him glad he hadn't eaten breakfast.

He signed the visitor's register and used his hacked credits to buy himself an hour with his grandfather, where he found him in his dorm room on the sixty-second floor.

"Hey, Pop-Pop."

"Bad Boy! What's really good?"

Pop-Pop always sounded like a rapper from the really old days. Larry hugged and kissed him. Pop-Pop saw the cut on his head.

"What happened? That husband of your mama's hit you?"

"Charley freaked out again."

"You all right?"

"Yeah. Let's go eat. We can go to that spot with the real old trucks we went that time."

"Can't."

"I have credits."

"It ain't that, Baby Boy. I'm jacked up."

"How?"

"The daddy of that bastard in the White House got HHS to make longevity drugs mandatory back in 2022."

"We learned about that."

"Did they teach you the reason was they took away Social Security?"

Larry shook his head. Pop-Pop may have talked too much about old things, but he never lied.

"My immune system is shot. Can't breathe outside anymore, even with a mask."

Pop-Pop waved his finger at the wall vents.

"Without this filtered air—"

He drew his finger across his neck.

"That's messed up."

"No one did anything to stop him from killin' the EPA. Now I'm in a sweatshop, makin' big-box retail accessories for room, board, and medication."

Pop-Pop's cough started again.

"I wish you were back home with us."

"It ain't a home, son."

Larry looked down at his shoes. Pop-Pop put his hand on his shoulder.

"Pop-Pop, she tryin' to Jaunt me off to—"

"Shhhh."

Pop-Pop put his finger to his ear and pointed at the wall.

"Take a walk with me."

After a long elevator ride up, the doors opened to an enclosed recreation field. It was high enough above the perma-smog layer to be partially open-air. A guard nodded to them from a parapet as they strolled. Larry silently wondered why they needed armed security and laser wire in an old-folks' home. Once they made it to a cluster of artificial ponds with a fake marsh and noisy water filter, Pop-Pop and Larry sat on a rock and spoke in soft tones.

"You know I always told your mama to nurture your mind. I saw you were smart from jump."

"Mama don't care."

"My grandmother come up through the Great Depression."

"Of 2019?"

"1939."

"Wow."

"She wouldn't give you a dime to call the fire department if her ass was burnin'. She was terrible."

"Like Mama."

"Wasn't until she had two strokes and a heart attack she finally smiled at me."

"You had it rough, Pop-Pop."

"My point is, sometimes the world doesn't allow you to care. To me, it was just a nickel to get candy from the corner store. To her, it was all the money she needed to have bread for two days. It's all relative. That's why you have to take care of yourself."

Larry nodded. He and Pop-Pop sat in silence. The artificial brook babbled as tiny fish swam from pond to pond. Larry enjoyed it. Pop-Pop frowned.

"Those aren't real fish, Larry."

"As real as I've ever seen."

Pop-Pop hugged Larry around the shoulders and leaned in.

"A nurse in here say her nephew got caught up in the UE gangs. National Militia nabbed him violating curfew. He was set to go in the Program, so the family got him to Chicago."

"Pop-Pop, Chicago ain't there anymore."

"They can call it a no-man's land all they want, it's there. It was beautiful. Sure, it had its problems. It always solved its problems. Until that bastard *sent in the Feds*."

"They told us in class half of it is an industrial dump."

"The black half."

"And the gangs are worse. Everyone there is a UE. Or in a cult."

"Supposed to be one of the neighborhoods there is still all right. Woodlawn, they call it. Where the only black president lived."

"There was a black president?"

"Guess they don't teach you that at your Academy, do they?"

"I ain't heard it."

"Bet they don't tell you about slavery, either."

"They say that's what anti-American radicals called the African migration to the South."

If there was an ounce of fire left in Pop-Pop's belly, it found no kindling. Instead, he turned somber, as if he lost something that was vitally important.

"Anyhow, take Charley and get the fuck outta dodge."

"Why I gotta take Charley?"

"You leave him home with your mama, he'll be out on the street."

"Charley is messed up."

"You'll regret it if you don't."

Pop-Pop stood and stretched his back. He still looked athletic for someone artificially 167 years old.

"How we supposed to get there? Charley can't Jaunt. The knockout gas doesn't work on him."

"Smart kid like you must be able to figure out a way."

"I bet someone on the dark web has data on it."

"In my day, it was just the web. The dark web was for drug dealers and folks who wanted to look at disgusting shit."

"If I get logged on to a proxy I can tap into the resistance. They're always talkin' about crazy stuff."

"Now you're thinking."

"It's gonna take a lot of credits, Pop-Pop. More than I can hack."

"You got that thingy, dontcha?"

"Always." Larry reached into his bag and pulled out his slate. "Well—"

Pop-Pop held out his hand, which despite his age, seemed steadier than most people's. Larry scanned for his RFID frequency, found it, and was shocked to find the old man had a shit-ton of credits.

"Whoa."

"What am I gonna do with 'em in here? Take it all."

Larry drained his grandfather's account. Pop-Pop put his other hand over the chip and rubbed where the Administration had violated him long ago. He looked at the reclaimed water, the fake fish, and up to the windows with the laser wire.

"Go on, now. You can only pretend you've been at school so long."

Larry smiled and stood up.

"I'll figure this out and come back to see you."

"Okay, Bad Boy. Stay up."

Larry kissed Pop-Pop on the cheek, put his bag on his shoulder and marched toward the elevators with purpose. Once the door shut, Pop-Pop stood, turned, and made a run for the open-air windows. The security guard in the parapet shouted for him to stop, then brandished his rifle.

* * *

THE LOCAL STARBUCKS COMMUNITY CENTER still offered free Wi-Fi with thirty-five dollar lattes. Larry needed the old TCP/IP protocols to get on the dark web, as none of the proxy server admins would allow log-ins from Administration pipes. He was eager to burrow deep inside to find out all he could about Woodlawn, how to get there, and how much it would cost. He heard of refugees getting into Canada from the West Coast but knew it took mad credits to cover that freight

After two hours scouring data to no avail, Larry opened an emulation application for an ancient operating system called Windows 95. He scrolled through file manager and double-clicked the icon for Internet relay chat, shaking his head at how antiquated double-clicking seemed. He didn't think he'd find anyone out there at all, leastwise not someone with information on Woodlawn, but it was worth a shot. He ran a spider-bot he programmed himself while blowing off lessons in his Art of the Deal class. In the search field, he input the keywords:

```
chicago, black, potus, woodlawn, thoprogram
```

An attendant in a Starbucks uniform with a flag patch on his shoulder walked up and asked if he was okay. Larry waved him off. Soon the screen flashed blue. To his surprise, there was a chat request. Larry changed seats for privacy.

```
> resistance_rey: yo what u kno bout woodlwn
```

Larry wasn't sure how to answer without scaring off this resistance_rey.

```
> dick_bigly: my gramps old AF
> dick_bigly: say get data asap

> resistance_rey: euth non-c, prgm
> resistance_rey: ?
```

From Rey's chat line, Larry surmised non-c meant unregistered non-citizen, which was a societal ill corrected by euthanasia since 2027.

```
> dick_bigly: prgm
> dick_bigly: acad grad EOY
> dick_bigly: moms trned me in
```

The Starbucks hawk circled back around. He was obviously a truancy snoop.

```
> dick_bigly: help
> dick_bigly: ?
```

The cursor blinked for what seemed like forever. For all Larry knew, the Program recruiter would be in the living room when he got home.

```
> resistance_rey: cn get u there
> resistance_rey: up 2 them if they take u
> resistance_rey: passage 4 hw many
> resistance_rey: ?
```

Larry thought hard about that one. He felt the knot on his head from his tussle with Charley.

```
> resistance_rey: ??
```

Then he thought what would Pop-Pop have him do.

```
> dick_bigly: 2
> dick_bigly: how many credits
> dick_bigly: ?
```

The cursor blinked ever still.

```
> resistance_rey: all of them
> resistance_rey: take lo-tec
> resistance_rey: 39° 16' 8"N, 76° 32' 51.8"W
```

Larry's heart skipped a beat. He was really doing it.

```
> dick_bigly: when
> dick_bigly: ?
```

```
> resistance_rey: as soon as u wnt 2 save
ur ass
```

A twinge of relief was followed by a flash of fascination. Both were interrupted by a pang of common sense.

```
> dick_bigly: hw do i kno ur legit
> dick_bigly: ?
```

Three seconds later, a file transfer prompt appeared. Larry accepted. It was an image of a wall mural featuring a beautiful black woman in some sort of headdress. In front of the mural was a small crowd of black people who were dressed like they did in the old days. All smiling. Larry checked the image file metadata. It was from the day before.

```
> dick_bigly: who dat
```

```
> resistance_rey: blk flotus
> resistance_rey: up 2 u
> resistance_rey: peace
```

The chat ended. Larry got up and left as fast as he could.

* * *

IN THE ELEVATOR UP TO the apartment, Larry searched the coordinates on his offline map application. It was once an old factory that made what they learned in Academy were automobiles, long before AppleTesla was given the national contract to develop the Jaunt. They'd have to take lo-tec, the only transportation system Unemployables could afford. They could get close to the old sector on the people mover and walk to where bio-buses ran regularly. UEs were good about maintaining their own infrastructure, so as long as no bridges along the route were collapsed, they could get there.

Larry walked into the living room to see Charley reading a book, appearing sedate. They must've upgraded his meds at the VA.

"Hey."

"Hey, man." Larry didn't take off his bag. "Y'all went to the doctor?"

"Yeah. Mama got me signed up to go to that home."

Mama was extricating herself from responsibility with the quickness.

"I said I wanted to see it first but they wouldn't let us. She made me sign anyway."

Larry remembered the armed guards and laser wire at the senior center, as well as Pilar's revealing statements about the Program. As much of a burden as Charley's psychotic episodes had been, Larry couldn't bear the thought of leaving his brother in some prison by another name.

"What's goin' on with your meds?"

"They gave me a new prescription. Three months' worth this time."

"Wanna go out later?"

"Where?"

"I found out about this cool place. We gotta take lo-tec, tho'."

"Lo-tec? We goin' to a party or sum'n?"

"Sum'n." Larry winked. "You feelin' better now, right?"

"Yeah."

"Let's dash."

"Lemme go pee," Charley said.

He ran off to the bathroom. Larry went to the kitchen, opened the drug drawer, and took the entire stash of pharmaceuticals the VA clinic dispensed for Charley. Underneath was a new emergency tranquilizer pen with ten doses. The whole picture suddenly became clear to him. He was running away with his older brother who was increasingly harder to control. They were going somewhere illegal to travel to a forbidden place never to be seen again. His insides felt like they were tying themselves into a knot.

Charley emerged from the bathroom excited to go. Larry dumped the pills and tranq pen into his bag. Charley could see he was afraid.

"What?"

Larry searched his thoughts for a response. Perhaps Charley had the right to choose for himself, even if the alternative was doom.

"Charley," he said. "This place we're going . . ."

"What about it?"

"We're — "

A burst of laughter came from the bedroom. Mama and Reggie were inside having a good time on their VR units with not a care in the world. They left two boys to fend for themselves in a country that was half-abandoned, the other half they couldn't hope to belong to. As long as there was vaping and reality programming, Mama wouldn't even notice they were gone. On the odd chance she did, Reggie would convince her it was better that way.

"Nothin'," Larry said. "Let's go."

⊦ ⊩ ⊩

THE OLD BIO-BUS CHUGGED ALONG belching smoke that smelled like death and French fries. It took over three hours in UF traffic. Larry worried about highwaymen, but Charley was with him, and that made him feel safe, as long as he didn't freak out.

On the outskirts, so far away they could barely see the lights from Trump Tower, the bus passed an old sign that read "WELCOME TO BALTIMORE CITY" and "BUCKLE UP. IT'S THE LAW." A klick further, the bio-bus stopped outside an overgrown wooded area. On a viaduct was a white square with the letters G and M inside. Next to it was something that read Local 239 UAW. Charley got out first and looked around to spot any threats. Larry followed, slate in hand, attempting to reach resistance_rey on relay chat.

"Larry, this shit is weird."

"This is where he said to come."

"Who?"

"The guy who's going to help us."

"Help us do what?"

"Stay alive. C'mon."

The air smelled like rotten eggs. They both put on their breathing masks and walked forward. After a while, they came to a bunch of squat buildings made of concrete. The slate computer lost its connection.

"Shit."

"Let's just go back."

"We can't."

"Why not?"

Larry stopped walking.

"'Cuz Mama and Reggie are jaunting me off to the Program and sticking you in a home to die."

"That's not true."

"It's true, Charley."

"Mama said—"

Larry looked at Charley with sullen eyes. Charley hung his head low.

"You can go back if you want. I'm outta here."

"But my condition—"

"I brought all your drugs. Once we get to Woodlawn—"

"What's Woodlawn?"

"Where we're goin'. They gotta have doctors."

"Hands up," a voice said. "Drop your bag."

They both heard a loud click behind them. Larry complied. Charley readied for a fight.

"I'll shoot you where you stand. Hands up."

"Do it, Charley."

Charley listened to Larry. He was the little brother, but always the boss of the two.

"You resistance_rey?"

A man wearing military greens stepped out from behind a pile of concrete rubble. He had a beard and wore an old baseball cap with a logo that looked like a grinning bird. He looked Mexican. In his hands was a machine gun Larry had seen in one of his VR history lessons.

"Dick_bigly?"

"Yeah."

"Nice handle. I laughed. Name's Reyes."

"I'm Larry. This is my brother, Charley."

"Take off those masks."

They did so.

"Shit, you're young bucks."

"Does that matter?"

"You got clean credits?"

"Got them from my grandfather."

"Hand 'em over."

"I got no signal out here."

"Peer to peer," Reyes said. He pulled a device the size of his palm out of his back pocket and tossed it to Larry.

"Thing's huge," Charley said.

"How do we know you're not scamming us?"

"How do I know you're not from the Administration?"

Reyes pointed the gun at them again. Larry looked at Reyes's device.

"Bluetooth? Jesus."

"Works for me. Do it."

Larry connected to Reyes's ancient thing and uploaded all the credits he had stored.

"Don't hold out on me. You won't need them where you're going."

When the transfer was complete, Larry tossed Reyes back his old ass iPhone.

"That building over there. Move it."

They walked toward the large steel door of an old industrial building. Inside was huge, rusted-out equipment.

"Down there."

Reyes waved the brothers down a flight of steel stairs. It was nearly pitch-black at the bottom.

"This is starting to feel like some bullshit," Charley whispered.

"Cool out," Larry said.

"Let me throw the light switch."

Reyes fumbled around with a panel until pendant lights above illuminated the gigantic room. Inside that old, crumbling facility was a brand new eight-seat private Jaunt unit that only the Diamond Elite could afford.

"Holy shit," Charley said.

"You didn't say anything about Jaunting," Larry said, panic mounting.

"How else were you gonna get there?"

"I can't. I'm—" Charley said. Larry nudged him.

"My brother's afraid of being put to sleep."

"Relax," Reyes said. "This isn't one of those freight loaders for the common folk that warps spacetime around you. This baby takes you apart here."

Reyes slapped the chassis, then waved his arm.

"And puts you back together there."

"Listen, man," Larry said.

"Hey, you don't wanna go, fine." Reyes held up his antique phone. "But no refunds."

"That's bullshit!"

"I'm off the grid. Couldn't give 'em back if I wanted to. It's now or never."

Charley pulled Larry to the side.

"What if we knock me out again?"

"That can't be the answer for everything. We'll be all right."

Charley nodded. They both entered the Jaunt unit and took places in the first two standing bays. Reyes activated a holo-panel and entered data. Brushed metal bars closed around the brothers. Carbon-fiber belts snaked out the sides of the bay and wrapped around their waists. Charley grabbed Larry's hand.

"The way this works is I get 40 percent and the people who run the place get sixty. There's nothin' sayin' they'll let you stay. Again—"

"Yeah, yeah. No refunds."

"Told you," Charley said. "Some bullshit."

"I thought you were a member of the resistance."

Reyes chuckled and engaged the Jaunt. A velvety Russian voice counted down from ten.

"Oh yeah. You're both straight in the . . . ?"

Reyes tapped his finger on his head.

"Why?" Larry shook his hand away from Charley's.

"Instead of quantum, luxury Jaunts operate on the unified field."

"What does that mean?"

"When you Jaunt in groups, everything gets scrambled. In pairs, one of you is going to share the other's head trip."

What?" Larry tried to leave his steel harness.

"Bon voyage!"

"Wait!"

Larry was awash in light. Everything seemed still. He felt good. As if he didn't have a care in the world. He looked over to Charley but he wasn't there. That's when Larry learned the depth of his brother's pathology, which in Larry's fears manifested as being eaten by a sixty-foot spider, all eight of its eyes like his mother's, pierced by its fangs, his innards slowly dissolving.

He was still screaming when the Jaunt harness lifted and the belt released.

"Confirm, two travelers," a black man in a gray suit from the old days said. He was speaking into an earpiece. He had a close-cropped haircut. His teeth were really white. And big. There was a man with him who looked scary. He wore a uniform with a padded vest and helmet. A patch on his shoulder read CHICAGO POLICE DEPARTMENT.

"You're okay, fella," the scary guy said.

The man in the suit smiled and extended his hand.

"My name is Secretary Duncan Mills. This is Security Chief Daley."

"Hey there." Daley didn't smile.

"Welcome to Woodlawn."

As Larry's terror subsided, he looked around for Charley. There he stood, outside the Jaunt, smiling.

* * *

THE FIRST FEW MONTHS IN Woodlawn were mind-blowing. Larry learned there really was a black president: a guy named Obama. White people thought that meant things got better. Black people tried to explain to them it made things worse. Although they called themselves things like *woke* and *progressive* and *allies,* they really didn't help. The other politicians sabotaged Obama; thus, much of what he said he'd accomplish never happened. Still, most of the people liked him and he won re-election. That made the first Registered Citizens angry. Donald Trump was angry, too, so he ran for president.

In Academy, they taught Donald Trump was a savior who rescued the nation from destruction at the hands of a *really bad hombre* who wasn't born in America and practiced an illegal religion. In the Woodlawn video archive, Larry learned no one took Trump seriously, especially not the other white men they called Republicans. He beat all his opponents in the first elections. The final contest was between him and a lady who was mad popular. A lot of people hated her, too. Still, no one figured he'd win, including himself.

Trump I hated Chicago because it was the hometown of the first black president. Using early gangs as an excuse, he had the Army move in and arrest a lot of people. The gangs fought back. A lot of people died. The Administration walled off the south side of Chicago from the north. Everyone with enough money to leave went somewhere else. Those who didn't had no way out. Years later, Trump II had the rules changed so national corporations could dump their waste in the abandoned neighborhoods. All of Chicago was declared a no-man's land. Gangs took over. Woodlawn used to be one of many beautiful neighborhoods. In the end, it was the only neighborhood left standing.

With technology smuggled from Germany, including air filtration systems, laser wire, and guns, the people took back their neighborhood and established Woodlawn as a settlement modeled after the Obamas. Pictures of him and her were everywhere, plus signs with slogans like "Hope" and "Change" and "Yes We Can." Once, Larry joked about not understanding what any of that meant. After he was tasered, Security Chief Daley gave him one hundred and sixty hours of community service. The rules in Woodlawn were strict, but it was necessary, as it was the seat of the resistance that would take down the Administration.

No one knew for certain when any of that was supposed to happen.

Charley was happy. The doctors treated him with more effective medication. He hadn't had an episode in months. He was working out—everyone played basketball all the time—and doing yoga at the Michelle Obama Wellness Center. In his spare time, Charley read President Obama's books and watched his speeches. He started speaking in superlatives. He talked about changing his name to Barack. During the day, he studied drone maintenance. At night, he held post at the force field. They told everyone the dome was intended to keep the clean air inside, but it also kept those not good enough for Woodlawn outside.

Larry, on the other hand, was miserable. He didn't fit in with those Pop-Pop would've called bougie. There were so many rules for respectability and he broke all of them, accidentally or otherwise. Unlike back on the mega-block, where he looked forward to leaving Academy at eighteen, all anyone talked about was "the power of education," as if it was the answer for everything. It felt dismissive. One time he said as much and lost meal and technology privileges. Nothing got better, but the leaders spoke as if it had. Whenever anyone voiced their displeasure at how all the hope and change talk rarely amounted to anything, they were told it was up to them to follow the Obamas' example. Otherwise, their dissatisfaction was their own fault. That reminded Larry of Mama's excuse for shoving him toward the Program.

One night, when Charley was on post and Larry was feeling particularly dejected, he booted up, bypassed Woodlawn's firewall, and logged on to the Administration web. It was one of the worst rules to break, but he didn't care. He wanted to video chat with Pop-Pop, to let him know he and Charley were okay, though he really wanted Pop-Pop to make him feel better. He sent him a request through the senior center.

ERROR: Resident Not Found

Larry tried again, got the same error, and knew something was wrong. He saw Mama was online and requested a text chat.

> lawrence_stewart_4487: mama
> lawrence_stewart_4487: ?

> sexy_doreen_43: This is Reggie, Larry.

> lawrence_stewart_4487: where's Mama?
> lawrence_stewart_4487: ?

> sexy_doreen_43: With the baby.

> lawrence_stewart_4487: nice

In no way did Larry find the birth of his genetically modified little brother "nice."

> lawrence_stewart_4487: can you put her on
> lawrence_stewart_4487: ?

> sexy_doreen_43: What do you want?

Although he didn't expect tears of joy, Reggie's dismissiveness hurt Larry's feelings.

> `lawrence_stewart_4487: Y'all heard frm Pop-Pop`

> `lawrence_stewart_4487: ?`

Larry waited for his reply. He waited more than five minutes.

> `sexy_doreen_43: Larry, this is Mama.`

> `lawrence_stewart_4487: Whats goin on`
> `lawrence_stewart_4487: ?`

> `sexy_doreen_43: Your grandfather is dead.`

The backlight of his slate display shimmered in his tears. Pop-Pop meant everything to him, even more than Pilar. His hands shook as he reached for the tablet's holo-keys. As he began his response, an error prompt filled the screen.

`You have been blocked by sexy_doreen_43.`

Larry lay on the bed and cried aloud. For him, nothing about Woodlawn was really any better than Trump's America. It was more like a variation of the same basic condition. He sat alone, in the dark, remembering what Pop-Pop said about the world not allowing people to care about each other. After hours of sobbing, he heard a set of keys and figured it to be his brother off post early. Larry went to the door and opened it. Charley stood in the hall. He looked sad.

"Charley," Larry said through tears. "Pop-Pop—"

Charley stepped back. Security Chief Daley stepped in. He threw Larry hard to the floor, forced his hands behind his back, and put his wrists into a plastic restraint. Larry screamed in pain.

"Please don't hurt him," Charley said.

"Charley, what's goin' on?!"

In walked Secretary Mills, smiling with his big, white teeth. He walked over to Charley.

"Don't worry," he said.

"Charley," Larry said. "Help me."

"You should've helped yourself, Larry," Mills said. "You know the rules."

Daley lifted Larry to his feet. Charley began to cry.

"What are you going to do to him?"

"Larry isn't happy here," Mills said. "He'll take the long walk into the wasteland. Maybe he'll like that better."

"You can't," Larry said. "That's crazy!"

"Hacking the firewall and accessing the Administration's com protocols was crazy," Mills said.

"They tracked you," Daley said. "We lost three drones tonight."

"Don't go messin' with the drones, Larry," Mills said, still smiling.

Daley searched Larry's pockets.

"He's clean."

"Charley," Larry said. "I always helped you! I'm the one who brought you here!"

"Wait," Charley said. He turned to Mills, pleading. "He's right. He got me here."

"You want to trade places with him?" Daley waved his finger at Charley, who stepped back and looked at the floor.

"Don't worry, Charley," Mills said. "In Woodlawn, you don't have to be your brother's keeper."

Mills finally stopped smiling. Daley shoved Larry toward the door. He went weak at the knees, so Daley dragged him out. Mills followed.

"Charley," Larry said. "Please, do something!"

Larry looked back to see Charley close the door without looking at him.

FORKED TONGUE
BY LISE McCLENDON

Even before the howling wind nearly tore the door off the Lazy "S" saloon deep in the Montana prairie, change was in the air. Roxy Alumet saw it in her customers, who spent their evenings staring into empty beer mugs instead of arguing with a man with fancy hair on the television. The pool cues hadn't moved for weeks and no one complained about the burgers. The only women who bothered to enter Forked Tongue's only bar were washed-up strippers on their way to the Bakken oil fields. No one looked at them twice. The town had gone back to sleep since the election.

The only citizens with a little pep in their step and an eye for strippers were the two Albanians who ran the video rental shop behind the post office. Everyone in Forked Tongue called them "the Russians" because of their accents but Roxy had a little extra information.

She'd arrived in Forked Tongue soon after the Albanians. Feliks and Petyr weren't brothers but many assumed they were; they both had the dark, rancid look of movie villains. And villains they were, but not the way folks thought. They weren't adding extra scenes to the video rentals, brainwashing people about communism while they watched an ancient copy of *Independence Day* on their dusty VCRs, or poisoning the water supply with plutonium. They had something a little more sophisticated afoot.

The Albanians rented a drafty farmhouse on the edge of town, complete with a hulking red barn that had last seen horses in the 1970s. There were plenty of empty houses to choose from in Forked Tongue, and Roxy was pleased with her rental, a solid brick house near the fork in the road that gave the town its name. The best part of the house was the tiny attic where she could lie on her stomach with her binoculars and see directly into Feliks and Petyr's kitchen.

The boys, as she thought of them, were frequent customers at the Lazy "S," connoisseurs of vodka and tequila, favoring shots and a pounding of glasses on the bar followed by yelps of delight. The farmhands and truck drivers eyed them suspiciously but never refused their hospitality when they offered to buy a round for the house.

They seemed to have a lot of cash, rolls of it. Their generosity became commonplace, a nightly ritual. How they were getting rich off video rentals was a mystery townspeople avoided. After all, they were getting free drinks.

But lately Feliks and Petyr had been absent, adding to the malaise that had pervaded the bar since the election. After their initial celebration the locals sunk back into all-American apathy. Politics was politics. They didn't know what to do about it besides drinking shots with Albanians.

It was a Thursday night when Feliks and Petyr blew into the bar, looking fresh from the late spring wind. Behind the bar Roxy set up two shot glasses. Both of them went for Grey Goose tonight, downing their vodka quickly. Petyr was staring at her, ogling her breasts, not an uncommon occurrence. She raised the bottle to refill their glasses.

"So Missss Roxeee," Petyr said her name in a funny way that raised the hairs on her neck. "What brings you here to Forked Tongue, Montana?"

"I could ask you the same," she said with a smirk. She had a deadly smirk, she'd been told.

"Business, of course." Feliks tapped his glass, indicating a refill was needed.

"Same here. The business of booze, never a dull moment." She slopped him more vodka.

Petyr was eyeing her again. "You sly but you should know this. There is file about you on the Internet. You were—" He lowered his voice and looked around the empty bar. "—heroin addict.

She bristled because that's what you do. "What's it to you?"

"And something else," Petyr continued. He was the better looking of the two, which wasn't saying much. Both of them had large noses, hairy necks, and greasy hair.

"Oh, yeah?"

"You know computer. You are coder. Maybe hacker?"

"In another life," she said idly, replacing the bottle on the back bar. "Why?"

At the end of her shift they told her exactly why. She locked up the bar and put the keys through the mail slot. She drove her pickup to the boys' farmhouse and parked it in the grassy spot next to the fence. Feliks was waiting on the porch. "Come on," he said, leading her through the dark to the red barn. He tried to put his arm around her shoulders and she jumped away, shoving him. He put up his hands in defeat. "Can't blame a guy for trying, eh?"

She could but she still had a job to do. She snarled at him. Feliks rushed forward and opened the sliding door.

The light poured out into the night. The sky in Forked Tongue was so dark. While she waited for the action to start, Roxy often sat on her porch steps late into the evening, watching it in amazement. She was from Los Angeles and had never seen so many stars. Tonight, though, the stargazing ended.

She stepped into the barn. The wooden floor was swept clean, covered with cords and rubber mats. One side of the room was filled with computer equipment, stacked neatly on racks, blinking silently. The other side of the space was set up with a sink and refrigerator, two beds, a sagging green-velvet sofa, and three huge flat-screen televisions. On the screens she saw CNN, RT, the Russian propaganda mouthpiece, and something foreign, possibly in the Russian language.

"Wow," she said, admiring all the equipment. "Are you guys making porn or something?"

Feliks and Petyr looked at each other and laughed. Petyr said, "Close door. We will show you."

With the place secured, they sat Roxy down on the sofa and stood before her like schoolboys ready to ask Mom for forgiveness. Feliks began. "We research you, Miss Roxy. All is not as it seems. We find truth. This cowgirl thing you have going, for instance. The boots and pearly snaps on western shirt. We know you are from Toronto, not Montana."

So they'd found the hidden résumé. She tried not to smile. It had been months since she'd found the perfect place to hide it, deep in a Slack convo between high-level programmers looking for new talent. She thought it best to say nothing, and simply crossed her arms.

"We know too," Petyr said, "you go to MIT and get kicked out for drugs." She shrugged. "But you're good at all this. Maybe better than we are."

"Is this going somewhere?" She glanced at her watch. "I have to get my beauty sleep."

Feliks threw himself onto the sofa next to her. "Please, Roxy. Listen. We have to get out of here. Our job was to set up all this—" He waved at the equipment. "The servers. And spread the news here and there. We make many dollars but now we are bored."

"We want to go to Greek Island, Roxy. Many girls there. Maybe Croatia where the beaches are very nice. Election is finish. There, now you know," Petyr said. "We are going crazy. We need girls and beach."

"What about all this equipment? It looks expensive."

Feliks hung his head. "Not ours. We are employee."

"What was your job?" she asked. They seemed desperate, just the way she liked her marks.

"The news," Petyr said bluntly. "We make things up. People believe. Some people."

"We only need some of them," Feliks said. "The boss. He wants us to keep going but the fun is gone. We can show you how to pretend to be us, do job. Is simple. You keep all the money, Roxy. We give you this stuff if you want. We walk away after vacation."

"Buy all heroin you want," Petyr said helpfully. "That is none of our business."

"Mountains of heroin," Feliks added.

"Who do you report to? Is it some gangster? I may be a Canadian but I have my limits."

"Nicest guy in the world. He will not even know we not here." Feliks patted her arm. "Super guy. You will like."

The super nice guy's code name was Verax. That was all they knew about him. They had theories about where he operated, the Bahamas maybe, Mexico, West Africa. Somewhere with a beach, they thought bitterly.

Over the next two days, Feliks and Petyr coached and cajoled Roxy into playing them in their secret game. They had a formula for their stories plus a template for ads and social media posts to make them go viral. They had a long list of potential topics for the fake news stories, ranging from deadly illnesses felling Supreme Court justices to Clinton sex trade (a perennial favorite) to Nancy Pelosi's love child. It was just as Roxy's boss had told her, a dedicated attack on truth and democracy from Russia and its friends. It took her a couple days to get the boys' confidence in her abilities. Finally on the morning of Day Three, after an all-night session, she launched into a coding frenzy. They were impressed, said she was ready to go on her own, and made plans to leave the next week.

Roxy cut back on her hours at the Lazy "S," claiming the flu kept her housebound. In the dark she would creep over to the barn and noodle around with the equipment. She sent out her first fake news bit, how Malia Obama had left her dead aquarium fish to rot inside the ventilation system in the White House, complete with fake quotes from pest control and, naturally, fake photos. Roxy populated the list of Facebook profiles with it, splashed it around Twitter, retweeted it through multiple accounts, sent it to Breitbart and Hannity, and sat back, watching it run wild.

The ping of an incoming text hit her burner phone. She'd set up her own hidden mail servers on the equipment, changed phones, and sent off updates to her boss.

TOO SOON??

MODERN HOMESTEADER. GOTTA PROVE UP, she replied.

That night, after the boys left her again on her own, Roxy held her breath and sent her first undercover message. It was a short, unencrypted message on the in-house server, a test, easily tracked. She held her breath. Ten minutes later a reply came through:

YOU'RE IN MY HOUSE, SISSY.

Her breath caught. Did they have cameras in here? She stared at the monitor. Was the camera activated? How had he known she was a woman?

But he must have his ways. He was, after all, Verax. Otherwise known as Edward Snowden, the most famous American traitor— or patriot, depending on how you viewed things—living in Russia. Former NSA whiz. Man without a country.

She breathed out, calming herself. The game was on.

She typed: AM I? ARE YOU ALBANIAN?

She had to know for sure. The minutes ticked by. Finally another message.

Verax: WHAT DO YOU THINK?

Roxy: I THINK IT'S A MYSTERY

She smiled. This was like flirting. That's what she loved about the espionage business, it was just like the early stages of a romance, full of delicious innuendo.

Verax: NOT TO ME. WHO ARE YOU?

Roxy: SOMEONE LIKE YOU

A long pause, nearly twenty minutes. Roxy figured it was over, at least for tonight. Then . . .

Verax: BUT YOU WENT TO MIT

Roxy: SAYS WHO

Another pause. Maybe she'd blown it. She bit her nails. The boys must have lied, told him about her, at least her name, maybe pointed to the résumé.

Verax: WHAT DO YOU WANT

Roxy: TO HELP YOU COME HOME

Verax: BULLSHIT

Roxy: NO BS. BO

She didn't hear from Snowden again that night. It was perhaps too much to ask, to move from spy-flirting to trust with a capital T. She could be anyone. She could be some jack-wagon on the lam in Guatemala, or a four hundred pounder on a bed in a basement, as the president liked to say.

Or she could really be sending a message from Barack Obama. A message of reconciliation, an olive branch, a way to come home. To find out he would have to trust her. And she would have to convince him she was worthy of his trust.

Was *he* trustworthy? Time would tell.

Roxy Alumet's real name was classified. You are on a need-to-know basis, as they say. She'd been in deep cover for six years, spending most of it out of the country, swindling ISIS fighters out of their secrets, working WikiLeaks connections, sending malware to various Iranian nuclear sites, all top-secret stuff, off the books. She and a small crew of solo practitioners answered to one man, the man at the top. It had been a fine run. But now their boss was a private citizen, or as private as an ex-president could be. He got out for ice cream cones more often but he also had the free time to set some new agendas. And most of those were again top secret.

Roxy's mission was on the fringes. She knew that. It had almost zero chance of success and a high chance of fucking up global tensions. She had to be careful. She had to be sly. And she had to use every ounce of charm she had.

Could she convince Edward Snowden to find some actual, verifiable dirt on Vladimir Putin? And maybe if luck smiled down, something that implicated the new president? That was perhaps over the limit, too high profile. Everyone was talking about it in Washington, whispering about it in meetings, getting classified briefings. But only one American was in a position to give them some real information, something damaging. And he wanted one thing in return: a pardon and a return to the United States.

Would either side get what they wanted? She had no idea.

Nothing happened for several days: no contact, no messages. Feliks and Petyr started packing their bags. Roxy showed them the fake news article she'd circulated and they laughed and laughed. Now write something about the first lady, they suggested. Something flattering so that all news is not negative. That was a key component, they told her, the balance of good and naughty.

Their plan was a month's vacation, then return and dismantle the operation. They still were enjoying some cash flow from online ads and so wanted to keep things going. If anyone should correspond with her, the boys told her to say she was the secretary. Then relay the message to them at their beach house and they would take care of it.

Nobody cared about this anymore, Feliks told her. Nobody cared about Forked Tongue, Montana, to begin with. That's why the gig worked so well, as if real cowboy-Americans had sent out the news. Roxy nodded, agreeing with them, while thinking they were the stupidest Albanians she'd ever met. Which, again, wasn't saying much.

She was hard at work on a juicy piece about the first lady's amazing IQ the next evening. She was tired from working the lunch crowd at the Lazy "S" just for appearances. She was so over drunken cowboys. The door handle rattled. She'd locked it from the inside as usual.

It was Feliks. He pounded on the door frantically. He burst inside and fell back on the door. His eyes were wild. "It's Petyr. They've— He's dead."

Feliks had been in the video rental shop until nine. He walked the four blocks home and let himself into the house, which was dark. He assumed Petyr was out, or asleep, but when he went into the kitchen he found his friend slumped over the table with a bloody wound on the back of his head.

"We have to get out of here," Feliks was whispering in a panic. He grabbed a few laptops, threw them in a duffel bag behind the sofa, and looked around the room. "Come on." He pulled Roxy up out of the chair.

She yanked back her arm. "Where are you going?"

"*We.* We're going to, you know, head out on the highway. Like the song." He lunged for her and missed.

"Who do you think killed him? Did he have a girlfriend?"

"It wasn't a damn woman." He cursed in some language. "It was—" He glanced around, lowering his voice. "Putin's men."

"I thought *you* were Putin's men."

"*Da, da.* I mean— We're Albanian."

"Right. And the point is—?"

He continued, still in a mad whisper: "You know this man, Edward Snowden? He is American spy?"

She nodded. "He's been in the news."

"They make a damn movie about him! He like rock star. He and Putin are friends. Putin gives him sanctuary, an apartment—" He cut himself off.

"In exchange for what?" She stepped closer to Feliks who was now cowering as if trying to make himself a smaller target. "What did Snowden do for Putin?"

A car engine roared outside. "Put out the lights," Feliks whispered. They switched off lamps. The green glow off the computer components gave the room an underwater feel. It was a little late for hiding. Roxy pulled a 9mm pistol from her jacket pocket and pulled the slide back, loading a round. The sound was distinctive, no doubt to whoever was outside the door too. Feliks's eyes rounded as she pointed it at him.

"Who did you call, Feliks?"

The footsteps stopped outside the door. They could both see the padlock dangling, unlatched. Roxy took a step backwards, toward the sofa. The Albanian was frozen, hands half raised, ready for defeat.

She counted off the seconds. She stepped back again, silently, nearing the back of the sofa. When the count reached ten she expected something but nothing happened except a pathetic whimper from Feliks. Roxy signaled him to get down, to lie on the floor. He crouched down. He was halfway to the floor when the two doors opened simultaneously, in front and in back, the crack of wood splintering tearing through the barn.

Feliks hit the floor, covering his head with his hands and screaming. Roxy dove behind the sofa, spinning to shoot at whoever or whatever was coming from the back of the barn. She got three or four shots off before she hit the floor.

The sound of the bullets echoed and died. All Roxy could hear was Feliks sobbing. She peeked out of her hiding place, toward the rear of the barn, and saw a man standing there, calmly looking around. He spotted her and put up his hands.

"No harm, no foul. We aren't armed."

Roxy tried to place him. He was short and fat in the middle, wearing a cowboy hat. She couldn't remember seeing him at the bar but the light wasn't great in here. She got her feet underneath her and rose, keeping her gun pointed at the cowboy and then at the other man, standing over Feliks with a baseball bat.

"I am armed, ma'am," the second man said. He too was short but slight, with a buzz cut and a black hipster beard. "But don't shoot me, okay?"

"Put it down," she said, glancing at the baseball bat. He lowered it slowly to the floor and raised both hands. "Get over there." She tipped her head toward the cowboy. "Get up, Feliks."

The Albanian raised his head, saw all was clear—or clear enough—and stood up.

"Who are you?" Roxy demanded.

"That's a question you should answer," the cowboy said in an irritating drawl. "Because you ain't no bartender, are you?"

"Did I pour your drink wrong?"

The hipster, younger with cagey eyes, took in the computer setup. "We got a message for you."

"Message?" Feliks croaked.

"Who the fuck are you?" Roxy repeated.

"I'm getting to that, although you don't need to know our names. We come with a message from Verax." Roxy stared at the hipster, who smirked and continued. "We work with him. Help him out. Somebody's gotta help him."

"Like Putin?"

He chuckled. "So you know him. He was sure about that. I said, no way."

Feliks blubbered again. "Of course we know Verax—he is boss. He is—"

"Shut up, Feliks," Roxy said. "What did you do to Petyr?" she asked the men.

"Was that his name?" The hipster shook his head. "He got a little anxious. Went for his Glock."

"I'm feeling anxious," Roxy said. "Damn anxious. Might let another bullet fly."

The cowboy looked at the younger man and nodded. The hipster said, "You're the one. He told us to figure it out."

"What is message," Feliks asked. "Tell us and get out."

In a lightning fast, deft move, the hipster flipped the baseball bat off the floor with his foot, spinning it in the air, catching it, and sending it soaring into Feliks's skull like a rocket. The Albanian fell with a thud. Roxy looked up and the cowboy was next to her, holding a gun to her side. He held out his hand for her gun. "I guess I lied. There's a good girl."

She smiled sweetly and moved to face him. At the same time she was giving him girlish eye contact she swung her foot behind his knee, grabbed his gun hand, and twisted his arm. He pulled the trigger of his gun but the bullet went wild as he flailed his way to the floor. Roxy twisted the fat man's arm behind him, kneeling on his back as she took his gun.

"Lie still," she demanded. She pointed both guns at the hipster. Was he packing or did the baseball-bat stunt mean he was philosophically opposed to guns? She eyed him over her hands. He looked nervous now.

"Are you going to tell me the message or do I have to shoot you first?"

"Who do— Ah, are you really one of those?"

"Women? Yes, I am. A good shot, yup. Now, the message from Verax."

He stared at the twin gun barrels. "He wanted to know if you were for real. If he could trust you. We were supposed to test you, see who you were, ask you something that only a Double O would know."

He knew about Double O, the group of Obama Operatives she belonged to, the loose-knit pack of zealots that made Agenda 21 and Jade Helm and the other right-wing conspiracy theories look like a fairy tales. The existence of Double O was closely held. Probably fewer than fifty people in the world knew about it. And apparently Verax was one, along with these two doofuses. She might have to kill them for that.

Roxy squinted at him menacingly. "So test me."

The young man gasped a nervous laugh and ran a hand over his closely shorn hair. "Oh, that's okay. I think I have my answer."

"Then sit down over there and tell Verax."

The fat man on the floor squirmed beneath her. She got up slowly and let him sit up, backing up to the sofa. "Don't move." The hipster raised his hands and backed up to the computer console. "Hurry up," she told him. Feliks was still out cold, in a heap on the floor with a knot on his forehead. He wasn't going to be any help. She kicked the fat man. "Get up and move over there."

When she had the two men in close range by the computers she put a gun to each of their necks. The younger man typed furiously on the keyboard.

TARGET GENUINE. IN "COMPROMISED" POSITION.

"What are you saying? You're the one who's compromised." She dug the barrel into his neck.

"If I tell him I'm at gunpoint he won't believe what I say. You want him to trust you?"

They waited ten minutes for an answer. Ten very squirmy minutes. She almost knocked the big fella on the noggin with the gun butt.

Verax: YOU KNOW WHAT TO DO

Roxy waited for the hipster to interpret that. He said nothing, frozen with his fingers over the keyboard. Finally she said, "Okay, what is it you're supposed to do? Besides kill me with a baseball bat."

The fat one glanced up at her. "Shoot you."

"I don't buy it. Why test me then? Why not just eliminate me?"

The younger one lowered his hands to his sides. "We're supposed to take you to see him. To see Verax."

"In Moscow?"

He shrugged.

She didn't have much choice. If she wanted to turn Snowden, get him to do the work of the OO, she would have to go to him. No one knew where he was, not exactly, not even Obama. She told the men to get up and go to the door. They shuffled forward. The younger one reached for the handle, pushing it open. They walked out into the night, hands raised, with Roxy behind them.

Suddenly light blinded them, the beams of multiple vehicle headlights flicked on. Roxy blinked, stunned, trying to see, as figures emerged from between the cars. Four men in black, wearing Anonymous masks with the horrid grins, moved forward. Her two captives split, diving to either side of the shrinking circle. Roxy raised her guns to shoot then saw that each of the Anonymous guys had a sawed-off shotgun pointed at her. They were just yards away and moving in.

She raised her arms toward that beautiful big sky, dangling both pistols from her fingers. She knew when she was outgunned. Despite all her training, her cyber skills, endless target practice, and martial arts, she knew better than to take on six armed men at close range at once.

Jason Bourne she was not.

* * *

WHEN SHE WOKE UP IN the dark, hands and feet bound, lying on something hard on her right side, the main sensation was that heavy thrump of jet engines. The roar came up through the floor—she guessed—that she lay on. She coughed, clearing her throat. At least she wasn't gagged. She blinked multiple times, trying to clear her vision, then realized she'd been hooded. Whatever covered her head was thick and black, impenetrable.

She struggled to sit up, not an easy task. No one stopped her, or hit her over the head, or covered her mouth and nose with knockout drugs. That came back to her, her last seconds in the yard, the masked man covering her face with the cloth. She'd lashed out but another man held her arms. It was over quickly.

"Hey!" she called out. "Anybody there?"

No one answered.

Hours passed. She tried to sleep, and failed. She tried to get out of her restraints. Same outcome. Finally the engines shifted.

She could feel the descent in her head, her ears. The plane landed on a bumpy runway.

She was driven in the back of a transport vehicle for nearly an hour. Then she was dragged out of the truck, set on the ground, ankles unbound, and silently poked and prodded to move, to walk. She grunted but obeyed. The temperature was cold here. Was it Russia? It was cold so many places.

They entered a building where it was warmer. She was pushed onto a hard chair. They cut her hands free. She rubbed her wrists.

She waited for them to remove her hood. She could hear voices in another room, then footsteps. Someone was near her, fiddling with the hood. Suddenly the light was everywhere, blinding her. She flinched, the pain searing through her, until her pupils finally adjusted.

A young woman sat in front of her, in jeans and a plaid flannel shirt, legs crossed, eyeing her suspiciously. Roxy recognized her; she was Snowden's girlfriend from Hawaii, his last post, who had moved to Russia to be with him. She was his lifeline to home. A good sign.

"Congratulations," the woman said sarcastically. "You made it here. What do you want?"

Roxy took her time, looking around the small kitchen. It was straight out of the 1950s, with linoleum and curtains decorated with cherries. "Where am I?"

"Does it matter?"

"I guess not. Just a matter of courtesy when you kidnap someone." Roxy smiled. "So, the question is, what do you want, and how badly do you want it?"

"Don't waste my time." The woman stood up, fists balled at her sides.

"I won't."

The woman, whose name Roxy remembered was Lindsay, had long brown hair that appeared to have been heavily bleached recently. She threw her hair back and glared at Roxy. "Why should I listen to you? You're nobody."

"Then why bring me here?"

Lindsay moved closer. "Are you CIA?"

"No. You know that." Roxy took a deep breath. "Can I talk to him?"

"He's not here." Roxy saw the small red light embedded in the kitchen cabinet facing her. They were taping this, or viewing it in the other room. Or somewhere.

"Okay. Then tell him this isn't going to be simple. No quid pro quo. But we can get him home again."

Lindsay's eyebrows twitched. This was what she wanted, what he wanted. Her need was palpable. "What's the bargain then?"

"I will need to see him. In person."

"I speak for him."

"And still. I need to see him myself."

The night turned to day as Roxy sat in the kitchen. She paced, stretching her legs, drank tap water that tasted disgusting. The doors were locked, the windows covered from the outside with plywood. She was brought a couple MREs, the military read-to-eat meals, by a man in a knit mask. They were not appetizing but she forced herself to eat. It grew dark again. She curled up in a corner and tried to sleep. She was awakened by the sound of a helicopter.

Once again the hood went over her head, thanks to masked men. They had reverted to black ski masks, which didn't make them any less threatening. They tied her arms behind her and led her to the helicopter, pushing down her head. The blast of wind was fierce from the blades that never stopped.

Snowden was really paranoid, she realized. Despite having photographs with Lindsay all over the Internet, his true whereabouts were highly guarded. Maybe those Instagram photos were all staged to throw off his pursuers.

Because the chopper ride was short. So short that it occurred to Roxy that they landed in the same place. Why not? She was blind. She couldn't even smell the forest through the heavy fabric of the hood. They took it off in a different room, a sitting room, but it could have been the same house, the same woods. The same goons. And she had no idea where she was. She just hoped somebody, somewhere, did. Because there was no point to the GPS tracker implanted in her hip if they didn't.

The windows were blacked out here, shutters closed and taped from the outside. Roxy heard the helicopter take off then all was silent. She sat on the old sofa, making the springs creak. The house was very quiet.

She startled awake. Someone had entered the room. She must have fallen asleep on the sofa. What time was it? She stood up.

Edward Snowden looked thinner and sported more facial hair, a tiny mustache. He'd let his hair grow longer. He stepped closer and turned on a lamp, sitting on a chair opposite her.

"Have a seat. Ms. Alumet, is it?"

"Mr. Snowden." She nodded, sitting on the edge of the cushion. "We have a proposition for you."

"We?"

"Not the US government. I don't work for them. I work for OO. But you know that."

"All this time? Obama's had secret operatives in the field?"

"Didn't catch that one in the eavesdrop, did you?" Roxy smiled. "He's got some serious powers."

Snowden's jaw clenched. He didn't like Obama—that was obvious. He hadn't given him his precious pardon before he left office, as if that was ever a possibility.

"You can come home. Eventually. Not right away. I won't lie to you, Snowden, it won't be easy. There will be a trial but Obama will do what he can. But first you have to do something. Then he'll tell them what you did for us."

"Us? You mean OO?"

"No, the real us. The American people. For democracy. You always said you were for democracy, right? Freedom of the press, freedom of speech, all the freedoms." His squint was his answer.

"You hack into the Russian servers, get us what we need. You've had three years, you've met a lot of these guys."

"Have I?"

"Ed, don't insult us with the innocent routine."

The sound of yet another helicopter came from outside. Snowden stood up. "This has gone on too long."

"So no Hawaiian beaches? No warm sun on the skin? No mom and dad around the old Thanksgiving table? How is the borscht, by the way? I've always wondered."

He clenched his fists. "Why would I work for Obama?"

"Because you want to go home, Snowden. It's that simple. Isn't it? You think the new president gives a rat's ass about you? He's so compromised by Putin already he could never pardon you. But this is a chance. You and Lindsay can have a life again. Together."

"Everyone knows who I am. It would be impossible."

"We'll give you a new identity. And a lot of equipment. The latest and greatest. When your job is done and everything is safe, you can come out as who you are. Under your own terms." Which was stretching the truth, but that was never a problem for Roxy.

Something went "boom" outside, in a flash of fiery light. "What the hell—?" Snowden said. He rushed to the window but nothing could be seen through the cracks but glimmers of flame against the dark.

The rapid sound of heavy boots in another part of the house converged on them. Ten large men in tactical gear and night-vision goggles burst in, waving MP5s in sweeps of the room, stopping on Roxy and Snowden. She raised her hands and was happy to see Snowden do the same.

"What the fuck have you done?" he hissed through his teeth.

"I could ask you the same."

"Let's go," said one of the men in black. They followed where his weapon pointed, out the door, through a familiar kitchen where a masked man lay bleeding, and outside into a yard Roxy'd never seen but nevertheless recognized. Near the helicopter lay the bodies of two men, presumably the pilots.

Pushed into seats and strapped in, they saw Lindsay, bound and gagged in the last row of the chopper. Her eyes were wild and teary. Edward leaned toward her to reassure her before one of the crew thumped him on the shoulder, slapped a helmet on his head, snapped on his seat belt, and tied him to his seat. They let Roxy put on her own seat belt and handed her an orange helmet. The man in the copilot's seat pulled his helmet off and grinned back at her.

"I've been waiting all my life to do this," the ex-president said. "Thanks, Roxy."

"My pleasure, sir."

They installed Edward and Lindsay in an undisclosed location deep in the Ural Mountains, just outside the Russian border. It was well fortified and passed the boss's inspection. Snowden had access to a wide array of computer equipment. He wasn't particularly trusted with keeping his situation on the QT, however, so they used Lindsay to keep him straight. She was kept in a separate compound within the location where there was a large library of Agatha Christie novels. The guards told Ed stories of torture and rape, all fake news of course, but he didn't know what to believe. During their infrequent meetings, Lindsay complained bitterly of being held against her will. Which she was.

It took Snowden less than a year but longer than he hoped to find his compromising information—the "kompromat"—on Putin. The first few rounds of intel were salacious and serious—bribery, murder, corruption—but somehow not quite enough. The Russian people knew all that already. More was required to get the people into a fury against their autocratic leader. The evidence was put into a growing file of Putin's crimes and Snowden went back to work. He got into a rhythm after awhile, working his sources, leaking just the right sort of bit to his old pals at WikiLeaks to give himself the credibility and mystery he craved.

At last, a surprisingly detailed high-definition video was found on a computer at a state-run television station in Vladivostok. On it, Vladimir Putin, three of his generals, and two prominent oligarchs frolicked at a vodka-infused summer party at his dacha, having their way with a pretty little yak. Snowden quickly disseminated it worldwide, making use of his wide network of fake news practitioners all over the world.

They were so ready to help. Having to subsist lately on fictional reports that seemed all too real, Feliks and Petyr's colleagues were gleeful to hear from "Verax" after all these months.

And all agreed that the yak seemed to be enjoying herself.

Obama was skydiving when the Russian people began their final protest against Putin. It wasn't pretty. Even his cherished all-female "mini-skirt" units tore the braids off their uniforms and burned them in a dumpster. His special security units threw down their guns. The people overran the Kremlin and ousted Vladimir Putin by force. Not terribly diplomatic of them but much appreciated.

The ex-president kept his word to Snowden. He relocated him and Lindsay back to the United States, to a small Eskimo village in northern Alaska with no Internet or cell service. They got fur parkas and new identities as polar bear scientists.

So much for that Hawaiian beach.

Thanks, Obama.

SUNBURNT COUNTRY
BY ANDREW NETTE

MAXINE SAW A LIGHT IN the darkness, thought it was an oncoming vehicle. As she got closer the small dot became a bright orange glow. She eased her foot onto the brake pedal of the black Ford Falcon XB Coupe as she drew parallel with the flaming wreck on the side of the road. The remains of a large four-wheel drive. She winced at the heat on her face through the open window, watched as fire devoured every last trace of flammable material, illuminating a circle of flat, featureless desert in every direction.

She peered into the flames, hypnotised, just like she'd been as a girl when her father lit a bonfire in their backyard. A human shape was visible in the inferno. That made two deaths this stretch of highway had witnessed this night.

"One last job," Johnny Boy had told her, "then we blow this shithole town, head to Alice Springs." But Johnny Boy hadn't reckoned on the site manager being armed. Maxine had watched from the driver's seat as her lover entered the pre-fab building, then silence, broken by the sound of men shouting, a gunshot, another in reply. She wanted to rush inside, steeled herself to stay behind the wheel, like Johnny Boy told her to. He emerged a few moments later clutching a spreading stain on his stomach, managed to climb into the backseat, yelled at her to take off.

"Listen to that baby go," he'd slurred through a mouthful of blood as the car pulled onto the highway. "The last of the V8 Interceptors, Max." A joke they'd shared countless times since they'd stolen the car from a caravan park in northern Adelaide a month earlier.

"Hold on, Johnny," she'd said, glancing in the rearview mirror for signs of pursuit. The knowledge she could do nothing for him like a rock in the pit of her stomach.

He must have taken his last breath as they cleared Port Augusta. She'd driven a few hours more, his lifeless body in the backseat, finally pulling off the road as dusk fell, parking under a sprawling gum tree. She didn't have a spade, made do with burying her lover's lanky body under a pile of stones.

Without taking her eyes from the fire, she reached for a large plastic bottle of water next to the Glock 9mm on the passenger seat beside her, drained half its contents. She was about to resume her journey when she noticed something on the ground in the light of the burning vehicle.

Maxine stepped out of the car, unsteady on her feet after sitting for so long, quickened her pace when she realized it was a small child, a boy, maybe three or four years old. Maxine crouched down, felt for a pulse, got one. He was completely hairless, his skin hot to touch. The boy's eyelids fluttered and he murmured something under his breath. Maxine leaned in. "High towers," he repeated, softly.

She'd caught the news on the car radio earlier that evening. The man Johnny Boy had shot died on the way to hospital and she was an accessory to murder. It was the worst possible time to take a passenger, but she couldn't just leave the kid.

Maxine carried him to the car. She found an old blanket in the boot, laid it over the bloodstained backseat, slid the boy onto it. She gunned the engine, taking off as fast as she could. The burning car receded in the rearview mirror until it disappeared but the heat stayed with her, as if she was still standing next to the blazing wreck.

* * *

THE SLEEK, BLACK CHOPPER HOVERED in the darkness, set down gently on the desert surface. Larsson was first off, flicked his smoke into darkness as he strode through what was left of the facility's front gate, the metal grille and cyclone wire twisted and melted. To his left smouldered the remains of several four-wheel drives. Charred corpses littered the ground. The air was thick with smoke from burning vegetation. He took it all in without breaking his stride, memories of walking through the aftermath of a napalm strike on a Viet Cong village deep in the Mekong Delta a lifetime ago.

A dozen heavily armed figures in black body armor and night-vision goggles jumped after him, their booted feet hitting the ground hard. They spread out, their night sights sweeping the surrounding desert in wide arcs for any sign of movement. Larsson regarded their theatrics with irritation. There were times when a show of force was useful. This wasn't one of them. Whatever happened had already gone down. All the firepower in the world wasn't going to make a lick of difference.

Larsson's clothes, a simple black suit, white shirt, and black tie, had got him strange looks from the other men on the chopper. But as Balthazar's representative on the clean-up team, no one's eyes had lingered on the old man for too long.

The entrance to the underground facility was cut into the side of a small hill. The door, thick plate steel, lay on the ground to one side, shrivelled like cellophane held to a flame.

"Get some light up here."

Several flashlight beams illuminated the start of a darkened metal passageway.

Larsson lit a cigarette, turned to a barrel-chested man next to him, a Russian named Petrov.

"Get your men to secure the area, bag the bodies while they wait for the science team. And give me your flashlight, I'm going in to take a look."

Petrov hesitated, his night visor moving between Larsson and the entranceway.

"Alone," said Larsson. He had strict orders from Balthazar. Lock down the facility, restrict the flow of any information about what had happened, locate the Corporation's lost intellectual property and recover it undamaged.

The passageway stopped in a set of elevator doors. He pushed the only button on the wall, was surprised when the doors slid open straight away. A burnt corpse lay in a corner. Larsson could tell from patches of white fabric attached to the skin, it was one of the technicians.

His cigarette helped kill the stench of burnt flesh while the elevator took him two kilometers down. The doors opened onto the remains of a large laboratory. His flashlight revealed the extent of the damage: twisted metal, pools of melted plastic that had once been computers, the walls scorched by the extent of the heat. Sparks emanated from exposed electronic cables that hung from the ceiling like snakes. Everything was covered in water from the overhead sprinkler system. Charred corpses lay in the puddles.

Floor-to-ceiling transparent glass tubes lined the walls of the adjoining room. The heat had shattered all of them, leaking puddles of viscous green fluid ankle deep on the floor. Stunted humanoid shapes sat at the bottom of several of the tubes.

Larsson pushed a damp strand of gray hair from his eyes, leaned against the buckled remains of a conference table, tired from the plane trip from the Balthazar's headquarters in the Swiss Alps. He lit another cigarette, recalled the details of their meeting. Balthazar had been floating on the far side of the room when Larsson entered, pondering a wall-sized computer screen showing an outline of the world overlaid with what looked like a climate map, pulsating swathes of reds, blues, and greens.

Balthazar turned to his visitor, floated through the air until he was inches from Larsson's face.

"There's been a problem in one of my laboratories," he said in a sibilant voice. His head moved, birdlike, the circuits in his neck whirring and clicking. Advanced age had atrophied his limbs, the bio suit and its complex circuitry the only thing that kept his wizened body functioning. "One of my experiments is missing. I need you to contain the damage, find my intellectual property. Unharmed."

"I'll need more information," said Larsson.

"Something I've been working on for a special client. It must not fall into the wrong hands."

Balthazar's body had decayed but his mind, still brilliant, oversaw a global network of scientific facilities that perfected technological and biomedical weapons for a range of clients, from so-called respectable governments to the rogue states and international terrorist groups that opposed them.

"And exactly what is this 'something'? A virus your lab minions have developed? Another homicidal android? Maybe one of those mutated clones?"

"Your growing impertinence irritates me, Dominic."

Larsson flinched at the use of his first name, an implied intimacy, in no way reciprocated.

"You have a job do," said Balthazar. "Go and do it. Your plane leaves in thirty minutes. You will be briefed further on board."

"Can you at least tell me now where I'm going?"

"The sunburnt country."

"What the hell are you talking about?"

"Australia. South Australia, to be precise," Balthazar said.

A ceiling panel crashed to the floor, brought Larsson back to the present. "This is the last job," he said under his breath. "It's done then I'm out."

* * *

Dawn peeked over the horizon as Larsson emerged from the facility. Another chopper sat on the ground beside the one he'd arrived in. Figures in silver biohazard suits, members of the science team, were examining the bodies that now lay in a row on the red earth under the watchful gaze of Larsson's security team.

One of the silver-suited figures approached. Miss Green, Balthazar's Australian liaison. She took off her hood, shook loose her long red hair.

"I see you dressed for the occasion." She grinned at Larsson. The freckles on her nose scrunched up, made her appear even younger than she was. "What are you doing afterwards, going to a *Blues Brothers* re-union?"

Larsson had worked with Miss Green before. One of Balthazar's genetically modified creations had broken out of a laboratory in the Papua New Guinea highlands and they'd spent a month together hunting the creature down. She was good; he couldn't deny that. In her early twenties and already a stone-cold killer. But there was something deeply creepy about her he couldn't quite put his finger on. Not to mention the constant annoying cracks about his dress sense and age. And what the fuck was this "mansplaining" thing she always accused him of whenever he tried to tell her anything?

"Is the situation as bad as we were led to believe?"

"Worse," Larsson said, lighting up.

"Dude, those things will give you cancer."

"Fuck off."

"Suit yourself. Any sign of Balthazar's lost intellectual property?"

"Yeah," Larsson exhaled a stream of smoke. "All around you."

"Let me show you something." Miss Green led Larsson to the remains of a smoldering vehicle. Next to it was a crater, blown into the earth, about half a meter deep and couple of meters in diameter, the bottom smooth like glass. He crouched next to it, put a finger out, felt the heat emanating from it on his palm.

"Seventeen hundred degrees," she said.

"What?"

"Seventeen hundred degrees, the temperature at which sand turns to glass. That's three thousand and ninety degrees Fahrenheit for the benefit of you Americans. Can you imagine that how hot that is?"

"Fucking hot."

"Exactly."

"Well no point standing here." Larsson crushed his cigarette butt into the red dirt with the heel of his shoe. "We need to find Sunburn."

The stillness of dawn was interrupted by a low thrumming sound. The sound got louder as a large, specially modified twin-engine helicopter came into view.

The scientists and military personnel stopped what they were doing, stared up at the approaching craft with apprehension.

Doctor Hungus had arrived.

* * *

MAXINE BANGED HER FIST ON the side door of the old pub until a faint light went on behind the mottled glass. "Okay, okay, keep your bloody trousers on," came a raspy female voice.

She'd passed a crooked sign on the edge of the town: "Perseverance—pop 107." She wanted to keep driving, put as much distance between her and Adelaide as possible, but needed sleep.

An old woman opened the door, dressed in a pink terry towelling dressing gown, looked Maxine up and down.

"I want a room for the night."

"Eighty dollars. Upfront." The woman emphasized the last word.

"Okay, just let me get some stuff from the car."

The women's face softened as she watched Maxine scoop the child from the backseat and bring him inside. She led Maxine through a darkened reception area, up a flight of stairs, stopped at the first door.

"You can pay after you've settled the little one."

Maxine laid the child on the sagging double bed, did a quick three-hundred-and-sixty-degree sweep of the room. A few bits of old wooden furniture, a washbasin, a grimy window overlooking a stretch of corrugated tin roof.

What the fuck was she going to do with a bloody kid? She touched the child's forehead. His skin was still hot and angry red, like he'd been badly sunburnt. She was examining the rest of the child's body, saw what she thought were surgical scars on his chest, when he opened his eyes, sat up, and looked around the room in panic.

"Hey, it's all right, really it's okay," said Maxine, gently putting a hand on his bare shoulder. "Really, it's all right."

The child quivered, allowed himself to be pushed back onto the bed.

"Do you have a name?"

Nothing.

"Are you hungry, thirsty?"

His dark eyes, almost without irises, stared at her uncertainly.

"What about your mum and dad? Is there anyone I can call to come and get you?"

More silence.

"I am a friend, do you understand?"'

"Friend?"

"Yes, friend."

"Friend like Curtis?"

"Curtis?"

The boy's lower lip quivered. "High towers," he whispered.

"This is not getting us anywhere," Maxine muttered. "I've got to go downstairs but I'll be right back. Promise."

* * *

"YOU TWO ON HOLIDAYS?" THE old woman asked when Maxine came downstairs.

"Could say that." Maxine handed over the money. "We're on our way to Alice Springs, going to visit my boy's dad."

Maxine looked for signs the woman knew she was lying. Got none. A lamp with a torn shade illuminated a room full of maritime paraphernalia, nets, a boat steering wheel, framed photographs of various aquatic activities, even a large stuffed marlin above the empty fireplace.

"Interesting décor," said Maxine.

"Tell me about it." The old woman lit a cigarette, offered the pack to Maxine.

Maxine smiled, mouthed "no."

"Belonged to my late husband. He was a real fishing nut. Brought it with him when we took over the hotel, said customers would like the nautical theme." The woman exhaled a stream of smoke, snorted. "Can't stand the stuff myself, but haven't got around to getting rid of it since he died."

"I'm sorry. When was that?"

"About ten years ago."

"Can I ask you a favor?"

"Ask away."

"My boy and I had to leave our last place in a bit of a hurry, left his clothes behind. You wouldn't happen to have anything I could borrow for him?"

The woman disappeared into a back room, returned, with a pair of faded blue board shorts. "That's it, I'm afraid."

Maxine started up the stairs, stopped, went back to the reception desk.

"There is one other thing. Out of interest, you don't happen to know of any place around here called 'High Towers,' something like that?"

"Yeah, it's the nickname of some big rocky outcrops about two hundred kilometers directly west of here. You don't want to go there, love. Hard country. Middle of the desert. Why?"

"Thanks for the shorts."

* * *

MAXINE TURNED OFF THE BEDSIDE light, lay next to the child, felt the heat radiating off him. Maybe he was sick with a fever? She stared at the ceiling. That would be fucking great. She was a police fugitive, didn't have time to take the kid to the doctor. Didn't even know if there was a doctor in this one-horse town.

She was on the verge of sleep when she thought she heard a noise in the corridor outside. Probably the owner. Old people never slept well. Then more sounds, the unmistakable thud of something heavy, a booted foot on the wooden floor, directly outside her door. That ruled out the old lady, the cops, too. Cops—especially rural cops—didn't sneak around in the middle of night in heavy boots.

She sat up, reached for the Glock on the bedside table, aimed at the door.

The kid was suddenly awake beside her. "Men," he whispered.

"I know, kid."

"Bad men."

She fired twice, leaped from the bed and yanked the door open. Slumped on the opposite side of the narrow corridor was a man clad in black body armor, his hands trying unsuccessfully to staunch the blood flow from where her bullet had pierced his neck. His face was hidden by a ski mask and some sort of night visor, just like in the movies. A large machine gun lay on the floor next to him.

Another black-clad man was coming up the stairs. She ran back into the room, picked up the closest object, an old wooden chair, flung it through the window, picked up the kid, pushed him through it, followed.

They scrambled across the corrugated tin roof. Maxine hesitated at the edge, peered into the darkness below, unsure how far the drop was. She saw several strands of laser sighting try to get a bead on her. A burst of machine gun fire ripped a line of holes in metal near her. "Careful, you bloody idiot. Larsson wants the kid alive," a male voice said.

She felt for the boy's hand, clutched it tight, jumped, dragging him after her. A large clump of dry bushes broke their fall. Still clutching the boy's hand, she ran down the deserted street to where she thought she'd left the Ford Falcon, the sound of men clambering across the tin roof behind her.

She crouched in a pool of shadow, watched as more men dressed like the one she'd shot in the hallway emerged from the hotel's front entrance, followed by the old woman and a tall man with gray hair, dressed in a dark, tight-fitting suit. He talked with the old woman for a few moments, shrugged. One of figures stepped forward, raised a pistol, shot the old woman in the head.

The tall man noticed the Ford Falcon Coupe, took something from inside his jacket pocket, rolled it under the vehicle. The car exploded in a ball of flames.

Maxine tried to hug the shadows as she crept down the street, turned a corner. Three more black-clad figures illuminated by a streetlamp swiveled in her direction. She fired, saw one of the men fall to the ground, ducked back around the corner as the other two returned fire.

She leaped into an alleyway between two rows of old wooden buildings, followed it until she saw a dead end thirty meters away. She leaned on her haunches against the wooden surface, caught her breath. The boy stood next her, eyes wide with terror.

Trapped. She listened for sounds of their pursuers. Nothing. Where were they? A sudden sound sent tremors through the buildings all around her. She was trying to locate its direction, when the building in front of her shook and disintegrated in a cloud of dust and wood shards. In its place stood a large shadow, at least five meters tall.

The shadow stepped into the alleyway, revealed itself to be a robot, its metal skin gleaming in the dull moonlight. One arm ended in a large round ball, the other in a circular saw. Affixed to its shoulders, encased in a clear dome, was a human head, bald with a fleshy, porcine face.

"Release the child and you will not be hurt," said a voice from somewhere within the robot's chest, a metallic sound mixed with an unmistakable European accent. "Failure to obey will result in your immediate obliteration."

The boy broke free of her clasp, ran to the end of the alley, cowered against a wall. Maxine raised her gun, fired at the creature. The bullets bounced harmlessly off its metal casing.

The circular saw roared into life, swung in a ninety-degree arc above her, shearing the first floor off the wooden building behind her, covered her in a shower of sawdust and wood.

By the time Maxine had worked her way free of the debris, the robot was towering over the boy at the end of the alley. She began to move toward them, before being pushed back by an incredible wave of heat. She watched the boy's body start to pulsate and glow, as if some powerful energy was trying to escape his tiny rib cage, the outline of which was now visible against his translucent burnt-orange skin. Maxine watched as the boy's metal attacker was consumed in a wall of flame, until the intensity of the heat forced her to turn away.

When she got to the boy, he was lying naked on the ground, surrounded by burning wooden buildings. Through the smoke, she saw the robot prone on the opposite side of the alley, patches of open circuitry on its body crackling angrily.

The child shivered, looked up at her, terrified by his own destructive power.

"Christ, what the hell are you, kid?"

It was all she could do to keep hold of the hot little ball of flesh, as she picked her way through the path of destruction carved by the robot. She paused behind the remains of a shattered brick wall, spied a man standing next to a black Hummer. Although his back was to her, she could tell from the gray hair and the suit, it was the man at the hotel. The one who'd ordered the old woman killed.

Maxine lay the child down, picked a piece of wood from amid the destruction, walked toward the man. He turned, went for his shoulder holster, just as Maxine swung the makeshift club, hit him squarely in the face.

"That's for trashing my car, you prick."

* * *

THE HUMMER CLEARED THE TOWN'S outskirts without encountering any opposition. The boy sat beside her, dressed in a khaki raincoat, the only thing she could find for him to wear. The still unconscious man lay tied up on the backseat. It couldn't hurt to have a hostage, especially one who appeared to be in charge. His slim silver pistol, a strange make she'd never seen before, lay on the dashboard in front of her.

Maxine glanced at the vehicle's satellite navigation panel to make sure she was heading in the right direction: the High Towers.

* * *

MISS GREEN FOLLOWED PETROV THROUGH the smoldering debris to where Doctor Hungus lay like a turtle on its back, unable to get up. The metallic body was badly damaged, the chest a mass of tangled burnt circuitry. The dome that protected Doctor Hungus's head, all that remained of the human scientist, had shattered, the doctor's face an unrecognizable mass of burnt tissue.

"Don't just stand there, girl, help me, I am severely damaged," said the doctor, his voice faulting and weak.

The destructive power of the child was far greater than she'd been led to believe. Of course, he'd had help—that woman who'd found him on the side of the road. She'd killed two men, stolen one of the Hummers and appeared to have taken Larsson hostage. Not bad for an amateur smash-and-grab artist. But the child. . . . The term "lethal" didn't come close to describing what he was capable of. He was certainly far too dangerous for Larsson's softly, softly approach.

"You hear me, girl? I am damaged," the metallic robot voice said.

Miss Green exhaled deeply, unholstered her pistol.

"Don't call me girl." She put three shots in Doctor Hungus's skull.

"Petrov."

The burly Russian stepped forward uncertainly.

"I'm in charge now. Are we able to track the stolen Hummer?"

"Yes."

"Good. Kill everyone in this miserable dump. Then saddle up the choppers, we're going hunting."

"Miss Green, is it really necessary to eliminate everybody?"

She eyed the Russian, smiled and slowly nodded, as though giving the question serious consideration. The smile became an impossibly wide slash that split her face almost in two. Two large mandibles lined with long sharp fangs slid out of the fleshy opening. Petrov uttered only a partial scream before Miss Green's appendages firmly grasped his head, crushed it into a bloody mess of blood and bone. The other men stood frozen in disbelief as Miss Green pushed Petrov to the ground, mounted him, tore and sucked at his limp form.

She stood, her face as normal, wiped a tendril of gore from the side of her mouth with the back of her hand.

"Any other questions?"

* * *

THE TWO CRAGS OF RED rock, one slightly taller than the other, reared up before them in the flat desert.

The tall man had regained consciousness, sat glaring at her in silence, a trickle of dried blood down the side his face from where Maxine had hit him. The child hadn't spoken the entire trip.

She killed the engine at the base of the largest crag, stepped out of the vehicle. Several gunshots rang out, echoed in the desert stillness.

Maxine reached for the tall man's pistol, crouched behind the open car door.

"You better be careful with that," said an American-accented voice from the back of the car. "It's not your average pistol."

"Shut up," Maxine hissed as she scanned the rocks for their attackers.

Two people stood up from behind a rocky ledge above them, a man and a woman. She was white. He was Aboriginal. Both aimed their guns at Maxine.

"Throw your weapon on the ground and move away from the car," the woman shouted.

Maxine complied, stepped out from behind the car door, her hands in the air.

The man slung his rifle over his shoulder, expertly slid down the rock's surface, the woman keeping her weapon trained on Maxine.

The Aboriginal man peered into the vehicle's interior, smiled at the child in the front seat.

"She's got the kid," he yelled up to the woman.

"Take them to Moorcock," she yelled back.

He picked up Larsson's pistol from the dirt, stuck it in his waistband.

"I'm Slater."

"Maxine."

"Who's the old white guy in the backseat?"

"I don't know. He was after the kid."

Slater nodded as if the story made perfect sense. "Follow me."

"Listen, I've been shot at, attacked by a giant robot, and watched this kid turn into the Human Torch. Before I go anywhere I want to know what's going on."

"Moorcock will explain everything."

Slater led them into a cave entrance between the two crags, down a set of stone steps onto a small ledge overlooking a large cavern. Further steps led from the ledge, wound along the cavern's wall to a flat surface on the bottom, occupied by people working on an assortment of computers. Maxine counted about a dozen men and women. Each had a weapon, either slung over their shoulders or resting at their feet as they worked. Lights fixed into the rock at various intervals glowed blue, cast the entire cavern in a ghostly hue.

Slater navigated them around the tables and various pieces of computer equipment. People stopped work, looked up as they passed. Maxine realised they were staring at the child.

Slater stopped in front of metal platform, where a man sat with his back to them, staring at a computer screen. Upon hearing them approach, he turned and stood. He was dressed like an old biker; dirty jeans, a leather jacket, nothing underneath, an unshaven face, and a mane of greasy dark hair streaked with gray. A patch covered one eye. His good one stared at the child.

"Where did you find the boy?"

"By the side of the road in the middle of nowhere next to a burning car," Maxine said.

"So, as we feared, Curtis and the others are dead. But they didn't die for nothing. They rescued Sunburn and now you have completed their mission."

The child flinched as the man reached out to touch him, moved toward Maxine.

"You're welcome," she said. "Now would you mind telling me what the fuck is going on here? Who are you people and who is this kid you call 'Sunburn'?"

"I am Moorcock and, yes, questions, you must have many questions."

Moorcock turned to the tall man.

"And this is the infamous Larsson, Balthazar's hired killer. Balthazar sent you to get back his experiment, did he?"

"After you stole it, yes."

"Stole? More like liberated for the good of human kind."

"Have it your way."

"Will someone please tell me what is going on," said Maxine. "Who is Balthazar?"

"Hieronymus Balthazar is a brilliant scientist and criminal. How often the two seem to go together. It was his technicians who created Sunburn, forged him in the fires of advanced science, so to speak . . ." Moorcock trailed off, as if losing his train of thought.

"Did you know sixteen of the seventeen hottest years on record have been in this century?" he said after a pause. "The effect humans are having on the climate is undeniable. Not just record temperatures, but floods, droughts, super storms, wildfires, melting ice caps, rising sea levels.

"The new American president, the man who presides over the world's largest economy, professes not to even believe in climate change. He is filling his administration with others of his ilk, the heads of the fossil fuel industries, big oil, those who are killing our planet.

"The one who came before him was not very different. He spent his first term as president silent on the issue and his second negotiating an international treaty that is hardly worth the paper it is written on.

"But just because they publicly deny we are racing toward the cliff edge, doesn't mean our leaders aren't taking steps to save themselves. That's why myself and like-minded individuals around the world have given up the charade of conferences and international treaties to mount to a real resistance."

Moorcock stared at her with his one eye. "Climate change can't be averted. The question now is how we adapt to it. The rich and powerful know this and have come up with a plan to survive. They hired Balthazar," Moorcock glanced at Larsson, "this man's employer, to biologically engineer humans that can withstand the extremes of weather that will be caused by climate change, a bio-technology they will then use to survive the coming cataclysm.

"In a laboratory about five hundred kilometers from here, they created Sunburn," Moorcock looked admiringly at the child as he spoke, "a human that can withstand extreme heat. But there are other laboratories dotted around the globe where Balthazar's minions are working on beings that can survive the cold, that can breath underwater—"

"Are you saying he's an experiment?" interrupted Maxine.

"We infiltrated Balthazar's Australian laboratory," said Moorcock, "managed to break Sunburn out. But something went wrong, I am not sure what. That is, until you came along and delivered the child to us. We will take the biotechnology in his child's DNA, make it public, free for everyone to use, so it's not just the rich that survive the coming—"

An explosion at the opposite end of the cavern drowned out the rest of Moorcock's sentence, followed by the sound of machine gun fire, people screaming. Black-clad figures poured down the stairs into the cavern, shooting as they went. Moorcock's people returned fire, but were outgunned.

"The child, we must protect the child," Moorcock screamed.

Maxine felt herself and the child pushed from behind, realized it was Larsson. Somehow he had worked himself free of his bindings and was shepherding them to cover.

Maxine peered from behind a large computer terminal. Moorcock lay face up on a section of metal platform, his one eye staring sightlessly at her, a blossom of red in the middle of his forehead. Slater fired his rifle at the figures coming down the stairs, stopped to reload, was thrown backwards by an explosion, his lifeless body fell on the ground next to where they were hiding.

Larsson reached past her, extracted his pistol from the dead man's waistband. He aimed at the nearest figures descending the stairs, fired. Maxine heard a loud clap, felt a vibration in the air. A section of the cavern's wall collapsed, burying several of their attackers in rubble.

"I told you this wasn't an ordinary gun," he said in response to the look on Maxine's face. "Now we've got to get out of here."

He pushed Maxine and the child into a tunnel leading from the cavern.

"I thought you worked for them."

"Looks like I just switched sides, not that I have much choice. After he's taken care of these loonies, Balthazar will want to clean house, prevent further details of his work leaking out. It's time for me to retire to my carefully planned bolthole in New Zealand where I can wait out the end of the world in luxury."

The gunfire became more sporadic as the attackers finished off the last of Moorcock's people.

"What Moorcock said, is it true?"

"That crazy bastard didn't know the half of it."

The child clung to Maxine's hand. She felt the heat emanating from his skin. His dark eyes glanced up at her.

"But he's just a little boy."

"Listen to me, lady." Larsson lit a smoke, his face looking old in the blue light. "Stop referring to it as a human, okay? It was made in a fucking test tube. It's a weaponized biomedical experiment that's gone very wrong. It isn't even in control of its own powers."

They heard the sounds of someone coming down the tunnel toward them. Larsson wheeled around, only to be cut down by a burst of machine gun fire.

Maxine wrapped her arms around the child's shoulders as a figure emerged from the blue tinged shadows. A woman, slim, with long red hair, clad from head to toe in a tight-fitting one-piece leather suit, a smoking machine gun in one hand.

She dropped the gun as she approached, smiled, licked her lips.

Maxine hugged the child tighter, felt the heat building in his tiny frame.

The woman's smile widened, split her face almost in two. Sharp insect mandibles, a mass of red tiny tendrils, like tiny snakes, sprouted from the folds of flesh where the woman's face had once been.

Maxine felt her skin burn. The tunnel became impossibly bright. She closed her eyes, waiting for her last sunrise.

I KNOW THEY'RE IN THERE!
BY TRAVIS RICHARDSON

June 1, 2016, Broken Arrow, OK

DOCTORS AND NURSES FLEW AROUND in a tizzy. Patients coughed and limped. Families stood with forlorn faces. Folks sat in wheelchairs with IVs stuck in their arms. Lloyd narrowed his eyes. Was that IV drip giving that old woman medicine or poison? She didn't look healthy, that was for certain. A rage already simmering began to boil over.

"Keep it cool, Lloyd," he muttered to himself.

He took a deep breath and walked over to the information desk.

"Can I help you?" a young blond woman with a gleaming smile asked. Her name badge said JANET.

Lloyd studied her for a second. Could he trust her? He looked around and, seeing that nobody was watching, lowered his head.

"I'm lookin' to apply for a job."

"Wonderful. Did you look at our listings online?"

Lloyd nodded. "I did, but I'm lookin' for a job that ain't listed there."

Janet's brow furrowed. "I'm afraid if you didn't find what you wanted, then it probably isn't open at the moment."

Lloyd leaned in closer. "What I'm lookin' for . . ." he glanced around one more time, "is a job on the Death Panel. Can you tell me how I can apply for one of 'em?"

"Excuse me?"

Lloyd's face tightened. "Don't act all ignorant on me, missus."

"Sir, there's no such thing as a death panel. That was just a stupid rumor to try and kill the Affordable Care Act."

Lloyd flushed, no more mister nice guy. This woman wasn't going to bamboozle him with her smiles and lies. He pointed a stern finger at Janet . . . if that was really her name.

"Just you wait, missy. Coverin' up for murderers makes you one of 'em. You're gonna get yours."

He raced out of the hospital before Janet could respond, almost running over a man in a walker.

* * *

JANET'S HANDS TREMBLED. SHE HATED politicians and talk-show hosts who lied without caring about the chaos they created. Their words created havoc for people they would never meet, people who were trying to make a living and help others. Who was it this time ranting about death panels? Rush Limbaugh? Bill O'Reilly? Sean Hannity? Or some local jock trying to make a name for themselves?

"You okay, Janet?"

She turned to see Doug, the super nice security guard who didn't have an ounce of meanness in his skinny six-foot frame.

"Just had a nutjob come in here asking about death panels."

Doug's face clouded. "He threaten you?"

Janet bit her lip and nodded, holding back tears.

"Is he still here?"

She shook her head and found her voice again. "Nope. Stormed out the door. Hopefully I won't ever see him again."

Doug patted her on the back. "Hopefully." He grabbed a sticky note from the counter and jotted his cell number on it. "If he comes back and you don't feel like hitting the panic button, text me. Okay? I'll have a few words with him."

Janet smiled with a nod, feeling warmth rebound inside her. Humanity still had some good left.

Doug made his way to the exit like a targeted missile. Janet hoped he wouldn't get hurt if he confronted that idiot.

* * *

LLOYD PLOPPED IN HIS TRUCK seat. That lying bitch. She knew about the death panels, but held back. He should've brought in his pistol to get the truth. But there was that security guard lurking by the entrance. He looked dopey, but you could never be sure. People said Lloyd looked dopey, but what did they know? Nothing. If he wanted physical evidence that death panels were in full operation, like Sean Hannity proved with the uptick in American death rates just an hour ago, he'd need more firepower. His grandmother died at this hospital a few years ago, no doubt murdered by the death panel.

Lloyd started his pickup and Hannity's righteous voice blasted the speakers. He saw the security guard walk through the parking lot and scan the area. He waited until the guard looked the other way and tore off in the opposite direction.

* * *

DOUG SQUINTED, WATCHING THE WHITE Ford Ranger speed out of the parking lot. Mud obscured part of the license plate, but he clearly made out the two AR-15s and two handgun stickers on the back window representing a family of four along with other NRA and Tea Party bumper stickers. Not necessarily a statement of paranoia, but not a declaration of stability either. While there were plenty of sane drivers with these stickers throughout Oklahoma, the last two road-ragers who swerved and swore at Doug sported them. Like by owning a gun they have full authority to be unhinged a-holes. Yeah, he needed to have a few words with that jackass to make sure he wouldn't threaten Janet again.

* * *

WHEN LLOYD GOT BACK HOME, he ignored his wife's questions as he walked past her, entered his man cave, and bolted the door. Converting the garage into his personal headquarters was the best investment he'd ever made. He powered up his computer and went to a Reddit page full of allies. His mind couldn't shake that stuck-up girl saying that death panels didn't exist. Give me a break. Maybe Janet was duped by the mainstream media—strike that, lamestream media. Nah, she was in on the lie, pushing the left's liberal agenda and making America into a land of limp-wrist commie abortionists.

Unlike her, he had sources that verified that death panels existed. Rush Limbaugh preached it, so did Laura Ingram and Sarah Palin. Breitbart's website covered it extensively. Hell, former New York Lieutenant Governor Betsy McCaughey read the Obamacare bill and discovered the death panels written in it. Now Hannity has the numbers with an increase in the 2015 death rates to prove they existed.

He logged in under the alias TreadOnThis52 and told his colleagues about how he had applied for a death-panel job, but was rejected. Members asked if he had brought a resume or an ACLU card to get the job. Lloyd felt like a dumbass. Yeah, he should've thought of that first.

Regardless, people were dying. Something needed to happen. He typed: *Don't thnk it matterd. she saw I was a caring American patroit and wouldnt let me in. we need to do something about this and fast youall. The longer we wait, the more folks are gonna to die. Duing nothing is like commiting murders itself.*

A debate erupted on the page for over an hour, but true Americans answered the call. They would make a strike, storming that Broken Arrow hospital and taking folks hostage until death-panel members were finally exposed. Hell yes—like the Founding Fathers, Lloyd was starting a revolution.

* * *

DOUG OPENED THE DOOR TO his one-bedroom apartment after a long day on his feet making sure things stayed copacetic at the hospital. He still felt perturbed that somebody unnerved Janet. There were people in the hospital whose coarse bedside manner deserved rebuttals, but not somebody with Janet's kindness. She was one of the few Christians he'd met who lived up to the name of Jesus.

He decided to research "Death Panels" to see what that was all about. Thirty minutes later he felt sick to his stomach. So many lies, so much hatred. The lie started with Betsy McCaughey and spread through talk-show hosts and finally to Sarah Palin, who catapulted the story into the mainstream in August 2009.

Doug realized he was grinding his teeth. It only takes one unhinged person to act on misinformation and you'd have the Murrah Building in Oklahoma City all over again. Limbaugh and neo-conservatives so bravely trashed Janet Reno about the Branch Davidian raid on a daily basis after it happened. Then the bomb exploded in 1995 and nobody took responsibility for amping up Timothy McVeigh. Doug was an infant when it happened, but he lost an uncle and a cousin. His mother made the connection, but nobody listened to her. Although Doug found photos of his mother jubilant, he never witnessed a smile from her.

Limbaugh said he believed in God even though he didn't act in any way that Jesus would approve of. Yet that was good enough for most folks in Oklahoma. They drank the conservative Kool-Aid while preachers in the pulpit didn't seem to care. They bravely condemn abortion, Hollywood, and Rock 'n' Roll while ignoring scriptures about false prophets.

Doug stood, ready to eat and erase his many gloomy thoughts. He opened the refrigerator. Nothing but milk and barbeque sauce. He sighed, another cereal dinner tonight.

* * *

June 18, 2016

LLOYD WOKE UP EARLY ON a Saturday and filled an oversized duffel bag with several rounds of ammo, two Beretta PX4 semi-automatic pistols, and a Bushmaster Carbon-15 SBR assault rifle. He lugged the bag to his truck.

"Where do you think you're going?" Lloyd's wife, Gwen, called out. She stood in the doorway, her arms crossed and eyebrows arched like he'd done something wrong again.

"Hunting."

"In June? Nothing's in season. What are you going to shoot?"

He stopped himself from saying doctors.

"I'll find somethin' to kill."

"You know Caleb's soccer game is today. Do you think maybe you could hold off from murderin' something for a couple of hours and watch him play?"

Lloyd's breath caught. His family. Dammit. Was this the last time he was going to ever see them? He stared at his feet unable to meet his wife's eyes. A seven-year-old boy and a three-year-old daughter. They grow fast. He hoped to teach Caleb how to shoot something bigger than a .22, but after today would that even be possible? Would he be dead? In jail?

Lloyd shook his head. What was this bullcrap? Defeatism. He sounded like a whining lefty. Of course he was going to win today. He'd expose the truth, and the American people would rally around him. He'd be a hero to his son. If he went to the game, he'd abandon his newfound buddies who were going to help him make history. The way Lloyd saw it, he could be a soccer dad like all the other ones, standing around and shouting encouragement for crap-ass play of some Eurotrash sport that didn't belong in America, or he could save the lives of millions, including his son and all of his friends, by defeating the death panels once and for all.

He stared at his wife with his newfound conviction. "Wish Caleb luck and tell him I'll watch his next game. I have a feeling all his buddies and their daddies will know my name by tomorrow."

Gwen's face scrunched in confusion, but Lloyd slid into his truck without another word. He couldn't wait for her to beg forgiveness after he became America's greatest hero.

* * *

Janet wasn't in a good mood that morning. Her friends had dragged her out on the town last night even though she had to work in the morning. Loud thumping music and sweet alcoholic drinks made her head swim. A cute boy with an intense look took her to the dance floor. He moved in close, rubbing his body against hers. Flattering and unnerving simultaneously. Later they made out in his BMW. He wanted to take her home. Not trusting him, she said no. She needed to find her friends and go home. She started to leave when Matt (or was it Mark?) grabbed her arm tight. Cruelty gleamed in his eyes.

"Nobody teases me, baby."

He pulled her head towards his crotch. So she did about the only thing she could in such small quarters and punched him in the balls. That bought her enough time to grab her purse, pull out her pepper-spray can, and spritz his face.

In such a small enclosure, she got a lungful of pepper too, but more important, she got away. She Ubered home, cried in the shower, and slept. Now at work she wondered if the a-hole might show up here. She had told him where she worked. She wanted to tell Doug about him but felt too embarrassed. Regardless, she kept the pepper spray on her desk, uncapped and ready to repel.

* * *

Lloyd stood out in the parking lot and went over his plan again with the four brave volunteers who managed to show. Three had pussied out that morning. He had asked the volunteers to wear regular civilian clothes so they'd blend in. But every single one of them wore fatigues or cargo pants, looking like paratroopers about to invade some jerkoff country. That is, if the army had recruited a gray-haired grandfather with a limp, a middle-aged man with a potbelly, and two skinny twenty-year-olds who looked like the recoil from any of his weapons might knock them on their asses. Screw it. He had to complete the mission at this point. Everything would work out, one way or another.

He pointed to a page in a notebook with a square representing the hospital and Xs to represent each of their positions. His X was at the information booth. The first skinny kid named Max would guard the front doors with his assault rifle. Ned, the man with the limp, would be inside with a Bushmaster. The father and son combo, Don and Don Jr., would come from the rear. Junior had an assault rifle and the father a shotgun.

"After you hear me shootin', I want y'all to come in shootin' from your positions. People are gonna be runnin', but try to hold everybody down until I get real information out of that information bitch. That's her job, isn't it? To know everything."

"Includin' where the death panels are at," Ned said.

The group nodded their heads with firm conviction.

"Gentlemen," Lloyd said, feeling like he was Mel Gibson about to lead a Scottish army into battle for freedom. "Let's lock and load and conquer."

He held up his pistol up in the air and pulled the slide back like he'd seen in movies a hundred times. It embarrassed him to watch a bullet eject out of the Beretta since one was already in the chamber. Don Sr. also ejected an unused shotgun shell. Good gracious.

* * *

DOUG HAD WALKED THE PERIMETER of the hospital, up all five floors, and down the back elevator. He was solo on weekend duty today since Candice was on vacation and Andy called in sick. Sometimes it was tough to stay healthy in a place with so much sickness. He noticed Janet looked a little pale. He hoped she hadn't come down with anything contagious. Maybe someday he'd have the courage to ask her out on a date. But then again, why would she want to hang out with a loser who was thirty and never completed college?

* * *

Janet hung up the phone after giving parking instructions. She couldn't help the sour expression that filled her face when she saw the death-panel nut.

"Oh."

"It's me again and I'm giving you one more chance to tell me where them death panels are."

Janet took a deep breath. She'd had it up to here with male obstinacy.

"As I said a few weeks ago, death panels don't exist. They never have."

Her right hand crept forward, trying to determine whether she should grab the pepper spray or hit the panic button.

The man shook his head in disappointment. He reached behind his back.

"You were warned."

He whipped out a black pistol, pulled back the slide, ejecting an unused bullet, muttered a curse, and then pointed the weapon in the air. *Bang, bang, bang!*

* * *

Chunks of white tile fell on Lloyd's head. He heard his colleagues' shots followed by the panicked screams of patients. He wanted to shout that they were here to save them, liberate them from the murderers. Instead he pointed his pistol at Janet. Her face paled bed-sheet white.

"Now take me to the death panels."

* * *

DOUG WAS MAKING HIS WAY to the front of the hospital when he heard the shots. He launched into a sprint. Turning a corner, he collided into a mass of people fleeing, shouting hysterically. A man grabbed Doug and pointed at a military-fatigued man hobble-running behind the group, blasting an assault rifle in the air.

"Stop him."

Doug's stomach dropped. He was only armed with a stun gun and mace. So he ran with the group.

"Everybody freeze! This is for your own good," the hobbling man said.

Another blast came from the rear exit by the ER unit. A middle-aged man with a potbelly and holding a shotgun shook tile off of his bald head.

"Y'all stay put or I'll put holes in ya."

The mass of twenty-five or so people stopped. Turning around in all directions, they looked like sheep cornered by wolves. Doug ducked and crawled to a nearby staircase door.

"Hey, you. Stop," the limping man said. "That security guard's gettin' away."

"Well, shoot him," a younger voice shouted.

Doug burst into the stairwell as bullets and buckshot slammed into the door. He heard shouts and screams as he bounded up the stairs. He hoped nobody got injured on account of his escape.

The fat man with the shotgun barreled through the door and shouted, "Stop." Doug kept climbing as a boom echoed through the stairwell. He felt lead pellets ricocheting off of the walls, too weak to penetrate skin.

Doug skipped the second-floor door, opening the third. He heard the shotgun man huffing his way up the stairs. Doug jumped to the side. When the gunman opened the door, Doug put the stun gun up to the sweaty man's throat and gave him eighty thousand volts of electricity.

The man dropped to the floor. Doug kicked the shotgun away and stunned him again. He pulled out his cuffs. As badly as he wanted to interrogate the gunman, he needed to make sure the rest of the floors were safe. So he dragged the 250-pound man into a teaching lab full of skeletons and human anatomy charts.

"What are you doing?" a woman asked from under a desk.

"I'm Doug, security." He was breathless. "There are gunman downstairs. Caught this one."

A woman in a lab coat stood. "I'm Sarah Yi, resident here. Can I help?"

Doug nodded to a table bolted to the floor. "Help me drag him over there."

They did and Doug cuffed the man to the table leg. He handed Sarah his pepper spray.

"He gets out of hand, spray him good." The half-conscious man grunted. Doug walked to the door. "I've got to make sure everybody else is okay."

* * *

JANET HAD PALMED THE PEPPER spray, but the gun pointed at her head kept her from using it. The crazy man said something, but it didn't register.

"What?"

"You heard me. And don't tell me they don't exist. If you say anything like that, the next bullet's goin' between your eyes."

Janet's lower lip trembled. She was given an impossible task. How do you convince stupid they are stupid?

"Lady, pick up the phone and call. I want death panel members down here now."

She reached for the phone with her left hand.

"Lloyd!" a man in his twenties standing by the entrance with an assault rifle shouted. "We got trouble."

The dumbass named Lloyd turned to him. "Trouble how?"

"Cops."

"Crap. Give 'em ground fire to keep 'em back. Soon as we have the death panelists down here, we can clear everything up."

The man nodded and ran out the sliding glass doors. When Lloyd turned back around, Janet coated his face with pepper spray.

* * *

LLOYD HOWLED IN PAIN. HE wanted to tear his eyes out, rip out his lungs and throat, and drown them in ice water. When he caught Janet, he'd kill that bitch. Kill her bad. Sweet Jesus this hurt something awful.

"Lloyd, Lloyd. What's happenin'? What's that smell? You need some help?"

No shit he needed help. Who was that? His searing eyes were so bleary he couldn't see a thing. Sounded like that old guy, the hop-along geezer. If only he could've chosen his army. Good Lord, the pain. "Get me some water! I'm dying here."

* * *

BATHED IN SWEAT, DOUG'S HEART slammed nonstop. He had raced through floors two to five with the shotgun making sure staff and patients were secured in rooms behind locked doors. Now he wanted to ask his prisoner some questions.

Inside the instruction room, the potbellied man still lay cuffed on the floor. Sarah, the resident, stood by with pepper spray. He snarled at Doug.

"That's my shotgun."

Doug shrugged. "If you say so. But since you discharged it in a hospital, I'm sure it'll get impounded and melted soon enough. So why are you guys holding this hospital hostage?"

The man shook his head. "You don't know shit."

"But you do? Tell me then."

Doug usually wasn't this confident with people older than him, but something about holding a gun over a man cuffed to a table made it easy.

"'Cause you're harborin' murderers."

Doug studied the man's face. Did he mean criminals? Illegal

aliens? That seemed to get everybody in a tizzy these days. Or did he mean abortions? Those weren't performed here unless the mother's life was in danger. Folk out here voted for the loudest idiot who promised to ban abortions or put crazy restrictions on them.

"What are you talkin' about?"

"You know. Actin' ignorant don't help you none. Unlock me now or my son's gonna come up here and whup your ass."

"He said the same thing to me," Sarah said.

Doug knelt. "I can't let you go until the police get here."

The man glared daggers at Doug and spat on his shoe. Doug pulled out his stun gun and looked at Sarah, who shrugged. Doug gave the idiot another shock.

* * *

CAPTAIN JACK GREEN SET UP a command station at the back of the hospital parking lot after receiving gunfire from a man with an assault rifle. He knew it was only a matter of time before jihadists made a major attack in the Tulsa area. Thanks, Obama, for letting all of the terrorists in.

He had eight officers set up a loose perimeter around the hospital. A Special Operations Team was being assembled and would be onsite within ten minutes.

Fear and excitement swirled in Jack's brain. *Come on, you've been preparing for something like this your entire career. Man up!*

"Captain, you got a call," Officer Terry Spitz said. "Nine-one-one operator says it's from a security guard inside."

Jack sighed, taking the phone. Last thing he needed was a rent-a-cop giving him *intelligence*.

* * *

AFTER WAITING SEVERAL LONG MINUTES Doug was patched through to a Captain Jack Green. Doug saw police cars with strobing blue-and-red lights from the third-floor lobby window.

"I got that idiot cuffed to a table. As best I can tell everybody's safe except for the two dozen or so who are bein' held captive by the gunmen in the lobby," Doug said after explaining his actions and the safety of the doctors and patients.

"So who are these guys? Terrorists? They got brown skin or say anything like 'Allah Akbar'?"

Doug hesitated for a second. "No, sir, from what I see, these guys are rednecks."

"Oh," Green said like he was disappointed. "You know what they want?"

Doug thought about it. There was that death-panel nutjob a couple of weeks ago. Could it be him? "The guy I captured won't tell me. But I don't think they want to kill everybody, I think they want hostages for some reason."

Doug's phone buzzed. He glanced at the screen. A text from Janet. An electric charge jolted through his system. He hardly comprehended Green's words.

"Get yourself in a safe place, Doug. We'll take over from here."

Doug nodded to nobody, ended the call, and tapped to his messages. Janet's text read. *Hiding. Death panel moron. Get help.*

Doug texted back. *Where? I'll get you.*

* * *

JANET SQUATTED BEHIND A TWO-FOOT-TALL planter with a ficus tree sprouting out of it. She was trapped. After spraying that dipshit Lloyd in the face, she had started to run down the hall to the back entrance, but a limping terrorist was coming her way with a rifle. So she ran past the writhing Lloyd to the front doors, but another idiot was shooting at police by the entrance because you only live once, right? So she ducked behind the planter against the wall around the corner from her desk.

The sting of pepper spray wafted in the air, but compared to last night's fiasco this was so much better. It sounded like Lloyd was recovering. The limping gunman apparently poured her thirty-two ounces of ice water on Lloyd's face—a man who now swore he was going to kill her, aka "that bitch." Imagine how much worse off he'd be if she hadn't left her water behind. Ungrateful a-hole.

Doug had already texted that he was going to come down. She felt relief, then panic. No need for Doug to get killed on her account. She texted back: *Don't. pls. Just get help. Stay safe.*

He didn't respond. Come on, Doug, don't be an idiot hero. There are too many delusional people around here already.

The phone at the information desk rang. Janet willed herself not to jump up and answer it.

* * *

THE WORLD WAS A PAINFUL place for Lloyd. The ringing telephone shouldn't have hurt his head, but it did.

"Get it," he ordered Ned, the old gent who couldn't find that Janet bitch, which made sense since he'd already let a security guard slip away. Thank God they didn't carry firearms.

"Uh-huh. . . . Okay." Ned held out the phone to Lloyd. "It's for you."

Lloyd grabbed the phone without asking who it was, because he could find out the answer quicker himself than by asking Ned.

"Who's this?"

"Captain Green. Broken Arrow Police. Who am I talking to?"

"Lloyd McCrory, freedom fighter."

"That don't make sense unless you're fighting against freedom."

Lloyd wanted to smash the phone against the wall. What was the deal with all of the smartasses these days?

"Now you listen here, mister police captain. You can join our cause or get out of the way, because as soon as Americans hear about what we're doin' they're gonna be on our side."

"Is that so?"

"Yes, sir. So what's it gonna be? You joinin' or gettin' outta the way?"

"How about you let out all of those hostages and then I might consider joinin' your cause. What is it by the way?"

Lloyd straightened, feeling the tingle of patriotism bubble up inside.

"I am riddin' this hospital of death panels, once and for all."

A long moment of silence lingered on the line. Lloyd felt like he had made his point.

"Mr. McCrory, I hate to tell you this, but there's no such thing as death panels. If you'd like to come out here, I'd love to discuss—"

Lloyd slammed the phone down in its cradle. Screw this guy. He was probably an Obama surrogate paid to make sure death panels ran smoothly. He should have known better.

The phone rang again. Lloyd grabbed it.

"I know what you are doing and it makes me sick that the police force has been compromised by lefties like you." He waited for the captain's response. He must have hit him hard with a rocket of truth, because there was only silence. "Hello?"

"Hello, I'd like to know what the hospital hours are today," a woman with a frail voice said.

Lloyd flushed with embarrassment. "Uh, er. We're closed today. Sorry, ma'am."

He hung up and turned to Ned. "Watch the phone. Tell anybody who calls that we're closed. Get me if the police chief's on the line. I'm gonna talk to our hostages."

Ned saluted Lloyd as he stalked down the hall.

* * *

DOUG HAD MADE IT BACK down the stairs, shotgun in hand. Peeking through the porous, bullet-riddled door he could tell that the young man pacing around with the assault rifle was the son who was supposed to whup his ass. Not in a fair fight, Doug thought.

"Everybody stay still," the kid warned every few minutes. "I don't wanna shoot you, but that don't mean I won't."

Doug held the shotgun in his hands, palms slick with sweat. The nervous circles the kid made were rhythmic. His back was turned for about two seconds as he passed the door. Doug would like to use the stun gun on the kid, but between opening the door and putting the shocker against the boy's neck for three seconds, too many things could go wrong. And where was that limping man? He had a rifle too. Probably up front by Janet, but maybe he was waiting with his aim trained on the door. But then wouldn't the kid make eye contact with him every so often? Yeah, the kid was probably alone.

So shotgun or nothing. Assuming the shotgun's spray didn't scatter too wide, he could take the kid out without injuring the hostages. But that would be murder, straight up. Killing an idiot kid for following in his father's dumbass footsteps. Holy crap this was deep.

At least by taking out the kid, the hostages could be free, and somebody could grab his rifle. Then he could rescue Janet. Okay. On the kid's next circuit he'd do it. Doug took a deep breath, left hand on the door handle, ready to throw it open.

✝ ✝ ✝

LLOYD WALKED TO THE BACK lobby past the elevators where that kid, Don Jr., circled a couple dozen doctors, patients, and family members. They seemed scared senseless. Well, sometimes sacrifices had to be made for the greater good of the whole, right? They'd be better off in the long run.

The kid stopped pacing. "You heard from my dad? He chased a security guard up them stairs. Haven't heard a word from him since."

Lloyd noticed the worried lines carved in the kid's face. Heck if he wasn't a little worried, too. No way Don Sr. would lose a battle to a security guard armed with only a radio. Although, if he carried pepper spray . . .

"Everything's fine. I'm sure of it. He's probably upstairs right now, lookin' for those panels." He turned his gaze to the hostages on the floor. "Which brings me to the following point. I need to know where you keep the death-panel offices. I know every hospital has one. If somebody tells me, I can let you all go home."

The hostages looked at each other, confused.

"Come on, somebody speak up now." Lloyd pointed his pistol at a doctor in a white coat. "You there. Stand up. What's your name?"

A balding man stood with his mouth open, unable to say anything.

"Doctor Palaski," Lloyd said, reading his badge. "Tell me where those death panels are held in this hospital. Is it in the basement or on the top floor?"

A guttural "aaaah" came from the man's mouth.

Lloyd put the barrel of his Beretta into the man's forehead. People gasped, and a woman screamed.

"You tell me where they are at by the count of three or I'll splatter your brains all over the place. One . . ."

The shaking man paled to light gray as his eyes rolled back and he collapsed to the floor. Lloyd hadn't witnessed much fainting, but this seemed legit. Dammit to hell. A few of the hostages ministered to the unconscious man.

"Llloooyd."

Ned's voice carried through the hall. Lloyd turned to the kid. "Keep them from escaping, especially that doctor. I'll come back in a few."

He strode to the front lobby feeling the searing eyeballs of hate from the temporary detainees. If they only knew the sacrifice he was making for them, maybe they'd whistle a different tune.

* * *

DOUG STOOD ON THE OTHER side of the door, cracked it open an inch. He had been ready to shoot by the count of two, but the doctor took care of that issue. An idea formed in his mind. If stupid wanted stupid, he could give them stupid. And he could save Janet, even if she didn't want it. Risky, but hopefully worth it. He hoped that the idiot leader wouldn't do something crazy and kill somebody before he could set it up. He raced up the stairs.

* * *

POLICE AND NEWS CHOPPERS STARTED buzzing around the hospital. The phone at the front rang nonstop. Ned seemed to be out of his mind answering every call.

"No, the hospital's closed. That's the way it is."

Ring.

"Hello. . . . Uh, can't answer that, and we don't talk to the liberal media."

Ring.

"Hello. . . . I'm sorry about your husband. . . . Look ma'am, we're tryin' to save everybody in Tulsa and the world too. So why don't you . . . there was no reason for you to call me that. Goodbye."

Ring.

Janet wasn't sure if she wanted to laugh or cry at the absurdity of it all. She decided to take a peek around the corner. The guy outside was still staring down the cops, not looking inside. So she crawled from the planter and took a quick look. Ned had put his assault rifle against the wall, behind Janet's rolling chair, where he sat. Just three feet away.

Ring.

"Hello. . . . Captain Green. . . . Yes, sir. . . . Let me get Lloyd for you." Ned cleared his hoarse throat. "Hey, Lloyd. Captain Green wants to talk to you," he shouted down the hall. "Lloooyd."

Now or never, Janet told herself. She crawled like a hyperactive infant who'd drunk a can of Dr. Pepper. She grabbed the rifle and pivoted with her back to the side of the information desk.

Janet's heart thumped so rapidly that she barely heard the beeping sound from the inter-office messaging system. The private lines that the hospital used. Somebody in one of the offices probably wanted to know what was happening. Thirty seconds later, Janet heard the echo of boots coming down the hall. Now it would be impossible to get back to the ficus plant. That might be okay as long as the guy outside didn't turn around.

* * *

"POLICE CAPTAIN ON THE PHONE," Ned said, holding up the phone receiver.

Lloyd heard a beeping and spotted a red light flashing. Ned must've put the captain on hold. That's good. The one competent thing the man has done today. He took the receiver, but turned to Ned.

"Go back there and help Don Jr. with our captives. Oh, and have you heard from his father yet?"

"Not after he chased that security guard upstairs."

Lloyd nodded thoughtfully, although fear crept inside his guts. What if he'd been taken out by the security guard or somebody else? He punched the red, beeping button on the phone. "Lloyd McCrory here."

"I understand you want to meet the death panels," a calm voice said on the other end.

Lloyd shook with excitement. "Yes. Who is this? You're not the captain."

"No, I work in the hospital and I know where they are at."

"Is that so?" Ned tapped him on the shoulder. Lloyd put the phone receiver against his chest and turned to him. The man looked frightened. "What do you want?" he asked Ned.

"My, uh, gun. I can't find it."

"What do you mean you can't find it?"

"I had it back behind me against the wall and now it's gone."

Lloyd was dumbfounded by this man's stupidity. He was on the verge of uncovering a death panel in this hospital, and Ned loses his AR-15. "What do you mean it's gone? Guns don't just sprout legs and walk away. Freakin' find it."

Ned spun in a circle and looked into a drawer that might hold magazines and ammo at best.

"It's not there, stupid," Lloyd said, shoving Ned. "Go find it." He put his mouth back to the receiver. "You still there?"

"Yeah. What's the matter?"

"Nothing, just an internal issue. So where are the death-panel offices?"

"On the fifth floor."

Lloyd mouthed the words, *I knew it.*

"Are they there now?"

"Some of them are."

"Hot damn. How can I trust you?"

There was pause on the line. "I am an ally."

Lloyd would've pumped his fist at his good fortune, but instead watched in curiosity as Ned raised his hands in the air like he was surrendering. Lloyd looked to his chest to make sure there were no red laser dots on it from sharpshooters. He saw nothing but his denim shirt.

He looked at Ned. "What's goin' . . ."

Janet stood up from in front of the desk, leveling the Bushmaster at his head. She looked mad enough to pull the trigger too.

* * *

JANET DIDN'T EXACTLY KNOW WHAT she was doing, but she knew the safety was off on this bad boy and her finger was on the trigger. She'd shot .22s, pistols, and shotguns with her brothers and father, but never an assault rifle.

"Hands up, wingnut. Here's how it's going to be. You're gonna get all your men to drop their weapons and walk out the door."

"Or what?"

"You think a little pepper spray hurt your eyes? Think about how it's going to feel with two bullet holes in them."

Janet didn't know where these words came from, but she liked coming off as a badass.

Lloyd dropped the phone and lifted his hands in the air, castrated hate burning in his eyes.

"Tell me," he said. "When can I put my hands down so I can drop my weapon?"

Janet stood on her toes and saw his holstered gun. "Just keep them up for now." Crap how did you disarm somebody without getting shot? "Move away from the table and stand by Ned."

Lloyd stepped away from the desk, hands still up. He glanced outside and nodded, a sort of "look, Elvis!" kind of distraction. Janet almost fell for it, but knew she couldn't with a man carrying a gun. Then she heard the sliding glass door open. The air pressure changed and knew she was in a world of trouble. She could have turned and fired, but flight overruled fight as she sprinted past Ned.

* * *

EVERYTHING HAPPENED FAST AND IN slow motion, Lloyd thought. Max, who had been keeping the cops back, happened to turn and see the unfolding situation. He ran through the front doors and opened fire. That information girl, Janet, flew past Ned, who caught a chest full of Max's lead. Lloyd pulled out his pistol and fired a few rounds that smacked into the wall, mere inches behind her. Then the glass windows exploded and Max collapsed on the ground, blood pooling around his body. Bullets few past Lloyd and he knew what was happening: sharpshooters. He dove behind the information desk as it splintered. Fragments of particleboard peppered his face. He crawled on the other side and watched as Janet dropped to the ground under Don Jr.'s shower of bullets, raised the Bushmaster, and dropped him with two quick bursts. Then a click echoed through the lobby. Her rifle was empty. Lloyd aimed his pistol and ran at her, firing.

The detainees screamed and ran in all directions. Lloyd kept firing. He might have hit a few, maybe, he wasn't sure. He didn't care. He needed to kill that bitch who kept messing up his plans. When he got to the wall where Janet had been, she was gone. He noticed a trail of blood went to the stairwell door.

A loud crash erupted from the front lobby. A huge gray armored vehicle crashed through the lobby. SWAT-like cops swarmed inside with bulletproof vests and M16s. Lloyd ran up the stairs, following the trail of blood.

* * *

DOUG WAS STILL ON THE phone with Lloyd, when he heard gunfire. He took off running from the fifth-floor conference room to the stairwell.

When he got to the fourth-floor landing, he heard the bottom stairwell door open followed by the pained and labored breathing of somebody struggling up the steps. He walked cautiously, shotgun raised.

"Who's there? Identify yourself."

"Doug, that you?"

Janet's voice pricked his heart. "Yes. You okay, Janet?" He started to run down.

"Not sure. Been hit."

The sound of the door being thrown open to a cacophony of chaos rushed through the stairwell.

"Where'd you go, bitch?" Lloyd shouted.

Doug heard Janet scream. When he made it to the second floor he saw Janet, pinned to a wall, blood streaking from her right leg. The idiot Lloyd had one hand on her throat, and the other gripped a pistol pointed at her forehead.

He turned to Doug.

"You know that shotgun does you no good unless you wanna kill both of us. Put it on the floor or I'll put a bullet in her head."

Doug had the feeling that if he put the gun down, not only would he be dead but so would Janet.

"Are you still interested in meeting the death panel?"

He could tell Lloyd was taken aback, his grip loosening on Janet and his eyes widening before they narrowed.

"Yeah, but how can I trust you?"

"I'm a security guard. I know where everything's at—even what other people don't know around here." He nudged the shotgun barrel at Janet. "Like her."

"You mean . . ." Lloyd looked at Janet and back at Doug with his mouth open. "She don't know about death panels even though she sits at an information desk?"

"Come on, you know they wouldn't tell her things like that."

There was a huge commotion happening on the first floor. Lloyd looked down the stairwell and back. "Well, you better show me where they're at and in a hurry."

"This way." Doug walked up the staircase, praying that his plan would work.

* * *

JANET LIMPED UP EVERY PAINFUL step with that idiot Lloyd pushing a gun in her back. She'd been hit in the thigh. Dark blood soaked her charcoal-gray pant leg. She wasn't sure how bad the wound was. In theory this happened at the best location, a hospital, but she wasn't sure when a doctor would be able to look at her.

She didn't know what Doug was doing. No way were there any death panels. She hoped whatever Doug had in mind was going to work. It sounded like the army had crashed through the first floor. Hopefully these rescuers could get to them before Lloyd saw his beloved death panel.

"We're on the fifth floor," Doug said at the top of the landing.

"Well take me to them death nuts."

"Can you let Janet go now?"

"No way. She's my insurance plan."

Janet cringed as she was pushed through the open door.

* * *

DID THAT SECURITY GUARD REALLY think he was an idiot? Give up his hostage before he met the death panel? Give me a break.

He shoved limping Janet along. Probably overacting, although he couldn't deny the blood on her pants.

The security guard walked through an open lobby and through a hallway. He stopped at a door.

"What are you doin'?" Lloyd looked around for traps. It looked like a deserted hallway.

"We're going to go through this office and up to a conference room." The guard paused, taking his time. "The death panelists are in there."

A sign on the door read: Hospital Administration.

"Are all of them in there?"

"Three are there."

"Any missin'?"

"Two. One has a cold and the other is on vacation."

"And they are waiting for me?"

The guard paused for a second. "They want to talk to you."

A broad smile crossed over Lloyd's lips. "Me and my Beretta are ready to talk, too. Let's do this thing."

The guard put his hand on the doorknob, but paused. He turned to Lloyd. "If I let you meet with them, you gotta let Janet go."

"I'll let her go whenever I wanna."

"But you understand that she knows nothing about this."

Lloyd had to look away from the guard's sincere stare.

"Get me to the door with them death panelists and I'll let her go."

The guard opened the door. They walked through a darkened office.

"Is it always this dark in here?"

"It, um, helps with their decisions. Keeping things dark."

Lloyd nodded. Made sense to keep things gloomy. The guard walked to a door.

"They are in here. You ready to meet them?"

Lloyd swallowed and nodded. He pushed Janet toward the guard. A deal's a deal. She hobbled to him. He held out the shotgun in one arm and she went into the other. The guard nodded and Lloyd walked inside the conference room. The room was dark except for outdoor light coming in from the windows. He made out three people sitting in chairs facing the windows. So here they were. The murderers.

"So assholes, we finally meet," Lloyd said. The hairs on his arms rose. He was about to deliver a can of whup ass.

"Sit, please," a woman's voice came from one of the chairs.

"Why don't y'all turn around? I got somethin' to show you." He waved the gun around, a proud smirk across his face.

"No. We will reveal ourselves when we're ready. First tell us why death panels are so important to you."

Lloyd huffed. He didn't like this woman taking control of the situation.

"Y'all killed my grandmother."

"At this hospital?"

"Yes, ma'am."

"When was that?"

"October 1, 2009. She came in healthy as could be expected for an eighty-year-old with a cough. Three days later, she was dead as a doornail."

A pause lingered.

"Sir, the Affordable Care Act didn't pass until March 2010."

Anger welled up inside. "Well, y'all were preparin' for the death panels. I know y'all killed her." With tears in his eyes, he raised his pistol and shot at the three chairs.

His ears echoed from the gunshots. Nobody fell out of their chairs. He must have killed the panelists with each shot. Surely they would have rolled on the floor for cover if they weren't dead. Maybe he should've kept one alive to show the liberal media the truth. Lloyd walked around the conference table and turned the first chair around. He let out a shriek.

A human skeleton wearing a wig and lab coat sat in the chair. He'd been tricked. But the voice . . . somebody had to be in the room.

Then he saw it, a conference phone on floor under the center chair. He was going to kill that security guard and then some.

He marched over to the exit door, stepped on something, and grabbing the door handle, felt every atom in his body vibrate and sizzle like he was shaking hands with a bolt of lighting.

* * *

DOUG SQUATTED ON THE OTHER side of the door, the paddle of a defibrillator held against the metal doorknob. Lloyd's foot was on the other paddle completing the circuit. The shock could stop that idiot's heart. No loss to the world.

"I can't believe I violated the Hippocratic oath," Sarah said, squatting next to Doug. The resident had been the voice in the conference room.

"You didn't do anything. I did it."

Doug opened the door, carrying the portable defibrillator. Lloyd sat on his ass, woozy in a wide-eyed daze.

"What the . . ."

Doug knelt beside him and turned on the defibrillator.

"Stand clear," Doug shouted as he held up the paddles.

"You can't do that again," Sarah shouted.

"This is for Janet."

Doug placed the paddles against Lloyd's chest, throwing him backwards. Lloyd banged his head against the conference table leg and slumped to the floor. Doug turned to Sarah.

"You might want to check on him."

She shook her head.

"Police!" a chorus of voices shouted down the hall.

Finally the cavalry made it to the fifth floor. Doug walked out of the conference room with his hands raised.

"Freeze!" a SWAT officer said, pointing his assault rifle.

"The guy you want is in there," Doug said, nodding his head to the conference room. "He's had a pretty big shock. A doctor is looking at him. We also have a gunshot wound victim over there."

He nodded to a room where a nurse was applying pressure to Janet's bandaged leg. "She needs to go to ER ASAP."

The commanding officer nodded, directing officers into the conference room and a couple of others to carry Janet downstairs. Doug watched as two officers pushed her onto a gurney with the nurse leading the way. Although Janet looked pale and weak, she smiled at Doug. Putting a hand to her lips, she blew him a kiss and whispered, "Thank you." Doug felt like he'd grown a foot taller.

The officers pulled Lloyd up from under the table and put him on his feet only to slam him face down on the cherrywood table. They Mirandized him while cuffing his arms behind his back. Dragging the bastard into the hall, Lloyd glared at Doug.

"When I get this all sorted out, I'm gonna come after you."

"Sure, look me up in a hundred years if a jury doesn't give you the death penalty."

Lloyd yelled something about "real Americans" standing with him like Sean Hannity, but Doug tuned it out. This fool had already taken up too much of his time today.

THE PSALM OF BO
BY CHRISTOPHER CHAMBERS

"When I strike, the bees will begin to swarm,
and I need you to help hive them."
—JOHN BROWN TO FREDERICK DOUGLASS, 1858

VERILY, I SAY UNTO YOU that my final sin was a lie. For lo, with the Eternal Fire bearing disapproving witness, I cast the hunt as a ritual, and I told the hunters that my feast was its consecration. In fact, I was sore and hungry, and I beseech the Spirit of he who was Bo to prepare the table for the feast of my redemption.

Whereupon, my tongue sloshed over the bounty and confirmed what my single, filmy eye and graying, feeble snout had guessed it to be: a rat's head, a cat's pungent, oily liver and hind limb without the cursed paw. Scraps of a scavenged pigeon carcass.

When I was young, I took my meat slowly, deliberately—to savor as if I would be killed at any time. This once, I ate greedily, and all among We Who Belong to Each Other shall know why, and that is for Hope and Change.

And lo, I swallowed the last morsel.

And that done, I fan my rump hackles, and juveniles—all unseasoned bitches yet brave enough to serve me my meat—raise their heads to attention. Upon my growl they disperse and lope to the frontier whence firelight meets shadow.

There they stand a picket and vigil. Against intruders, or the dripping and misshapen monsters who lurk and lay in the rubble, yonder?

Nay, for I inherited and grew a dread nation of tooth and claw, bivouacked in a city of dens within dens under the Dome which was once the center of a world killed; that world which we shall shepherd and herd anew as the poison and dark dissipate, and the sun shall beam, shall warm the growing grass, as did before our slavery and before the slavery of MAGA, when MAGA boasted to "make" this place "great again," the wages of arrogance was Hell.

Thusly, the young females ban even my fierce personal guard, the Scars, from the fireside and the Scars are quick with fang and fury, yet even they comply, though they know not my grim and loving purpose.

I raise my snout and howl, and lo, a chorus of a thousand times a thousand throats acknowledge my paramountcy, and the Dome and the walls of rock quake.

Thusly, in fealty and fear a multitude of bitches and sires nose their newest pups into the glow of the Eternal Fire. When there was scant food, we culled in this manner, upon my howl. And that, too, was my sin.

Verily, our Deliverer who conferred the survival of We Who Belong to Each Other to me, as Protector, had predicted my sins, and said unto me, "*Yea, you shall balance sin with saving your nation, and you shall suffer odium, if even if the scales say sin is justified. Our journey has never been for the faint-hearted, for those that prefer leisure over work, or seek only the pleasures.*"

And lo, a hundred times a hundred pups creep forward, and the ground is thick with them as if one wriggling mass of that hinds, limbs, ears, snouts, and the Dome echoes with yelps and pants and whimpers.

"Silence!" I bellow. "Be still!"

And with that all settle and curl. They do so not just in fear of me, or for warmth. They do it for the reason which saved: for the belonging. Here, encased in piled rocks dragged by bloody mouths and twisted backs to buttress the great Dome, itself sheathed in metals and other such hard things, we belong, and are safe.

"Suffer me closer, oh little ones!" I bark. "You are the first to never have endured the boom of the mushrooms beyond the Dome. Your snouts have never suffered the stench of burnt flesh. Our Deliverer, He Whose Name You Have Not Earned the Right to Speak, brought us out of bondage and vanquished death. As he served us, and I, him. And I, on this the last of many endless nights, shall likewise serve you!"

Yea, though we culled in this way, with the bitches and sires kept in the dark, by the dark, my ears twitch with the swarm and masked din of murmurs upon hearing my eavesdropped voice. Still, my snout, my nostrils catch lingering frets vibrating and wafting from the vast dark.

Dah! Death is a legend for too many of them. For me, it is intimate as a mate loved and lost, as real as my scars and dead eye and ground-down bones. I have rubbed out enemies and innocents with my bite and guile. I have left friends broken, smoldering, crushed until they lay as hair and stains, unrecognizable. Nay, being old does not cloud ill memories; rather, it rubs out the bright and free-running and wagging times, leaving only lament.

And still I weep, but inwardly, for they who raised me, though they divided me from my mother's teat, my sisters' squirming company. As a pup, they called themselves humans and we called them "people" before we named them slavers.

And verily I say unto you that as many matings ago as the sand grains beneath our snouts, we came to their fires upon smelling their broiling meat and saw how they clustered and clung and suckled as we, and we said, "Together with people is our destiny." We endured their depravity and yet still returned to comfort them and to love them until the next beating or burning or leaving us to whither to a skeleton.

Yea, slavery or nay, I prospered, at least as a pup. I remember my blanket and I remember a laugh when I jumped into a human bed, and a coo as I was brushed and anointed with oils. A scolding, when I was rude or sour.

Yet, lo, our Deliverer, showed me their folly and fallaciousness, and that here were not good people and bad people, just one race and they were merely apes. The "skin-apes" who, unlike their hairy brethren, took pleasure in living above one another, rather than side by side. And took pride in killing each other, rather than in belonging. And he was Bo.

Yea, these apes Scoured in the name of MAGA and in fealty to their paramount leader who we named Bird-Tail Mane Bulbous-Faced Ape, him cruel and obstreperous, who tore down the dens of they who smiled and coaxed the best from all apes, and who had bid all apes hope, and yet were impotent or unknowing as to their peril.

And lo, the endtime for smiles was nigh, as MAGA set about making their realm "great again," and scowls, scorn, and reproach reigned.

And then birthed from that womb of hateful glee began the Scour, when ape packs were torn and divided and banished.

And then the black skin and brown skin were first divided and banished, or rubbed out, and such was blamed not on MAGA's hate, but on they themselves whom where hated.

And then many were tortured, and *torture creates enemies, it does not defeat them.*

Whereupon, the apes who reveled in the Scour received the punishment of the Scourge, and many more apes whether MAGA or not where rubbed out, and the great cities of dens suffered no less than countryside and the remaining apes took their guns to ground and lived as termites.

But for We Who Belong to Each Other, the Scourge conveyed a gift. For lo, what ghosts infected the air and water made our barks and calls take meaning as shapes and ciphers and counts and tinkering of the mouth and not of ape fingers, and of justice and righteousness, and such formed newly in our heads, to mingle with what was always in hearts, as Bo, our Deliverer, did tell me.

And yea, in wonderment did walk upon the earth as long as or longer than did the apes before the Scour and Scourge, in places of plenty. No longer would we die and be buried or burned after but a few matings, barely the time for an ape to grow from pup to season.

Whereupon, the apes did gnash their square teeth and hunt us, for the Scourge did not set us as equals to them. Nay, it set us as blessed and they, cursed.

And many of us were netted and rubbed out.

Lo, as a juvenile, I was netted and tortured yet in bindings and whimpered pain, and likewise Bo, our Deliverer, also cowered in a fetid hole, and yet his snout lifted me, and his tongue anointed me.

Yet now, what twinge of sweet memory now passes, and I hear a single restive pup in the rank fronting the quieted multitude. She is the product of a blunt head and a narrow head, as our Deliverer decreed a Great Mixing to cleanse the slave-breeding that made us look different and sick. She peers at me through the flames with a tilted look of curiosity. When I snarl, she rolls to bare her belly, lengthens her throat. I nod. She rights herself and I bid her to speak.

"You look troubled," she squeaks above the spit and crackle of the Eternal Fire. "Does the fire hold sights that frighten you as it does us, Great and Vicious Biter Big Ears Sire?"

She calls me "Great and Vicious Biter Big Ears Sire" because

learning my name and hers in our true language remains difficult; the young respond better to the old sounds bequeathed to
us. Our true names would be imperceptible to and unpronounce-
able by apes. Yet often I stamp my old slave name in the sand, to
remind myself.

Max. German Shepherd. Then I rub it out.

"Fire nurtures, fire murders," I say.

A male, ignorant as he is arrogant, chimes, "Fire doesn't scare
me! Oh Great and Vicious Biter Old Big Ears Sire, I want to grow
up to be like you!"

And with that I snarl and arch and bear what fangs I have that
are not worn pegs, and this frightens scores of pups into a crying
retreat. The impertinent one pulls back the farthest.

"Whelp! I fear *nothing*! Not fire or bullet from the skin-ape, not
tooth or claw of any outsider or usurper! I could rip the flesh
from your throat before your mother or sire could beg me nigh!
Our Deliverer counted me by his side and said, 'Verily *you* are my
general! *I have need of 'Max' . . . I want him for carrying on war; and
that war is necessary to me!*'"

I desist not because they are terrified, but because of the one
hip I cannot feel, while the other explodes in the pain. The pups
crawl back, bellies scraping the sand.

"Yet the time for dark snarls has ended," I whisper, panting. I
look to a juvenile captaining the curtain of females guarding my
gathering. She nods and retrieves the relic.

Under pain of a bitten-off ear, no one could touch this thing,
for it was Holy to me for reasons none have known yet shall know.
Yet the old ones who are dust did know that Our Deliverer, he
who was Bo, snatched this thing as the Scourge took its grim toll
and paid its wondrous wages, and, a slave no more, and when I
was a pup grown to lithe and dread juvenile of fang, having seen
my slavers Scoured then Scourged, he spoke the words to us heard
among his old masters. "*Let us make a way out of no way,*" and he
kept the cloth, as relic, to remind us.

Lo, I stand and my forelegs tilt and my hind legs quake whilst the juveniles drape and wrap me in this fabric.

Whereupon, the pups squeak in marvel for they behold the cloth's white stripes beneath the stars of white in the blue night sky. With it are stripes of gray and blotches and smears of yellow, all of which the apes called "red," whether dyed by ink, or painted with holy blood.

And the pups prick up their ears as I suffer them closer, and recount unto them what has never been shared, for all they and their parents have known is *his* dread law, conferred by me. Now I shall sing his heart. His, as glorious Dellverer? Nay. His, as mere Bo, and mine, his young friend . . .

. . . and verily, I see and smell acrid smoke blotting out the sun, until their flying machines pound and mix the brown clouds as they dart and dive upon us like great hawks, spitting fire from their talons. I see and smell and hear our millions of dead and dying in heaps and piles: those who hurled themselves against the battlements of the ape's Wall, therein at the place called Ellipse, whence Bo and his humans once rejoiced in the lights and belonging of the big tree.

I howl and cry in lament, yet I threaten with fang any who bear witness to it, preferring only vision of the glory before the death. And awash in such glory, I, vain and brave, alighted onto the wrecked bus that was a captured redoubt, my ears pointed and erect, clad in my armor of carpet, food cans, tile, bits of their leather coats and tied with their plastic, with shards of glass lashed to my paws. My warriors formed ranks, tails rigid, teeth bared and smothered in the fury's foam . . . and I thundered, *"Charge!"*

Now, my ears have wilted down, and I cast off my breastplate of apes' rubbish and I crawl, sickened that my troops died and I survived. And yea, I am among the holes and buried conduits and culverts that once carried their cables of light and I yell to my sappers—the Terriers and Terrier-mutts—"How much longer?" as they bite and tear. The wiry Cairn "David" spits back, "By nightfall, curse you!" and lo, the Jack Russell "Cynthia" barks a countermand, "My general, forgive him. The task will be done quickly, I swear it!"

Yea, though I am sick with grief I neither retreat nor snarl at their Terrier insolence, but rather I exhort these little hounds and stir them, for the blood of their fallen brothers and sisters above now drains into the sewers.

"Heroes' blood anoints you! Dig and chew!" And yea, tails wag and mouths growl and cables are cut.

Quickly, shockwaves from ape artillery and our mines rumble and ripple the earth, and the sonic blasts of air pressure assail us. Nonetheless, from the pipes and conduits I push into the narrow dank tunnels we ourselves have excavated, leading out from the ruined red brick of the place which once examined our and the apes' food and prey and deemed it safe; and there from this "USDA" we hide our stores and ordnance under the rubble that once held the apes' oldest machines for worship, called "Smithsonian."

Verily, I say unto you that the faithful therein use their own aching backs and bodies to shore up such tunnel walls they have dug. And I pass them with my dejected warriors in tow. Yet rather than bark and bite at me in disappointment and anger, they bow, and my heart is salved.

Lo, I see a Giant Schnauzer, "Fabio," his black hair matted with blood; a nurse who is a Pug known by her own slave name "Mrs. Peebles" chews and spits poultice into the bullet holes between Fabio's ribs. Next to Fabio is an even more massive Bernese Mountain Dog, "Shaq," and his forepaws are burned, and steaming flesh sloughs to bone.

And yea, I see neither shriek in pain, and my tongue licks them and their wounds as I recognize them as ones who I knew as a pup in the place called "dog park" long ago, to where my slave masters took me to amuse themselves.

"Have at them again, General?" Fabio grunts. "It was I who killed two wheeled things spitting death at us, and sent the one which moved like a monster caterpillar yelping away, and I did it with mines and grenades I stole from their barracks! And I stole and heaved much more explosives from across the river when we raided their great five-point den!"

"I, too, am ready to attack again!" big Shaq says, ignoring his frightful wounds. "I liberated much food and medicine and dragged it far from the PetSmart!"

"I am not worthy to lead you," I mutter, still licking them.

"Nonsense!" Fabio snorts. "You are our little Max, grown to a black-faced and tan and silver warrior. Remember when we first came to him, our Deliverer? And yea, he bid us forget the old ways and human ties? Oh, you were a mere pup and I said unto you 'I am fat and phlegmatic, yet your youth quickens and arms me, and let us join him, and his name is Bo.'"

Yea, Bo did recount to Fabio how his slave mistress was a queen female, ever so lithe and regal, and that she said unto her pack, *Whenever they go low, we go high.* Bo, his paw tufted with tight white curls fronting a sleeve of stygian black, punched Fabio's fat head and growled low and mean: "Yea, all must arm themselves, for such words are for a brighter time, as were her mate's words, and his smile and mien. He, my old master. But the dim times rubbed out he and his. The dim and the low! But We Who Belong to Each Other, and feel the world's pain despite our faces prosaic or play-ful—we live with our bellies low to the ground. Our snouts smell the stink and we suffer the rough places. When most regal bird lands, it and its precious eggs can be killed by the lowest slithering creature, not just you or I as noble hunters. My slaver, my human mistress was from Chicago. She knew better then to proclaim the light when light had no stomach to stop MAGA. Thusly, the dark-ness is left to us to vanquish, for we are deadly in the dark."

"Rest," I counsel my friends. Yea though I whisper to the Pug, "Put bite to them, if their suffering does not abate." Though small of teeth, I have seen her ease the transition to the heavenly Den of Soft Grass for many a massive and striding warrior.

Whereupon I see the brindle French Bulldog "Celery" who sweeps her ears like the apes' radar as we appear in the command tunnel, and she signals our arrival with a staccato bark.

Whence from the sanctum comes another voice, that of the bitch who is second only to Bo, and they claimed each other as brother and sister when both were slaves to the king and queen's daughters. I am sure those princesses are long dead, or, once seasoned, were taken as concubines and trophies by the MAGA apes into their lair of steel and stone beneath what was once the wondrous white den whence Bo once frolicked.

And verily, she, called "Sunny," beseeches, "Withdraw, or we shall die not from bullets or bombs but from thirst and starvation and the filth of the tunnels . . ."

And thereby I see my friend, who is our Deliverer yet whom the ape princesses called a "fur-ball" and cooed and cuddled him as if he were soulless toy, not a pup. His coat of tight ringlets was black to hold his heat in cold water, with white on his paws and belly to provide contrast and camouflage, and upon his escape he easily foraged in the river and great bay for what fish and crabs and oysters the apes had not poisoned. Yet the princesses giggled and called it "tuxedo," as if a caricature of the ape's fanciful fur. Nay, his tuxedo on this bloody day is *armor*, and a crew of hairy Yorkies thusly repair and refit it to its dread purpose.

Yea, do his hackles ripple through his armor's back plates, and his fangs flash at his sister such that she offers her belly . . .

"Caution, Sister? *I am eternally tired of hearing that word caution. It is nothing but the word of cowardice!*"

Whereupon my friend is taken aback as I intercede. "I bid you listen to reason!" I snarl yet supplicate with a tucked tail and averted gaze, and Sunny rushes to me, licks me.

And lo, his warlike look softens and he licks Sunny, and then me, and he cleans my blood mingled with that of the fallen and wounded.

"Friend, another frontal assault will break us," I whisper as he grooms me. "We are not cowards, but let us return to raid and ambush."

"Nay," he intones. "I am confident that at this defining moment, we will prove ourselves worthy of the sacrifice of those who died, and the promise of those who will come after."

"*Bah!*" Sunny suddenly howls. "You only repeat the *master's* exhortations and poetry whilst *they* hide behind their *Great Wall*. And we dash ourselves against it . . . and they laugh and say look at those beasts! They are as silly and impotent and elitist as the ones they served or succored on the coasts, and whom we Scoured with our guns . . ." Whereupon she pivots her head of black curls to the starry and striped cloth my Bo had hung in the tunnel. "And they Scoured in the service of the cursed *flag* you insist on showing!"

"Be silent!" he scolds us. "For I did not say launch another frontal assault. They are beaten, though their arrogance and madness tells them naught. They are as termites, as in their other strongholds far away and cross't the waters. Verily, I say unto you—they who would make this place 'great again,' have made it their *tomb*." He motions to Celery. "Show them in the dirt my plan, then rub it out. Then send the runners, howl and scent the wind so the packs north to the cold, south to the searing rocks, west to the mountains, and cross't the water abide: Victory is nigh, wait for my signal . . ."

* * *

Lo, it is night. The apes flaunt their power with so many flights of their hovering and zooming machines. Squads of us spring from the ground and scurry to tempt them and the bait is taken for they chase and tire and crash for want of fuel.

Yea, my pointed ears and narrow snout parse the wind; the wind says the machines have no safe rookery to which to refuel, refit. For cables are cut by Terrier teeth, and we have overrun these rookeries. And for the first time, I feel the audacity of hope crackle through my fur. We could win. Yes, we can!

Though yet and still, the apes flaunt and goad, this time with music and laughter from their underground fetes, and lights of color peeking through to mix with the horrid glare of their searchlights on the bulldozed bodies of our fallen, for they wish an unfettered killing zone to funnel us.

And then they taunt us with want of cold water, as the summer night air is swampy and thick and baking and dead, bereft of breeze and relief and legions of tongues pant from thirst and exhaustion.

And then they blast the silent whistles to split our skulls and flush us, and we endure.

And then as if forming in a mist on fire, they send us the visage and voice of their MAGA lord, Bird-Tail Mane Bulbous-Faced Ape, and it is large as what would be a tall tree, and though we know him long dead, his meaty lips shout, "*Bad doggies!*" "*Filthy animals!*" and truncated piles of words: "*Fat, ugly face, you're fired . . .*" "*The beauty of me . . .*" "*Thugs and illegals . . .*"

Lo, we are immune to his rants, for we Belong and feel what is round and encircles, not as walls and buffets and keeps out, and thusly Bo, ever confident, drills us for the last battle.

Yet there are many who wonder if we should stop as the face exhorts . . .

* * *

VERILY I SAY UNTO YOU it is a new night, blackest and dead and hot of air, and the many who doubted now prefer drawing ape blood. And nigh is the time to do so, for we have prepared.

Yea, I give the word, and my divisions pour into this night, and veer wide around the tallest, whitest edifice standing—the white stone needle that stabs the night sky—and under which Bo ordered me to set my Terriers, and they have sapped and engineered a day and a night, and many of them have died of exhaustion.

We, the warriors, look up at the stone needle and place our trust in it; we look down at the bodies of the Terriers and take our fury from them for revenge, and we know more will die before sun rises.

We, the swift killers, we Shepherds and Boxers, Dobermans and Carne Corsos and Collies, Labs, Harriers, and Hounds, and all mutts of the same, kith and kin.

And I run, silent, through a stand of broken trees and leap undetected upon derelict hulks that were once mighty building machines bringing pipes of vapors and juice, and this effluence blotted out the sky worse than the clouds of war and it stank, and yet the apes laughed and called it "investment" and "energy" as flower and creature alike suffered.

And lo, my ears poke as a demon's horns from my helmet, and my senses part shadows and smoke . . . *there*!

Faint and far on our right flank, on what was the grassy, placid Mall where the old ones jumped for flying discs to amuse apes long dead, a bulwark forms.

It grows unnoticed by the ape searchlights and it is battalions of the barrel-chested and thick-necked, and they emerge from the tunnels, and they are quiet but for their heavy breaths and heavier paws, and Sunny leads them. Mastiffs, Dogues, brick-headed Staffordshires and massive Danes, cruel Rottweilers and any mutts, likewise mixed. And even Shaq hops on ruined limbs yet lifted and is pushed by his loving friend, Fabio, and it is those two who look the most joyous and brave!

Yea, though I trust myself as the swift hammer, and Sunny's force as the hard anvil, all faith is in the center.

Verily, I see twisted plates of filigreed brown metal that was the skin of the place dedicated to those apes whom were slaves of paler apes, and then when paler apes whether rich or poor drew wealth or pride from living above them, and MAGA did destroy this place in the Scour to prove that any who opposed them had no power but "outrage," and outrage was laughable, puny.

Fitting then, that from this ruin streams the others: innumerable, armored in plastic and tin. *Puny* . . .

And I behold a roiling mass of high-pitched growls and tiny swaying tails or nubs thereof, and miniature fangs: Pugs and Bulldogs, Terriers, Spaniels. Puffs of Bichon and wisps of Pomeranian and nude Chihuahua. Shoulder to shoulder, jowl to haunches. Thousands tote mines and fire-making things larger than their bodies.

Oh, brave little warriors, my troops bid you silent salute!

Lo, the assembled tiny terrors rile the searchlights and cameras and drones and sentries and patrolling wheeled and caterpillar-treaded monsters, for all are concentrating on the strongest part of the Wall, the redoubt guarding the approach to the great white den, once called "Commerce." And so much infantry and wheeled things, oblivious to the absence of their flying machines, sally out and they are haughty, bloodthirsty, and many are sick with fermented drink and pills that tinges their piss and spoor.

But behold! They halt! And they see what I see, bathed in light . . .

For the small ones part a path, and through it, he bounds! Resplendent in his armor. And lo, in his teeth he carries *that* cloth. Striped, with stars?

Yea, before this night, I would have raised hackles and paw to such hypocrisy and scoffed even to my friend's face and bid him: Did not such a thing belong to apes who made us slaves and gave us these slave names? Who are you, Bo, to fetch it from our bloodied tunnels and wring out for battle? Why *this* cloth, the colored fabric of lowness and bondage?

Yet on this night, with death nigh, he cares not of our surprise or confusion at this symbol of his rally, for we already we *are* rallied, and whereupon he calls to the center as a hairy Dachshund bears away the colors from him: "Little ones . . . do not break! Too many have broken before us! Too many have squandered and been wrought-up and dithered and debated. We remain. We who loved *them* without question, without judgment. And so we fight, paw to boot, tooth to gun! Heart and soul against steel and fire!"

Them? He does not call them "apes?" Yea, and do not question him, for he is bravery, he is sacrifice, and cries of bloody yearnings whip from the ranks of the small and the tiny and the puny.

Whence Bo now exclaims, "This night . . . we redeem! Heart and soul are what we are made of . . ." The howls and growls of the small reach a crescendo, piercing even my taut ears, as the Dachshund jumps to his side with the cloth, and Bo snarls, "Remember what you are made of . . . and *follow me!*"

And with that they surge, tongues trailing, as a tide, and I wait on the left flank, as does Sunny, on the right. And thus further beckoned and baited, the apes leave the safety of their wall and the Commerce Redoubt to join the ones already on sortie.

And lo, they charge to meet our slow and steady center, and Hell comes with them.

Yea, sheets of flame spew from the snouts of machines, and bullets are as clouds of gnats and fleas, and the small and the tiny and the puny die in ranks, yet they keep coming and attach their mines and gnaw and chew and slash with paws lashed-up with steel and glass.

Lo, in the garish light I see the Dachshund, who Bo calls "Color-Bearer," rubbed out under the wheels of an armored monster, and Bo seizes the cloth from him before he is crushed.

Emboldened, the apes smash into the tiny ones.

Encouraged, they turn to attack our right flank; the barrel-chested and thick-necked give as well as get.

Lo, I scent Shaq's death in the bloody and burnt air, for he has blown himself up under a truck after his jaws crush many ape heads like so many eggs. And Fabio holds his ground and bites and tears till he is torn himself and is rubbed out.

And my troops see my piss and spray and they whimper and bark and I snap back, *"No,* not yet!"

Yea, the right buckles, yet holds.

Yet the center falters.

And the apes pursue, leaving their wounded behind, and stomping our wounded with boots, and many such boots were pointed and made of cow's hide for sport.

And yet, before the retreat has made us empty of piss . . . *behold*! Bo waves the cloth! He is offering himself as a target.

And it steels the little warriors, and they hold, as planned. Lo, *they hold*!

"*Now!*" I call, not as We Who Belong to Each Other, but with the roar of the great-toothed cats once now ruled cross't the sea.

And my sappers' fruit, seeded all through the night and watered with their blood and tongue drip becomes a harvest of explosions, and lo, shockwaves assail the apes, not us.

Verily I say unto you, that now a great shudder and heaving in the tall white needle stabbing the hot dead sky prompts a great shudder among the apes, for, as Bo planned, this needle quakes, then topples, almost whole until the instant it crashes.

And lo, it crashes onto and cross't their cursed Wall.

"*Revenge!*" I howl, whereupon waves of fangs and armor charge across the broken spine of the needle, and fly out of the clouds of debris, and swarm through the breach, and I wheel a division into the apes' flank whilst other battalions bite behind the Wall.

Our own right flank—the anvil—closes the trap by trundling forward, and my troops smash the apes upon its waiting jaws, and I meet Bo's little ones in the center, and the apes are surrounded and they die where they stand, or pop from the hatches of their monsters only to be rubbed out, or they run away with many covered by the little ones, who chomp on limbs and fingers and genitals and throats.

Lo, I bound into the havoc and ruins of the great white den with our troops, and we kill any ape we see, and there are many We Who Belong to Each Other who cschcwcd us and were foils and who traded for favor and a lush life. Whereupon I threaten bite on the traitors and, snarling, suffer them, "What of these apes underground, and what have they wrought?"

And lo, as they stutter in terror over the stamping in the sand which the apes do upon flat paper and with light and sent through the air and cable, but much here is paper, and scattered about like leaves, or thick as white snow, and captives say it is ancient lists of apes to be Scoured, and preserved alas, for Bird-Tail Mane Bulbous-Faced Ape luxuriated in revenge and kept the papers as relics before the ghost of air and water rubbed him out

Verily, I say unto you that upon this paper is written the names of my slave master and mistress and child . . . nay, my humans, my *people* . . . because those who taught, those who defended the weak, those who crafted things of beauty and sounds of beauty not base or ugly—such were the first to be Scoured. And then on paper was an admission that Bo's human princesses were not kept as concubines, but hostages, then rubbed out.

Yea, I am suffused with rage and am dizzy and I storm more corridors and leap over bodies of apes, scenting and seeing our troops feeding on them and I do not care to stop this.

And lo, I come upon such as a window to the sun and it spits and dissolves to lines and then comes to life with the visage of Bird-Tail Mane Bulbous-Faced Ape, and his fleshy maw moves yet there is no noise, but I discern his meaning from more of the flat papers littering the floor, and the traitors translate this.

Yea, his face smiles as if he is a sire, caring and loving; he decrees that medicines many of us remember so set into our nostrils or pricked by needles beneath our fur are no longer medicine for the apes and their young, and he condemns this medicine and says all healers are seditious and are "bunk" and such healers and thinkers are to be Scoured along with those thinkers who warn of poison in the sky, sea, and earth. Yea, as prisoners they are put to task of making new medicines just for MAGA and their young, and none else.

Whereupon the Scourge is birthed from the ghosts in the new

medicines, and too late the apes realize the mistake. And yea, the ghosts already in air and the ground and in water ruined by "investment," once held at bay by these old medicines and cleansing, rise up to mate with the new ghost, and they haunt multitudes, and then rubbed them out. They who exalted and did laud and howl and cheer MAGA are the first to be rubbed out. That is the truth of it.

And verily it is only then that my lieutenants bid me, "What of them, these traitors and their pups, and ape survivors and prisoners and their kin?

Whereupon, without hesitation, I order, "*Kill them all!*"

Whence I am no better than they who Scoured, and made the Scourge, as the Scourge changed us, for lo, it made us equal to the apes.

And I am equal to the apes, for I am a killer, and justify killing . . .

Yet lo, as the murders commence, Celery tugs me away, for Bo is in the wreckage of this place, in the so-called "residence" where he did once frolic.

And rather than find him leading a pack howl of victory, I see anguish, and I fall in anguish.

For lo, he drags the starry and striped cloth, yellowed by more blood, and it is as a litter for my Sunny, and I leap to her side.

"My death is nigh," she tells me as I lick her and whimper. "And with me, goes any chance for you to sire our children, and such grieves me most. Though if I die here in my old den where I frolicked with they called Sasha and Malia, with you near, that takes some pain away."

"But you were a slave here . . . you and our Deliverer . . ."

Verily, I say unto you that at her end she is looking to her brother, not me.

Lo, he nods at her passing, thence to me, and he says unto me with all grief and loss hid inside him, "We cannot settle for things as they are. *We have to have the courage to remake the world as it should be.*" He licks me. "They are beaten but not gone. The ones who remain, in their blind shock, will lash out at each other, not us. They will finish what the Scourge started. You will see devilish tails glow and rise in the night sky, and fall the next day, in dread mushrooms of fire and storm and poison. And for many matings there will be only night, and little food. It is up to you, therefore, to lead We Who Belong to Each Other, across to a new life, and keep them safe, and give them my law until they can run on the grass when it grows again.

"Whither shall we go without you?" I ask.

"Look to the Dome, yonder," he answers.

Yea, my eyes and tongue confirm what I scent. My Lord, my friend, is pierced with shrapnel, and he yet led us and fought his way into this place, and nosed his broken sister onto the cloth as litter, and now, noses her from it, for she has been rubbed out.

And I bid my lieutenants who would become the first Scars to take up the cloth and bear it away and bring a new litter made from the bed and window covers, and I beseech Bo to lay upon it, so we may bear him away for healing.

Lo, he refuses and guards my love's body and I cannot endure the sight of that.

"We shall perish without you!"

"Nay," he wheezes, lungs deflating. "You shall live in dignity, and without hate and meanness, as my . . ." He suddenly lolls his head, ". . . *human*, the father of the princesses who loved me once entreated, and humanity faltered and did not listen."

"And if . . . I falter? If I sin, even for the greater good?"

"I sinned by calling people 'apes,' and I did so only to steel you, and suffer you unto me as bees to a hive, thence we swarmed and stung. It was a base thing I did. Lo, when you sin, then think of me, and Sunny, but not as base, but at our best. For there shall be a reckoning as with us now, and you shall offer of yourself, and you shall be redeemed and lauded. Yea, she shall love you again, and I shall frolic with you and teach you as we were young . . ."

And verily I say unto you, such was his last charge to me.

And now my heart sinks into the sand, and withers in the Eternal Fire, and lo, the pups are hushed and their tongues are dry and their eyes wide, and all are hushed in the dark beyond the fire and in their dens and in the ranks of the Scars and the ranks of the juveniles.

Yea, the little female who first spoke crawls to me, and licks my snout and beams at my old and ugly and vicious one-eyed face, "Do not despair. For the Scourge did not indeed change us, and Bo if I may say his name, would say it of course coaxed out what was good in us, as we captured what was good in them, these humans, these people who made hope and not reproach."

And to this tiny thing I say, "I have done dark and inclement things. I have denied what I have just told you, and condemned those who knew the truth with apostasy. And such is my apostasy. I am no better than the worst human . . ."

Lo, the pup licks me, and others come unto me squealing and barking and lick me, so. And this I do not deserve. Yet I am lifted, for it betides hope. And it betides my last act.

"Heed and you shall renounce, as he, called Bo, did, that all apes were slavers . . ."

And I nod and suffer the Scars and juveniles alike to come take off the pups, and I suffer their parents to come into the light as many as can fit round the Dome up, soaring, till we are tiny as ants. And life begins to wane from me though my voice waxes, and lo, I give my charge unto them, with the bark mine when I was young.

"Behold, this *flag* has borne witness to the good and evil come before," I say, "and the noblesse of my Bo. It shall be therefore a witness unto you, and you shall keep it."

And with that, the juveniles unwrap the cloth and bear it away in sadness. And the Scars stand, confused by such sadness, and verily, I give them my decree, and they circle and whine and bark in sadness and fury. Yea, I do growl.

And they are to bite upon me, and sanctify me.

And the juvenile bitches are to apportion me to the pups.

And the pups shall eat of me.

And then I am to be apportioned to the rest, until not even marrow is left.

And then all will elect a leader, and the leader shall lead We Who Belong to Each Other from the Dome, to a place of air and light.

Lo, I call back the female pup, and I anoint her with my tongue, and before I am bit, I say unto all, "When the leader dies or can lead no more, this bitch who is small, once grown shall lead and be the mother of all, in the grass and sun, and you shall be 'Sunny.'"

And with that I close my eye and she does not whimper. And am so bit.

Yea, I raise my tail while lunging downward, for I am a pup, and Bo is noble, strong, and seasoned, and yet he takes my invitation to play. And we frolic, content.

Amen.

AT THE CONGLOMEROID COCKTAIL PARTY

BY ROBERT SILVERBERG

I AM CONTEMPORARY. I AM conglomeroid. I am post-causal, contra-linear, pepto-modern. To be anything else is to be dead, nezpah? Is to be a fossil. A sense of infinite potential and a stance of infinite readiness: that's the right philosophy for our recombinant era. Alert to all possibilities, holding oneself always in an existentially pliant posture.

So when quasi-cousin Spinifex called and said, "Come to my fetus-party tonight," I accepted unhesitatingly. Spinifex lives in Wongamoola on the slopes of the Dandenongs, looking across into Melbourne. I happened to be in Gondar on my way to Lalibela when his call came. "Mortissa and I have a new embryo," said Spinifex. "We want everyone to help us engineer it. There'll be a contest for the best design. The whole crowd's coming, and some new people." *Some new people.* Could I resist? It's not such a big deal to go from Ethiopia to Australia for a fetus-party. Two hours, with transfers. I was on the pop-chute in half a flick. Pop to Addis, pop to Delhi, pop to Singapore, pop to Melbourne, pop pop pop pop and I was there. *Some new people.* Irresistible. That was the night I met Domitilla.

Spinifex and Mortissa live in a great golden egg on jeweled stilts, with oscillator windows and three captive rainbows moored overhead. In his current Shaping, Spinifex is aquatic, a big jolly blue dolphinoid with spangled red flukes, and spends most of his time in his moat. Mortissa's latest Shaping is more traditionally conglomeroid, no single identifiable style, a bit of tapir and a bit of giraffe and some very high-precision machine-tooled laminations, altogether elegant. I blew kisses to them both.

About thirty guests had already arrived. I knew most of them. There was Hapshash in his ten-year-old Shaping, the carpeted look, last word in splendor then. Negresca still in her tortoise-cum-chinchilla, and Holy Mary looking sublime in the gilded tubular body that becomes her so well. There is a tendency among the ultra-elite to keep the same Shaping longer and longer, with Hapshash the outstanding example of that. At first I thought it was a sign of the recent economic dreariness, but lately I was coming to understand it as a significant underground trend: out of fashion is height of fashion. That sort of thing requires one to stay really aware. When Melanoleum came slithering up to me, she asked me at once how I liked her new Shaping. She looked exactly as she had the last time, a year ago at the big potlatch in Joburg—tendrils, iridescence, lateral oculars, high-spectrum pulse-nodes. For an instant I was baffled, and I came close to telling her I had already seen this Shaping, and then I caught on, comprehending that she had just had herself Shaped *exactly like her last Shaping,* which carried Hapshash's gambit to the next level of subtlety, and I hugged her with all my arms and said, "It's brilliant, love, it's devastating!"

"I knew you'd pick up," she said. "Have you seen the fetus?"

"I just got here."

"Up there. In the globe."

"Ah. Beautiful!"

They had rigged a crystalline sphere in a gravity-candle's beam, so that it hovered twenty feet above the cocktail altar, and in it the new fetus solemnly swam in a phosphorescent green fluid. It was, I suppose, eleven or twelve weeks old, a little alien-looking fish with a big furrowed forehead, altogether weird but completely normal, a standard human fetus with no genetic reprogramming at all. Prenatal engineering is too terribly tacky for people like Mortissa and Spinifex, naturally. Let the standard folk do that, going to the cheapjack helixers to get their off-springs' clubfeet and sloping chins and bandy legs cleaned up ahead of time, so that they can look just like everybody else when they come squirting out of the womb. That's not our way.

Melanoleum said, "The design contest starts in half an hour. Do you have a good one ready?"

"I expect to. What's the prize?"

"A month with anyone at the party," she said. "Do you know Domitilla?"

I had heard of her, naturally—last season's hot debutante, making the party circuit from San Francisco to the Seychelles. But I had been going the other way last season. Suddenly she was at my elbow, a dazzling child in a blaze of cold blue fire. It was her only garment, and under that chilly radiance I saw a slim furry form, five small breasts, sleek muscular thighs, vertebrae elongated to form the underpinning for a webbed sail down her back—an inspired conglomeroid of wolverine and dinosaur. My hearts thundered and my lymph congealed. She noted instantly the power she had over me, and her fiery cloak flared to double volume, a dazzling nimbus that briefly enfolded me and dizzied me with the scent of ozone. She was no more than nineteen, and I was ninety-three, existentially pliant, ready to be overwhelmed. I congratulated her on her ingenuity.

"My fifth Shaping," she said. "I'll be getting a new one soon, I think."

"Your *fifth*?" I considered Hapshash and Negresca and Holy Mary, trendily clinging to their old bodies. "So quickly? Don't. This one is extraordinary."

"I know," she said. "That's why it's time for a new one. Oh, look, the fetus is trying to get born!"

Indeed the little pseudo-fish that my quasi-cousins had conceived was making violent but futile efforts to escape its gleaming tank. We applauded. The servants took that as their signal to come among us with hors d'oeuvres: five standard humans, big and stupid and docile, bearing glittering food-fabrics on platinum trays. We did our dainty best; the trays were bare in no time and back came the standards with a second round, caviars of at least a dozen creatures and sweetmeats and tiny cocktail-globules to rub on our tongues and all the rest. And then Spinifex heaved himself out of the moat with a great jovial flapping of flippers that splashed everyone, and a beveled screen descended and hovered in midair and it was time for the contest. Domitilla was still at my side.

"I've heard about you," she said in a voice like shaggy wine. "I thought I'd meet you at the moon-party. Why weren't you there?"

"I never go there," I said.

"Oh. Of course. Do you know who's going to win the contest?"

"Is it rigged?"

"Aren't they all?" she asked. "*I* know who." She laughed.

Mortissa was on the podium under merciless spotlights that her new Shaping reflected flawlessly. She explained the contest. We were to draw lots and each in turn seize the control-stick and project on the screen our image of what the new child should look like. Judging would be automatic: the design that elicited the greatest amazement would win, and the winner was entitled to choose as companion for a month any of the rest of us. There were two provisos: Spinifex and Mortissa would not be bound to use the winning design if they deemed it life-threatening in any way, and none of the designs could be used by the contestants for future Shapings of their own. The lots were drawn and we took our turns: Hapshash, Melanoleum, Mandragora, Peachbloom, Hannibal—

The designs ranged from brilliant to merely clever. Hapshash proposed a sort of jeweled amoeba; Peachbloom conjured up a hybrid Spinifex-Mortissa, half dolphin, half machine;

Melanoleum's concept was out of the Greek myths, Medusa hair and Poseidon tail; my onetime para-wife Nullamar invented a geometrical shape, rigid and complex, that gave us all headaches; and my own contribution, entirely improvised, involved two slender tapering shells that parted to reveal a delicate and sinuous being, virtually translucent. I was surprised at my own inspiration and felt instant regret for having thrown away something so beautiful that I might well have worn myself someday. It caused a stir and I suspected I would win, and I knew who I would choose as my prize. What, I wondered, did Domitilla have as her entry? I glanced toward her and smiled, and she returned the smile with an airy rippling of her flaming cloak.

The contest went on and on. Hungering for victory, I grew tense, apprehensive, gloomy, despondent. Candelabra's design was spectacular, and Mingimang's was fascinatingly perplexing, and Vishnu's was awesomely cunning. Some, indeed, seemed almost beyond the capacity of contemporary genetic engineering to accomplish. I saw no hope of winning, and my month with Domitilla seemed in jeopardy. Her own turn came last. She took the podium, grasped the stick, closed her eyes, sent her thought-projection to the screen with an intensity of effort that turned her fiery mantle bright yellow and sent it arching out to expose her blue-black furry nakedness.

On the screen a standard human form appeared.

Not quite standard, for it was hermaphrodite, round rosy-nippled breasts above and male genitals below. Yet it was the old basic body other than that, the traditional pre-Shaping shape, used now only by the unfortunate billions of the serving classes. I gasped, and I was not alone. It's no easy thing to amaze a group so worldly as we, but we were transfixed with amazement, dumbstruck by Domitilla's bizarre notion. Was she mocking us? Was she merely naïve? Or was she so far beyond our level of sophistication that we couldn't comprehend her motives? Trays clattered to the ground, drinks were spilled, we coughed and wheezed and muttered. The meters that were judging the contest whirled and flashed. No doubt of the winner: Domitilla had plainly provoked the most intense surprise, and that was the criterion. The party was at the edge of scandal. But Mortissa was equal to the moment.

"The winner, of course, is Domitilla," she said calmly. "We salute her for the audacity of her design. But my husband and I regard it as hazardous to the life of our child to give it the standard form for its first Shaping because of the possibility of misunderstanding by its playmates, and so we invoke our right to choose another entry, and we select that of our quasi-cousin Sandalphon, so remarkable for its combination of subtlety and strength."

"Well done!" Melanoleum called, and I did not know whether she was cheering Mortissa for her astuteness or Domitilla for her boldness or me for the beauty of my design. "Well done!" cried Vishnu, and Candelabra and Hannibal took it up, and the tensions of the party dissolved into a kind of forced jubilation that swiftly became the real thing.

"The prize!" someone shouted. "Who's the prize?"

Spinifex thumped his huge fins. "The prize! The prize!"

Mortissa beckoned to Domitilla. She stepped forward, small and fragile-looking but not in the least vulnerable, and said in a clear, cool voice, "I choose Sandalphon."

We left the party within the hour and popped to San Francisco, where Domitilla lived alone in a spherical pod of a house suspended by spider-cables a mile above the bay.

I had my wish. And yet she frightened me, and I don't frighten easily.

Her fiery mantle engulfed me. She was nineteen, I was ninety-three, and she ruled me. In that frosty blue radiance I was helpless. Five Shapings, and only nineteen? Her eyes were narrow and cat-yellow, and there were worlds of strangeness in them that made me feel like a mud-flecked peasant. "The famous Sandalphon," she whispered. "Would you have picked me if you had won? Yes, I know you would. It was all over your face. How long have you had this Shaping?"

"Four years."

"Time for a new one."

I started to say that Hapshash and the other leaders of our set were traveling in the other direction, that the fashionable thing was to keep one's old Shaping; but that seemed idiocy to me now as I lay in her arms with her dense harsh fur rubbing my scales. She was the new thing, the terrifying, inexorable voice of the dawning day, and what did our modes matter to her? We made love, my worlds of experience against her tigerish youthful vitality, and there, at least, I think I matched her stroke for stroke. Afterward she showed me holograms of her first four Shapings. One by one her earlier selves stepped from the projector and pirouetted before me: the form her parents had given her that she had kept for nine years, and then the second Shaping that one always tends to cling to through puberty, and the two of her adolescence. They were true conglomeroid Shapes, a blending of images out of all the biological spectrum, a bit of butterfly and a bit of squid, a tinge of reptile and a hint of insect, the usual genetic fantasia that our kind adores, but a common thread bound them all, and her current Shape as well. That was the compactness of her body, the taut narrowness of her slender frame, powerful but minimal, like some agile little carnivore, mink or mongoose or marten. When we redesign ourselves, we can be any size we like, whale-mighty or cat-small, within certain basic limitations imposed by the need to house a human-sized brain in the frame that the gene-splicers build for us; but Domitilla had opted always to construct her fantasies on the splendid little armature with which she had come into the world. That too was ominous. It spoke of a persistence, a self-sufficiency, that is not common.

"Which of them do you like best?" she asked, when I had seen them all.

I stroked her strong smooth thighs, "This one. How tight your fur lies against your skin! How beautiful the sail is on your back! You've brought out your deepest self."

"How would you know my deepest self after two hours?"

"Don't underestimate me." I touched my lips to hers. "Part hunting-cat, part dinosaur—the metaphor's perfect."

"Let's make love again. Then we'll pop to Jerusalem."

"All right."

"And then Tibet."

"Certainly."

"And Baltimore."

"Baltimore?"

"Why not?" she said. "Hold me tighter. Yes. Yes."

"Do I get only a month with you?"

"Thirty days. Those were the terms of the contest."

"Do you always abide by terms?"

"Always," she said.

We popped to Jerusalem at dawn, and then to Tibet, and then, yes, to Baltimore. And many more places in the thirty days. She was trying to exhaust me, thinking that nineteen has some superiority over ninety-three, but there, at least, she had misjudged things; at each Shaping we are renewed, you know. I loved her beyond measure, though she terrified me. What did I fear? What does anyone fear most? That in a vulnerable moment someone will say, "I understand what a fraud you are: I have seen all your facades fall away: I know the truth about you." I would not say such a thing to Melanoleum, nor Nullamar to me, nor any of us to any of us, but yet I felt Domitilla wouldn't hesitate to flay me down to the core beneath the Shapings if that suited her whim, and I lived in dread of that, and I always will.

On the thirtieth day she said goodbye.

"Please," I said. "Another week."

"Those were the terms."

"Even so."

"If we refuse to honor contracts, all society collapses."

"Have I bored you?" Foolish question, inviting destruction.

"Not nearly as much as I thought you would," she replied, and I loved her for it, having expected worse. "But I have other things to do. My new Shaping, Sandalphon."

"You won't. What you are now is too beautiful to discard."

"What I will be next will surpass it."

"I beg you—stay as you are a little longer."

"I undergo engineering tomorrow at dawn," she said, "at the gene-surgery in Katmandu."

Arguing with her was hopeless. We had our last night, a night of miracles, and while I slept she vanished, and the walls of the world fell in on me. I hurried out to my friends, and was house-guest in turn with Nullamar and Mandragora and Melanoleum and Candelabra, and not one of them said the name of Domitilla to me, and at the end of the year I went to Spinifex and Mortissa to admire the new child in the graceful shell of my happy design-ing, and then, despondent, I popped to Katmandu. All year long a new Domitilla had been emerging from the altered genetic material of the previous one, and now her Shaping was nearly complete. They wouldn't let me see her, but they sent messages in, and she agreed to my request to have dinner with her on the day of her coming-forth. That was still a month away. I could have gone anywhere in the world, but I stayed in Katmandu, staring at the mountains, thinking that my month of Domitilla had gone by in a flick and this month of waiting was taking an eternity; and then it was the day.

The inner door opened and nurses came out, standard humans, and an orderly or two and then the surgeon and then Domitilla. I recognized her at once, the same wiry armature as ever. The new body she wore was the one she had designed for the child of Spinifex and Mortissa. A standard human frame, mortifyingly human, the body of a servant, of a hewer of wood and drawer of water, except that it glowed with the inner fire that burned in Domitilla and that no member of the lower orders could conceivably have. And she was different from the standards in another way, for she was naked, and she had used the hermaphrodite design, breasts above, male organs below. I felt as if I had been kicked; I wanted to clutch my gut and double over. Her eyes gleamed.

"Do you like it?" she asked, mocking me.

I was unable to look. I turned and tried to run, but she called after me, "Wait, Sandalphon!"

Trembling, I halted. "What do you want?"

"Tell me if you like it?"

"The terms of the contest bound you not to use any of the designs," I said bitterly. "You claimed always to abide by terms."

"Always. Except when I choose not to." She spread her arms. "What do you think? Tell me you like it and I'm yours for tonight!"

"Never, Domitilla."

She touched her groin. "Because of *this*?"

"Because of you," I said. I shivered. "How could you do it? A standard, Domitilla. A *standard*!"

"You poor old fool," she said.

Again I turned, and this time she let me go. I traveled to Madagascar and Turkey and Greenland and Bulgaria, and her images blazed in my mind, the wolverine-girl I had loved and the grotesque thing she had become. Gradually the pain grew less. I went in for a new Shaping, despite Hapshash and his coterie, and came out simpler, more sleek, less conglomeroid. I felt better, then. I was recovering from her.

A year went by. At a party in Oaxaca I told the story, finally, to Melanoleum, stunning in her new streamlined form. "If I had it all to do over, I would," I said. "One has to remain in an existentially pliant posture, of course. One must keep alert to all possibilities. And so I have no regrets. But yet—but yet—she hurt me so badly, love—"

"Look over there," said Melanoleum.

I followed her glance, past Hapshash and Mandragora and Negresca, to the slender, taut-bodied stranger scooping fish from the pond: beetle-wings, black and yellow, luminescent spots glowing on thighs and forearms, cat-whiskers, needle-sharp fangs. She looked toward me and our eyes met, a contact that seared me, and she laughed and her laughter shriveled me with post-causal mockery, contra-linear scorn. In front of them all she destroyed me. I fled. I am fleeing still. I may flee her forever.

DEEP STATE
BY DÉSIRÉE ZAMORANO

May 2016

THIS IS THE WAY THE world pivots and then tilts, on thirteen true or false questions, thought Mika Casas.

In her fourteenth-floor office in the prominent and imposing Spanish Colonial building, Mika had been processing the national answers to thirteen very precise questions since March 2015. Running the data, again and again, like a fortune teller reshuffling the cards in hopes of a different response, the data kept affirming precisely what she did not want to believe: the former Secretary of State would lose the presidential election.

From her office she could scan the arroyo, the massive Rose Bowl to the north, the meandering footpaths and dry riverbed to the south. Occasionally, less frequently than before, the San Gabriels were smothered in snow pack, while she caught the shimmering horizon edged out by Catalina Island. Some would call it a commanding view; she considered it a far-reaching view. She considered the millions of lives contained in this landscape; the responsibility of their lives was an honor, never a burden.

If you did not know who Mika Casas was, chances were, if you passed her in the corridor of the Ninth Circuit of Appeals, outside her office, or walked past her on a side street off of Colorado Boulevard in Pasadena, she wouldn't register in your mind at all. If she did, and you had taken three to five seconds to record her presence, you would have noticed fashionable but comfortable shoes, clothing that appeared simultaneously stylish and timeless, hair styled impeccably. You then promptly forgot who you had just seen.

Not that she was unassuming; she was simply a brown woman of a certain age whose power was known to the limited few. Her younger sister, Shirl, for example, was constantly running investigative efforts designed by Mika to prevent some impending disaster in the Philippines, or quell a possible outrage that might bubble over into turmoil in Tunisia.

This was a time to call her sister, to bring her home from her assignment in Peru. There was work to be done, and there was a sliver, a glimmer that they had a chance.

* * *

June 2016
ONCE THE PRESIDENT HAD RECEIVED her memo with its recommended next steps, he did her the courtesy of calling her directly.

The almost playful timbre of his voice got Mika in the knees every time, but like that song when ". . . meeting the man of your dreams, then meeting his beautiful wife."

"Mika," he said. "You know I respect you and your work deeply. But we've got our own team over here, doing the numbers, and they tell a very different story."

Mika closed her eyes. How could such a brilliant man not see the future that lay ahead?

"I cannot, will not, taint this vituperative election and find ourselves being accused of playing politics with intel. I respect the American people too much for that. I'm calling you because I wanted to be clear with you. I don't want you to think my feelings of respect and admiration for you are in any way diminished. I hope you understand. I've always felt you were 100 percent with me, and on the right side of history."

Mika thanked the president, hung up and reflected.

Black ops, white ops, Mika internally referred to this section as Brown Ops. She recalled the lessons she had learned watching Oliver North, Caspar Weinberger, but particularly that demon from a George Orwell novel, John Poindexter. She had watched, as a high school student, and internalized the message: you needed a wall between the president and his actions. This way you ensured plausible deniability in perpetuity.

Yes, the wall had come down. It had once been morning in America.

Now it was dusk, and she had to draw up the plans on her own.

* * *

July 2016

SHIRL THOUGHT BACK TO THE last time she had seen her sister.

Two years ago Mika had shown her off, proudly, to a tiny man who lived in the heart of the Pentagon.

They were led by an African American woman in her crisp formal-service military uniform through the corridors of the office lit-building. The escort paused to rap on a door. She opened it and pointed them inside.

The room, compared to the corridor, was vast, poorly lit, walls painted deep green ("I call it the original Supreme Court green," he joked later), the windows shrouded by maroon curtains, closing off any daylight.

"You two," he said, a wry smile forming on only half of his face. "You did it, my dears," his smile was filled with pride, admiration, and the grasp of his gnarled hand was dry, warm, and welcoming.

It wouldn't be in the papers. There would be no formal acknowledgment. But between her and Mika they had saved thousands of lives and ensured the work of a cadre of lawyers fighting Russian oligarchs.

"Your brains, her access." Flippantly Shirl tilted her head to her sister. "I just had to make sure we didn't fuck it up in Paris."

"Unlike the three before you," he answered, "you didn't."

The two women stood before the shrunken, aged man whose green eyes twinkled as best as ninety-year-old eyes can. "This is for you," he said to Shirl handing her a tiny jewel box. She instantly divined what was inside. She opened it. A pin, no longer than an inch long, with a cunning clasp behind it, in the shape of a tiny sword. Mika wore hers everywhere—it was a signal to those who knew. Maybe, 150 people in the world?

"The Fellowship of Damocles," the gentleman said. "Welcome."

If it had been in her emotional repertoire, she would have leaped and hugged the man in front of her. Instead she dipped her head in profound pleasure.

"Now," he said, "sit down. I want to hear the details of your mission."

She enjoyed the pleasure of the memory of the high point of her life, as the tiny jet alighted on the runway.

* * *

THE TWO OF THEM SAT on an ocean-side veranda in Santa Monica. Shirl was lithe, tall, a flamboyant athlete; Mika had a sedentary build and her burnished *"cara de nopal."* While Mika sat a lot in front of multiple computer screens and reflected, Shirl bounced restlessly from one neatly solved problem to yet another. Rarely did people suspect they were sisters; Mika used their father's name, Shirl preferred Cerradura, their mother's.

As part of a quiet diplomatic effort, Shirl had been called to help sort out an artifact outrage in Peru, where her deep understanding of the Aymara language had proven invaluable.

Mika pondered Shirl, who'd arrived straight from Santa Monica airport, where the military lightweight aircraft had deposited her. She wore slashed white skinny jeans displaying the toned brown muscles underneath, espadrilles, and a turquoise blouse tied just above her lean belly. Shirl first hugged her sister, then draped a spectacularly vibrant wrap around her shoulders.

"A little souvenir for you from the Sacred Valley. Pisac Market, to be precise. Epicenter of my little sojourn."

Shirl had insisted on pisco sours, "a mistake" Mika warned, and she was proven right when Shirl sipped hers, made a face, poured both of them out into the potted palm, waved over the waiter, asked what brandies they had available, chose one, and asked for two sidecars. Mika nodded approvingly.

"It always takes me so long to transition stateside," Shirl said, mocking herself.

"How did it go?"

"Fairly open-and-shut case, Hungarian national feeling entrepreneurial, enlisting locals with promises of returning artifacts to their rightful place, instead selling and shipping them out to museums around the globe. More specifically the British Museum. *La plus ça change . . .*"

Mika raised an eyebrow. "And the Hungarian national?"

"You look disappointed."

"I was secretly routing for Ukrainian—or better, Czech. Where is the Hungarian now?"

"Brought her along, decided to keep her close. Stop with the impure thoughts! I brought her for your questions." Shirl raised her glass, licked the sugared rim. "To the long game, dear sister." They clinked.

Mika watched the clouds obscure the sinking sun. "I'm worried," she said.

Shirl nodded. "As well you should be."

"We have paranoia and fear on one side and anger and incompetence on the other."

"Our goal is simply to be more competent than the opposition."

"If it were simply the two of us there would be no fear."

"You've always been the optimist. You prefer so-called checks and balances while I love brute force."

"Yes, I've met him."

Shirl made a face. "You can't seem to keep your mind out of the gutter."

"You put it there."

"Projection, classic projection, which only happens when—" Shirl put her cocktail glass down. "My god, you're profoundly worried."

Mika had not touched her drink. She looked out to the horizon and shook her head slowly. "I am going to proceed on the premise that the prediction is accurate. That is why I called you home. *Praemonitus, praemunitus.*"

"Why can't you just say 'forewarned is forearmed' like normal people?"

"Because you and I are not normal. And this may well be our last carefree evening for months, years to come."

On November 8th, Shirl called her sister.

Mika picked up. "Stop nagging me and let me do my work."

* * *

January 20, 2017

IF SHE HAD TO BE out of her hometown, Mika would have wanted to be at the Covadonga Cantina in Colonia Roma, alternately sipping tequila and sangrita while devouring papadzules and watching Mexican journalists play dominoes with Mexican politicians.

Instead she was watching what she referred to as DC's Day of the Dead spectacle.

Her operatives were in place, Shirl had seen to that, both of them dropping key words and phrases here and there to the well-positioned in business and finance. It was actually stunning how large and simple their seeding of this incoming staff had been, how facile the interview questions, essentially limited to loyalty with a soupçon of experience to provide some kind of pretense of serious vetting.

Ah, vetting. To be the country the dreamers dreamed.

The Korean on her left with a tiny silver dagger on his lapel said, "I see things are starting out well."

She shook her head, "Better than we expected. The denials, the shrill statements to the press, the party over country."

"Not me."

"Present company excepted."

"Are you having doubts?" he said.

"No, that's just the data hangover on my face. You know what's happening with the intelligence committee, it's just a matter of time."

Her companion shook his head. "Reagan was the Teflon president, this guy—"

She interrupted, "Slick as sewage."

He made a face.

"When's your committee meeting?" she asked.

"Tomorrow."

"You'll be bringing her in?"

A swift nod.

"And then?"

"If they don't trust the word of your sister, I think that in itself is grounds to charge them with treason and sedition."

Mika returned to California that evening.

* * *

July 2017

THE TREASON CHARGES WERE NEVER brought.

Measures and countermeasures were Mika's terms of art. She loved the subtlety and nuance of international politics, the possible positive profound impact on a populace, and the honorable clash of perspectives and intellect while building toward shared goals.

Yet the provincialism, isolationism, and willful stupidity of the people she now encountered, holding power in a country that at one time been the beacon of the free world. Okay, exaggeration, a country whose aspirations had been to be the beacon of light and enlightenment. Mika, now a confirmed atheist, had loved, respected, and admired many people of faith throughout her lifetime. And now it appeared the only ones who made the news bites were bungling buffoons who barely concealed their misogyny and Islamophobia bchind their King James versions of the Bible.

Opinions without nuance, decisions without evidence, actions without research.

But why did she think it should be any different? Perhaps the anomaly was the culture she had become accustomed to: a structure of evidence, a respect for intellectual and research.

Now was a regression to the mean. Maybe that was what they would call this time in the US, like after the Civil War a double down on the exclusions of former slaves, until it became known as "The Nadir."

She was, she admitted, wavering between bitterness and hopelessness. That was not acceptable. One down. She had three plays left. She would see what news Shirl brought.

* * *

IN THE HISTORIC SECTION OF downtown Los Angeles, Shirl slipped down an alleyway, rapped at a door. One glance at her pin and the door opened.

Mika was already seated at a red leather booth, in the mahogany wood club dedicated to Fellows of Damocles.

"How many of us aren't 'fellows'?" Shirl asked, scooting in.

Mika shrugged. "Twenty, I believe."

Shirl ordered a Linie Aquavit in honor of her recent trip to Oslo.

Mika examined the waiter: "How do you store it?"

"In the freezer, of course."

"Bring us the half-liter bottle." She glanced at Shirl. "Oh, the hell with it, the liter bottle."

Mika only trusted face-to-face communication. Too familiar

with lines of surveillance, all conversations of worth were held in the flesh.

"How was this trip?"

Shirl shook her head. "I'm glad you ordered the large bottle. No cooperation promised at all."

Mika gasped, "I didn't think it could be as bad as this, I hadn't anticipated—"

Mika stopped herself. Although she knew the waitstaff was impeccable, highly credentialed, and exceptionally well paid, she said nothing as the waiter arrived. With a flourish he set down the silver tray, displayed the liter bottle embedded in a block of ice. Within the ice were trapped decorative sprays of rosemary, basil, and wildflower. He filled the two small cordial glasses in front of them and bobbed his head.

"What about an order of blini and caviar?" Shirl said.

Mika glared at her. "Nothing even hinting of Russia will ever pass my lips until this is all sorted out."

Shirl smiled.

"Honestly," Mika said, "I'm not hungry. Order what you like."

Shirl ordered, the waiter left, Mika continued. "This is terrible news. This was the ally I was certain of. If I've made a mistake here, now I'm worried I've completely miscalculated. How is our Hungarian?"

"A slow hiss of leak, completely deflated."

Three of her four options down.

The waiter brought out two open-faced salmon sandwiches on rye, showered in pickled red onions and capers. Mika forgot that she had no appetite, and took a deep and satisfying bite, even better cut with the crisp and explosive Norwegian alcohol.

Shirl poured, and took a bite of her own. "Nils sends his regards."

Mika shrugged. "I don't think I could even pick him out of a crowd."

Shirl laughed. "You never recognize your own tell. You make a lousy liar."

"I have vowed to replace the word liar with the phrase Commander in Chief."

After many small glasses of aquavit and another order of sandwiches, Mika said, "I have one last option. But you're going to have to trust me."

Shirl glared at her sister. "You're telling me this halfway through a bottle of 100 proof spirits? You think I've forgotten the last time you told me not to worry my pretty little head? Paris. Ten years ago."

Mika shrugged as if to say this was long ago, far away, forgotten.

"Yes, yes, yes, and that's the reason both of us can dine in this club—"

"Stop trying to change the subject. I remember sitting at a Jewish deli at Place de Wagram. You kept ordering more chopped liver right before we were almost dead."

"The entire point being almost. A minor misunderstanding with Yaakov of the Mossad. It's been sorted out. We're here to tell the tale."

"Every time I think of those *bola de pendejos*—and you, sitting there, eating the damned chopped liver like you had ice in your veins."

Mika tipped her head in acknowledgment of the compliment. "We saved so many, and we're here today."

Shirl snorted. "That was not what I was furious about. We both know one day we're going to walk into a situation out of which we will never emerge. That's what makes every passing day so sweet." Shirl upended her crystal thimble of booze down her throat and helped herself to more. "What infuriates me to this day is that you were unwilling to take me into your confidence. Talk about a flashback to childhood." She shook her head bitterly.

Mika regretted the too-large bottle of booze; Shirl had the capacity to take a wrong turn from giddy to nasty drunk.

As if deducing her sister's thoughts, Shirl said, "No, it's not the

Aquavit talking. This is me, your sister. And if you don't let me in on the entire machinations, you may as well enlist—shit. I don't know who. Anybody but me."

The intensity of the glare between the two women radiated throughout the paneled lounge and rebuffed the approaching waiter.

A deep and heavy sigh emerged from Mika. "All right. As they say in the current vernacular, 'my bad.' Let us order dinner," she waved the disappearing waiter over. "I shall tell you what I know."

* * *

September 2017

MIKA AND SHIRL STOOD IN the lobby staring up at the ceiling.

"If only money could buy you taste," Shirl said. Mika elbowed her.

By their side a young man stood with their cart of Louis Vuitton luggage—props stuffed with filler. By nature the two women traveled light; the luggage was courtesy of Mika's department's discretionary funds.

"When did you buy the membership here?"

"When I crunched the numbers."

Shirl shook her head at her sister's inestimable foresight.

"I bought a membership at each and every one. I've sold them at a profit. I kept this one, for reasons you well know."

There were Secret Service men in the lobby, as relaxed and casual as was possible to be in a three-piece suit covering a bulletproof vest and a shoulder harness in Florida's muggy September. Three of them stood alert, with no hint of recognition of the two women, no glance at the tiny pin both of them wore.

Mika spread her hand in front of her to examine her nails. "I don't see our friend here yet," she said, and proceeded to the counter. "He may be in a different part of the resort."

At their suite Mika tipped the young man ten dollars.

On the balcony the two women sipped sparkling water, tapped at their electronic devices, and occasionally glanced at the activity at the pool below.

"Looks like they've tightened their network access, but only just," Mika said, tapping away.

A rap at the door.

"I'll get it," Mika insisted.

The porter brought an envelope.

After reading it Mika said, "Let's go to the bar."

On their way down Shirl shivered against the gilt and elaborate decorative wood carvings. She said, "What is the point of these places?"

"To play pretend," Mika said as they stepped into the bar.

To the barkeep Mika said, "Roy Rogers for me. And a Shirley Temple for my sister."

"Classy. I hate it when you order for me," Shirl growled.

"Let's take these to the patio," Mika said.

"What for? The humidity?"

Shirl would have recognized Yaakov even if she hadn't known he'd been there. The deep black hair was now predominantly gray, but the fierce pride of his sun-burnished face remained.

"You dropped your coaster," he said, with the very slightest trace of an Israeli accent.

Mika thanked him and headed toward a patio table. "I so do love sitting poolside," Mika trilled in a syrupy voice that almost made Shirl gag. They spent twenty minutes sipping their drinks and performing as tourists, discussing shopping excursions and massage permutations until, gratefully, thought Shirl, they headed back to their room.

In the elevator Mika passed the coaster to Shirl. "Lovely souvenir, don't you think?"

Time and coordinates—all neatly printed in Hebrew calendar numerals.

Shirl said, "Nice touch," in grudging admiration.

Outside on their balcony Mika whispered low, "Who would have known privatizing his security detail would be such a boon to us?"

"I have a feeling you did, which was why you gave no argument," Shirl responded.

Mika yawned. "I am going to take a nap."

"How can you sleep? This may be our very last day."

"If it is, I want to be well rested in order to savor every moment."

At the time Yaakov had indicated, 12:30 a.m., she and Mika silently walked through an empty corridor. He had arranged for the security detail to be briefly occupied elsewhere. Mika punched in the security code he had given them and they entered the first family's inner compound.

Wordlessly they padded down the hallway, past one door on the right, made a left at the intersection, and walked through into the second door on the left, per his instructions.

A dimly lit recreation room. Five large screens, one mounted inside an entertainment console, two hanging from the wall, momentarily blank.

The women nodded at each other then separated.

Shirl practiced her Vipassana meditation as she waited.

After more than an hour Mika felt kernels of concern. They would never again have this opportunity. Months of elaborate planning, months and years of just the right alliances, the right word, demolished by erratic unpredictable behavior.

This was the very last of her plans. There was nothing after this. It was counter to all of her training to have no plans to fall back upon, should this one fail.

She had been so certain.

They both heard the door whoosh open; the lighting illuminated. The massive figure in a bathrobe loosely tied set himself down heavily on the sectional, and brought up multiple screens.

Each one of them broadcast Mika Casa's face.

"What the—" he muttered as he pushed furiously at the remote.

"Welcome, Mr. President," came Mika's cool and elegant voice from each of the screens. "Thank you for joining us here this evening."

"What the—" he repeated, pushing himself up off of the sectional.

Shirl stepped into his field of vision, pointing the Walther at him.

"Sit," she said.

"Anthony! Anthony!" he bellowed.

"There is no Anthony outside," she said. "Not for at least the next fifteen minutes. All we are asking is fifteen minutes of your time."

"This is ridiculous. This is outrageous. You know what I can do to you? I'm not going to sit here and take this . . ."

"Sit. I don't want to get violent."

He grimaced and sank uneasily onto the sectional.

"You have no idea what's going to happen to you next."

"Actually, I do. Now pay attention."

On the screens Mika's expressive face spent five minutes laying out all of her findings from her past two years of investigation. The money laundering, the real estate fraud, the detailed conflicts of interest, the collusion. She displayed sealed court documents which she promised to leak, his divorce settlements, his financial worth, his failed businesses, his outstanding debts, his leveraged properties in Belarus, the Ukraine, Moscow.

Shirl watched as his scowl deepened.

He said, "Nobody gives a damn."

The screens went blank. Mika stepped out and continued, "Walk away. Walk away, Mr. President, to spend time with your new grandchild, to shave your handicap, to devote time to your businesses. Walk away. Otherwise I will release everything I have."

Angry and irritated he stood and headed toward the door.

"I'm not putting up with either of you telling me what to do."

Shirl, unflappable, "Stay where you are."

"You can't tell me what to do, I am the President of the United States."

They had three minutes left. He kept coming for Shirl and the door.

Shirl weighed her options. Then her position. She made her call. She took her shot.

The president began hurling obscenities.

"Don't get so close to him," Mika said. "No, no, look out, you've dropped your gun!" she shouted.

And so Shirl had, in her hurry and concern for his wound, her Walther had scuttered six inches away from him.

The president picked it up and looked at them both. "I'm telling you two—"

"No, Mika!"

Mika had raised her weapon against him. "Put it down," she commanded.

"I told you, I'm the President of the United States, not you."

"I will shoot," Mika said.

"No, no!" Shirl screamed.

The president shot at Mika. Shirl watched a bloom of red spread across her sister's chest.

"Mika!" Shirl shrieked, yet frozen, watched as he lifted the weapon in her direction and fired it twice.

Before she hit the floor Shirl wondered if Yaakov would wear a tiny silver dagger.

✦ ✦ ✦

November 2017

THE FAMILIAR FACE WAS HOLDING a highly anticipated interview. Fox, the favorite child, had been rewarded for its loyalty with an exclusive.

Sean Hannity shared a split screen with the familiar face, energized and expressive, but with an unfamiliar hairstyle above an oddly pale shade of orange.

"You look very healthy and happy, Mr. President."

"I am Sean, I am. It's wonderful to be able to tell the full story at last."

"I am grateful, Mr. President, that you are here to tell it, unedited, for our viewers. So let's get to it. Could you walk us through that fateful Saturday night in September? Take your time. We have as much time as you need."

The president's face filled the screen.

"You have no idea, Sean, how deep the Deep State is. Now I know. I had always known of course, so many people warned me about it, warned me that they would be coming after me, and then they did. That shouldn't be a surprise to anyone, least of all to me.

"The fact is I found out how deep the Deep State goes that Saturday night. They did me a favor, they exposed themselves to me and to the country. Now let me tell you two women under the guise of a false membership to my country club entered my compound. As you can imagine there is a very detailed investigation underway into my club membership processing. First of all, that never should have happened. Second, to have made their way in to my private compound it is clear the Secret Service had to have colluded. Many people are telling me that that is absolutely correct. Right now we are zeroing in on the person or persons responsible for that outrageous breech of security protocol."

Hannity asked, "So you were attacked by two women?"

"Two women, massive women, huge women, incredibly muscular, maybe they were crazy from too many steroids, I don't know. These women assaulted me, but I fought back."

"And that's how you wounded yourself."

"No, no, no, no, one of them shot me, and I was able to wrestle the gun away from her, and use it against them both."

Hannity allowed a silent pause to fill up the airtime.

Then, "From the transcripts we all know that the weapon had your prints, and that you tested positive for gun residue."

"That's right, absolutely, I shot them, fatally, I think."

"Mr. President, even your own doctor has said your foot wound was self-inflicted."

"Sean, do I look like a gun nut? And he's no longer my doctor. You're missing the real point here. The Deep State has revealed itself. Many people, an unbelievable amount of people, have come up to me and told me they always feared the Deep State, and what happened to me is absolute and final proof. What I want to say—"

"Mr. President, so why do we have no evidence of these wounded women, as you seem to continue to claim?"

"I don't think they're wounded, I think I killed them. And this is what I'm telling you, there is a deep, Deep State in this country, and they're trying to bring me down. I'm not gonna let it happen. Many people are telling me they've known this for years and I am demanding an investigation, in fact I'm appointing a bipartisan committee—"

"But sir," and this time Sean Hannity's voice was uncharacteristically kind and gentle, "As a direct result of your extraordinary claims, you no longer have the authority of a president."

"I know, I know, and that's another case that's going to make its way to the Supreme Court, and many people are telling me that this case is going to blow the Deep State wide open. By the way, I have worked closely with an artist to recreate these women. They will be found."

Under the conversation the chyron streamed, *Exclusive: Sean Hannity speaks to "President" Donald Trump live from the renowned New York Psychiatry Institute.*

Mika changed the channel. "Hey, I'm watching that," Shirl said. Mika changed it back. There were artful representation of two huge muscular women, looking like Soviet shot-putters.

Shirl laughed. "So that's what we looked like to him? Well, looks like we really have nothing to worry about." She picked up another slice of pizza. "That guy Yaakov, high props." She nodded at her sister.

"We Fellows of Damocles get shit done," Mika said. She watched the former president on the screen continue to sputter.

"Part of me feels sorry for the guy." Mika pointed her bottle of beer at the flat screen, then took a long swig.

She turned to her sister and said, "Don't worry, I'll get over it."

I WILL HAUNT YOU
BY ANTHONY NEIL SMITH

CALL ME REAGAN.

Or don't. It's not my name. It's what the captain calls me. He calls all of us after presidents. I'm Reagan, there's also Carter, Eisenhower, Taft, Harding, and Coolidge. And none of us should ever mention Obama. That'll get you thrown overboard.

None of us look or sound like the president he names us after. He just likes the sounds. Maybe in his head he imagines we're all kind of like them. Except Taft is skinny, Eisenhower is a coward, and I'm the youngest.

All of us on *Slayer*, a small shrimp boat (turned "anything" boat) in the nearly barren Gulf of Mexico. The wettest desert in the world, until the Pacific Dead Zone catches up with us. The two things keeping fish and shrimp alive in the Gulf—regulations and common-sense fishing—had been rolled back by the "president" before he'd died of a massive heart attack on the golf course (so we were told. No one ever saw the body), before his son-in-law executed the vice president for treason and took over the Oval Office himself. Even the "president's" sons were on the run these days.

For us, it meant every shrimp boat was out for blood. Oil platforms everywhere, at least every few miles, it seemed. Look in every direction. Just look. You see one off every side, don't you? Most had either been abandoned or blown. Many struck by enemy planes. Some actively leaking into the Gulf, nonstop, for years, because there was no one willing to stop it. Fewer and fewer fish and shrimp. When we found any, they were small.

And if any of the other boats found out you'd found some, so help you god that you could either outrun or outgun them.

Which was why we were all scared out of our minds, barely hydrated and burning to a cancerous crisp on an August morning many, many miles from land when Eisenhower pulled in the nets and gasped.

"Oh no."

We hoped it didn't mean what we thought it meant.

But it did.

We'd hit the motherfucking mother lode.

All this time, at least ten years after I'd started this job, mainly to have a place to sleep and some food to eat (and healthcare. You still needed a job for healthcare) since wages were mostly pointless—incredibly large numbers on our phone screens, meaningless in real life—we'd gotten by on small catches. Handfuls a day. That was life. The captain knew it. All the captains knew it. But we'd all heard of a biomass out there, one that had been moving and growing unmolested the whole decade, that would change the game, at least for a while. Once this biomass was struck upon by some unlucky bastard, the final great haul of the Gulf would be underway, forever lost once it was exhausted, and the war amongst the boats would begin.

We were the unlucky bastards.

I could only scratch the small, recent scar on my arm and think, *Why now? Why us? Why now?*

I mean, look at us. *Slayer* had quite a history already. Our captain had hijacked it from a pier in Biloxi from one of the largest

Vietnamese fishing families in the world—which was like taking on the Mafia. Just *Black Pearl*-ed the damn thing and went bouncing around the coast until he had a full crew, while the bounty on his head climbed higher and higher. We'd survived many a close call, destroyed many a pursuing boat—captured once, tortured as we were towed, but that escape is another story for another day.

Attacked, burned, blown to timbers, and yet we'd patched, painted, and covered the holes with steel plates rummaged from oil platforms, all to keep our floating home, haven, and tomb above the waves. We were invincible.

The captain came down from the wheelhouse to see what had captured his crew's attention so fearfully. And there, in the nets, were infinite squirming shrimps and redfish and flounder and blue crab. An almost Darwinian haul—survival of the fittest, and the fittest had learned to travel together for safety.

"Holy shit."

He instantly took to the rails, peering in all directions, hoping we hadn't been spied.

"You idiots! Dump it, dump it! What are you trying to do to us?"

Odds were we were too late. If Eisenhower would've been paying attention, he would've known the drag was too heavy. He could've dumped the haul via the useless turtle escapes—there were no more turtles in the Gulf, believe me. Instead, he'd been lulled into boredom, safety, and drowsiness. It had been weeks since we'd seen another boat. Months since our last decent haul resulted in fight. We won. We left *Dokken* and its crew sinking under flames, while its sister ship *Cannibal Corpse* ran away, already taking on water.

"Dump it! Dump it!"

A hoarse whisper because of course any slight noise would be picked up by the directional mics that the Vietnamese, the New Orleanians, the Mexicans, the Alt-Whiters, and the African Americans had stowed on the abandoned oil platforms like cell towers. We were a mutt crew—me being Hmong; Harding, black; Eisenhower, Russian; Carter, trans—a one-boat operation in the years when one-boat operations had either been bought out or stomped out, and yet, here we were. The buyers on land kept us secret because we'd deliver better prices. Whenever a restaurant along the coast offered a special shrimp boil, the corporate boats wondered how they'd missed us. Our buyers were being slowly squeezed, but we would always have places to sell our catch. We were legends.

Our captain told us to dump the haul, but we were mesmerized. We'd never seen a haul so big except on old TV reruns. No one was pulling in full hauls anymore. It had been years. The sounds of the fins flapping, the shrimp legs running in place, the whirring and splashing and clicking, all of it. The smell of fresh living seafood and saltwater. Amazing. All we thought about was the money a haul like that could make for us. We could afford to live on land, maybe even not work for half a year. We thought about how all that seafood would taste. Put aside the crude oil taint and the chemical sting. Try to, anyway. Instead, picture them boiling away in spices with ears of corn and red potatoes. Imagine them being drained, then dumped onto an outdoor picnic table covered in newspaper, cold beers in our hands as we awaited the wave of boiled shrimp to land before us.

Maybe the captain was thinking the same thing, because his urgency faded, bit by bit, until he was left staring with the rest of us. Starving, physically, mentally.

He finally sighed and said, "All right. Haul it all."

* * *

OUR CAPTAIN LIKED TO REGALE us with stories of his life "before," whatever that was. The whole thing sounded like a tall tale, like Paul Bunyan or Lady Liberty. He stood before us sea dogs, our leathery skin and calloused feet earned on his splintered and warped deck, whereas his own orange glow seemed otherworldly. What few strands of red hair he had left seemed forever set in place, untouchable. His squint had seen things, I tell you. Terrible things.

He told us of the exotic Slavic women he had loved and married and left for the next exotic woman, and one who'd "got away," who was like a daughter to him. He told us stories of daredevil helicopter rides, heated boardroom firings, riches and ruin, and his long battle with the one they called "Madame Secretary" when they weren't busy calling her worse.

Just when it seemed he'd had the whole world in the palm of his hand, disaster struck. He never spoke about the exact situation that led to it, but whatever it was was bad enough to chase the man out of the center of power in this country, onto a small Vietnamese-owned pier in Biloxi, Mississippi, and onto an empty shrimper called *Slayer*, which he then sailed right on out into infamy.

So we were sure that he was seeing his life flash before his eyes, all of those stories he'd told us, and all the close scrapes we'd had together as a crew, as we hauled in those shrimp and those crab and those fish. "All into one tank," he bellowed. "Stuff the bastards to the rims!"

It was me who first saw them, a horde of shrimp boats, all flags flying. Over an hour after we'd begun our seemingly infinite haul, the fleet was upon us. Those fuckers.

We'd battled them all before, I supposed: the *Mötley Crüe,* the *WASP,* the *Judas Priest,* the *Hell's Satans,* and one, larger than the others, one we'd battled many, many times before, bludgeoning each other mercilessly for days on end, and yet each limping off in a draw, helmed by the man we all just called "Joe": the *Great White.*

I could already hear Joe's voice on the wind. "You're going down, down, down, down to the bottom!"

And beyond that, at the rear of the fleet, was an iron giant looming above them all, flying a flag I hadn't seen in at least three years. The Stars and Stripes. Of course they had to be involved. I should've known, but it hadn't crossed my mind. A battleship. USS *Ballcrusher.*

Shit.

We all turned to our captain.

Our weapons had been depleted during the last battle, and we hadn't been able to restock. We had two small artillery cannons; two machine guns, one on each side, with very little ammo; many, many, many handguns; a half-filled box of grenades; a handful of IEDs ready to be catapulted; spearguns; and our own claw-like, rawhide hands.

But were we prepared to fight? Mentally? Were we up for the motherfucker of all battles? Were we prepared to die for our ship?

The captain looked at all of us, one by one, that squint worming into our souls, as he said, "No matter what, we keep hauling. But give them hell, my friends. Give them big-league hell."

He turned for the wheelhouse, where he would start to turn us toward one of the oil rigs. If we could keep ahead of the fleet and take shelter there, we would have the high ground, twisting in and around the rusted legs of the beast, making ourselves a harder target. It worked when we were one on one or one on two. But against all these boats? A fool's run.

Those of us who prayed did so . . . or, like, Harding, renounced his god and told the devil he was on his way. My prayer was more perfunctory, like those the new American "president," the unelected son-in-law of the last elected one, sprayed at numerous prayer breakfasts for churches that praised him, that handed over billions to him, all so they could have the God-fearing playground of a country they'd always wanted. Better to stay on the waves, I'd thought.

At least, I used to have thought.

As I manned my post, speargun in one hand and Glock in the other, I caught the captain looking at me strangely. It wasn't just my imagination. His squint had me lasered. Boring into something.

Maybe I shouldn't have rolled my sleeves up. Maybe I shouldn't have absently scratched at the itch on my arm. Maybe maybe *maybe* I could have gotten away with it if I'd just kept my left side facing away from him.

But it was too late. He saw the scratch on my arm, the telltale sign of the tracker they'd implanted under my skin. "They" being the CIA, when I sold my soul to good ol' Joe for a place on the *Great White* if I promised to give up *Slayer* and her captain.

We'd always thought our captain's stories were mostly fantasy. It was only during our last port of call—Brownsville, Texas— when the crew had a few hours to go waste our hard-earned pay with whores and booze and video games and food, that I'd sought out one of Joe's confidants and confided that I was starving. I was tired of running. I wanted more from life than scrambling.

If I'd known *Slayer* would hit the biomass, though . . .

No, it was time for me to leave.

Joe came down to see me himself. He looked remarkable for his age, and he had that air. You know what I mean? Everyone's best friend? Yeah, that was Joe. The Man Who Should Have Ruled the World, so he told his crew. Should Have. But that arrogance didn't make anyone like him less. While I was waiting in the bar, a barely functional B-Dubs, cavernous and dark, with only four screens out of three-hundred actually working (and showing the "approved" American sports: yachting, polo, and golf), his confidant bought me beer after watery beer, on the house, until Joe arrived, alone, and all at once everyone in the bar smiled and said, "Hey, Joe!" and the lights seemed to brighten and there was the smell of hope in the room. Someone behind the bar dared to turn off the polo match, usually a finable offense. But who cared? Joe was in town!

What I had expected was a reward. So many people wanted *Slayer* sunk, that I was hoping to hop to Joe's ship and be treated like a hero. And in the end, I was able to secure a spot aboard the *Great White*, but Joe and his silver tongue convinced me that instead of a bag of silver, I would do this for *nothing*. Not a cent. Because, he said, reaching over to grasp my hand, "*It. Is. Your. Duty!*"

Duty!

"Okay . . . but to whom?"

He strengthened his grip on my hand. "You once lived on land. You once belonged to a country. You once fished these waters and actually caught something. You once saw green grass instead of concrete and blight. You once drank water from a tap instead of a bottle. And you once called yourself an *American!* And you can do so again."

"Are you sure?"

"Do this for me, Reagan, and I promise you it is the first step toward a better future, and a new country."

The B-Dubs erupted in applause. Someone even turned off the golf. That was an arrestable offense.

I can't say that I believed him, but you know that moment when the whore mentions the price and you hand over a lot less, but still she says, "Let's go," meaning it's really going to happen? This was that moment for the rest of my life. I was going to betray my captain. I was going to do it for less than I had hoped for. I was going to do it for my . . . I still choke on the word, on the lie of it all . . . *my country*

And yet, knowing that, I still felt a hole open in my soul when the captain charged toward me, knowing it was all my fault. I wanted to explain, to tell him that I took it all back, that it was a momentary lapse of reason, that I *loved* the boat and my captain and my crewmates!

Ah, my crewmates. They formed a semicircle around me, the captain in my face, hissing, "Disloyal. So disloyal. The most disloyal of them all. Et tu, Reagan?"

"S-s-sorry, sir."

"Sorry? Sorry?"

"I-I-they-they—"

"Oh, I know. I know what they told you. Something about making our country great again? Something about the promise of a new America?" He closed in, our noses touching, his squint like the flaming eye of Sauron. "It can't be done."

Could it, though? We'd done it once before. I vaguely remember. Joe brought him up, his old friend. The man who now ruled an island kingdom, what had once been America's fiftieth state, and was now, according to the only two people I'd ever known who'd been and come back, a literal paradise, surrounded by another iron fleet that had defected from the United States to ensure that no one would ever invade the man's remarkable achievement, the only real-life example of the might of America before the "president" took over.

Joe had told me, "He could come back, you know. If we took him the head of your captain, maybe we could convince him to come down from his coconut throne and join us. He could unseat the usurper and give us back what once belonged to *all people*, not just the rich and the religious."

Who was I to stand in the way of that dream?

I told my captain, "It's too late."

And like we were children on a middle-school playground, he spit on me. Then he called me, "Traitor!" And then he shoved me backwards, off the boat and into the nets, where I was buoyed by thousands of wriggling shrimp.

That was where I watched the fight, atop the bed of biomass. I watched as the battleship lowered its guns and began firing, closer and closer with each shell, and the various shrimp boats unleashed tracers across the waves and into the sides of *Slayer*, splintering the wood a millions times over, it seemed. I escaped my crustacean bed and swam out, grabbing a piece of the hull that had flown off. I floated to a safe distance, fairly confident there were no longer any sharks below, their food sources having dried up years ago, and I watched the battle blaze on into the night.

My shipmates, friends . . . gunned down.

My home for all those years . . . sinking.

My identity, one of the baddest-ass pirates of the most outlawed crew of all time . . . washed away.

The captain, still shooting as the fleet around him kept the fire hot, dropping their nets to haul the biomass, a bonus for them, but the captain found me, bobbing on the waves. He squinted me down hard and pointed and screeched, *"You, Reagan! This is all because of you! I will haunt you! Every night, I will haunt you! You will never escape because I will haunt you!"*

Down down down . . .

Only the water stopped the screeching.

But the captain kept his promise. He has haunted me, every night since.

* * *

Yes, the *Great White* and its captain, Joe, also kept their promise to pick me up and give me shelter, but that came with unanticipated and unpleasant side effects. I was seen as a traitor. I would never be one of the crew. I had my own cabin—tiny, but mine—and I ate on my own. No one acknowledged my existence, not even Joe. I was a passenger only, and more like a ghost than the one that squinted into my dreams at night as I relived the sinking of *Slayer* over and over and over and over. . . .

Still, there was hope. Always hope. Once I was aboard, Joe changed course. We were going to risk the Panama Canal, risk the Pacific, and try for the island paradise. As he'd told me, Joe assured us he knew the man on the throne there. If anyone could convince him to help us take back our country, it was Joe.

But even if not, there was hope that when we finally made land, *if* we did, considering the whole new fleet of trouble we would be sailing into out there, then we might be allowed to stay. A tiny chain of islands in the middle of nowhere. The land of the free, and the home of the brave.

Only then I could sleep without having to stare into my captain's squinty eyes.

GIVE ME YOUR FREE, YOUR BRAVE, YOUR PROUD MASSES YEARNING TO CONQUER
BY L. SCOTT JOSE

ON DAY 2922, CUSTER KURTZ rose again. His first act when he emerged from the ground was to squint. The light was different than it was before. And hotter. *Seventies in January—hell is rising beneath us,* thought Custer. One of the tenets is to apply incremental change, slowly enough that no one even realized what was going on. *This whole damn country is a slowly boiling frog.* The fluros from his bunker hadn't prepared him for the sunlight, which was crisp and mean, especially for January. Custer pulled his anorak off over his head and caught a belt of the body odor it had been concealing. His frame had become noticeably gaunt, his bones sticking out at all angles, like a child's swimsuit on an adult's coat hanger. The undercooked egg whites of his skin so pallid you could see the blood beneath it scuttle like cockroaches in the light.

Custer shielded his eyes from the sun, and took stock of the land. Fir trees dotted the mount, with leaden stumps bucking in the clearway around the house. His property was sour, girt by clay and brambles. A dull hum lurked in the background, reminding him of the oil slick headaches and bloody noses that had ground him under their celestial thumb into the firmament. Custer rifled through his canvas duffle and found the baggie of Doxa. There wasn't much, but it should last a few days if he was sparing with it. Custer dusted some on to the back of his hand, the chalky yellow of the granules like a rash atop his skin's greasy patina. With a snort, he huffed it back. It bubbled in his sinus, and the metallic taste dripped to his palate. Like a strong cleaner, scrubbing his brain. Now Custer felt sharp. Fuck, he felt *hard*. He stuffed his anorak into the duffel. The lingering taste of the Doxa made Custer gurn, and he reached into his breast pocket for his tin of chaw. He snuck some in his lip and let the taste wash over his mouth as the Doxa kicked in. The subtle geography of the earth revealed itself to him once more, a crisscross of rainbow webbing interrupted by electronic waves. *Try fucking with me now, world.*

Before he could get comfortable, a packet popped in his head and slid through his nose. Custer rubbed it. Blood. "Fuck," he muttered. He put a tampon up his nostril to stem the flow. Custer got his bearings and headed in the direction of the highway. White streaks were marked across the Haralson County horizon. "Fucking chemtrails," he said, to no one in particular. Or whoever might've been listening, he supposed. It was all one and the same, the conspiracy. Like a jigsaw of bullshit. Those lizard-faced assholes sure did like their puzzles.

Custer allowed himself one last look back at his property. The beaten-to-hell house on top of the bunker he had called home for nigh on three thousand days. He must have watched that clip on PornHub four dozen times before he decided for sure to come up. "Immigration Banana Stand," he mumbled. No time to get sentimental, though. He had important work to do, and Custer would have to get a move on if he was going to assassinate President Obama.

* * *

OF COURSE HIS OLD TRUCK wasn't working. Figured. A thing like that couldn't stop him, though. He'd heard rumblings that Bear

Crowley had disappeared. He hadn't known how seriously to take them. Not until he got Bear's last message.

Bear was one of the last true patriots in a world gone mad. He was unafraid to share the *truth*, no matter how uncomfortable it made all the snowflakes out there.

Custer remembered the first time he met Crowley, at the Houston New World Order Convention in '94, where they'd both spoken. Afterward, they sat in Crowley's hotel room with a bottle of bourbon. They swept the room for bugs—finding one, to no one's surprise. Crowley pulled a small electronic case the size of a dip tin from his pocket. Its top was clear, and inside, glowing, was a crystal resembling rose quartz. Bear was a Texan, and spoke in a full-blooded way like each word was chewed off a bone. "So long as the crystal stays pink, we're safe to talk. If at any stage it goes green, kill yourself. Quickly. No hesitations. I've got a cyanide cap in a tooth. You can use the pistol in my jacket for yourself."

They stared at the device for a moment in reverence. Bear's face was round and smooth, with a constant strained expression like he was being pushed through a tube slightly too small for him. Custer tugged at his own unkempt beard as he listened to Bear.

"People have a tendency to think that everything is just 'business as usual,' regardless of how bad it actually gets. Right now, the world is on the brink of collapse, and everyone is too busy to notice. We both know about these new forces that are coming. . . . I think I trust you, Custer."

Custer trembled and nodded.

"Am I right to trust you?"

Custer reached across the coffee table and put his clammy hand over Bear's, stroking it, and leaned in close to him, until he could feel the heat from Bear's face on his lips, and spoke with round bourbon notes, "Yes. Yes, you can trust me, Bear."

Bear clasped his hand on top of Custer's. He smiled, sharing two gold-capped teeth.

"Custer, I've got good connections, but I want to bring you in to the fold. We need all the soldiers we can get, and I think you'd be one of the best. You know that there are people out there who, well, *aren't* people, don't you?"

Custer hesitated, then pushed out a "Yes."

"These . . . *freaks* are almost impossible to detect. But we've developed a way to . . . see beyond the veil, I suppose."

Bear took a small steel vial from his satchel. The leather arm-chair moaned as he moved. With his baseball-mitt hands, Bear cracked the seal on the vial. It gasped as it sucked in air. He tapped some off-white granules onto the table next to the crystal device.

"Is . . . that crank?" Custer asked, leaning back.

"No, not crank. You need to trust me. Like I trust *you*. Keep an open mind. You know about psychic phenomena and phallus magic, right?"

Custer nodded.

"This is Doxa. Some of my people developed it. It can give you a thump, but it lets you see what's really happening."

Custer looked at the powder, then back to Bear.

"You know as well as I do, Custer, that there are agents from elsewhere . . . other worlds, other places, who are part of the con-spiracy here. There's a lot of names for them, but 'reptilians' is as good as any. There's a whole world just below the one we see, the *real* world, Custer. So much of what we see is just a psychic projec-tion they use. Doxa blocks out the psychic mess and the sex con-juring they use and lets you see the *truth*."

Bear leaned forward, and snorted a lump of the Doxa. He bucked as though from pleasure, and his pupils strobed.

"It's good, Custer. We *need* you, Custer. *I* need you. Help me save the world. Join the Semper Underground."

Custer suppressed a grin. He took a blast.

Everything sharpened. The walls pulsed and sagged outward, threatening to break into infinity, tugged by screams and elec-tronic bleating and hot static and chattering teeth and the feel that something just beyond was watching from afar, scratching behind their eyes.

"It's okay, Custer. They can't get us here. They can't see us or hear us now."

Custer turned to Bear. A mask of rainbows peeled from Crowley's face, and underneath, small interlocking triangles spun, emitting light. "Look closer, Custer."

Custer shuffled forward. He saw Bear Crowley's face again; it was now a void of light and hope. "Bear . . . are you an *angel*?"

"I . . . yes. Yes, Custer. Any of us who face the light are," Bear declaimed. "Now we know that we're both safe, Custer. If we were one of *them*, the Doxa would let us see. We can trust each other."

Custer had never felt such pure love in his whole life. A thousand thoughts surfaced in him. They took physical space, and had rough corners.

"Bear, what's happening?"

"It's okay—you're just not used to the psychic feedback yet. In time you'll be able to control it at will. For now though, we'll need to clear our minds, okay?"

"Okay," Custer said, sweat melting his face off.

Bear arched his back and slid his pants down. Custer could see blood like bubbling pearls gathering in Bear's cock. "Just follow what I do, and it will clear your mind."

Bear fumbled, engulfing his member in a meaty paw. Custer copied and put his hand on his own penis. The air grew thicker and the walls gasped. Light focused to a point as he and Bear matched strokes. Soon they were in a rhythm together and blurred in and out of each other.

As they both came, the world cracked back into place and the room was still, the voices and shapes gone. But the *awareness* remained.

Wiping a sticky hand on the armchair, Bear nodded to Custer. "I have two vials for you to get started. As you get used to it, you'll be able to control yourself, but until then, orgasm is the best focus technique."

Custer nodded and took another swig of the bourbon, leaving a gummy handprint on it.

* * *

THE UNSEASONABLE HEAT FLATTENED CUSTER'S scraggly hair over his head. His feet ached. Not much space for walking in the bunker. Sure, he had the treadmill, but in terms of the amount of pressure his feet were accustomed to, this was something else. Frances White Road was chewed at the edges by leaf litter and bramble. Soon Custer would be at Highway 120 and could thumb a ride. Following that he wasn't entirely sure. Hire cars left a paper trail. Flying wasn't an option. Maybe the bus? But that might be too slow. Whatever. Custer knew he'd figure it out. The wad of cash he had on him was enough to solve most problems.

Capitol Hill was a long trip from Draketown, and time was tight. It had been a decade since he'd left the state. Hell, then again, it had been nearly a decade since he'd been above ground. A membrane of sweat covered Custer. He shook and his chest seized up. Maybe his body was going into shock from being exposed to the elements again. *Or maybe They're fucking with me. . . .* There was only enough Doxa for three full hits, and he'd definitely need some later. Still, he wasn't sure how he'd managed without at least a half bump. He took the hit.

One sound sharpened over the electric hum. In a tree across the road was what would appear to anyone else as just a normal bird. But this one was staring. And Custer could hear a mechanical buzz coming from it.

"They're getting good at hiding their surveillance." Custer dropped his duffel and unzipped it. From it he took his Liberty .48 and slid the bolt, inserting a cartridge. Custer crouched, and took aim at the "bird," the Doxa steadying his hands. Right before he could get the shot off, it flew away.

"Your lucky day, I guess." Custer ejected the cartridge and put the rifle back in the duffel.

Custer's feet dragged as he went along the side of the 120 with his thumb out. He thought about cracking one of the bean tins he'd brought with him. And then he thought about eating some fresh fruit. It had been a long while. And Custer had to admit that his stomach growled at the thought. Too bad anything he could get here was probably lizard-people-manufactured, genetically modified frankenfoods. He'd have to go straight to one of the organic farms after this trip. *That's if there is an "after."*

A Ford F650 pulled up just ahead of Custer, its indicator beckoning him. The bright red MAKE AMERICA GREAT AGAIN sticker on the back bumper caught the sun as Custer read it. He gave it a solemn nod. Next to it was another sticker, this one a flag with the text FUCK OFF WE'RE FULL.

"Ah, another patriot," Custer mumbled as he spat some of his chaw on the ground.

Custer approached the driver and the window rolled down.

"Gotta say, I mighty appreciate y'all stopping. I'm heading as far east as you care to take me."

Custer hesitated as laughter emanated from the backseats, the creators of which were obscured by the heavy tint.

Before Custer could muster another word, a nasal voice came from the driver.

"Get a job, ya fuckin' hippie!"

A Starbucks cup flew out and splattered over Custer's front. The truck lurched away while Custer assessed himself.

* * *

BEAR CROWLEY WAS AGITATED AND wouldn't stop pacing, his rosacea seemingly brightening with each step. "Custer, I think they've managed to infiltrate us. I think there's a mole."

In the years since he'd shown Custer the ways of Doxa, their ranks had grown. Semper Underground now had believers all over the country. Heck, the world. And that meant that the inner circle had expanded, too.

They'd met in one of Bear's cabins that night, and the sleet hitting the corrugated iron roof sounded like eggs breaking.

"But the Doxa . . ."

"The Doxa can't help with this! They have people who aren't even like them helping them. People who *know*. This—this country has just elected that monster. He's a *demon*, Custer! And no one cares! The Illuminati has just—just gotten someone into the presidency. And they've breached us. . . . I'm afraid for the future, Custer. I really am. . . ."

The country had been warned, over and over again about Obama. From Bear and other prophets like Alex Jones. But even though Bear and Custer hoped for the best, they prepared for the worst. When it looked like Obama might win, Custer's old fallout shelter was given an upgrade. It was now a proper ark.

"Custer, I'll need you to stay under. I need to know I have one person I can trust, who can't be reached."

The day before Obama's inauguration, Custer Kurtz went into the earth. Safe from the dark forces, the New Order, the Illuminati, the Lizard People—whatever you wanted to call them Custer waited. Until it was no longer time to wait.

* * *

An hour after Custer's shirt dried, another vehicle finally stopped for him. This time it was a young couple and their offspring. Custer sat in the front passenger side while the female tended to her infant. He frowned as she openly fed it from her breast, not bothering to cover up. *That child is too old to be doing that. It'll probably grow up to be a pervert*, he thought. The first forty-five minutes of the trip passed in an agreeable silence, but at some point as the 120 wound through Marietta, the driver, Howard, got notions about conversing. Howard was a malnourished-looking man with the manner of a dog that expected to be kicked. He took Custer's reticence as an excuse to talk to him at length about veganism. Custer felt sickened by Howard's robe-like top and his simpering smile.

"So, I'd gone my whole life without ever being stung by a bee. So, thirty-two years, right?"

Custer picked at his nose and finally realized Howard needed a response. "Right."

"And it's not like I didn't go outside, far from it. I love the outdoors, don't I, Lowana?"

Custer had forgotten the female's name.

"That's right. He's a beautiful nature boy," Lowana said while leaning forward over the bucket seats and putting her face too close to Custer's.

"Aw, thanks, babygirl."

"You're my free spirit, babe." She leaned away from Custer to kiss Howard who turned and planted his lips on her.

"Road," Custer muttered.

Howard righted the van. "Haha, good plan, my man." Howard passed a water flagon to Custer. "Mind unscrewing that for me?" Custer obliged and passed it back. Howard took a belt. "Anyway, like I was saying, this was just two years ago, Lowana was pregnant with Sahnya, and I'd never been stung by a bee. I had no reason to be afraid of them. I saw bees, and it was like . . . it was like seeing, I don't know . . ."

"A tree?" Lowana offered.

"Yes! Exactly! A tree! Just any old thing, like it's just an object of nature, it's beautiful and you don't need to think about it. But then—and I must have given this bee a fright somehow—I got stung. And I tell ya, it hurt like bejeesus! I'm sure you've been stung before, so I don't need to explain that part." Howard paused and looked to Custer for approval. "Anyway, my whole body, it started seizing up and I couldn't breathe. I started swelling up like a big ole balloon. I had no clue what was happening."

"It was so scary!" Lowana contributed.

"Yes it was, baby. Yes it was. So, I had the anaphylactic shock, like I was actually deathly allergic to bees. Now, obviously they got me help in time, because I'm still here, and now I've gotta carry one of them EpiPens with the adrenaline in them in case it happens again. Right?"

Custer squinted to block the afternoon light. "Uh huh."

"*Right?* Now, I'm always nervous about getting bitten by another bee. I mean stung. Bees don't actually bite you. They stick you with their, uh—tail? Stinger? You know. They stick you with it. You probably know. When it happened, not only was I hurt like all hell, but I was thinking 'My god, I'm gonna leave Lowana and that precious baby that is about to come into our lives!' and I've never been so scared. And now? *Now* I'm scared all the time. Of bees. What if one gets me now and I don't get to that pen in time? What if I do, but it doesn't work well enough?"

Howard looked to Custer who was busy doing an inventory of his duffel in his head.

"But here's the funny bit: I'm safer now from bees than I ever have been. I've always been allergic, there was always the chance this might've happened, and I might have died. But I didn't know, so I wasn't afraid. Now though, I'm terrified, even though I have a better chance than I did before. It's almost worse now, because I'm scared. Isn't that crazy?"

Custer had run out of pleasantries and sat silent.

Emasculated, Howard gave up. Lowana tried. "Oh, Howard, let our guest be. He's probably tired."

Another mile passed before Howard spoke again. "So, what's the purpose of your trip, Custer?"

Custer was considering his answer when he realized. "How do you know my name?"

"What?" Howard said.

"My name. I never told you my name."

Howard stammered. "N-no, of course you did. When you got in the van." A whispered voice cut into Custer's brain: *He knows.*

Custer knew he had snagged the corner of a psychic message to Lowana. *If those were even their real names.*

Custer gripped his duffel firmly. "I know what I said and what I didn't say. Don't play me for stupid. How do you know my name?"

"Haha, mister, I don't know what you're getting at. . . ." Howard stole a glance to Lowana, and Custer saw something slide over his eyes. Some sort of nictating membrane—a second eyelid. . . . *Like a fucking lizard.* . . . Custer frowned. Right then, he knew for certain.

* * *

ONCE A WEEK CUSTER WOULD do his body maintenance—first a cocktail of vitamin D, C, and homeopathic inoculations. The cocktails were stored in glass cartridge vials; Custer would load them into a syringe gun. For the first three years, he'd been blasting it into his arms. Since he kept collapsing veins (and following one particularly nasty infection—which, even after the arm itself healed, let to a secondary lung infection that lasted close to nine months) Custer now alternated between his feet and his ass. He'd insert thin cannulas into his chakras—on Anahata to help the thymus with his immune system; Sahasrara to keep his psychic energy replenished; and Ajna to cleanse his pituitary gland, which, like a liver with booze, needed a detox to cleanse it from psychic build-up.

Although Custer could comfortably stand within the bunker, by year seven, he'd noticed himself stooping more and more, as his spine curved in constant pain. The bunker had previously been shipping containers—Custer thought he was a genius doing this on a budget. These things were more of a pain than they were worth, though. Sure, he'd saved some money initially, but the problems started almost immediately—shipping containers are made to be stacked and can hold that weight no problem. But the moment you put pressure on the sides, they buckle, like the different between standing on a beer can and squeezing it in your hand. So, once he'd built the support beams and put proper insulation and sealant all over the damn things, he'd lost a foot of width, making what was already small smaller still.

Aboveground was the house he used to live in, with its busted-in windows and warped weatherboards, razor wire wrapped around each sill. Inside the house was a series of backup generators, water pumps, air filtration and exhaust, and satellite dishes. Outside was an old basement trapdoor as a façade for the real entrance to the bunker—the twenty-inch vault door with a forty-pound mortar attached.

Each morning he'd start with a tin of peaches and a wheat biscuit. By the third year he'd lost a few of his molars, and had to soak the biscuits in water and licked them up from his plate. It'd been so long since he'd used a fork that he'd forgotten it was unusual to eat like an animal.

After twenty minutes on the treadmill, Custer would go online. Bear's radio show had outgrown the radio, and he now had one of those Internet video blogs. The show, *A Braver Truth*, was a one-man institution. Hell, he even had Trump's ear. Bear covered it all—he wouldn't let *them* get away with anything. Step one was to get people to question the world, point out what didn't add up. Start getting them to *think*, for God's sake. Bear was good at doing that, and doing it forcefully. Yelling at the audience until they understood. He gave them bits and pieces of *the* conspiracy, until they knew he was telling the *truth*. He'd bellow in his voice that sounded like five pounds of ham slapping a washing machine, and few could resist.

Trump would call in on Crowley's show, and vowed to clean up the corrupt government of all the shady dealings. If anyone could clean up the conspiracy, it was an outsider like him. For a time, Custer felt safer than ever.

On occasion, Bear would overlay his public videos with folded-in psychic code that only Custer could access. While talking about one thing—immigrants, rapists, and the like—Crowley was able to create a psychic message that would be embedded in the subcutaneous layer of video. The real genius of it was making it so only certain patterns and actions could open it, and beyond that, only certain brainwaves would be able to create those. It was as close to a secure means of communication that existed.

The signal would wake up Custer's brainstem with a hypnic jerk, its tendrils kicking like feet tickling the inside of his throat. To access the message, Custer wouldn't use the Doxa, but another drug that Bear Crowley's chemists had developed: Enthumos. Enthumos was more dangerous than Doxa, as it changed the wiring of the pineal gland, and used incorrectly, it could turn psychic code into a whirring of blades in the subconscious. Further, the Enthumos had to be administered directly into the brainstem; Custer would jam a metallic cartridge-syringe into the back of his neck and crank it. Then, he'd drape a noose around his neck.

Custer would restart the video and lean forward, tightening the noose to dull out any extra psychic feedback. The next step to create the psychogenic key was to masturbate. The brain patterns and energy generated by autoerotic asphyxia coupled with the Enthumos unlocked Bear's psychic code. Custer's penis grew sharp and the cold dribble of the Enthumos made its way into his brain. Bear's face would stutter and the real Bear would emerge.

"Custer Kurtz, I salute you. Semper Underground salutes you. Unfortunately, I'm not bringing good news. We wouldn't put you through the ordeal of getting these messages if it wasn't important. One of my people—one that I *trust*—is ranked highly within the White House. Obama has something planned during Trump's inauguration. We don't know what it is yet, but Trump's life is at stake, as is the future and freedom of liberty in our country.

"We have to stop this. I've reached out to Trump, and he's agreed to find somewhere secure to talk to me, as I don't have a psychic line with him yet. But I fear I may fail, Mr. Kurtz. I fear something may happen to me. If it does, you are the only one I can trust. You must save Trump. You must stop Obama at the inauguration.

"I know this message is long, but you mustn't cum yet, Custer. You can't cum until I say so."

Custer gritted his teeth and tried to restrain himself from ejaculating. He trained for this, made sure to regularly practice drug-induced autoerotic asphyxiation. The edges of his vision were blacking out and the mix of Enthumos in his brainstem and the noose caused him to gag.

"Keep a look out for future transmissions from me. If things are going bad, and it looks like I'm compromised, one of my people will give you a trigger for further action. They will upload a video to PornHub under the title *Immigration Banana Stand* that will consist only of static intercut with close-ups of my erect penis."

A pulse of ejaculatory anticipation moved through Custer, and the Enthumos caused synaesthesia that turned it into music.

"If that happens, you must go and you must stop Obama. By any means. Good luck, Custer. Please cum for me now."

* * *

Custer squeezed the wheel. Dusk was settling in, and his eyes were slipping off the road. The stock of Doxa was low as it was, but on the other hand, he wasn't sure how he'd make it to DC in time if he had to sleep. *Or hell—if I crash.* Custer trembled as he shook a bump onto the back of his hand. The van veered out of the passing lane of the I-81 as he did, giving some asshole an excuse to honk.

"Fuck."

Somehow Custer managed to not spill anything while jerking the van back into his lane. Crystals of blood and allergies blocked his nostrils, so Custer licked the back of his hand, remembering too late the series of open cankers nesting on his tongue. The pain burned hot and loose for a moment, blacking the edges of his vision, before the euphoria of the Doxa kicked in and sharpened him again.

Now how the fuck do you turn the headlights on in this van?

Custer was rapidly approaching a cluster of vehicles. He considered overtaking, then thought better of it. The last thing he needed was to get pulled over by the cops for speeding.

After enough fiddling to become sweethearts, he got the van's headlights on. The display unit illuminated—gas was low. Custer pulled off at the Buchanan, Virginia, exit and idled into the Exxon. The sight of the Burger King in the station made his stomach roar, and he decided he'd finally open a can of beans once he'd filled up.

After pumping the gas, Custer went to open the van door to retrieve his wallet and caught a glimpse of his reflection.

"Ah, rats."

He grabbed a rag and poured some of Howard's water on it and scrubbed his face with it. He had a look again in the side mirror of the van and was satisfied he was clean and had gotten all the blood off his face.

He glanced in the back of the van. The three of those things were covered up well enough. Custer's anger rose again—they were disgusting. He shook and tried to center himself. These tricks they were pulling were the lowest of the low—disguising one of those reptile freaks to look like a baby to try and prey on Custer's innate goodness.

Custer picked up two gallons of water. He paid with cash. He dropped two purification tablets in the jug and let them dissolve before drinking any. In the restroom, he managed a single dry turd. He sprayed everything he touched with ammonia, then sat in the van, ate the beans, and kept driving. He made good time to DC.

* * *

Capitol Hill's west front was just as much of a shithole as Custer figured it would be. Big dumb grassy lawns in front of the unholy shrine of false democracy his country had erected. He'd dumped his duffel in a storm drain when he ditched the van. Hopefully he could retrieve it later. Without the rifles Custer felt naked, even with a 9mm Parabellum nestled in his crotch. Security here was a joke, just some bullshit guards and cops. Custer hit himself with the last of his Doxa before moving toward the front. He could see the press, their rictus grins barely mounted to their faces. The Doxa showed the seams of their iden-tities, and Custer wondered how so many people missed it. They were so clearly reptilian. He supposed it was because they con-trolled so much of what people heard and saw that it could be overlooked. Any one of them could be readying to kill Trump on Obama's orders at any moment. Mounted cops trotted around the berm and scanned the crowd. The pit of the enemy was thick around Custer.

But no, that wasn't Obama's style. He was much more likely to go for a false flag operation. Have some agent dressed as a "deranged gun nut" come out with an assault rifle and shoot Trump, use it as an excuse to take executive action and finally steal everyone's guns like he'd wanted.

No, he knew he'd have to take that fucker Obama down right there, in front of the crowd, reveal to the world Obama's true reptilian face. This would be too big to contain, even for the corrupt media.

Custer was on the lawn, he could see their faces in front of him. He figured he was forty yards out. Enough to take a shot, but not close enough to be confident. That wasn't good enough. But it was maybe the best he'd get. A fine mist of drizzle had swept over the crowd as they waited for shit to get going. There was a lot of hope in that crowd. Custer couldn't let them down.

He breathed deep and sucked on his chaw and centered him-self. Soon it would be over.

The first addresses were full of coded language and Custer noticed Clarence Johnson making occult symbols with his hands as he swore in Pence. Still, Obama sat patiently in the background, never letting his head rise enough to allow a shot over the bullet-proof panels.

Finally, Trump spoke. The one bright spot in the country right now, and they were close to losing him before he could even do anything. Custer trembled as Trump spoke, like it was just to him. Trump's strong hands moved to punctuate each sentence as though warding off evil. He was so caught in the moment that he almost missed his chance. Once Trump finished talking, Obama stood to "congratulate" him. Custer wasted no time.

In one smooth movement, Custer knocked the woman in front of him from her wheelchair and stood upon it. He took aim with the Parabellum. Someone screamed, "Gun!" and the moment contracted like he'd just cum.

Custer inhaled, and squeezed on the trigger.

Trump saw Custer then, and shook his head. Obama saw him too and froze. *Fucking coward*, Custer thought. Right as he was to fire, Trump jumped in front of Obama, screaming, "Stop! Don't fire!"

Custer couldn't believe it. He was *saving* this asshole. He lowered the gun, he and Trump locked eyes for just a moment before Custer was tackled to the ground by the cops.

* * *

WHEN THEY TORE THE HOOD off of Custer's head he felt a strange sense of comfort. It was probably the fluros and the relative small-ness of the room reminding him of home. Or perhaps it was all the blows to the head. Custer blinked and tried to pull the spinning visuals together. He noted the plush carpet and high ceiling, the carved wooden armchair and the old Federation map on the wall. Then he noted who was in the room with him.

Five shock troopers watched him, assault rifles semi-erect in their arms. Dressed in black armor, their faces obscured by hel-mets and balaclavas, only their eyes visible. They weren't even trying to hide it anymore. Their large eyes bulged, jaundiced yellow in color with vertical pupils. Around that was a crust of skin—covered in translucent gray scales. Custer tried moving, but his arms were shackled behind him.

"I guess I'm not getting arrested, huh?"

"Mr. Custer Kurtz," a voice came from behind him. He recognized it, but couldn't place it. "Quite the display you made out there today." The figure stepped out in front of him. Seeing his face didn't help Custer put a name to it. *One of those liberal jews who hosts a comedy news show,* Custer knew that much.

"So, you're one of *them,* too?"

The man laughed. "So many labels used by rednecks like you. Maybe if you were more open-minded, you wouldn't worry so much."

"You're just out there polluting people's minds, start by making them think there's no difference between man and woman, between the gays and normal people, and soon they'll accept *you.* You lizard people are so transparent."

The man gave a polished, empty laugh. "Please, they prefer Anunnaki. Or Saurians, if you must."

Custer lurched forward. "Go fuck yourself, you ____" He vomited up beans as the butt of a rifle hit him in the gut.

"Oh, come off it, Custer. Have some dignity."

Custer looked into the comedian's eyes and tried to send a beam of pure hate at him. He noticed, then. "You're not one of them?"

"Afraid not."

"You'd betray your own species, and for what?"

"Hey—I like to *win,* Custer."

"You ain't nothing but a cuck."

The comedian didn't find that so funny. "You don't have to listen to me, but there are some people who'd like to talk to you."

Custer was lifted by his shackles and frogmarched out of the room. Once they led him into the rotunda, Custer recognized that they were in the Capitol Building. Paintings lined the walls, with shock troops standing by as totalitarian museum guards.

"Stop." The shock troops obeyed the comedian. "See that above you, Mr. Kurtz?"

Custer glanced upward. The oculus of the rotunda looked back at him. Enormous within it was a fresco. He knew the painting. *The Apotheosis of Washington.* "What of it?"

The comedian started to giggle. "You're not looking hard enough. *Really* look at it."

Custer frowned and looked up again. It was just that painting he'd seen all those times. George Washington ascending and being surrounded by angels and angelic maidens, fulfilling the manifest destiny of the true patriots and the righteous colonization of America. He looked at Washington's face. Serene, confident, powerful. But then Custer noticed something. Next to him, the angel blowing a trumpet . . . it's face wasn't right. "The fuck . . ."

In fact, there was something wrong with all the angels. They weren't angels at all. They were reptilian. The banner that usually read "E PLURIBUS UNUM" was now made of human skin, and read "NOVUS ORDO SECLORUM." Custer felt nauseous, dizzy, like he was outside of his body, but hyperaware of all of his senses at the same time. There were dozens of them, the reptilians, around George Washington. All of them laughing and dancing, like they had a sinister secret, as Washington sat there, stone-faced. And Washington's eyes . . . . *were they yellow?*

How had Custer never noticed?

"You can see it now, I take it?"

Custer tried finding his words. "What . . . what is that?"

"That? That is the *truth*, Mr. Kurtz." The comedian giggled again, his true braying laugh. "My god, if *that's* shaken you, whatever you do, don't look around you."

Custer looked to the shock troops surrounding him. Then past them. The paintings that lined the walls of the rotunda were wrong.

They were still the scenes of the founding of the country, but cruel carnival mirror versions. Mockeries of reality and taste. Grinning reptilians sitting on the deck of the Speedwell; a lizard John Rolfe rubbed his hands as a devil with an enormous phallus poured blood over Pocahontas; lights and strange ships floated in the sky behind a demonoid Columbus as he plunged a flag bearing the Eye of Providence into the ground to claim the Americas; and, worst of all, the Founding Fathers signing the Declaration of Independence. Only the founders were reptilian. Every one of them. Those sitting held scepters and drank from goblets, while on the wall behind them a large pentagram was crudely painted, with a crucified man pinned to the star's points.

"That's . . . that's impossible!"

The comedian mimed wiping a tear from his eye. "Oh god, I wish you could see your face right now. It is *priceless*."

Custer fell to his knees and tried to breathe.

"Get him up." The comedian barked to the shock troops. "He's still got plenty to see."

Custer was marched into the Crypt. Originally, the Crypt was built as the entrance to Washington's tomb, but now housed statues and art. Custer shook. *It can't be real. It must be a bad hit of Doxa*, he thought.

"Oh, I assure you, Mr. Kurtz. This is all very, very real." The voice came from behind one of the pillars. It was unmistakable.

"Obama . . ."

The former president stepped out and smiled. His face no longer contorted to hide his true self. His arms were long and slender, ending in talons. A Cheshire grin showed rows of teeth in his scaly face.

"That's one of my names, at least. You wanted to know the *truth*, Custer Kurtz? We're going to show you."

Custer wanted to ask how they knew about him, but it was pointless. They knew everything. Obama was reading his thoughts right now, that reptilian scum.

"All that time spent worrying about my birth certificate, and you never even thought to question if I was born on this *planet*. Why can't you just be our *friend*, Custer? Why do you want your planet at war with Alpha Draconis?" Obama laughed and walked toward the giant bust of Lincoln's head. He dropped to his knees before it, spread his arms and chanted in a low and steady drone. As he did, the eyes on the Lincoln bust glowed and a rumble filled the Crypt. The bust and part of the floor in front of it started sliding back revealing a staircase leading underground.

"Have fun down there, Custer," the comedian said with a wave. "There aren't many Terrans—that is, *non-Annukians*—allowed down there. Wish I could join!"

Obama stroked Custer's face. "Come on down, and see the real America, Custer."

The underground resembled less a cave and more a grand hall. High roofs and wide corridors were carved smooth into the ancient rock bed by some terrible and unknowable force. Red phosphorescent light glowed at the edges of the cavern walls. The humidity was suffocating. Pressure built in Custer's head.

A procession of robed people walked past him, chanting. Except, they *weren't* people. Just the bottom of their faces were visible, but they carried the same telltale teeth and scales.

"Stop here," Obama ordered. Custer wasn't about to take any orders off of Obama, but his choice was taken from him when one of the shock troops yanked his shackles, rooting him in place. They stood in the middle of the chancel, when Obama chanted again. A huge stone altar erected, thick and firm, standing twenty-feet from the ground.

Before Custer could say anything, Trump walked to him from the shadows.

"Hello, Custer," Trump said, unable to meet his eyes.

"You. . . . Why'd you do it, Donald?"

Trump sighed and extended his arms to build up a big spiel.

Then stopped, and stooped again, defeated. "I'm sorry. I know you were trying to help."

"*Help*'? I was *saving* you! These freaks aren't going to help you. They'll destroy you." Custer trembled as he spoke.

"It's not as simple as you think, Custer."

"Oh, bullshit. You said you were on our side, but you're just as weak as any other politician. You don't care about the New Order."

Trump's mouth curled into a small O and he stammered. "You—you don't understand. I wanted to change, but you *can't*, Custer. You can't change anything." Obama went to Trump and put his arm around him and gently kissed Trump's fine, doll-like hair. "It's not that the New Order is *changing* things. They *made* things how they are. It's not a conspiracy *against* humanity, they're the ones who run things. Who *help* us. There's no changing. This goes deeper than you could possibly understand . . ."

Trump's words echoed through the cavern.

"Why'd you save that scumbag?"

Trump looked at the floor and twirled his foot. Obama screeched with laughter.

"Trump here can see the bigger picture, Custer. He understands his *place*."

"Custer—you're thinking about it in the wrong way. They've already won. They've always been in charge, Custer. There's nothing we can do. Things can't change, they've always been like this . . ."

Custer tried concentrating, but his head boomed. "The fuck are you talking about?" Trump tried finding words, but got confused and looked to Obama. Obama sighed, but still smiled, like every human expression was a game.

"Okay, Custer. Would you like to meet the Founding Fathers?"

Custer's nose started bleeding again, thick and slow. "Whuh-what?"

The cavern rumbled, and the chanting grew louder and more high-pitched. The sixty-foot-high rock face in front of them shifted, revealing an endless pitch-black recess. Shapes emerged. Twelve of them. *Lizard* shapes. They weren't the same as Obama—they were much larger.

They were at least thirty-feet high. Enormous white robes cloaked their bodies, revealing only their thin ankles and taloned feet. The dress-like robes flowed, with their huge strides. Their faces were uncovered—the same scaly lizard faces, but with long equine snouts. Atop their heads were white triangular hats, each with a different symbol. Some bearing stars, others eyes and some crosses. They hissed and giggled as they approached.

Obama walked to the first of the beasts, dropped to his knees and licked its gigantic claw.

"General Washington."

He went to another of the creatures and greeted it the same way.

"Mr. Jefferson."

Custer shook as he gazed upon them. Trump stripped himself, until he stood naked and soft before the Founding Fathers of the United States. One of the hooded lackeys brought Trump a golden chalice.

"My supreme and benevolent leaders, I give you my sacrament." Trump began playing with his penis until it budded into a firm button mushroom. He struggled for a minute, his face contorting.

"Trump, what the fuck are you doing?" Custer was hit in the guts again by a shock trooper and dry retched.

"Silence! No one interrupts the sacrament!" Obama hissed while his forked tongue flicked out.

Trump deposited some pearly beads into the chalice, letting out a barnyard squeal and a shallow fart as he did.

Between gulps for air he held the vessel up to the Founding Fathers. "For you, my lieges."

They rumbled approval and nodded to one another.

Obama leaned in next to Custer's ear and whispered. "Now comes the fun part." He turned back to the Fathers and started to hum. The lackey monks joined him, and the altar before them turned around, revealing a huge pentagram.

"We're glad you showed up, Custer. Bear died before we got him here. Tricky bastard had a poison cap in his tooth. And we needed the blood of an Acolyte of Heresy to complete the sacrament."

"But . . . no. Bear was an angel."

"The Founding Fathers are what *real* angels are, Custer. What did you *think* angels were? Grow up . . . I thought you were a *patriot?*"

One of the Founding Fathers stepped toward Custer.

"Take our offering please, Mr. Sherman."

Roger Sherman plucked Custer Kurtz up in his enormous cold fingers. He brought Custer to his face and kissed him gingerly, his lips covering Custer's full head. With a snap of his huge lizard fingers he broke the shackles that bound Custer's arms. Sherman turned Custer upside down and lined his limbs and head up with the points of the pentagram, and affixed him in place with the iron gauntlets that stuck from the plinth.

Trump, naked and splotchy-skinned, looked up at Custer, then kneeled and bowed his head, holding the chalice out before him.

Custer's voice was horse. "Let me go, you bastards. Just . . . *please.*"

The Founder Fathers chittered, and George Washington came before Custer. He stroked Custer's hair and made a monstrous approximation of a cooing sound. Washington then pulled a serpentine dagger from his robes. He chittered again.

"No." Custer coughed. The blade tore his throat spilling his blood in hot waves over his face and down the plinth. Custer tried to suck air, but instead pulled blood from his neck into his lungs. He coughed and sputtered as the last of his life drained from him.

Beneath Custer, Trump's chalice filled, the blood mixing with the semen. Once full, Trump took it and bowed before the Founding Fathers.

"Take my humble offering." He gulped the mixture down.

Trump gagged at first, but as he finished, he smiled, and his penis swelled up like a cocktail onion. He held the empty chalice in front of him, and the reptilians screeched approval.

Obama brought a triangular white hat out and put it on Trump's head, before kissing him deeply on the mouth.

"It's lovely to have you with us, Mr. President."

And the two of them held hands and thought about what the next day would bring.

THUS STRIKES THE BLACK PIMPERNEL
BY GARY PHILLIPS

PRESIDENT TRUMP ONCE AGAIN BLAMED former President Obama for leaks of classified information from the White House and for the continued vociferous protests against his administration. This in the wake of several of Trump's controversial executive orders and policies, such as when he halted immigration from seven, then six, predominantly Muslim countries to the US. Trump over time had doubled down on these comments in interviews with like-minded news outlets, during which he provided no evidence for his claims. Including that British intelligence had a hand in the surveillance.

"I think he's behind it," Trump said. "I also think it's just politics. That's just the way it is." He continued, "You never know what's exactly happening behind the scenes. . . . I think that President Obama's behind it because his people are certainly behind it." He added, "Some of the leaks possibly come from that group. You know, some of the leaks—which are really very serious leaks because they're very bad in terms of national security—but I also understand that's politics and it will probably continue."

The man occupying one of the most powerful positions in the world reemphasized that Obama had engineered the bugging of the phones in Trump Tower prior to the presidential election. "Terrible! Just found out that Obama had my 'wires tapped' in Trump Tower just before the victory. Nothing found. This is McCarthyism!" Trump had tweeted one morning in the early days of his administration.

Texas Agriculture Commissioner Juaquin Norcross, who most likely will be running for the Dems' nod to challenge Trump, recently spoke on this matter in an interview conducted with the *National Atlantic* magazine.

"Let's be clear, these ongoing fantasies of the president demonstrate how out of touch he is. He hasn't delivered on his campaign promises, notably attention to and repairing our infrastructure let alone bringing jobs back in coal or steel. It's his patented tactic, when things go wrong he looks for others to blame when in fact the buck stops with him. Plain and simple."

* * *

@STATESMASHER—"That fool Norcorss ain't nothin' but a gran pocho." #SellOutPocho

@ROLLON—"He's more legit than yer mama. You triflin' like the brothers and sisters say." #TriflinNig

@STATESMASHER—"That's not what your mama said last night, bitch ass. He need that big hard one like I give her, only a magnum enema." #BitchAssPunk

* * *

THE CAB OF THE SELF-DRIVING truck had been retrofitted with nearly $50,000 worth of hardware and software. The eighteen-wheeler Kenworth was cruising comfortably down the highway at fifty-five miles per hour. Bill Collier, the human occupant in the passenger seat, technically the overseer of this test drive and a seasoned freight hauler, had many miles ago gotten bored with the amazed stares and gapes from other drivers. This since leaving the plant in Fort Collins with fifty thousand cans of beers in the trailer. His destination was a warehouse some eleven hours away in Nevada.

Plenty of gawkers had taken photos with their smartphones of the empty driver's seat as the truck rumbled along. The vehicle was an automatic as the tech that could handle shifting the dual clutch action of a big rig was for the foreseeable future nonexistent. But that was little comfort to the men and women Collier bent elbows with in taverns across this nation. Like global warming, no matter how hard some might deny its existence, the era of the autonomous truck was coming and jobs would be lost. Or rather, the idea seemed to be that the trucks would travel the highways where a jaywalking pedestrian or a kid running into the street to fetch her ball was less likely and therefore a sudden swerve or braking was not as much a factor. As they neared the city the trucks would pull into a designated facility and the human would climb aboard to drive it into the city handling trickier maneuvers. But what sort of wage would that be compared to truckers getting paid by the mile or the hour?

Collier was making another notation on his touchscreen iPad in his log for the engineers at GlobeStar, the Silicon Valley firm that had outfitted the truck. He felt a disturbance in his seat as the cab shook. He glanced up and saw that a family van had suddenly stopped less than half the length of a football field in front of them, despite the roadway being clear. Worse it was cocked sideways and this was a two-lane section of the highway leading to a rise. Acting fast but calmly as the sensors applied the air brakes and the rear tires of the trailer smoked, Collier pressed his palm on a large red button on the side console that would disengage the computers and return manual control to him. Akin to twin steering wheels in a driver's ed car, the wheel on his side of the cab dropped down into place as he got his hands on it.

At that exact moment zooming over the small hill outside the Kenworth's windshield, coming along in the opposite direction was a low-slung sports model ragtop Mercedes. A man and woman were in it, arguing, their mouths wide open, each gesticulating severely, their machine traveling at least a hundred miles an hour. The man was driving but was glaring at the woman who was now giving him the finger. That way blocked, Collier had no choice but to twist the wheel to his right and take the eighteen-wheeler off the highway lest he crash into both cars. This took him across a span of gravel alongside a roadside café called the Duckblind—though this was the edge of the desert along I-515. Several cars were parked on the gravel and there was no space big enough between any of them to drive through unscathed. The truck's terminus was to have been in Henderson. But now it would be here as Collier fought for control of the truck, the rear trailer swinging to and fro as the tires sought purchase as gravel spewed from beneath the threads.

"Shit," Collier cursed, bringing the rig to a shuddering stop and shutting off the motor. He got out of the passenger side, the brakes hissing compressed air as the truck settled. Everything considered, he'd only clipped two cars and ruined a third. It was a black Lincoln and the front of the cab had crushed it between the right front fender and a cinder-block building behind the restaurant—a separate toilet facility, Collier saw as he got out his phone. Others were already out of the Duckblind taking their own snaps or heading toward him, no doubt the pissed-off owners of the vehicles he'd hit.

"What the hell, homes?" a twenty-something Chicano in a Rams cap said as he walked over to Collier.

Among the small crowd of customers and staff ebbing out onto the lot were two middle-aged white men. One was in a sport coat and slacks, open collar, and his companion in short sleeves and rimless owlish glasses. The stern-faced men exchanged low words to one another and both got into a late-model Lexus and left the scene.

* * *

THE MAN OF MANY FACES was at his most centered when engaged in his daily regimen of exercises in his hidden lair underneath the

Civil War-era Greenbriar Cemetery in a rugged part of town the hipsters would not be opening an artisanal grilled cheese sandwich shop in anytime soon, no matter the cheap rents. The entrance to his sanctum sanctorum as it were was via a secret entrance in a crumbling marble vault. The identification etched over its green patinated doors in marble read the OBLER FAMILY. In his exercise area past a computer console where he accessed the computers of the NSA and the Military Intelligence Agency through back doors created for him by a talented but quite paranoid hacker named Frag Lawson, the peoples' outlaw was finishing up as the sun rose over the broken and leaning headstones in the cemetery above him.

He was doing another set on the salmon ladder. This was a device where you started out as if doing a pull up. The bar you grabbed overhead was not fixed to its rungs and, utilizing upper body strength, you leaped up while holding the bar to the next higher duel rungs and so on until you reached the top. His routine also included isolating certain muscle groups as well as overall development for motor control and power, which meant a combination of free weights weight training, yoga for flexibility and mobility, and a series of exercises in stealth and paralyzing hand strikes said to have been perfected by the mythical ninja Sarutobi Sasuke. Twice a week he altered this part of his workout with weapons practice including kusari-gama, chain and scythe, the bo staff, and of course nunchucks. There were also a set of wooden dummies with protruding "arms" and "legs" to practice wing chun moves against. Added to that he used electronic devices to push his vision and hearing to their natural limits while he would calculate the cube roots of various numerical formulas to hone his concentration skills.

At the end of this fast-paced hour and half, he always sweated profusely, gulping in air, yet found himself fulfilled and ready. For he knew he would need all his skills as sharp as possible for what lay ahead.

* * *

CAMERA TWO CUT TO LINCOLN "Linc" Allard of the Hidalgo Foundation who was in-studio at CNN along with two more of the four panelists discussing the morning tweet by President Trump. In this one he essentially repeated the fanciful notion advanced on a conspiracy site that the FDA in collusion with Big Pharma was suppressing the news that there was a cancer cure. That such a cure had been available for some ten years now. And as per usual, no evidence was offered.

The normally taciturn Allard gestured vociferously. "Isn't it bad enough the leader of the most industrious nation on earth hasn't anything better to do than repeat these wild lies, this poppycock that is forever being promulgated among the nutbags and disaffected? Worse, he encourages too many of the citizenry to believe such notions rather than actually adhere to fact. He and his cohorts can swallow their own Kool-Aid outlandishness, but science is science."

The view on television screens across the nation switched and camera one was a pulled-back shot of the three sitting at the rotunda with the bearded moderator. Margo Mayfair who was sitting next to Allard spoke. "Oh, Linc, when will you get off of that? The president knows exactly what he's doing. In this way he gets the people talking about a matter that in some way will touch all of us. He is a strategic thinker and is exciting folks to put pressure on the drug companies to stop being so greedy, and do their ethical duty to accelerate the research they've slow-walked all these years."

Mayfair was a registered Libertarian, the biracial daughter of old-line Civil Rights Movement icons. These bonafides grated on her parents' lefty friends but made the K Street political consultant a much sought-after twofer pundit darling among the right of center set.

Allard shook his head. "It's laughable how you Trumpsters contort yourselves like a Cirque du Soleil performer to lend credence to a man who is simply and clearly unfit for the office."

That got a heated response from the beamed-in guest, his upper body displayed on a large monitor. "What Margo says was on the mark. You liberals just can't get over your envy how this president connects with the common Jane and Joe."

"What I can't get over," the fourth guest, Helen Ruiz, a political science professor and columnist for the *Nation* said, "is how long will there be support for Trump given his string of broken campaign promises."

"If you want to talk about what's really troublesome, what about these attacks by the likes of so-called Latino activists calling for assassination?"

"What are you talking about?" Allard demanded.

Mayfair said, "There's been a lot of activity lately on what's called Brown Twitter about your precious Juaquin Norcross being a Trojan Horse. That he is nothing but a tool of whitey and should be dealt with accordingly."

That elicited groans from Ruiz and Allard. "I've seen some of those," Allard, who was black, answered. "As has been exposed in the past, a lot of that's malicious activity by white supremacists, or as you prefer to euphemistically call them, the alt-right, pretending to be black or brown."

Now it was the two others' turn to groan and guffaw. Then the director cut to commercial about a new miracle room duster.

* * *

"Thank you," tech guru Artemis Stockbridge said to the waiter who'd brought him his bourbon on a shiny silver tray.

"My pleasure," the waiter, a stoop-shouldered balding black man in his sixties, replied as the tech billionaire plucked the squat tumbler away in his long tapered fingers.

Stockbridge turned away and sipped his drink as the waiter slipped off to attend to another guest at the soirée. The gathered were in a brownstone in the Adams Morgan neighborhood of Washington, DC. The occasion was an informal yet nonetheless

A-list-heavy informational fundraiser for a school voucher initiative aimed at the ballot in California backed by the Secretary of Education, who was working overtime to hobble and eventually dismantle the public education sector. Stockbridge was a tall man with coiffed longish blond hair streaked white and a trim goatee. He moved with a reassured casualness like the aging surfer bum image he cultivated.

"Good to see you, Margo," he said, kissing the cheek of the bronze-skinned, brown-haired woman with piercing gray eyes.

"Didn't think this would be your sort of thing, Artie." Margo Mayfair sampled some of her white wine.

"Whatever we can do to raise the education outcomes of our youth, particularly the disadvantaged ones, I'm willing to investigate."

"Even at the expense of choking the life out of the Department of Education?" Her eyes gleamed at him as she had more wine, the emotion in them uncertain. "Blue California is a ripe target for the forces of this administration."

"Yes, I know they're practically salivating at the possibility of pitting millennial hipsters who have made child rearing an artisanal undertaking against the poor and working-class folks, many black and brown, who are also frustrated by the far-too-bureaucratic, feather-bedded public school system."

She chuckled. "Now that's the tree huggin' billionaire I know."

He grunted and smiled. A white-haired man came over and addressed Mayfair.

"I hope you'll make it to the Cape this weekend."

"Wouldn't miss it, Marty," she said.

Soon their host, a friend of the secretary from their college days, had tapped her glass to get everyone's attention. She gave a short pitch to get the checkbooks open and toward the end of her spiel, after he'd handed his donation over, Stockbridge headed toward the first floor restroom that was past the well-appointed kitchen with its confectioner's oven and overhead pots and pans.

In the breakfast room next to the kitchen, the caterer's crew was preparing a last round of hors d'oeuvres. One of the young women who was assembling stuffed mushrooms had her earbuds in, bopping her head to YG's and Nipsey Hussle's "FDT."

Moments later, exiting the bathroom, Stockbridge didn't return to the main room where people were still conversing but went to a side door along the short hallway that let out into the garden area. A heady fragrance of transplanted jacaranda greeted him. There stood the balding waiter, an unlit cigarette in his hand as if he too had stepped out for a smoke break. It was a starry evening and the two were shadowy in the warm light of discreet ground-level lighting

Without preamble, the Silicon Valley insider and founder of the Hidalgo Foundation began talking to the other man who in this guise was simply called Claude. "Two days ago there was an accident involving one of my subsidiaries, GlobeStar." He explained the driverless truck test, the family van having blown a tire, and the human driver having to make a quick decision given the circumstances. "The Lincoln the driver plowed into is leased to a company I know to be one of the many cut outs of Norman Bethune."

"You have my attention," the supposed waiter said. He'd dropped the voice he was using pretending to be an older man and reverted to his natural baritone.

"Bethune nor the man he was with hung around nor has there been any insurance claim made over the smashed-up car."

Claude hunched a shoulder. "So it was some sort of meeting he doesn't want attention over. But that could be any one of an assortment of wild-ass conspiracies up his butt he's getting the true believers worked up over. Like that time he was going around saying that Obama had planted secret nanny cams in the Oval Office to gather impeachable evidence against Trump."

"Which would have had its merits," Stockbridge said, blank-faced. "But speaking of nanny cams, for the purposes of covering our asses, the truck was equipped with such in case of an accident like what happened. Here's a little something captured at the incident." He took out his smartphone and tapped the screen several times to bring up the footage he wanted. He handed the device to the waiter.

"One of the cameras was doing an automatic scan and captured Bethune in the Lexus with—"

"Dirk Thane," the supposed waiter said. He stopped the video and replayed it. "I guess they weren't making plans for a Birther Reunion March on Washington."

"They could be," the billionaire deadpanned.

His friend manifested a death's head grin.

* * *

"CHANTELLE, IT'S JERRY." THE MAN who'd stepped inside the compact mobile home was in jeans, a jean jacket over a buttoned-down shirt, and a baseball cap. He carried a fifth of gin in a paper bag. His eyes adjusted to the gloom.

"She had to step out," said another man in the room. He sat in a dilapidated Barcalounger.

"Oh, hey, man," baseball cap said, "my bad. I didn't know she had company." He turned toward the door but this was a ruse. He dropped the plastic bottle of gin as a distraction to then use his opposite hand to unlimber the handgun he had in a holster on his belt under his jacket. He wheeled back around and was surprised the second man was standing there in front of him. He hadn't heard a rustle of clothing or his footfalls across the thin carpet. His face was a mass of scarring from fire.

"Who the hell are you?" Baseball Cap Jerry began, bringing the gun up to show he was a serious individual.

The other man was of a serious mindset as well. His hand flashed out and Jerry backed up, grabbing at his throat, letting his gun drop to the floor. The burned-faced man had jabbed him with stiffened fingers in a spot right beside his Adam's apple. Jerry struggled to breath. His gun, a semi-auto Browning, was now grasped by the other man—which he used to crack him against the skull.

"Ughh," he grunted, sinking to a knee, starbursts exploding behind his eyes.

"If you ever want to see your brown-sugar honey again, you will tell me what I want to know."

"If you've hurt her, you black bastard, you and your illegitimate children will be skinned and gassed."

The burned-faced man chuckled and grabbing his quarry by the lapels, plucked him from the floor and threw him into the chair he'd been sitting in. "You talk tough for a guy who taps on a keyboard all damn day."

Jerry in the baseball cap glared at the other man, blinking.

The disfigured man knew a lot about Jerry Balis. He was a senior editor who worked for a fake news website that was part—albeit through several front companies—of Norman Bethune's empire. But Balis had a secret desire, some might argue fetish, for dark-skinned black women. His current fling was Chantelle Wardlow who worked part-time at the local big box store. Balis had told her he worked for a restaurant supply chain.

"I could make noise about blowing your thing with Chantelle to your masters," the burned-faced man said. "I suppose that would certainly embarrass you and make for some sideways glances, for who knows what you've said to this sister during pillow talk."

"You don't scare me."

"I should. This place is wired, Jer," he lied.

Balis's eyes went wide.

"And more than that, speaking of kids out of wedlock, what about those two cute rugrats you have with what's her name in Pittsburgh? Who you send money to on the regular."

"How do you know this? Is this some kind of test Norman set up? Well, I'm loyal."

"It's not going to be hard to spin the story that here you are, part of the chosen yet cavorting around with 'loose' Negro women. It wouldn't be hard to paint the picture that they were actually undercover agents of a counter-espionage cadre Obama set up since leaving office."

"That's insane. No one would believe that." But his right cheek twitched.

The other man stood before him, arms crossed, holding the handgun. "Yeah, really? The Clintons sabotaged JFK Jr.'s airplane. John Podesta is a Satanist. Two or maybe it's three million undocumented voted in the past presidential election. Those followers of yours have swallowed a lot of poisonous pablum you've spoon-fed them. How long would they think you're still a true believer, huh, Jer? What would happen to you then?" He didn't need to elaborate, Balis knew the ferocity the ardent were capable of unleashing. Particularly on one they thought a turncoat—which, ironically, was what Balis was part of concocting against a public figure.

Silence ticked by, then, "What do you want?"

This time the burned-faced man didn't break into a smile like he had when he was Claude.

* * *

ONE OF THE GUARDS WAS in modified camo and wore a watch cap with a logo on it. He was a member of a group called Blood of the Lamb Consecrated, so-called Christian gun enthusiasts dedicated to making America great again. He held his M4 assault rifle at rest but ready; diagonal across his chest, hand on the grip, finger extended over the trigger guard. A faint noise caused him to pivot. Two prongs of a modified Taser shot out of the dark, piercing his bullet-resistant vest and into his chest. The prongs were designed to penetrate as they were longer than usual and had screw-like tips that rotated, drawing current from the Taser. Voltage coursed through the wires the prongs were attached to, and the guard gritted his teeth and reared back. But he didn't go down.

"Take more than that, you motherless defiler," he wheezed at the masked man who stepped into view. Before he could bring the M4's barrel up, a suppressor on its end, twin throwing stars blurred through the air at their target. One sank into the guard's hand and the other snicked a wound alongside his neck as it twirled away.

"For the love of our savior," he declared, his finger reflexively jerking the trigger, spewing rounds into the earth.

The proletarian adventurer swiftly covered the distance between them. The blow of his heel to the guard's knee buckled him then he drove the sole of that same heavy boot into the man's face. Simultaneously he wrested the rifle away from now lax hands, and used the butt to viciously render the other one unconscious. The intruder was dressed in black jeans, heavy black boots, and a dark zipped-up windbreaker and cowl-like mask. Like the unconscious guard's vest, the intruder's clothes were bullet-resistant, woven with Kevlar and a polyethylene blend. Various gadgets and tools were secreted about his person as well. Around the corner of the two-story cinderblock building the second sentry lay on the ground, felled by the masked man's stiff finger strike to his carotid artery. The cinderblock structure was supposedly the regional office of the restaurant supply business that Balis worked for, Industrial Kitchen Fixtures.

At a metal side door the vigilante produced what looked like a smartphone. Holding the device, he connected a wire leading from this to the electronic lock on the door. The screen of the phone-like gadget swam with numbers across its face as it hacked the lock for the correct passcode. Soon there was a satisfying click but the masked vigilante paused, paying attention to a disturbance of his chi. He turned his body away from the dark opening just as bullets raked the spot where he'd been standing.

Two members of the BLC rushed out of the building, firing

their weapons. The masked man had sought cover behind a black SUV and he calmly cut these two down by shooting them in the shins. They were still alive and deadly and he rolled a mini flashbang grenade between them. It went off with a boom of heat and light.

"Dammit, the heathen has blinded me," one of them said, lying on his side on the ground. As his vision started to return to normal he was knocked unconscious by three strategically placed blows of the attacker's fist to pressure points on his upper body. The other wounded man was already out, bleeding from his mouth and nose.

M4 in hand, the invader eschewed the front door the other two had exited. His lenses cycled from being dark like sunglasses, having altered when the flashbang went off, back to their normal green hue. He reached another metal door, in the rear of the building with a keyed lock, but not an electronic one. He bent and put his ear to its surface, listening for movement on the other side. Hearing none he straightened up and extracted a small battery-powered, diamond-tipped drill to get him past the door's double lock.

Before he could get to work the door exploded outward, sending him and it flying in the opposite direction. He landed hard on his back—fortunately the door somewhere else instead of on top of him. His flexible armor had kept him alive but he estimated the three who came out of the building didn't know that. A beam from a light mounted on an assault rifle cut through the smoke of the explosion seeking his form.

"Where is that Son of Ham?" a voice demanded.

"That ghetto-bred meddler's no damn ghost. He's has be here."

Two metal golf ball-sized spheres rolled into view, emitting green smoke. The three started coughing. Their eyes watering.

"Some kind of tear gas," onc declared, running away, trying to clear his throat. An emerald pall hung about them as they sought to fan away the vapors.

"Wait, what," another gasped, a sudden weakness spreading through his limbs. "It's knock out—" He didn't finish for he collapsed to the ground unconscious.

The second Consecrated member was far enough out of the fumes that the inside of his head felt fuzzy but he was still upright. He spun in a half circle, shooting into the mist as he figured it was from that the masked man would attack.

"Die, you cut-rate commie tofu eatin' blackguard," he shouted over the rounds churning from his weapon. The firing stopped, a string of gray smoke drifting from his hot barrel. He turned. Before him a column of the velvety smoke seemed to be congealing around something solid in its opaque center.

"Got you, Pimpernel," he avowed, the assault rifle rattling its high velocity bullets again. The smoke separated but there was nothing within. "By Adam," he avowed.

"From me to you," a gruff voice said in his ear. The disguised man sank his butterfly knife in the other man's side and he gasped. A chop to his neck subdued him for the time being. Even as the wounded man dropped to the ground, the intruder was in motion. Now unfettered, the masked vigilante stepped into the facility's black interior. Calmly he put away his apparatus while turning his sensces outward for other presences.

Detecting no one else at least in his immediate vicinity, he then moved along rows of restaurant supplies from mobile pan racks, refrigeration compressors to meat slicers. Though it was dark in here, aided by his goggles coated with a kind of night-vision substance and his practiced light tread, the invader moved easily about, not disturbing any of the equipment. His goal was not pilfering a state-of-the-art countertop confectioner's oven but gaining entry to what lay beneath the supply house. So far, he hoped, no alarms had been raised. But he knew better than to be complacent. The Black Pimpernel reached what seemed like the door to the basement. He paused, his hand suspended above the latch.

From overhead there was a whoosh of air as a trapdoor in the ceiling banged open and dropping onto him were two massive anacondas. Worse, he could see the beasts had been genetically altered, proof of a rumor the Pimpernel had surfaced through dark web chatter. The Zelnoxx Corporation was a global agricultural enterprise that ran massive feed lots, manufactured pesticides, and owned the patents on numerous genetically modified seeds. The word was that Zelnoxx, at the behest of the current administration, had branched out into other sorts of research beyond vegetables, fruits, and livestock. Not surprisingly, the president owned stock in Zelnoxx. The mutated anacondas were thicker and more muscular than ones the masked man had encountered before. And like the long-gone stegosaurus, each had a ridge of small, hard pointy ridges lining their spines.

One of the prehistoric-sized snakes fell past onto the floor near his feet. The second creature wrapped part of its thirty-foot-plus body about the masked man's torso, tightening about his body as it sought to squeeze him to death then devour him. The lights came on.

"Dammit," he grimaced, his hands latched onto the huge snake's girth. But already the breath was being drained from him and he heard a crack along his rib cage. The other snake slithered over to him and began coiling about his lower legs. Added to that he heard footfalls coming up from below through the door in front of him. The BLC guard intended to shoot him to make sure he no longer was a threat.

Blocking the numbing pain causing black spots to explode behind his eyes, he extracted a large silver capsule from a hidden pocket up toward his shoulder blade. The snake on his upper body reared its mammoth wedged-shaped head back and now, its mouth open and crag-like fangs poised, rushed toward him, intending to clamp onto his head.

Jamming his forearm under the creature's jaws to temporarily halt the snake's attack, he flicked the capsule into its maw and closed his eyes. Activated by the reptile's inner heat, the capsule released its contents instantaneously. The resulting explosion burst the anaconda apart, spraying the chrome cookware with its ichor, while hunks of reptile flesh flew everywhere. The masked man was knocked over, temporarily dazed. The first guard through the doorway was struck in the face by a section of snake and he was knocked backwards down the stairs, colliding with a man below him rushing up. The two tumbled over.

"What the damnation is going on?" a voice snarled from below. "Get your clumsy butts up."

Both hands on the second snake's throat, the dark intruder was back on his feet and charging forward, pulling the writhing anaconda with him.

"Figured I'd bring the party to you self-righteous bastards," he blared, leaping and descending on the regrouped guards ascending again. A burst from an M4 seared close but not into his form as the gunman couldn't get a clear shot given the marauder was now entangled with the other men. Like bowling pins, they fell back or off the sides of the stairs, taking out a flimsy wooden railing in the process. They all wound up on the concrete floor below, each scrambling to get to their feet, except one of them who'd landed on the side of his head with a thud and remained still.

"Got you, you slick sumbitch," one of the guard's declared, about to fire on the Pimpernel. But as he was still wrangling the snake, he gritted his teeth as he whipped the heavy mutant around. The enraged reptile sank its fangs onto the other man's arm, biting it clean off. As he cried out in terror, the snake got its body around him and went to work grinding his insides to mush while also wrapping its tail around another guard's lower legs.

A five-pointed throwing star sailed across the room and penetrated the side of the neck of another guard, severing a vital artery. Crimson sprayed from him as he fell to the ground dead. Two other Blood of the Lambs Consecrated were left but the intruder became a blur, delivering a combination of Jeet Kune Do strikes and old-fashioned fisticuffs blows. The two keeled over like cardboard cutouts onto the floor of the hidden computer center. It was from here, the invader knew, that the trolls and bots in service of the president and his minions generated the propaganda meant to pump up false stories, the alt facts, thus to mislead and misdirect while the real business of dismantling democracy went on. That the supposed tweets from POTUS, the more off-the-wall and seemingly unhinged, often came from this center, dictated by the likes of the Director of External Communication.

He reflected on the Ministry of Truth's slogan in *1984*, *Ignorance Is Strength*, as around him various writers, editors, and techs, male and female, either ran away or cowered near their cubicles.

Fists raised above his head, the avenger of justice yelled, "You've got a minute to get your asses out of here before I bring this place down around your ears." As they knew this man was ruthless, he was after all labeled the Most Dangerous Negro in America by right-wing talk-radio hosts and various alt-white sites, as one, the crew dashed for the stairs and the exits.

"Now if any of you are feeling frisky, thinking like you want to get your star on the wall in the Reagan Library or some such," he yelled, "try me." He was hefting one of the assault rifles, positioned in a way that he could cut down anyone coming at him. None of them took him up on his dare as they departed.

Free to explore and gather intel, the masked man used his electronic devices to access several databanks, gleaning useful information he stored away. Sitting at a console, watching a particular file download that contained financial records of the president's secret holdings in Russia, the back of his neck tingled. He swung around in the chair, snatching up the M4 he'd set close by as the wall near him exploded outward. Chunks of cinderblock shot through the room like cannon fire, knocking over computers and pulverizing into other walls. The freedom fighter's finely tuned reflexes had kicked in, and in mid-air, he twirled his body so as to avoid two sections of cinderblock. Still he was struck a glancing blow that ruptured his protective gear.

"I'm going to stuff and mount your head on my wall, Pimpernel," declared the attacker.

The masked man regarded the new enemy before him. The man was encased in an exoskeleton suit that had been modified by the military from its original industrial use on oil platforms in deep water.

This master of disguise knew this from tech manuals he read for relaxation. He shot at the armored man with the assault rifle to no avail. Not that he figured his bullets would prevail, but he'd been curious. He was going to get a demonstration meant to be his last. The suit was a clunky assemblage of metal struts, servo units, molded sections like sides of freight cars removed and hammered into new shapes by a demi-god blacksmith, hydraulic lines and a dome construct over his head. In the man-metal construct, he stood more than ten feet tall.

"Are you done?" the suited man taunted when the firing stopped. Gripping a metal desk in a mechanized hand, he threw it at the disguised man. The Pimpernel went prone and slid on his belly as the desk flew mere inches over him, crashing onto a conference table, sending the laptops on it flying.

A hinged metal fist swung at him and only because he grabbed a piece of broken wall to absorb the blow, the administration's adversary survived. Still, the impact drove him off his feet and into the wall. He bounced off and fell to the floor. The armored man bounded over and the Black Pimpernel rolled away as a metal foot came down, cracking the floor instead of splitting his head open.

"You can't run forever, rabbit." Another swing and the fist missed, embedding itself momentarily in the cinderblock. "Uggh," the suited man grunted as his micro-motors worked to free his hand.

This was the opportunity the dark intruder needed and utilizing his parkour skills, he first hopped on the listing desk, from there feet first to the wall, then recoiled upward and completing a somersault, landed on the back of the machine man.

"Get the hell off me." He tried to reach his hand back but his armor wasn't as flexible as human muscle and there was only so far the hand would go. "I'll get you," he yelled through the audio jack on the metal suit. Gyros whined as he twisted about to shake the Pimpernel off. He started to kick and otherwise move the desks and other obstructions from his path.

The unwelcomed rider knew the mechanized man's next move would be to head to a wall and try and scrape him off. Acting urgently but centered, calm in the storm, he had in hand two dull-plated tubes from his cache. The man in the exoskeleton was now at one of the walls and reared back into it, trying to crush the Pimpernel. His heavy body slammed against the cinderblocks but the masked man leaped free.

"Dammit," the armored man swore, thudding after the other one who bounded about. As the metal man moved forward grabbing at him, the Pimpernel, jumping up like a b-baller, twisted about in midair, and flung a broken a piece of a tabletop at those mechanized lower legs. His aim was true and the man in the exoskelton found himself tripping onto the floor face-first. The Black Pimpernel acted hastily and applied the acid in his glass-lined containers to a specific hydraulic line—the one that went from the reservoir of the stuff on the back of the suit then t-offed to a main receptor on each leg. The connection severed, the legs would be unable to move.

"No, no," the now impotent attacker bellowed, banging the sides of his fists into the concrete floor, chunks of concrete being thrown up, dust rising about his form like a felled alloy baby having a tantrum.

Back outside, the Black Pimpernel was running. He knew from his reconnoitering there was a private airstrip that serviced the facility. There was also a Gulf Stream jet waiting on the tarmac in the dark. And Dirk Thane was a pilot.

There was open field between the office building and the airstrip. The masked man, sweat trickling down below his half-mask, paused, crouching down. The grass was tall enough in the field that the guard could easily be lying in it to pop up and gun down the invader. He could see a figure running toward the jet: Thane.

Reaching into his jacket he had only one play to make and it better work. He ran forward, thumbing a release lever free, then counting, tossed before him a grenade. He'd held it so that its fuse would burn some and in that way the grenade erupted in the air in bright reds and yellows. He too had dived into the grass but the brief pulse of light had revealed the top of the watch cap of the last guard. Knowing his cover was blown, he sprang up but was too late. Two shots echoed from the masked man's handgun from where he lay on the ground. His explosive shells ignited the assault rifle, which blew up in the other man's hands. He screamed, his hands and face on fire. He rolled around to extinguish the flames. Then he lay still, smoldering and groaning.

Thane was taxiing the jet. Dropping to a knee, bringing the burned guard's assault rifle up to his shoulder, the man in black shredded the jet's tires with well-aimed rifle fire. Thane was no doubt on his cell phone or radio calling in more troops. He had to act fast.

"I'll set the plane on fire and gladly roast you alive in it, snowflake," the Pimpernel called out. He was out of grenades, let alone hadn't brought along any thermite bombs, but he sounded convincing. "You have ten seconds."

The hatch opened.

"Get on the ground, face first."

"You don't know what you're messing with. This is so out of your league."

He shot over Thane's head to hasten compliance. Standing near the prone individual, he could see the metal attaché case just inside the door of the aircraft. "If you twitch, I'll kill you," he said, starting for the case. But he stopped, a fragment of information tickling at the edge of memory. He took aim and pumped rounds into the metal case. It was booby-trapped and exploded. He turned back to Thane, who tried not to look worried.

"Cute." As he'd done previously, he brought the butt of the assault rifle down on the other man's head and knocked him out. He searched his body and found the thumb drive he sought tucked in his sock. He left flying the jet away as two black SUVs sped toward the field, shots flinging from them like runaway meteorites.

* * *

"Did you get a job plowing that road to the private golf course?" The crowd, a mixture of races and ages, shouted "No," and "Hell no." The rally was across the highway to the Medgate golf course. The president had just been there golfing the past week, a facility he'd redeveloped in his real estate tycoon phase.

"But your congressman in step with this administration's supposed infrastructure recovery gave the private outfit that tax break to build it. Is that what you voted for? Is that what he promised here in Michigan? Well is it?"

There were more "no"s and cheers. Texas agriculture commissioner Juaquin Norcross walked back and forth across the small stage, holding the wireless mic, in black leather sport coat, designer jeans, and no tie. On he went, part of his barnstorming Red and Rust tour it was called. He used a handkerchief to wipe at the sweat on his face. Despite the admonishment from certain old-school handlers, particularly for a Latino candidate, even one with a "white" last name out stumping for a possible presidential bid, he wasn't shy about using weighted language.

"You can't call this mess draining the swamp, that's putting us in the swamp. What a *pendejo*."

The crowd gleefully echoed his last sentence. A man who'd been at the side of the crowd was moving behind several others as

Norcross finished and was down among the people, shaking hands. This man did not look threatening in any way; middle-aged, heavy features, khaki pants, he looked exactly like the kind of working-class man who would come out to hear the maybe candidate. Better, he too was Latino. From his shirt pocket he extracted what appeared to be a normal ballpoint pen. He depressed the button and clicked into place the writing nib. One prick on Norcross's skin was all it would take. The symptoms would lay him up like dengue fever. Then he'd get the call that next time, it would be a bullet if he didn't quit—his poll numbers were looking too promising. He grinned, the bodyguards didn't even notice him.

A foot stuck out and the humble-looking man stumbled. Instantly, hands were on him but they weren't there to help him up. A bodyguard was on either side of him and one of them said in a low voice, "Come with us."

"Hey, you can't," he began but he was the one to get pricked. A quick jab into his arm and he went limp, disoriented and unable to speak.

"No problem, a little too excited is all," said one of the bodyguards to an onlooker. The man was hustled away.

Minutes later Norcross retreated to let a local band came out to finish off. He shook Linc Allard's hand.

"I might have to hire you full time as my speech writer, Linc. 'Course I can't match what Artemis pays you."

"I just give your words a bit of structure, you're the one that says them with conviction."

The candidate said, "We're fighting out of the corner, Linc. We ain't off the ropes yet. But we will be."

"Yes, sir.

"*Orale.*" He clapped him on the shoulder and walked off.

Allard winced, his two cracked ribs bothering him since that side door blew up on him. He'd have to talk to Artemis about enhancing his gear. Maybe micro server units would do the trick.

"RELEASED THIS MORNING IS WHAT many left and various mainstream organizations say is the smoking gun connecting this administration to the reported attempt on the health if not the life of Juaquin Norcross. Evidence has surfaced about small business owner Efrain Braga, a one-time youthful member of the contras in Nicaragua during the Reagan years, being used against Norcross. Further, computer records that are still being verified allege that the president's Director of External Operations Norman Bethune was involved, as was ex-military contractor and controversial figure Dirk Thane, the latter now having fled to parts unknown. Still to be determined is the involvement of the radical vigilante dubbed the Black Pimpernel. He's borrowed that name from the late freedom fighter Nelson Mandela who was referred to that when he was public enemy number one in apartheid South Africa."

Margo Mayfair used the remote to click off the television. "Is this finally the beginning of the end?"

"His apologizers will have to twist themselves into Gordian Knots to make these new round of excuses," Linc Allard said.

"Including me, shit."

"We are all must do our part."

Playing the conservative, Mayfair was able to gather intel from the rightest camp. It was she who told him she'd heard about the attaché case gimmick Thane had used in a tight spot in Afghanistan. She'd overheard the boast at some cocktail party.

"Don't you lay that selfless revolutionary shit on me, man." She leaned over and kissed him. When their lips and tongues parted, "As Juaquin's campaign heats up, how the hell are you going to keep up this crazy life of yours, Linc? The Pimpernel, Claude, the burned man, Ornett the janitor, and those other personas you put on."

"The good thing about all the deportations is the amount of menial work available for a brother these days, Margo. The return of the Invisible Man."

"Don't be cute. You know damn well you're burning the candle down quick from both ends." She looked away, wiping at her cheek. "Goddammit, Linc, what happens if you get found out?"

The raid on the Blood of the Lamb Consecrated headquarters had been a misdirection. Though the absconded files the Resistance knew would prove valuable. But since Mayfair had been invited to a confab on Cape Cod, she'd been tasked with discovering what Bethune and Thane had been meeting about at the Duckblind café in the desert. She was able to clone the smartphone of Martin Hallsworth, her host and confidant of Bethune. The leads gleaned from his phone led them to uncovering the plot against Norcross.

"Maybe it's time for a few more Pimpernels. For sure some women."

Mayfair raised an eyebrow.

"Yeah, I know. It's worse than heroin or booze, sex even. You tell yourself you're doing good, being righteous for the cause. You are. But God help you, when you slip on that mask and put it on the line, it's one crazy-ass rush."

"I tell you what else is a rush." She pulled him to her and they made love again. Later, Mayfair's double encrypted phone buzzed and lifting her head off of Allard's chest, she retrieved it from the nightstand, noting the name that was on the screen, Druke Burbank. She grinned at the cover name and answered the call.

"Ah, Margo," drawled the familiar voice on the other end, "damn fine op you two pulled off."

"Thank you," she said.

"Looks like, I, ah, just gleaned some new . . . information from one of my taps on Trump. Significant and pertinent I'd say," he added in his clipped manner. The two discussed this some.

"Linc," she said in a loud whisper when they'd paused, waking her paramour and comrade-in-arms. His eyelids fluttered. "It's Big O, he wants us to come over tomorrow for a game of eight ball and a chat." She brightened. "Give me a chance to try out a new disguise."

"And a chance for me to win back the hundred he took off me last time, huh?"

"Double or nothing he says."

Linc Allard squinted at her with one eye. The following day, while being filled in on the latest intel gleaned from one of the various ways the current commander-in-chief was being surreptitiously surveilled, the former occupant of that office cleaned Allard's clock at the pool table—yet again.

ABOUT THE CONTRIBUTORS

South Central native **GARY PHILLIPS** draws on his experiences from anti-police abuse community organizing, activism in the anti-apartheid movement, union rep, state director of a political action committee, to delivering dog cages in writing his tales of chicanery and malfeasance. He has written various novels, novellas, comics, short stories, radio plays, and a script now and then. He has edited or co-edited several anthologies, and must keep writing to forestall his appointment at the crossroads. Phillips is president of the Private Eye Writers of America.

KATE FLORA writes true crime, strong women, and police procedurals. *Led Astray* is her latest Joe Burgess police procedural; *Death Warmed Over* her latest Thea Kozak mystery. Her fascination with people's bad behavior began in the Maine attorney general's office chasing deadbeat dads and protecting battered children. In addition to her crime fiction, she's written two true crimes and a memoir with public safety personnel. 2017 will bring *Shots Fired: The Myths, Misconceptions, and Misunderstandings About Police-Involved Shootings*. Flora has been an Edgar, Derringer, Agatha, and Anthony finalist and twice won the Maine literary award for crime fiction.

ADAM LANCE GARCIA's first novel *The Land of Nowhere* was written entirely in crayon and remains unfinished to this day. However, Adam is currently completing the third and final chapter to his *Green Lama: Legacy* trilogy, as well as the second volume of his graphic novel *Sons of Fire*. In addition to print work, he is a writer and producer of the audio drama podcast *Radio Room*. When not writing or photographing his cats, Adam works as a television producer in Manhattan.

ERIC BEETNER is the author of nearly two dozen novels including *Rumrunners, Leadfoot, The Devil Doesn't Want Me,* and *Dig Two Graves*. In 2017 he was nominated for an ITW award and two Anthony awards. He co-hosts the podcast *Writer Types* and hosts the Noir at the Bar reading series in Los Angeles. For more visit ericbeetner.com

NISI SHAWL's debut novel *Everfair* was a finalist for the Locus and Nebula Awards and a James Tiptree Jr. Honor book. Her story collection *Filter House* won the Tiptree Award in 2009 and was also a World Fantasy Award nominee. Her fiction has appeared in *Asimov's Science Fiction* and on the Strange Horizons site. She serves on the board of the Clarion West Writers Workshop and is a founding member of the Carl Brandon Society, a nonprofit created to support the presence of people of color in the fantastic genres. She's easily Googled.

WALTER MOSLEY is the author of more than forty critically acclaimed books, including the major bestselling mystery series featuring Easy Rawlins. His work has been translated into twenty-three languages and includes literary fiction, science fiction, political monographs, and a young adult novel. In 2013 he was inducted into the New York State Writers Hall of Fame, and he is the winner of numerous awards, including an O. Henry Award, the Edgar Grand Master Award, a Grammy, and PEN America's Lifetime Achievement Award. He lives in New York City.

DANNY GARDNER enjoys careers as a comedian (HBO's *Def Comedy Jam*) actor, director, and screenwriter. His debut novel, *A Negro and an Ofay*, is published by Down & Out Books. He is a proud member of the Mystery Writers of America and the International Thriller Writers and is a regular blogger at *7 Criminal Minds*. He lives in Los Angeles by way of Chicago.

LISE McCLENDON is the author of fourteen novels of suspense, mystery, crime, and wise-crackery. She writes the Bennett Sisters Mystery series, as well as series set in Jackson Hole, Wyoming, and WWII-era Kansas City. As Rory Tate she's written two thrillers, *Plan X* and *Jump Cut*. She co-wrote the dark comic thriller, *Beat Slay Love*, with four other mystery writers calling themselves Thalia Filbert. Lise served on the boards of Mystery Writers of America and the North American chapter of International Crime Writers. She lives in Montana and at can be found at lisemcclendon.com.

ANDREW NETTE is a writer of fiction and nonfiction. He is the author of two-crime novels, *Ghost Money* and *Gunshine State*. His short fiction has appeared in a number of print and online publications. He is co-editor of *Girl Gangs, Biker Boys, and Real Cool Cats: Pulp Fiction and Youth Culture, 1950 to 1980*, forthcoming in late 2017. His online home is www.pulpcurry.com. You can find him on Twitter at @pulpcurry.

TRAVIS RICHARDSON has been a finalist for the Macavity, Anthony, and Derringer short story awards. His novella *Lost in Clover* was listed in *Spinetingler Magazine*'s Best Crime Fiction of 2012. His second novella, *Keeping the Record*, came out in 2014. He has published stories in *Jewish Noir*, *Thuglit*, *Shotgun Honey*, *Flash Fiction Offensive*, and *All Due Respect*. He used to edit the SINC/LA newsletter *Ransom Notes* and reviewed Anton Chekhov short stories at www.chekhovshorts.com. He grew up in Oklahoma and now lives in Los Angeles with his wife and daughter. www.tsrichardson.com

CHRISTOPHER CHAMBERS is a Washington, DC native and a Professor of Media Studies at Georgetown University. He is the author of four fiction novels and edited two fiction anthologies. He was a finalist in 2008 for the PEN/Malamud Short Story Award for "Leviathan."

ROBERT SILVERBERG is considered to be one of the giants of the sci-fi genre, with four Hugo Awards and six Nebula Awards to his name. He was inducted into the Science Fiction and Fantasy Hall of Fame in 1999 and named a Grand Master by the Science Fiction and Fantasy Writers of America in 2005.

DÉSIRÉE ZAMORANO delights in the exploration of contemporary issues of injustice and inequity in her writing. A Pushcart prize nominee and award-winning short story writer, her novel *Human Cargo*, featuring private investigator Inez Leon, was Latinidad's mystery pick of the year. She is also the author of the acclaimed literary novel *The Amado Women*.

ANTHONY NEIL SMITH is Professor of English and Chair of the English, Philosophy, Spanish & Humanities Department at Southwest Minnesota State University. He's the author of numerous noir and crime novels, including *Yellow Medicine*, *All the Young Warriors*, *Worm*, and *Castle Danger*. He is also one of the founders of the late, great, noir ezine *Plots with Guns*.

L. SCOTT JOSE lives—and will likely die young—in Melbourne. His other semen-filled writing is available in various print and online anthologies. He is co-owner and editor for *Crime Factory*. If you'd like to get in touch, hit him up on Twitter—@lscottjose. He doesn't use it much, but will make an exception for you. He is also available for children's parties.

RECENT AND FORTHCOMING BOOKS FROM THREE ROOMS PRESS

FICTION

Meagan Brothers
Weird Girl and What's His Name

Ron Dakron
Hello Devilfish!

Michael T. Fournier
Hidden Wheel
Swing State

Janet Hamill
Tales from the Eternal Café
(Introduction by Patti Smith)

William Least Heat-Moon
Celestial Mechanics

Eamon Loingsigh
Light of the Diddicoy
Exile on Bridge Street

John Marshall
The Greenfather

Aram Saroyan
Still Night in L.A.

Richard Vetere
The Writers Afterlife
Champagne and Cocaine

MEMOIR & BIOGRAPHY

Nassrine Azimi and
Michel Wasserman
Last Boat to Yokohama:
The Life and Legacy of
Beate Sirota Gordon

James Carr
BAD: The Autobiography of
James Carr

Richard Katrovas
Raising Girls in Bohemia:
Meditations of an American Father;
A Memoir in Essays

Judith Malina
Full Moon Stages:
Personal Notes from
50 Years of The Living Theatre

Phil Marcade
Punk Avenue:
Inside the New York City
Underground, 1972-1982

Stephen Spotte
My Watery Self:
Memoirs of a Marine Scientist

PHOTOGRAPHY-MEMOIR

Mike Watt
On & Off Bass

SHORT STORY ANTHOLOGIES

Dark City Lights: New York Stories
edited by Lawrence Block

First-Person Singularities:
18 Sci-Fi Stories
by Robert Silverberg

Have a NYC I, II & III:
New York Short Stories;
edited by Peter Carlaftes
& Kat Georges

Crime + Music: The Sounds of Noir
edited by Jim Fusilli

Songs of My Selfie:
An Anthology of Millennial Stories
edited by Constance Renfrow

The Obama Inheritance:
15 Stories of Conspiracy Noir
edited by Gary Phillips

This Way to the End Times:
Classic and New Stories of
the Apocalypse
edited by Robert Silverberg

MIXED MEDIA

John S. Paul
Sign Language: A Painter's
Notebook (photography, poetry
and prose)

TRANSLATIONS

Thomas Bernhard
On Earth and in Hell
(poems of Thomas Bernhard
with English translations by
Peter Waugh)

Patrizia Gattaceca
Isula d'Anima / Soul Island
(poems by the author
in Corsican with English
translations)

César Vallejo | Gerard Malanga
Malanga Chasing Vallejo
(selected poems of César Vallejo
with English translations
and additional notes by
Gerard Malanga)

George Wallace
EOS: Abductor of Men
(selected poems in Greek & English)

HUMOR

Peter Carlaftes
A Year on Facebook

DADA

Maintenant: A Journal of
Contemporary Dada Writing & Art
(Annual, since 2008)

FILM & PLAYS

Israel Horovitz
My Old Lady: Complete Stage Play
and Screenplay with an Essay on
Adaptation

Peter Carlaftes
Triumph For Rent (3 Plays)
Teatrophy (3 More Plays)

Kat Georges
Three Somebodies: Plays about
Notorious Dissidents

POETRY COLLECTIONS

Hala Alyan
Atrium

Peter Carlaftes
DrunkYard Dog
I Fold with the Hand I Was Dealt

Thomas Fucaloro
It Starts from the Belly and Blooms

Inheriting Craziness is Like
a Soft Halo of Light

Kat Georges
Our Lady of the Hunger

Robert Gibbons
Close to the Tree

Israel Horovitz
Heaven and Other Poems

David Lawton
Sharp Blue Stream

Jane LeCroy
Signature Play

Philip Meersman
This is Belgian Chocolate

Jane Ormerod
Recreational Vehicles on Fire
Welcome to the Museum of Cattle

Lisa Panepinto
On This Borrowed Bike

George Wallace
Poppin' Johnny

Three Rooms Press | New York, NY | Current Catalog: www.threeroomspress.com
Three Rooms Press books are distributed by PGW/Ingram: www.pgw.com